# STORM OF WAR

PETER GIBBONS

Boldwood

First published in Great Britain in 2023 by Boldwood Books Ltd.

Copyright © Peter Gibbons, 2023

Cover Design by Head Design

Cover Photography: Shutterstock

A CIP catalogue record for this book is available from the British Library.

Paperback ISBN 978-1-80483-466-4

Large Print ISBN 978-1-80483-465-7

Hardback ISBN 978-1-80483-467-1

Ebook ISBN 978-1-80483-464-0

Kindle ISBN 978-1-80483-463-3

Audio CD ISBN 978-1-80483-472-5

MP3 CD ISBN 978-1-80483-471-8

Digital audio download ISBN 978-1-80483-468-8

Boldwood Books Ltd
23 Bowerdean Street
London SW6 3TN
www.boldwoodbooks.com

Byrhtnōð mid beornum; hē mid bordum hēt
wyrċan þone wīhagan and þæt werod healdan
fæste wið fēondum. Þā wæs feohte nēh
tīr æt ġetohte. Wæs sēo tīd cumen
þæt þǣr fǣġe men feallan sceoldon.
Þǣr wearð hrēam āhafen. Hremmas wundon,
earn ǣses ġeorn. Wæs on eorþan ċyrm.


Byrhtnoth and his men, ready and waiting: he ordered them
To make the battle fence formation with their shields and
hold it
Firmly against their enemies. Then it was near to fighting,
glory in battle. The time had come
when fated men must fall.
A clamour was raised, ravens circled,
eagle ready for carrion; on earth there was noise.

— AN EXCERPT FROM 'THE BATTLE OF
MALDON', AN ANGLO-SAXON POEM WRITTEN
TO CELEBRATE THE BATTLE FOUGHT AT
MALDON IN 991AD

.

# GLOSSARY

**Burh** A fortification designed by Alfred the Great to protect against Viking incursions

**Byrnie** Saxon word for a coat of chainmail

**Danelaw** The part of England ruled by the Vikings from 865AD

**Drakkar** A type of Viking Warship

**Ealdorman** The leader of a shire of the English Kingdom, second in rank only to the King

**Einherjar** Vikings who have died in battle and have ascended to Valhalla

**Heriot** The weapons, land and trappings of a Thegn or other noble person, granted to him by his Lord and which becomes his will or inheritance

**Hide** An area of land large enough to support one family. A measure used for assessing areas of land

**Holmgang** A ritualised duel common amongst Viking peoples

**Njorth** The Viking Sea God

**Odin** The father of the Viking Gods

**Ragnarök** The end of days battle where the Viking Gods will battle Loki and his monster brood

**Reeve** Administer of justice ranking below a Thegn

**Seax** A short, single-edged sword with the blade angled towards the point

**Snekke** A type of Viking Warship, smaller than a drakkar

**Thegn** Owner of five hides of land, a church and kitchen, a bell house and a castle gate, who is obligated to fight for his Lord when called upon

**Thor** The Viking Thunder God

**Týr** The Viking War God

**Valhalla** Odin's great hall where he gathers dead warriors to fight for him at Ragnarök

**Vik** Part of Viking Age Norway

**Weregild** Compensation to be paid, for example to the family of a person who has been killed

**Witanagemot** Meeting of the Kings Council

# 1

990AD

Beornoth was hunting Vikings. It was a still day in early summer. There had been a chill to the morning, but now the sun broke through patches of milky cloud to warm Beornoth's neck. He listened to a sparrow's call in the trees and nudged his warhorse forward to the edge of the rise. His leather saddle and belt creaked as the horse plodded forward, nodding its head and snorting into the leaf mulch beneath its hooves. Beornoth patted the horse's muscled neck and leant forward to scratch his ear.

'It's quiet, Lord, no smoke or screams,' said Alfgar. The young warrior stood next to Beornoth holding a spear and shield and peering over the lip of the forest's edge where it fell away into a steep slope thick with brown and green bracken.

'It's because we are too late. The damage here is done,' said Beornoth, sighing heavily.

Beornoth waited at the edge of a copse, looking down into a shallow valley. The Vikings had landed a half-day march away on the coast, having sailed their fleet of fifty warships from their base in the broad estuary of the River Severn, which separated the shire of Somerset in Wessex from the headlands of Glywysing in Gwent, home of the Welsh. At the bottom of the valley and nestled between fields of ripening green crops was a village of five wattle buildings topped with damp grey thatch.

'I can see movement down there.' Alfgar pointed his bright spear towards the village, where armed men milled around the buildings with the ease that comes from the confidence of safety. But the men down there were not safe. They were as unsafe as the West Saxon villagers of that place had been before the Northmen had come to their homes with axes, hunger, vicious greed. The Northmen were not safe because Beornoth had come for them. They were Vikings and felt secure in the cloak of their army, which had landed in the River Parrett north of Athelney a week earlier. With so many ships the Viking fleet would be two thousand warriors strong, but this village contained only a handful of raiders. The Northmen swaggered through the captured village, villagers either fled or taken as slaves, gathering whatever valuables they could find. Beornoth's tongue poked around the gap in his teeth where an arrow had punched through his face years earlier. He watched the Northmen and their confidence angered him. He imagined them laughing at the West Saxons and their weakness, at how simple it had been to land their fleet and strike into the lush countryside to take whatever they wished. And it had been easy, until now. The Ealdorman of Somerset had sent urgent word to King Æthelred that the Viking army plagued his lands, and King Æthelred, alarmed at the size of the enemy force, had sent word to Ealdorman Byrhtnoth of Essex to bring his men, his Viking killers, to Somerset and expel the cursed heathen force. King Æthelred II ruled over the English from his seat at Winchester, and had done so since he was twelve years old. He was a descendant of Alfred the Great, a King of the House of Wessex, and the Ealdormen from Northumbria to Cornwall were sworn to his service. Beornoth had been summoned from his home at

Branoc's Tree, and had brought his warriors to join with Byrht-noth's hearth troop to march west. Beornoth was a Thegn of the East Saxons, and Byrhtnoth was his Ealdorman. That had been three days ago.

'Take the spearmen and follow the treeline north,' said Beornoth. 'Come down into the valley along that line of hedge. I will wait until the sun is above me and will meet you in the village.'

'You will ride alone?' asked Alfgar.

'Just me and Wulfhere.'

'Should we not wait for Ealdorman Byrhtnoth?'

'He rides west to join Somerset's fyrd, so we bring two shires' worth of warriors to the fight. We will punish the bastards here first, and then we will join him.'

'But Lord...' Alfgar started, but then noticed Beornoth's frown and nodded his understanding of the order. Alfgar barked a command and twenty spearmen followed him at a quick marching pace, their boots rustling in the undergrowth.

Beornoth waited until the sun had shifted in the sky, and until Alfgar and his spearmen filed down the thick strip of briar hedging which ran from the valley peak opposite him and down into the village itself to separate a pasture from a field filled with bright yellow rapeseed. He clicked his tongue and his warhorse, Ealdorbana, picked its way down the hillside. Ealdorbana meant 'life destroyer', and the name was fitting because he was the largest warhorse Beornoth had ever seen. He was every bit as brutal as his rider, and trained for war. Blood and weapons would not frighten the animal, and nor would the noise and terror of battle.

'They've seen us, Lord,' said Wulfhere, his hulking frame riding a piebald mare. A handful of men gathered on the fringe of the village, close to a pigsty, and pointed at the approaching riders. 'How many of them did you say there were?'

'I didn't.' Beornoth didn't care how many Vikings were in the village. They had hurt peaceful Saxon people who worked the land with bent backs to scratch a living for their families and King. Now Beornoth was here to hurt them in return, and he would kill or injure as many as he could.

'Let's hope we aren't outnumbered then.' Wulfhere shook his bald head and drew his axe from its saddle sheath. More Vikings emerged from between the houses. They wore hard baked-leather breastplates and carried axes or spears. 'I don't see any mail or swords amongst them.'

'Looters and pillagers then. Not warriors.'

There were twenty Vikings gathering outside the village, and a big man barged his way through them. He had two war axes, one leaning on each shoulder, and he smiled at Beornoth. His head was shaved along the sides, and a long blonde plait ran from the top of his head down his back. Beornoth dragged his sword free of its scabbard. He allowed the blade to scrape on the wood throat beyond the fleece lining and held the blade at his side. With his sword, byrnie and warhorse, the Vikings saw a Lord of War. Only the wealthiest and most successful warriors could afford such weapons. They were the signal of power and skill at war. The sword was also a warning. Beornoth kept Ealdorbana at a slow trot to allow the Vikings to watch him approach, for them to see and judge his war gear. The sword was his tool, his dealer of death, and he wanted the Vikings to see who was before them. Beornoth was a killer and a protector of his people. He was a Saxon Thegn, and he wanted the Vikings to understand that he came for justice, that he came to wreak vengeance upon them for the Saxons they had wronged.

'The mail and sword are mine,' barked the axeman in Norse. 'I'll take the leader, you others take the baldy one.'

'You have killed peaceful people who could not defend themselves. You must think yourselves brave men, killing farmers and taking their women and children as slaves. I have come to kill you all, so say your prayers to Odin, for there can be no surrender here,' said Beornoth, also speaking Norse. The Vikings murmured and looked at each other with open mouths, surprised to see a Saxon who spoke their language. Saxon and Norse words were cousins, and Beornoth had grown up in the north of the old Danelaw, where Norse was spoken as frequently as Saxon.

'What did you say?' asked Wulfhere.

'That we are going to kill them all.'

'I'll say a prayer to God and Jesus to give us the strength to fight the pagans then.'

'Keep tight hold of your axe and kill the bastards. That will serve you better,' growled Beornoth. And his heart quickened, his chest heaving. Beornoth ground his teeth and welcomed the fury and anger. He allowed it to wash over him and course through his body. The big axeman swaggered forward and opened his mouth to speak. Beornoth suspected the man wanted to challenge him to single combat, as was ever popular with the Vikings, so he dug his heels into Ealdorbana's flanks, and the warhorse sprang forwards, the immense power in the animal's bunched leg muscles propelling him forward at monstrous speed.

In two leaps he was upon them. Beornoth let Ealdorbana barge the axeman out of the way, and he hurled the Viking backwards before he brought either of his axes to bear. Beornoth tensed his right arm and flicked the tip of his sword upwards and let the warhorse's power drive the point of his blade through another Viking's chest, lifting the man from his feet as his breastplate and chest bones cracked under the weight of the blow. He dragged his weapon free, and blood splashed across Ealdorbana's flanks. The warhorse snapped his teeth at a warrior's face and kicked out with his forelegs, driving the enemy away with his ferocious size and strength. Beornoth swung the sword over his saddle and cracked the edge into a Viking's skull, splitting the bone with an audible crack and soiling the field with his brains. Two more slashes and Beornoth was through them. The suddenness of the attack, and the sheer size and ferocity of the charging warhorse, had stunned the Vikings, and now they were dying. He wrenched on Ealdorbana's reins, and the horse turned in a flurry of hooves and snorting. Screams and cries filled the valley, and the iron tang of blood was thick in the air. Wulfhere smashed his axe into a Viking's face and took a blow from a Viking spear on his shield. Beornoth glanced over his shoulder where Alfgar ran through the town with the troop of spearmen at his back.

'Make the shield wall,' Beornoth called, and he climbed from Ealdorbana's back to join his spearmen in the fight on foot. Wulfhere kicked his mount clear of the Northmen and joined Beornoth as they attacked the Viking line. Beornoth's charge had broken them and he relished the look of horror on their faces as they saw their deaths marching towards them. They thought themselves Viking warriors, peerless fighters from the harsh north who could raid and sack without fear, and yet an organised and fearsome Saxon force had torn them apart in moments. 'Kill them,' Beornoth growled, and joined Wulfhere and Alfgar in the front rank.

The fight was over before it had even begun, and Alfgar's spearmen marched with organised efficiency. A handful of brave Vikings charged the Saxon shield wall, bellowing war cries and hacking at the linden wood with their axes, but Alfgar's spear ripped one man's throat out and his men soon dispatched the others from behind their overlapped shields. The Vikings broke, fleeing across the fields, and Beornoth allowed his men to run them down.

'Bastard,' a guttural voice shouted in Norse from beyond the melee. Beornoth turned to see it was the axeman. He had recovered from Ealdorbana's blow and stood with his two axes pointed at Beornoth. 'I wanted to fight you, warrior against warrior. You are a coward and a turd.'

'I know you did. That's why you are still alive,' said Beornoth. He strode towards the warrior with his sword in hand.

'There's no need to fight him, Lord,' Wulfhere said. 'We've beaten them.'

Beornoth wanted to fight him. Killing Vikings soothed his tortured soul, and he hated them for all the pain they had caused him. He closed his eyes and remembered his daughters and called upon the furious anger of his vengeance. The Viking cried to Odin and charged. Beornoth snapped his eyes open and gripped his sword in two hands. The Viking came fast; he swung one axe in a high arc whilst the other came low for Beornoth's knees. Beornoth sprang backwards and the axe blades sang through the air. The axes came around together in a backswing and Beornoth parried them with his sword, and he kicked the Viking in the hip, driving him off balance. He tried to recover, but could not raise his axe with enough strength to block Beornoth's sword as he drove it down, overhand, and with his entire weight behind the blow. Beornoth's blade cut through the Viking's arm, connecting with the axe first but driving it downwards and away with the force of the blow. The axeman looked up at Beornoth, fear quivering in his blue eyes. His right arm was all but severed, lifeblood pumping out of the terrible wound to dung the grass, and the limb hung from his shoulder by grotesque threads. The warrior knelt, and nodded to Beornoth, grimacing and sweating from the pain but brave enough not to cry out.

'Who is your Lord?' Beornoth asked, holding the bloody sword so close to the injured Viking's face that a flick of his wrist would take the man's eye out.

'I serve Jarl Hakon of Vanylven.'

'Who is the leader of your army?'

'Olaf Tryggvason, of the Jomsvikings.'

'Keep hold of your axe,' said Beornoth. He slammed the tip of his sword into the warrior's chest and grunted as he smashed the iron blade through leather armour, bone, and into the soft flesh of the axeman's heart. The Viking had fought bravely, and allowing him to die holding his axe gave him the chance to go to Valhalla, his Gods' great hall for warriors killed in battle.

'Free the prisoners,' said Beornoth, turning to Wulfhere. 'We march to join Ealdorman Byrhtnoth. There are more Vikings to kill.'

# 2

---

'Fifty ships of the heathen bastards, laying waste to good Saxon land,' said Ealdorman Byrhtnoth. He stood with one boot on a marbled rock, one hand on the hilt of the sword strapped to his waist, and the other stroking the iron-grey spade of his beard.

'God is punishing us again, my Lord. He has sent the spawn of hell to scourge us for our sinful lives,' said Bishop Nothhelm. He crossed himself twice and mouthed a prayer to the heavens. Nothhelm was Bishop of Essex, a small wiry man with tightly curled grey hair sprouting from either side of his Bishop's mitre. He winced as the wind whipped his face, and his slender shoulders shivered beneath his gown.

'They are come for silver and slaughter, my good Bishop,' said Byrhtnoth. 'Whoever sent them here to kill our people and ravage our land, by God, it will be us who throw them back into the cursed seas whence they came.'

Beornoth stood with the rest of Byrhtnoth's Thegns, behind their Ealdorman and peering over a cliff and down towards the churning mass of the brown sea. The white-tipped waves rolled and drove at the harsh rocky beach below them, enormous slabs of

rock protruded from the earth like black and ashen knives stabbing into the relentless swell. The beach curved around a narrow
headland before sloping into the harbour of a fishing town. Long,
sleek Viking warships of different lengths, *drakkars* and *snekkes*,
choked the harbour. Their beast-headed prows snarled and
swayed on the sea's undulating rhythm, and the occupants of those
vessels, bloodthirsty warriors of far Norway, had spewed forth onto
Saxon soil. From their fleet in the River Severn they had shifted
south to occupy the coastal town of Watchet in the shire of Somerset. Beornoth frowned at the Bishop, for it was not God who had
sent the pagans to Watchet. They had come of their own will and
desire. A hunger for glory, blood and wealth drove them to leave
their harsh, cold homelands in search of the soft, plump riches of
Saxon England.

'Beo,' Byrhtnoth said, not taking his eyes off the bay. Beornoth
strode forward, the Bishop shot him a sour look through squinted
eyes, and Beornoth returned his look with a flat stare. He did not
care for priests, Bishops, or God for that matter. God had not been
there when Beornoth had needed him most, in the dark days
long ago.

'Yes, Lord,' said Beornoth. He called him Lord because Byrhtnoth was the Ealdorman of the East Saxons, and one of the most
powerful men in all England. Beornoth held lands in Byrhtnoth's
shire as Thegn and was therefore oathsworn to fight for the
Ealdorman whenever he called.

'You caught some of these pagan rats inland, I hear?'

'I did, Lord. Twenty of them, no Jarls or champions amongst
them. Just warriors clad in leather and carrying axe and spear.' Jarl
was the Viking word for earl, or leader, and they could be a Jarl
with fifty ships and as powerful as a King, or a Jarl with one ship
and a herd of goats.

'So, what did you do with them?'

'We killed them all.'

'Of course you did,' said Byrhtnoth. He chuckled and stood to his full height, which was of a size with Beornoth himself and taller than most men. Byrhtnoth was a bear of a man, broad of neck and shoulder and his chest was as thick around as an ale barrel. He looked Beornoth in the eye, and a smile played at the corner of his wide slash of a mouth. He held out his hand and Beornoth clasped his forearm. Byrhtnoth shook his arm warmly, and it felt like Beornoth was gripping the trunk of an oak. 'It's good to see you, Beo.'

'You too, Lord. I wish it were under better circumstances.'

Byrhtnoth grunted and turned to stare at the fleet of enemy ships in Watchet's harbour. 'Did you learn anything from them?'

'It's Olaf Tryggvason again. With more ships this time. Something new as well. The man I questioned said that Olaf's men are Jomsvikings. Some sort of tribe or organisation, not a place.'

'So, he is back. It must have stung when we killed his man, Skarde Wartooth, and routed his army on Mersea Island last year.'

'It seems this Dane, Olaf, has his sights set on our country, my Lord,' said a short but well-armed Thegn who came to stand with them. Olaf was a Norseman, but in the long and bloody history of Viking raids the terms Dane and Viking had become as one. At the Thegn's belt was a magnificent sword, its hilt chased with gold wire. His byrnie chain mail was of the finest craftmanship, each link smaller than a child's thumbnail, and its sheen caught the rays of the sun like scales. He had a strangely lopsided face, with one eye lower than the other, and a mousy beard.

'They are Norsemen, from Norway. Further north than Danes,' said Beornoth, and the Thegn scowled at him.

'Beornoth, this is Godric, son of Odda and a man of my hearth troop. He and his brothers are Thegns in Essex, and his youngest brother will swear his oath to me soon.'

'Beornoth, from the northern shires I hear, and a Thegn now in Essex. Your reputation and deeds are the talk of the country,' said Godric, and he inclined his head. Beornoth nodded to return his greeting.

'We will throw these heathens out of Watchet and show them the measure of Saxon steel,' said another of Byrhtnoth's Thegns: Aelfwine, Thegn of Foxfield.

Byrhtnoth grunted his agreement. 'They've killed Goda, a Devonshire Thegn, and have dug themselves into the old burh down there in Watchet. They have raided further up the Severn and will do more damage if we don't stop them.'

'How many men do we have?' asked Beornoth.

'We have the will of God behind us. The Lord of Hosts is with us,' said Bishop Nothhelm, and the gathered Thegns crossed themselves, all except Beornoth.

'With God's will, and the strength of our blades, we shall destroy the raiders,' said another of Byrhtnoth's hearth troop, the men of his personal war band. All were Thegns or sons of Thegns. Their boasting, mixed with the Bishop's rhetoric, made Beornoth tired, and he rubbed the weariness from his eyes with forefinger and thumb.

'I have brought my warriors, and the fyrd of Devonshire, to aid the men of Somerset,' said Byrhtnoth. 'And the King is here, with the warriors of Wessex.' The fyrd were laypeople, farmers, millers and potters who, in times of crisis, were called upon to fight for their Ealdorman and King. They were not warriors, and would be lucky to be armed with a spear rather than a hoe or sickle.

Beornoth watched as Byrhtnoth's men exchanged glances at that news. King Æthelred had marched to Devonshire's coast, and Beornoth hoped he had indeed brought an army of Wessex warriors with him.

'With fifty ships, Olaf has a long two thousand Norsemen down there. Each man of them a warrior, bred to axe and shield from the time they can walk,' said Offa, another man of Byrhtnoth's war band. 'We cannot count on the fyrd to help throw the Vikings out of Watchet, and who knows who or what a Jomsviking is.'

'Aye,' said Beornoth. 'If they took the place so quickly, like as not, the burh fortress had fallen into disrepair. It was one of the old ones, built by King Alfred himself. The Vikings will repair it and use it as their base to raid and murder across the remainder of Somerset and Devon. We should attack before they get the chance to secure the fortress.'

'The King will call the Witan together this evening, and all will be decided then,' Byrhtnoth said. 'We are here to kill Vikings, and rest assured that we will fight Olaf and his men, and we will avenge Goda the dead Thegn.' The hearth troop raised a cheer and Byrhtnoth marched off towards where the Saxon force had made camp on high ground south of Watchet. His men followed him with swords, byrnies and belts jangling as they marched across the hillside.

Beornoth stood on the edge of the rise, peering down into the bay. From this distance there was no sign of any work underway within Watchet's walls, but the Vikings would scour the local woodland for timber. War was their business, and in Beornoth's experience, they were both disciplined and organised. The longer the Saxons allowed Olaf and his men inside Watchet to prepare and repair, the harder it would be to get them out.

'Don't mind their boasting, they are young, but they can fight,' said Offa, standing next to Beornoth. The wind blowing in from the sea whipped his silver hair away from his lined face. Offa was Byrhtnoth's captain, and commanded the Ealdorman's hearth troop, much as Wulfhere was the captain of Beornoth's own warriors. Beornoth liked the old fighter, he had met Offa when he had first sworn his oath to Byrhtnoth and occasionally since. He had a reputation as a steady sword and had been a Thegn in Byrhtnoth's household going back to the time of Byrhtnoth's father.

'We did not fight Olaf himself last year at River's Bend or Mersea Island. He was on the south-west coast fighting the King's men. We fought one of his Jarls, and that was hard enough. Hopefully Olaf is not as fierce as those men.'

'You killed the leader of that force, Skarde Wartooth.'

'I did, and he was a savage bastard. Byrhtnoth's young wolves will prove the mettle of their boasts soon enough.'

'So, there's no chance the Vikings will just sail away once they learn the King and his army is here?' said Wulfhere, behind them. Beornoth and Offa both laughed awkwardly and Offa shook his head.

'They will not fear our gentle King,' said Offa. 'But they will fear Byrhtnoth, and you, Beornoth.'

'I do not think they fear us at all. They see our land as ripe for the taking. Or why would Olaf return this year? He raided last year, as did Skarde, and we thought they were plotting an invasion. Maybe this is that invasion? Not that I don't think you are fearsome, Beornoth, of course,' said Wulfhere, and Offa laughed again.

'We must kill them, invasion or not,' said Beornoth, and Offa nodded. They looked out again at the violent swell of the sea, and at the Viking fleet beyond. Beornoth ground his teeth and his stomach soured as he thought of attacking the enemy in the old fortress, and how many good men would die on its timber walls to stop the Vikings in their quest for plunder and glory.

King Æthelred had indeed brought the army of Wessex to face Olaf Tryggvason and his fifty warships of Vikings. The hillside teemed with warriors, women, horses and children, all busy preparing the camp as darkness drew in. Beornoth marched through the maelstrom of tent canvas, firewood, horse fodder and campfires. The King had ordered that the Witan council would meet in a wood-surrounded glade beyond the camp.

'Are we invited to the Witanagemot' asked Alfgar, striding alongside Beornoth and clad in mail byrnie, with a wooden crucifix bouncing on his chest as he walked.

'All the Thegns can attend the council, but it's the Ealdormen and the Bishops who will do the talking,' said Beornoth.

'So, it's just a meeting of the powerful men in the Kingdom?' asked Wulfhere, between crunches of an apple.

'Yes,' said Beornoth. 'The King only calls such councils in time of war, or where there is an important matter of law or land to decide.'

'So, why are we going?' asked Wulfhere.

'Because Byrhtnoth says so.'

'We're missing out on some warm grub. The lads will be eating, drinking and laughing in front of a warm campfire,' grumbled Wulfhere. 'And it looks like rain.'

The evening was dark and brooding, and it did smell like rain. The men would need to make shelters to keep arms and armour dry through the night.

'Will the Archbishop be there?' asked Alfgar, touching the cross at his chest.

'There will be lots of churchmen there, though they have never held a sword or a spear in their lives,' said Beornoth.

'Archbishop Sigeric is a wise and holy man, Lord,' chided Alfgar. 'He was a close student of Dunstan himself; God rest his soul.'

'No doubt he is as wise as he is rich in gold and rings,' said Beornoth, and shook his head as he saw Alfgar's face pale at the blasphemy. Beornoth had no time for the Church, or for God. Which was unusual in a Kingdom where every man, woman and child worshipped the Church, God and Heaven.

'Most men never get to see a King, lad. Remember this day,' said Wulfhere. He tossed his apple core away as they entered a light wood of rowan and hazelwood. Dozens of men approached the gathering place, streaming down the hillside dressed in their heavy war glory, or the fine cloth of the Church.

'Wynflaed will never believe me, that I have seen both the King and Archbishop Sigeric,' said Alfgar, and he grinned, his youthful face bright and beaming. Alfgar and Beornoth had rescued Wynflaed from a Viking slave pen a year earlier and she was now Alfgar's betrothed.

'Concentrate on the war, not on Wynflaed,' said Beornoth.

'How can he, with all that beautiful red hair of hers?' said Wulfhere, and Alfgar's face flushed. 'We all know you didn't approve of the engagement, Lord.' Wulfhere waved his hands and flopped his head from side to side. 'And we all know Alfgar is the bastard son of Ealdorman Aethelhelm of Cheshire, and that you think he should have waited for a better match. You have chided him enough on the matter.'

Beornoth frowned, and Wulfhere grinned at him, his forehead wrinkling and his bald head shining in the evening light. Beornoth ignored the jest, because the trees were thick with men. He weaved through the press of bodies, the warriors and Thegns of Essex, Wessex and Devonshire, until he came to the edge of the wood where the glade opened up before him. It was a bowl of grass intertwined with thick roots, and with a huddle of three pale boulders at its centre. An old man in a green Bishop's mitre and holding a crook stood at the rock, and men left the grass bowl clear, gathering around its edges.

'Archbishop Sigeric,' whispered Alfgar as they shouldered their way to the front so that they could see the space clearly. Sigeric was the Archbishop of Canterbury and the most powerful churchman in the Kingdom. A brass horn sounded, tinny and shrill, and the

Archbishop bowed his head and made the sign of the cross. The gathered crowd fell silent, and each man dropped to one knee in the presence of the King, anointed by God himself.

'King Æthelred,' said Sigeric in a croaky voice. The men, including Beornoth, bowed their heads, and a thin young man entered the clearing. He had long auburn hair beneath a circlet of gold, and his face was long and lantern jawed. He wore a fine tunic of red and blue.

'He isn't much older than you, Alfgar,' whispered Wulfhere, which was true. He looked to have seen only twenty-five summers, but Beornoth knew he had already been King for twelve years following the murder of his brother, King Edward. Two Lords clad in byrnies and with fine swords strapped at their waists flanked the King.

'Three cheers for the King,' shouted one of those Lords, and the gathered warriors gave three clipped shouts to acclaim their King. Beornoth cheered, but noted that many did not, and he saw more than one shaken head amongst the clamour of mail and helmets. The cheers were half-hearted, and the King's slender shoulders slumped a little. The men flanking him glared around the glade, baleful but not surprised.

'We come together at this Witanagemot,' said the King, raising his hand to acknowledge his people, and the gathered throng rose to standing at his gesture. He spoke in a timid voice, and Beornoth craned his neck to hear. 'To decide how we will attack the cursed heathens who now occupy our burh at Watchet. They have killed a Thegn and put many of our people to the sword.'

The King nodded to Sigeric, who stepped forward. 'Vikings have indeed landed at Watchet and are now ravaging lands across Devonshire. We have gathered the host of England here to stand up to them.' The warriors around the glade cheered and stamped their feet, but Sigeric shook his head and raised his crook for quiet.

'The heathens come in fifty ships of war and two thousand warriors. That is not a force to be taken lightly. Even with the fyrd of Devonshire and the warriors of Wessex and Essex, we might not have the numbers to face such a host.'

A murmur rippled amongst the men like the sigh of the sea.

'Are you saying we should not fight?' came a voice, hidden from view, but startling because it was a woman's voice amongst the clamour of warriors and priests.

'Who is it?' asked Alfgar, craning his neck to see who spoke before the Witan.

A small, grey-haired woman bustled into the circle, and the King's chin fell to his chest. She was bent-backed but held her head high, her lips pursed and her gnarled knuckles gripped a cane which she used for support as she strode forth in short, determined steps. The Lords flanking the King looked at each other, unsure how to act.

'Are you saying the Saxon fighters are no match for Viking fighters? Are you saying, my Lord Archbishop, that the heathen Gods are stronger than God and Jesus?' said the woman, and she wagged a finger at Sigeric.

'You should not be here, Lady Ælfthryth,' said the Archbishop, his wrinkled jowls quivering as he shook his head.

'It's the King's mother, the widow of King Edgar,' gasped Alfgar.

'I should be here, because I will not stand for such callow talk,' she said, and there was a rumble or ascension amongst the warriors.

'Lady Ælfthryth,' said Sigeric. 'We know the pagans are greedy, they come only for silver. So why not simply pay them without further bloodshed?' There was a roar of astonished voices amongst the crowd. 'Why not pay them now, and they will sail away with no more good Saxons killed?'

'Never! We should fight!' shouted a voice from the crowd, and the warriors cheered. Beornoth clenched his fists. He knew Vikings. He had grown up in the borderlands between Northumbria, the Kingdom of York and Cheshire. There, Vikings of the Danelaw were thick across the land and had been for generations since the Great Heathen Army had conquered much of north and eastern England a hundred years earlier. Beornoth knew that paying the Norsemen would just embolden them. Like wolves, they would smell weakness and fear. They would take the silver, laugh at the fearful Saxons, and then strike again, but harder and with more savagery, and take whatever they could until someone stopped them.

The King raised a hand for quiet and put two fingers on the bridge of his nose. 'Let us hear from someone who has fought Vikings. Ealdorman Byrhtnoth, come forth and speak to the Witan,' said the King. Byrhtnoth strode into the glade, and he looked huge in his mail compared to the King, the Archbishop and the King's mother. The warriors surrounding the glade roared their welcome to the Ealdorman, and the chanting of his name reverberated through the trees, every voice acclaiming Byrhtnoth. Beornoth could feel the power of it rising through the earth to shake beneath his boots. King Æthelred stared at his subjects with his mouth open, and Lady Ælfthryth fixed Byrhtnoth with an icy stare. It was a hard look from a ruthless woman, one Byrhtnoth should beware of, and it chilled Beornoth more than facing a Viking Jarl in single combat. Ælfthryth might have worn a gown and shawl, but she was as cold a killer as any Viking. There were rumours she had killed her husband's first son and heir, so that her own son Æthelred could become King. Æthelred had been just twelve years old then, and she had ruled the country as regent until he became a man. A warrior faces you with a sword in hand and the fight is where you can see it, but the King's mother fought her battles in the shadows with cunning and intrigue, and so the look she cast at Byrhtnoth sent a shiver down Beornoth's neck.

The King raised his hand again for quiet. 'Ealdorman Byrhtnoth, your reputation as a warrior is both well known and well earned. The tale of your victory on Mersea Island is told across the realm at firesides and feast days. You know these Vikings, so speak.'

Byrhtnoth bowed to Æthelred. 'Thank you, Lord King. I am not a man for fine words or speeches, so I will say only this. These Pagans do not come for silver alone. They worship Gods of battle and blood; Vikings want glory and war. They come for your mothers, sisters and daughters. They come for your land and your lives. If you pay them, they will take your silver and attack again. They will attack and murder and rape until we stop them. We must attack and drive our swords into their pagan hearts.' Byrhtnoth was shouting by the time he reached the end of his words, and the crowd had erupted into a storm of cheering and waving of weapons in acclaim. Beornoth too shouted his approval at the Ealdorman's words, for there would surely now be a fight, and he would get a chance to kill Norsemen and avenge their victims.

# 3

Drizzle leaked from a bleak sky. The rain swirled and danced amidst a blustery wind off Watchet's north coast. Beornoth stood with his men waiting for Byrhtnoth to take the field and give the orders for the line of battle. Wulfhere sat back on his haunches staring at where the burh rose from the flatlands like an earthen crown. To their right, the men of Wessex formed up before the King's banner of the white dragon. The big men came first, the warriors of Æthelred's hearth troop, King's Thegns, all picked for their size and skill at arms. They marched in good order, the white dragon of Wessex adorning their shields and their spears held at the same angle pointing towards the heavens, their boots stomping into the grass in perfect unison. Above them, a banner bearing the same snarling dragon hung limp, despite the wind. It was soaking wet from the rain and a small river of water poured from its edge onto the helmet of the square-jawed warrior who held it forth. Beyond those soldiers came the less organised men of the fyrd, the farmers, smiths, millers and potters of Wessex and Devonshire. These were the lay folk called to arms by their Thegns to fight for the safety of their homes and families. They milled about at the rear of the lines of warriors. Some carried spears and shields, but most bore mattocks, picks and clubs.

'If it's going to rain, I would rather it be proper rain,' said Wulfhere, wiping the rainwater from his bald pate and face with his hand. 'I hate this fine rain. It's a bastard that will fall all day. It'll get under our mail and into our boots.'

'I don't think the rain is our greatest concern today,' said Alfgar. He stared intently at the burh. 'It looks like they have repaired some of the palisade.'

'They have,' agreed Beornoth. The fresh golden timbers were prominent on the defences against the brown of the old dark stakes. The dull iron of spear points bristled above the wall, shifting and leaning as the Vikings patrolled the town, aware but as yet dismissive of the Saxon army. 'But whoever was responsible for this place has let it crumble. The ramparts are leaning and pushed out in at least four places I can see, and the ditch and bank have crumbled.'

'The dead Thegn, God rest his soul, will regret that laziness now that they have removed his head from his body,' said Wulfhere.

'These pagans are an affront to God,' said Alfgar. Olaf had mounted the slain Thegn's head on a spear above Watchet's main gate, along with the five other heads of men who must have been leaders amongst Watchet's defenders.

'Then why hasn't he cast them out of the town then?' said Beornoth. 'Why did God allow Olaf Tryggvason and his army of savage pagans to sack a town full of people who say endless prayers and pay endless amounts of silver to his church?' Beornoth did not expect an answer to that question. Alfgar's mouth opened, and he raised a hand, but thought better of arguing on God's behalf. Beornoth was beyond that, and his men knew it. 'At last, here comes Byrhtnoth.'

The Ealdorman emerged from the treeline on the hillside, which stretched away from Watchet's valley. He strode at the head of his hearth troop, dressed in his byrnie and with his sword strapped to his belt. A youth scurried behind him, carrying Byrhtnoth's shield and spear. There was no place on this battlefield for warhorses, and so Beornoth had left Ealdorbana at camp, as had the rest of the army's Thegns. Byrhtnoth raised a hand when he saw Beornoth and marched towards him.

'Any sign of the King yet?' Byrhtnoth barked, pointing at the dragon banner and the men of Wessex.

'Not yet, Lord,' said Beornoth.

'Well, we are here. And we won't wait around all day.'

'No Lord, the men have been drinking since first light, looking for bravery in ale. The longer that goes on, the drunker they will be.'

'Offa,' Byrhtnoth barked over his shoulder. 'Keep the Thegns off the ale until we fight.'

'Yes, Lord,' said Offa, nodding a greeting to Beornoth as he stood alongside his Ealdorman. 'And the fyrd?'

Byrhtnoth shook his head and sighed. 'Let them have their drink. They might need it, the Thegns will do the fighting today, not the fyrd. One man for every five hides. That fyrd is the bulk of our army, one farmer must come for every five farms, armed with a weapon to fight Vikings who are all warriors, every man of them as skilled as one of our Thegns.'

'If the Ealdorman here had taken a man from every five hides to stand the walls of the burh and maintain it, then we wouldn't be standing here now.'

'That was the law in Alfred's and Athelstan's day, Beo, not now. The peaceful reign of King Edgar made men comfortable. They forgot about the Danes, and the Norsemen and their dragon ships.'

'So, we must attack one of our own burhs now, Lord. And it will be terrible,' said Offa. The old warrior shook his head and stroked his grey beard as he contemplated assaulting the fortress.

'We must. So how shall we do it?' asked Byrhtnoth.

'Head-on attack, my Lord,' said one of Byrhtnoth's Thegns, and Beornoth saw it was Godric, the young man he had met the day before, standing with his chest puffed out and his chin jutting.

'We will have to approach the burh whilst the Vikings shoot arrows at us, then clamber down into the ditch, and scale the bank beyond whilst they throw spears at us. Then we must scale the timber walls and get inside to fight the enemy,' said Offa.

'I am not afraid of the fight, or of these pagans,' snapped Godric, placing his hand deliberately on his gold wire-wrapped sword hilt.

'Nor I,' echoed another.

'They should come out and fight like warriors,' said another.

Beornoth turned away from their boasting and looked again at the burh. 'It will have to be a feint,' he said.

'Where are you thinking?' asked Byrhtnoth.

'The main army will attack the main gate, as the enemy would expect. A small force can skirt around to the west. There is a place there where the palisade timbers are without fresh wood. Maybe they have not reinforced that section yet. A small force can attack that section and get inside the burh, maybe open a gate, or collapse the wall there to allow the rest of the army in.'

Byrhtnoth looked to the west. 'Send a scout on horseback around the valley summit, out of sight of the Vikings. Ask him to see what condition that part of the wall is in, and what terrain lies before it. Tell him to ride hard. I want to know before the fight begins.'

'Yes, Lord,' said Offa, and set off to execute the order.

A murmur rose from the gathering army, and the King rode from the treeline, mounted on a magnificent white stallion, as bright as a star in the gloom of cloud and drizzle. A half-score of mounted warriors surrounded him and he took his place at the front of the army, men bowing and kneeling in his wake.

'Will the King fight, Lord?' asked Alfgar, an awed smile spreading across his face.

'No, lad. He will go to the rear when the spears clash.'

'Looks like they want to talk,' said Godric, pointing to Watchet, where the twin oak doors opened slowly and six men marched forth, all armed in byrnies and carrying a leafy branch to show they came in peace.

'Offa, Beornoth. Let's see what they have to say,' said Byrhtnoth. Beornoth and Offa followed him to join the King and his Thegns.

'Ealdorman Byrhtnoth,' said the King from atop his horse.

'Lord King.'

'Seems they want to bargain. Perhaps they fear our host?'

'I don't think it's likely, my King,' said Byrhtnoth. A gaggle of Bishops who stood beside the King shook their heads and whispered amongst themselves, displeased at Byrhtnoth's words. Beornoth doubted there were many in Winchester who ever disagreed with the King. 'More likely they want to see if we will pay them to leave.'

'Maybe we should reconsider that,' said the King, in a drawling voice. Spears and shields appeared on the walls of Watchet's burh, and more warriors marched out to form a long line of men behind the six leaders who came to parlay.

'Do not, Lord King,' said Byrhtnoth, and now the King's Thegns turned to look at the Ealdorman, so harsh was his tone. 'Pay them now, and not only will we lose a fortune in silver, but they will simply strike somewhere else on our coastline. We must fight them and defeat them. They also come to glory their pagan

War Gods with the blood of our dead, and they will never sate their hunger for our silver and blood.'

'Watch your tone when you address the King,' barked a Bishop, and Byrhtnoth bristled.

'No doubt Ealdorman Byrhtnoth has the right of it,' said the King, shifting his weight in the saddle. 'So, how should we do it if we fight?'

'All-out attack, swarm the walls, Lord King,' said a short, stocky warrior in the troop of King's Thegns.

'A siege, my Lord. Starve them out, with God's will,' said a Bishop.

'Their walls are not fully secure, my King,' said Byrhtnoth, nodding to Beornoth and repeating his plan. 'The burh has fallen into disrepair and the Vikings have repaired some sections, but we can attack in the west where the timbers are rotting, and the banks are half-collapsed. I can lead my men in that attack, and your main force should attack the front gate as a feint. Once I am inside, it will draw the Vikings away from the gate and our main force can break through. And with God's will, we will cast the Norsemen out of Watchet. We have scouts up into the valley already and will have a report shortly.'

'Seems like you have it all worked out, Lord Byrhtnoth,' said a Bishop with a pointed nose. 'The army attacks the walls where the fighting will be thickest. You attack a weak point and cover yourself in glory. Again. The men will acclaim you. Your greeting yesterday did not go unnoticed, Ealdorman Byrhtnoth.'

The warriors around King Æthelred looked at the Bishop and then at Byrhtnoth and snapped their eyes forwards in uncomfortable embarrassment.

'You are welcome to join me in the front rank, Father, as we climb the ditch under a hail of arrows and spears and climb the palisade whilst Viking warriors try to plunge the cold iron of their spears and axes into our faces, necks and chests.'

'Now, now. The good Bishop is a man of letters and scripture, Byrhtnoth, not a warrior like you. Come, let us speak to these Northmen and see what they have to say,' said the King. 'Are there any amongst us who speak their tongue?'

'My Thegn Beornoth here does, Lord King.'

'Another hero of Mersea Island, eh? Come along then,' said the King.

The King stayed mounted, and his horse trotted across the grass, its hooves throwing up clods of soil. Byrhtnoth and Beornoth went with the King, as did three of his own Thegns and three of the Bishops, including Sigeric. They crossed the space between the Saxon army and Northmen in an uncomfortable silence until the King reined in ten paces away from the group holding the leafy branch.

'Tell them who I am, and that this is my town and my Kingdom,' said the King. 'Tell them they must depart or face the consequences.'

Beornoth edged forward so that he stood next to the King's horse and repeated Æthelred's words in Norse. The Vikings chuckled at the suggested consequences. The man at their centre was young, of an age with Æthelred. But where the Saxon King was thin and callow, this man was quick-eyed and assured. He was of average height, his waist was narrow where a belt cinched his byrnie to take some of its weight, and his shoulders were broad. He had a sharp, angled axe blade of a face, all high bones and flat planes. The other Vikings at the parlay were older, scarred and dripping in tattoos, elaborately braided hair and arrogance.

'I am Olaf Tryggvason. It seems that your King does not want this land, for he does not defend it properly. Maybe we will leave, if you pay us,' said the leader with a shrug, and his captains laughed.

Beornoth translated for the King and kept his eyes upon the enemy leader, a man whose name he had heard so often, a killer and rider of the Whale Road. Beornoth saw the daring in him, the confidence. That so many grim-faced growlers followed the young man marked him out as a dangerous enemy.

'Tell him that if he does not leave, we will attack this very day,' said Æthelred. His voice grew higher in pitch and Beornoth did not look up at him for fear that his face had grown red in front of his enemies.

'He looks scared,' said a hulking warrior next to Olaf. His black hair was shot through with iron grey, and creases lined his face at the eyes and forehead. 'I think he might cry if you shout at him, Olaf.' The others laughed.

Beornoth spoke the King's words in Norse, whilst the Bishops huddled around Æthelred's saddle and whispered urgently at him.

'You can attack, if you like. I should warn you, however, that Palnatoki here and I are Jomsvikings, and we have a crew of Jomsvikings within these walls. Your King faced a handful of us last year, and his men ran from us like children from a wrathful father,' said Olaf, putting his arm around the hulking black-haired warrior, and he smiled at Æthelred.

'What is a Jomsviking?' asked the King after Beornoth translated, leaving out the part about his warriors being children.

'We are warriors who follow the Jomsviking code, and only the finest fighters may enter our order. We defend our brothers, and avenge their deaths. We do not fall back from armies unless outnumbered. We live in our island fortress at Jomsborg, and no women or children may enter it. We are a brotherhood of the blade, and we are here. We fight for the glory of the Gods, and Palnatoki is our founder.' Olaf cocked his head towards the old, hulking warrior. 'There is no force in Midgard who can stand against us.'

'Tell him we have Byrhtnoth with us, victor at Mersea Island, and you Beornoth who slew Skarde Wartooth,' barked the King after Beornoth had translated the words.

Beornoth spoke the words in Norse. Olaf looked him up and down, and leaned his head to one side. 'He is truly the one who killed Skarde,' said a warrior, and Beornoth recognised the man.

'Einar Ravenhair,' he said, inclining his head in greeting. He had met and fought against Einar at the battle on Mersea Island one year earlier. Einar returned the gesture, the crag of his face impassive.

'So, it seems you have skilled warriors of your own. This is good,' said Olaf, and he nodded, the corners of his mouth turned down in appreciation. 'Tell your King I will fight him here, if he likes. Just him and I. If he kills me, my men will sail away. Or he can pay us forty thousand pounds of silver to leave. Your only other option is to attack our walls,' said Olaf. 'Skarde was my friend, Saxon.'

'He fought bravely, but he was a murderer, a raider, and a slaver. Like you. So I killed him with this sword.' Beornoth patted the iron hilt at his waist and kept his eyes locked on Olaf's. 'If you come before me on the field, I will kill you too, and this feeble grandfather,' Beornoth said, and looked Palnatoki up and down with disdain. Olaf's arrogant, calm manner in the face of the Saxon army was as kindling to Beornoth's anger. Olaf and his men had killed good Saxon people, simple people. They had already ravaged the countryside around Watchet, as well as the town itself, and had taken women and children as slaves to sell in the Viking slave markets at Dublin or in the far north at Hedeby. Their ships filled the sea off Watchet; the burh could not hold their vast numbers and those ships would hunt for more easy targets up and down the coast between Watchet and their previous base on the Severn. Beornoth was a warrior and a Thegn, and he was here to protect the people and exact vengeance on their tormentors. He wanted to fight, and he wanted to kill. Olaf fixed him with a stony stare, and Palnatoki ground his teeth, the muscles of his cheeks working beneath his beard. 'You have killed one of our noblemen and mounted his head on a spear point in front of his own burh. So, we won't pay you with silver. We will pay you with swords, spears, and axes. You must think yourselves great heroes, capturing a broken-down fortress and attacking women and children. You are cowards and nithings, and I will laugh when we cut out your black hearts.' Nithing meant a man of no honour, a coward who would not be permitted to enter Valhalla and would wander the afterlife as a wraith, and Beornoth knew it would needle at Olaf and his men.

Palnatoki lunged forwards and Olaf held him back. Einar Ravenhair and the other Viking leaders reached for their weapons, but Olaf laughed, throwing his head back. 'Good, I like this talk. Let's have our war then.' He looked at the King and barked like a dog. The Vikings laughed when Æthelred flinched, and turned on their heels, but Palnatoki turned back and touched his hand to his axe and pointed at Beornoth.

'What did you say to them?' asked the King.

'How dare you speak for the King of the Saxons without asking his permission?' said Archbishop Sigeric.

'Olaf said he wanted to fight you, Lord King. Just him against you, if you kill him, his men will go away. Or he says you can pay forty thousand pounds of silver, and he will leave. Or we must attack the walls.'

'The King would never lower himself to fight...' began Sigeric.

'Oh, shut up,' said the King, cutting him short. 'Me, fight Olaf? Dear God.' The King made the sign of the cross before the chest of his fine byrnie. 'Forty thousand pounds of silver, such a sum...' He trailed off, staring at the backs of the retreating Vikings.

'So, we fight then,' said Byrhtnoth cheerfully. The King slumped in his saddle and glanced at his Bishops who chattered amongst themselves like hens. 'Good. My scout will return soon, if the news is favourable. I will take my men to the western wall to attack the weak point there. For the plan to work, Lord King, the army must attack the main gate before midday.'

'Very well, Ealdorman Byrhtnoth. I will have my men attack, as you say. May God bring us victory over this heathen Olaf,' said Æthelred.

Byrhtnoth clapped Beornoth on the back as they marched back towards their men. 'Let's kill the bastards, Beo.'

# 4

---

Beornoth crouched in the damp leaf mulch and bracken at the forest's edge facing Watchet's western wall, leaning on the shaft of his spear whilst the army of Wessex formed battle lines opposite the burh's main gate.

'It's past midday,' said Alfgar. 'When will they attack?'

'Bloody soon, I hope. Any longer and the ranks will be stinking drunk. We should send a runner to the King,' said Wulfhere.

Byrhtnoth paced back and forth amongst his retainers, his brow furrowed and arms crossed. He pointed towards the army and threw his hands up in frustration.

'I think they are moving,' said Alfgar. The lines of the King's army were indeed shuffling forward towards the gate. A roar went up from the front rankers, the Thegns and warriors of Wessex and Devonshire. There was a loud thrumming sound, and suddenly the sky was thick with arrows, sailing silently towards the fortress. Then the dragon banner appeared high in the centre of the army, and the warriors picked up their pace, marching towards the Viking-held burh.

'We go on the Ealdorman's command,' said Beornoth. 'Keep

the men in good order. We must cover the ground between here and the ditch as quickly as possible, then climb in through that section of wall.' Beornoth pointed to where the earth bank had collapsed into the ditch and the timbers of the wall and palisade had therefore slumped. The palisade stakes leaned, pointing outwards towards the field like a splayed hand, rather than straight up. There was therefore no fighting platform behind that section of wall for men to stand on. Where the palisade was whole, defenders would stand on the fighting platform to hurl missiles as attackers tried to navigate the ditch, and strike from above as those men climbed the steep bank. Which was the horror the Wessex men faced as they attacked the main wall and gate.

'What do we do if we get inside the walls?'

'We kill as many of them as we can. Open the gate and drive the bastards back into the sea.'

'It will be grim work getting through that gap,' said Wulfhere, as he thumbed the edge of his war axe. 'Luckily for us, we have Byrhtnoth's men in their war glory.' He jutted his chin along the line to where Byrhtnoth stood ready to attack, and where his men clasped forearms and urged one another on to great deeds of bravery.

'Shield,' said Beornoth. Cwicca hefted the shield two-handed and Beornoth slipped his hand through the leather strap to grasp the smooth wooden grip which spanned the bowl of its iron boss. The iron tang from the shield's boss, rim and rivets, and the musty smell of its leather covering overpowered the freshness of its willow planks. Cwicca was a boy, only fourteen summers old, who Beornoth had rescued from the Vikings a year earlier, and he stood clutching a spear, a grin wide on his boyish face. He had a round face, chestnut eyes and curly hair falling around his ears.

'I have my spear,' Beornoth said.

'This is for me, Lord. Let me fight today. I am old enough. Oswi is with the warriors, and he is the same height as me,' said Cwicca, and Wulfhere laughed.

'Never mind what Oswi is doing, you will stay at the rear and guard our horses.'

'But Lord...'

'Enough,' Beornoth barked, and Cwicca scuttled away, his curly hair bouncing, and still clutching his spear in both hands. Beornoth liked the lad, and he had fought well in weapons practice back at Beornoth's hall at Branoc's Tree.

'You can't hold him back much longer,' said Wulfhere.

'I know. But today isn't the day for him to get his first taste of battle. This will be work for experienced fighters, not boys. I don't want to find his corpse on the battlefield.'

'What's wrong with him?' asked Alfgar, pointing to where one of Byrhtnoth's men knelt, doubled over, strings of vomit dripping from his mouth.

'Must have fallen ill,' said Wulfhere. Beornoth shook his head. It was Godric, the young, well-armed Thegn from the Ealdorman's hearth troop. A priest led the young man to the rear of the lines, whilst the Bishop of Ely, Byrhtnoth's favoured church, led the men in a prayer before the fight. Byrhtnoth knelt, and his men followed. Beornoth also knelt, even though the Bishop's words were hollow for him.

'Blessed is the man who hath not walked in the counsel of the ungodly, not stood in the way of sinners, nor sat in the chair of pestilence...' said the Bishop. Beornoth closed his eyes and allowed the voice of the Bishop to drown out. He knelt because he did not want to set a poor example to his men, who were all men of God. The words went through his nerves like a knife, words of an unjust God who had shown no favour to Beornoth. He had brought only pain to his life, as had raiding Vikings such as those in Watchet's burh. 'But his will is in the law of the Lord...' the Bishop continued.

Beornoth opened one eye and watched as the warriors of Wessex reached the ditch which formed the perimeter around the fortress. The men ran down its sides, and a hail of spears greeted them. The cries of the wounded began, and the front line scrambled up the bank with their shields held above them. 'And he shall be like a tree which is planted near the running waters which shall bring forth its fruit, in due season...' Beornoth closed his eyes again, ignoring the prayer. He thought of his two daughters, killed as children by Viking raiders in his old home in the far north-west of England. He remembered the joyous sound of their laughter, and their soft, round faces, and then the sight of their burned bodies, shrunken by the flames. Beornoth's chest heaved and the muscles in his neck tensed. He ground his teeth and welcomed the fury of his anger and his thirst for vengeance as it pulsed around his body. The men in the burh were not the men who had killed and burned his children years earlier, but they were Vikings just as those men had been, and so were fitting vessels for Beornoth's hate and revenge.

'To war, men,' Byrhtnoth shouted, and drew his sword. 'Death to the pagans. On me!' he roared and charged from the cover of the trees towards the burh's western wall. Beornoth followed, and he surged into a run across the field towards Watchet. The warriors of Wessex scaled the timber walls at the main gate, using axes for grip and hoisting each other up on shields to reach the sharpened stakes at its summit. The roar of battle was a tumult of screams, war cries and the thumping clash of iron on wood. Beornoth's shield was heavy in his left hand, and his helmet wobbled on his head as he ran. The younger warriors sped past him and Beornoth found himself in the fourth rank, racing across the gap to the ditch. Alfgar ran two ranks in front of him and wanted to cry out for his friend to wait for him, but he stifled the cry. Alfgar had fought on Mersea Island, and at the Battle of River's Bend. As much as

Beornoth still saw him as a youth not ready for the horror of war, he was, in fact, a hardened fighter and veteran killer of Vikings. Wulfhere puffed alongside Beornoth, his cheeks blowing and his legs pounding.

They reached the ditch, and Beornoth ran down the slope, his boot sliding in the mud churned up by the warriors in front. He cannoned into the crowd of warriors in the ditch's gulley with his shield in front of him. The warriors there gathered, waiting anxiously for the men before them to scramble up the collapsed bank, which was a mix of clods of grass and rocks, all made slick by the ceaseless drizzle. Those men clambered up the bank slowly, some slipping back in the mud and shouting curses, and others attempting to climb on all fours.

'Get up there, now!' Byrhtnoth bellowed from along the line.

'They have seen us,' said Wulfhere, pushing a younger warrior away from him because he had trapped Wulfhere's shield at his side in the crush of men in the ditch. Bearded faces appeared where the timbers poked from the earth at different angles atop the collapsed bank, helmeted and pointing down at the Saxons below them. A spear flew over the palisade and slammed into the thigh of a warrior five men down from Beornoth.

'If we stay here, we die,' Beornoth said. He barged his way through the warriors until he reached the bank. A man was stumbling there in the mud and Beornoth grabbed him by the collar of his leather armour and hauled him backwards, tossing him back amongst the crush of men. Beornoth threw his shield up the bank so that it landed at the foot of the splayed palisade timbers. He flipped his spear around and stuck it, blade first, into the mud of the bank. 'Wulfhere, your spear,' he called. Wulfhere handed Beornoth his weapon and Beornoth plunged it into the earth halfway up the slope. He pulled himself up the bank, using the spears to brace himself against the mud and the hill. Beornoth slipped and landed on his face, the wet mud slopping into his beard and against his cheek. Men screamed and died behind him as more spears came over the palisade. The Vikings had noticed the attack, and more Vikings would come from the front gate to plug the gap in their wall. Beornoth could not let the Vikings win. He would not let them kill more Saxons because he could not climb up a muddy hill. Beornoth gripped the spear and dragged himself up, then turned to grip Wulfhere's hand and pulled him to the top. A spear jabbed at him and scraped across the shoulder of his byrnie, and Beornoth grabbed the shaft with his right hand. He yanked it savagely towards him and it came free of its owner's grip. Beornoth swung it around in his hand and stabbed it upwards towards the bearded faces and a man wheeled away with a bloody slash across his nose.

More Saxons had successfully made the climb, following Beornoth's method of driving spears into the mud, and he knelt to pick up his shield. Wulfhere clawed his way up and hacked between two splayed timber palisade staves with his war axe and the bearded blade came away bloody. Without hesitating, Wulfhere reached forwards and pulled a ruddy-faced Viking towards him by his beard and Beornoth drove his spear into that man's guts and helped Wulfhere throw the warrior down towards the mass of Saxons in the ditch. Wulfhere hacked his axe into a palisade stake and hauled himself up and between two timbers which had spread in the collapsing bank. A roar went up from the Saxon ranks to see one of their men through the wall, and Beornoth followed Wulfhere through the gap. A rotten timber snapped under his weight as he forced himself between two posts and he fell to his knees inside the fortress, rising just in time to block a spear thrust at his face with his shield. Beornoth surged to his feet with a roar and drove his spear into his attacker's chest, smashing through the Viking's breastplate and throwing him backwards. Beornoth grabbed the hilt of his sword and ripped it free of its scabbard and slashed the blade across the hamstrings of a Viking who hacked at Wulfhere's shield with an axe. A warrior came for Beornoth, charging at a run with a spear point held before him, and Beornoth sidestepped the blow and slammed into the man with his shield. The Viking fell to the ground under the blow and Beornoth plunged the point of his sword into the warrior's gullet with such force that the sword went through the Viking's neck and into the ground below him. Blood welled from the wound and the Viking stared at Beornoth with dead, glassy eyes. Beornoth put his foot on the warrior's face and yanked his blade free from the grasping soil and out through the dead man's neck in a spray of dark blood. It was desperate work, blade work, and the thrill of battle pulsed through Beornoth's veins.

'Shield wall,' he shouted, and Wulfhere came to bang his shield next to Beornoth's. They were inside Watchet, and now he had to open the gate, or drive enough of Olaf's warriors away from it so that the King's men could swarm the walls there.

More Saxons poured through the damaged section of wall, and Offa, Byrhtnoth's man, brought his shield together on Byrhtnoth's left side.

'Here they come,' said Offa, and sure enough, a wall of Vikings was marching towards them along the pathway which ran along the inside of Watchet's palisade. Each man held a black-painted shield bearing a single white rune before him and came armed with a spear. At their head came Palnatoki, the old warrior who had been at the King's parlay. Beornoth recognised the black and silver hair poking out of the bottom of a fine helmet crested by a raven's wing, and the sheer size of the man's hulking frame.

More men joined the Saxon shield wall so that their shields filled the space between the palisade and where the wattle housing of the burh began. Beornoth edged forwards, and the line went with him.

'Keep the line, Beo. Kill the bastards,' Byrhtnoth shouted over Beornoth's shoulder from where he had taken up a position in the second rank.

'If we can't get through them, then hold them,' said Beornoth. 'Hold them and kill them so that more of their warriors come to join this shield wall from the gate. Fight hard, lads.'

The Viking shield wall came on in a determined march. They held their shields before them in a perfectly straight line, with spear points resting on the upper edges, all in exact formation. They grunted together with each forward step, and just before they reached the Saxon line, Palnatoki barked an order and they surged forward as one to smash their shields into Beornoth's shield wall. The force jarred up Beornoth's arm and halted his forward momentum. He braced himself for the inevitable pushing, which always came when the linden wood clashed, but almost stumbled forward as the resistance in front of him disappeared. Instead, the line of spears snaked forward, and the ashwood smell of a spear shaft filled his nose as it darted past his face to slam into the warrior behind him. As its owner withdrew the weapon, it snaked past Beornoth's cheek, splashing his face with fiery blood. He snarled and struck forwards with his own spear, but a Viking shield took the blow squarely. Another wall of spears darted forward like the fangs of a serpent, and Beornoth raised his shield to take the blow on the iron boss, where it clanged and drove his arm backwards. Then came a heave from the Viking shield wall. They barged the Saxon line with their shields and drove Beornoth and the other front rankers backwards. Beornoth put his shoulder against his shield and pushed back, but again the resistance disappeared. This time an axe hooked over the rim of his shield, and he braced his knee against the lower rim to stop the shield from being tilted away from him and leaving his chest and neck exposed. He heard a Viking opposite him grunt with disappointment that the shield had not come away, and there was a stench of stale ale and meat from the Viking's maw.

They dragged a body past Beornoth from the rank behind him, barging past his shoulder, too fast for him to release his blade and try to pull the man back. A Viking bearded axe blade had hooked around the warrior's shoulder and pulled him towards the Viking line. Beornoth let out a roar of despair as he realised it was Oswi, the youngest warrior of Beornoth's own men from his lands at Branoc's Tree. The boy hurtled towards the Vikings, and Beornoth saw the flash of Palnatoki's blade as he slammed an axe head into Oswi's face, smashing his teeth and nose with a terrible slapping sound and killing him instantly. The gorge rose in Beornoth's throat. These Vikings fought differently: organised, efficient and deadly. They had torn the Saxon shield wall to a ragged mess. Injured men groaned and cried out, blood mixed with shit in the muck beneath Beornoth's feet where the dying voided their bowels. Brave warriors, and brothers of the shield wall, like Oswi, were dead and injured and the Vikings made the grim wall of shields and spears once more, like a monstrous hedgehog coming for them with deathly precision. Beornoth realised these warriors must be the Jomsvikings Olaf had referred to. Palnatoki led them, and they were a different Viking. Brutally organised and effective.

'We can't hold them,' said Offa next to Beornoth, his face taut with effort as he braced himself for another attack.

'They are cutting us to bits,' agreed Wulfhere. 'They will trap and butcher us inside the walls.'

'Should we retreat?' came a voice from along the line. 'Before they slaughter us.'

Beornoth tipped his head back and roared. It was pure fury

escaping from his body, anger and frustration because the men were right, the Vikings were winning.

'No retreat. No slaughter,' he said. Beornoth dropped his spear and reached behind the neck of his mail to touch at the small wooden locket resting at his chest on a silver chain. It held two locks of golden hair from the heads of his daughters. The lights of his life, snatched away from him by Viking raiders. 'Give me your axe,' he growled at Wulfhere.

'Don't do it, Lord,' Wulfhere said, seeing the fury in Beornoth's eyes.

'Give it to me,' he shouted, and reached over to snatch the weapon from his friend and the captain of his household warriors. The Jomsviking shield wall smashed into the line again, forcing the Saxons back two paces, but this time Beornoth took the blow, and then crouched to sweep the axe below the rim of his shield at the ankles of the Viking in front of him. The man yelped in pain, and Beornoth rose to smash the iron rim of his shield into the injured man's face. Beornoth let go of his shield and forced his way past the falling enemy, dragging the blade of his axe across the face of the next Viking in line, slicing away his nose and ear in a wash of blood. Beornoth clawed his way into the Viking line, grabbing the wrist of a warrior who tried to stab him and twisting it with a vicious crunch. He headbutted that man twice in the face, and then he was amongst them. A blade scrape across Beornoth's ribs, and his byrnie stopped the cut from penetrating his flesh. A spear stave cracked across his helmet, and panic flooded his head, blood pounding in his ears.

'Palnatoki! Fight me, you nithing coward,' Beornoth shouted, and suddenly the resistance against him moved away. The Jomsvikings kept their shield wall intact to hold back the Saxon line, but pushed Beornoth to their rear. Palnatoki emerged from the mass of Vikings to face Beornoth behind their battle line.

Beornoth's heart pounded. The Jomsvikings were too strong, and he could see no way for his and Byrhtnoth's men to break through. Vikings could never resist a challenge to their honour or single combat, and his challenge to their leader was a gamble, but if they were going to drive the Vikings out of Watchet, Beornoth could not see any other way.

'You Saxons are as weak as grandfathers. You fight like my old mother back in Jomsborg,' said Palnatoki, and he laughed as the battle raged next to them, Oswi's blood still on his axe. The Norseman was as tall as Beornoth and broad at the shoulder and belly. Palnatoki sheathed his axe and took a spear from another warrior. He pointed the weapon at Beornoth, and fixed him with eyes as dark as black pools. Palnatoki opened his mouth to talk again, to boast and laugh at the Saxons' impending defeat, but Beornoth attacked him. He attacked with hate and savagery and roared his vengeance at the Jomsviking leader.

# 5

Beornoth whipped the axe up from where it rested at his side. The blade flashed at Palnatoki's face and the Viking leaned back, avoiding the blow by a hair's breadth. Beornoth followed up the swing by raking his boot down the Viking's instep and stamping on his foot, and with his free hand he grabbed Palnatoki's shield and forced it back towards the Jomsviking. The cocky look vanished from Palnatoki's face, and he tried to stab at Beornoth with his spear, but his own shield crowded the blow. Beornoth twisted around the shield and struck his axe against Palnatoki's helmet, and the Viking stumbled forward off balance.

Beornoth did not give his enemy a chance to recover and slammed his axe into Palnatoki's shield. He used all his strength to twist and wrench the shield out of his grip and tossed both axe and shield to one side. Beornoth drew his sword and reached behind him to slide his antler-handled seax from where it hung from the rear of his belt. Palnatoki found his feet and drew his axe from a loop at his belt, and came at Beornoth, swinging his weapon in a blur of speed and skill. Beornoth parried the strike, and the clash of metal rang out to shake the very ground. Before he could pull his axe back to strike again, Beornoth knelt and stabbed his seax into Palnatoki's thigh, and in three rapid strikes he stabbed his enemy in the groin and then jammed the tip of the broken-backed blade into Palnatoki's foot, pinning him to the ground. The Viking roared in pain and swung wildly at Beornoth, but he sprang backwards, away from the blow.

The Jomsviking leader fell to his knees, clutching at his foot, blood from his wounds dripping into the soil. Beornoth howled at the Vikings to watch, and their rear rank turned. When he was sure they were watching, he brought his sword around in a low, flat arc and the edge chopped into Palnatoki's neck above the rim of his mail byrnie, and the old warrior's head toppled from his shoulders. Beornoth kicked the head towards the Vikings as Palnatoki's corpse fell to the earth, pumping dark blood into the Saxon earth. A great lament went up from the Viking lines, and they hurled themselves at Beornoth. The whole rear rank of bearded warriors charged him and Beornoth parried, ducked and swayed from their blows. He believed he must die as shields pinned him and a spear shaft clattered him across the helmet.

'You killed our Lord,' shouted one attacker in Norse.

'The founder is dead. Where is Lord Olaf?' cried another Viking voice.

Beornoth heard a war cry to shake the heavens, and the pressure from the surrounding shields gave way. Byrhtnoth's strained face was there in the gap, and he stabbed his sword through an enemy's gut, and Wulfhere charged the Jomsvikings with his shield.

'You broke them, Beo,' said Byrhtnoth. 'They folded after you killed that big bastard.' The Ealdorman clapped Beornoth on the shoulder and grinned before setting off to pursue the fleeing Jomsvikings. Beornoth groaned and fell to one knee, his breath coming in quick gasps and his muscles burning from the exertion of the fight. An arm slipped under his shoulder and he looked up to find Alfgar smiling down at him.

'God bless you, Lord, but you did it. Look, Olaf breaks off his defence,' said Alfgar. Beornoth peered through the mass of bodies ahead of him and saw that Olaf's men streamed away from the walls, running into the central town area of the burh and making for the port, where their precious ships lay waiting for them.

'I thought we were lost,' said Beornoth through heavy intakes of breath. 'I thought the Jomsvikings would kill us all.'

'So did we all. Until you killed that big one.'

The men of Wessex swarmed over the walls and opened Watchet's front gate, and Beornoth and Alfgar followed the crowds of warriors as they surged through Watchet's streets. The rain stopped, and the sun warmed Beornoth's face and neck. He removed his helmet and pulled off his leather helmet liner, which was soaked with sweat, his hair beneath it plastered to his face. They reached a crowd of Saxon warriors and pushed their way through until Beornoth saw a Viking shield wall facing the Saxons and spread in two ranks across the length of the port, beyond which lay the Viking fleet.

'They are boarding,' said Alfgar, leaning in to speak into Beornoth's ear to be heard above the shouting and clamour of the Saxon army. 'Why do we not attack?'

'We have,' said Beornoth. Bodies littered the hard-packed earth between Watchet's dock buildings and the Viking shield wall. The men in that line of linden wood stood firm, their black shields locked, and spears levelled in perfect order. Jomsvikings. The shield wall parted, and Olaf Tryggvason strode forward, flanked by Einar Ravenhair. Both had the marks of battle upon them, sweating and splashed with gore, but stood with shoulders back and heads held high. Both men held swords upside down as a signal of peace. There was a surge from the Saxon lines, who stood

ten paces beyond the Viking line in a baying mass, hungry for
Viking blood but fearful to attack the ruthless Jomsvikings.

A group of warriors barged their way through the Saxon force,
to cries of: 'Make way for the King.' Six big men in byrnies coated
with the muck, blood and filth of the fight at the gate made a line
in front of the Saxon warriors, and faced Olaf and Einar. Beornoth
imagined the horror of that attack, the descent into the ditch
amidst the murderous missiles thrown by the Vikings on the walls,
then the slippery and treacherous climb up the bank to reach walls
defended by Norse axemen and spearmen. Blood and death
outside Watchet's gate, and that attack had been a feint to allow
him and Byrhtnoth to make their attack on the western part of the
defences. A slight figure strode through the Saxon ranks, and the
men there fell quiet. King Æthelred walked through the pathway
cleared by the six warriors, and his mail was unsullied and shining. He walked with hunched shoulders and kept his head down,
the bloodied and soiled men of Wessex and Devonshire watching
the man anointed by God as their King walking through them
unmarked. It was hard for a fighting man to see his Lord wait
behind the lines whilst he risked his life in combat. A warrior
fought for his Thegn, Ealdorman or King because of his oath, but
there had to be respect and loyalty for a man to fight hard and risk
everything to obey his master's orders. Byrhtnoth's men loved him
and would march into a hail of Viking spears because Byrhtnoth
fought amongst them, he risked what they risked. Beornoth imagined what it must have been like to fight alongside a great King,
like Alfred or Athelstan, a King like that could spur his men on to
great deeds of bravery. Little wonder they had fought so successfully against the Viking scourge in those days.

The King searched the front ranks until his eyes found Byrhtnoth, and the King beckoned him over to join him in the parlay
with Olaf. Byrhtnoth strode towards the King.

'Come, Beo. We will need your Norse tongue,' he said, and Beornoth followed him.

'Well done, Ealdorman Byrhtnoth,' said the King in a low voice. He offered Byrhtnoth a wan smile. 'A splendid victory. So many dead, though. So much pain and suffering.'

'They will want us to let them board their ships in peace, Lord King,' said Byrhtnoth. His eyes shone in his lined face, darkened by the filth of battle. The Ealdorman was huge and powerful, where the King was thin and frail.

'What is your advice, my *dux bellorum*?' asked the King, using the Latin phrase for 'lord of war'.

'We could slaughter them here on the quayside. But it would be a hard fight, these Jomsvikings are no ordinary fighters, they almost crushed us and might do so again, washing away what we have achieved today. We should let them go, but make them return what they have stolen, and leave hostages to keep the peace.'

'Very well, let us talk to this Olaf then.' The King walked towards Olaf and Einar, flanked by Beornoth and Byrhtnoth, and with his six warriors behind them, hulking and baleful.

'Palnatoki was as a father to me,' said Olaf as they approached. He spoke in Norse, and Beornoth could see his eyes glaring, and tears stained the battle dust on the sharp edges of his cheeks. 'They tell me you killed him, just as you killed Skarde Wartooth?'

'I killed him,' said Beornoth. 'Just as he would have killed me, and had killed many before me in battle. He fought with honour, and he died like a warrior.' Beornoth leaned towards Byrhtnoth and Æthelred and offered a translation.

'When I was a boy,' said Olaf, wiping the sweat from his brow with his palm, 'Harald Greycloak, who was the son of Erik Blood-axe, killed my family in a fight for the throne and sold me into slavery. A man bought me for the price of a cloak, and I was a slave for most of my early childhood. Palnatoki found me there, in that pit of misery and servitude, saved me and trained me to fight as a Jomsviking. He gifted me the ability to avenge my family's deaths and raised me up to the man you see before you. I should hate you for killing him.' He rubbed at his eyes with forefinger and thumb. 'But I do not. We are warriors and this is the life we choose. Now, we will leave this midden heap of a fortress. We will return to our ships and there will be no more killing.'

'Ask him why we should let him leave, the impudent pup,' said the King after Beornoth had translated. Æthelred did his best to look angered and haughty, but his clean weapons, unmarked armour and the pinch at his lips only made him look petulant.

'If you do not, many more men will die here on this dock. And we will still leave,' said Olaf.

'Tell him they can go if they leave us ten hostages, and they must be men of rank,' said Byrhtnoth. 'Tell him we want all the silver, goods and slaves they have taken since they landed in Watchet, and that I want to see it all before another man leaves this quayside. Otherwise, we will fight until not a man is left standing, and he will lose so many men that he cannot sail his fleet, and cannot raid for years. We will ruin him, and their blood will flow like a river.'

A smirk played at the side of Olaf's wide mouth as Beornoth translated. 'We agree with your conditions.' Olaf winked at the King, and turned to leave, but then stopped and looked around at Beornoth. His pale blue eyes fixed on Beornoth's own. They were cold in that angled face, harsh and cruel. 'When I said I do not hate you for killing Palnatoki, I was wrong. I do hate you. My men tell me your home is in the east, you and the old warlord here. Maybe I will come for you there, and make you pay for killing my friend, the man I loved like a father.' Olaf clasped the arm rings on his left arm as he spoke, as though making an oath on his warrior rings, and a chill ran down Beornoth's spine.

'What did he say?' asked the King, and Beornoth told him.

'We should kill the bastard here and soak Watchet with his blood,' said Beornoth, visions of Olaf and his warriors killing and burning in Branoc's Tree swirling in his mind.

'The fight is over. You will take one hostage, Beo, and we will spread the rest throughout my Thegns. If he attacks again, the hostages will all die,' said Byrhtnoth.

Olaf's men brought ashore piles of silver candlesticks, plates and rings. They returned women and children, captured in the environs of Watchet, and they left ten hostages, all well-armed men in byrnies. The Vikings boarded their ships, the long sleek warships like knives in the water. Their oar blades lowered into the grey water, like legs sprouting from monstrous sea insects. Beornoth wondered that such shallow ships could carry the Norsemen across the wild, deep sea. They were brave to make that journey, and as hungry as wolves for blood and glory. He hoped Olaf would sail away, to Frankia or Ireland or some other land to unleash the fury of his Viking warriors. But he had seen the glint in those cold blue eyes, and in his heart Beornoth knew Olaf would strike at Saxon lands again, and if there was a God, Beornoth hoped he would keep Olaf and his Jomsvikings away from the peace and safety of his home at Branoc's Tree.

## 6

'It's good to be home,' said Wulfhere as they rode over the crest of a high pasture overlooking Beornoth's lands at Branoc's Tree. He breathed in deeply and exhaled as though the very air of the place gave him succour.

'Look how the lambs have grown,' said Alfgar. The stumbling, black-legged lambs they had left two weeks earlier were now bounding playfully in the lush grass. Beornoth looked down upon his burh and heriot, the fortress Byrhtnoth had granted him following the Battle of River's Bend a year earlier. Beornoth was the Thegn of Branoc's Tree and the hundred hides around it, one hundred farms and families who depended on him for protection and justice. The heriot was the grant of land and weapons, which Beornoth held in return for his oath to fight for his Ealdorman when required. The burh itself was much smaller than the coastal fortifications at Watchet. It held his long hall and the rooms where he lived, a church with a high cross on the gable, a kitchen, and a bell house. It was ringed by a stout timber palisade, which he and his men kept in good order, and fronted by a ditch and bank below the palisade's timber poles. It was his duty, as Thegn, to keep

Branoc's Tree in proper order, and fight for the Ealdorman when he called. The people around Branoc's Tree would flee inside its wall in the face of an attack, where they would be safe unless the enemy could breach the defences. Alfred the Great had ordered such defences constructed across England to protect the people against Viking raids, and they worked because no Viking crew looking for easy plunder would test themselves against such stout fortifications and risk losing men they could not easily replace, men they needed to row their precious warships back to Jutland or the Vik.

'Aethelberga will be delighted to receive our guest,' said Wuffa, and the warriors laughed. Wuffa was a wiry warrior of Beornoth's household troop whom Beornoth had taken on with the Branoc's Tree heriot. He had a pockmarked face, ravaged by some childhood disease, and was a stout man in the shield wall.

'The old battleaxe will complain so much that the great tree will wither,' said Ead, a young warrior, and the others laughed again. Branoc's Tree had got its name from a sprawling oak tree, whose ancient trunk was as thick around as two men.

'Watch your tongue,' snapped Wulfhere. Wulfhere was captain of the warriors Beornoth kept in his hall, and Beornoth arched an eyebrow, surprised to hear Wulfhere defending Aethelberga, the widow of the Thegn who had died at the Battle of River's Bend, and from whom Beornoth had succeeded as Thegn of Branoc's Tree. 'She is the Lady of Branoc's Tree, and I won't have you hairy-arsed churls mocking her.'

'I think I can see Wynflaed down there,' said Alfgar, rising on his saddle and smiling down at the burh. Beornoth could not make out her red hair from this distance, only the magnificent tree which gave the place its name, and that the people seemed busy, safe and well. That was enough, for since leaving Watchet, visions of Olaf and his cruel hatchet-like face laying waste to

Branoc's Tree and the people within it had plagued Beornoth's dreams.

Winland and Alfgar were in love. They would be married soon if Beornoth permitted it. She had been married before, but the Vikings had killed her husband, and Alfgar loved her with the bright intensity of youth and did not hide it. At first Beornoth had frowned upon the union, Alfgar being the bastard son of an Ealdorman and therefore liable for a match of rank and wealth, but he could not deny the joy which poured from them both whenever they were together.

'Will we feast tonight, Lord? To celebrate the victory?' asked Wuffa.

'What victory?' said Beornoth.

'At Watchet, Lord?'

'An Ealdorman died, and Olaf Tryggvason put his head on a spike. We lost good men, three of our own men are injured, and Padda back there is dying. Olaf only left because he feared he would lose too many warriors defending Watchet once we were inside the burh. The Vikings will be back.'

'But we beat him, Lord?'

'Did we? Olaf lives, and I doubt he and his sea wolves have returned to Norway. We must practise harder with axe, spear and shield.'

The men fell silent at Beornoth's harsh words. He nudged Ealdorbana down the hillside towards his burh. They were joyous following the fight at Watchet, and they had fought well. Beornoth regretted being so dour, but he couldn't help it. A lifetime of war and death had made him that way. 'We will feast tonight; you have earned it, men.' They whooped and cheered and the younger men who had travelled on foot ran down the hillside to see their families and friends.

Beornoth rode through the main gate and raised his hand to

greet the crowd of people who had gathered inside the burh to welcome their warriors home. He dismounted, and a boy took Ealdorbana's reins. 'Feed him and brush him. I want fresh hay in his stable, and let him rest,' said Beornoth.

Aethelberga strode over to him, broad-hipped and ruddy-cheeked. She beamed, fussing at her dress. 'I knew you would be victorious. We prayed for your victory over the heathen.'

'Any problems whilst I was gone?' he said, after nodding thanks for her words.

'Everything is fine, Beornoth. We lost a pig to sickness, but other than that, things are well at Branoc's Tree.'

'And Eawynn?' Beornoth searched the courtyard, where his warriors now milled with the people and their loved ones, but could not see his wife.

'Eawynn is well. She tends to the garden, weaves and rests. She is sitting on a chair behind the hall watching the flowers,' said Aethelberga, and she smiled and put a hand on Beornoth's forearm. 'Eawynn is at peace, or has found some level of peace, at least.'

'We have a guest,' said Beornoth, and he turned to look at the man in mail and furs who rode alongside Wulfhere. 'This is Brand Thorkilsson. He is a hostage provided by the Viking leader. Brand will stay with us until next summer, as a guarantee that the Vikings will not attack again.'

'And what are we supposed to do with him?' said Aethelberga, and she made the sign of the cross and cast a sour look at the Viking.

'Find him a bed and feed him. He won't harm anyone.'

'How do you know? He might...'

'Because I will kill him if he does,' said Beornoth.

'Hello, my Lady,' said Wulfhere, after he had dismounted. Aethelberga looked at the big, bald warrior and her face flushed red. 'I made this for you.' He handed her a small piece of fresh golden wood carved into the shape of a swan. She smiled and bowed her head, and shuffled off, clucking with the other women and shouting orders for food and ale to be brought to the warriors.

'You should know better at your age,' said Beornoth.

'What do you mean?' said Wulfhere.

'You are sweet on her. You are like young folk at an Easter dance, all red faces and coy smiles.'

'She is a fine woman, and she has my respect.' Wulfhere frowned and looked at his boots.

'Aye, well. Her husband was Thegn here before me, don't forget. Before the Vikings put him in the ground at River's Bend. Tread carefully around her.'

'I will, Lord.'

'And Wulfhere?'

'Yes, Lord?'

'Don't let me catch you stealing a kiss behind the kitchens.' Beornoth laughed as Wulfhere cursed at him under his breath. His captain stalked off and the farmers and womenfolk of the burh greeted Wulfhere warmly as he moved through them. He hugged one girl and shook hands with a shepherd. He ruffled the hair of a dirty-faced child and pinched the cheek of a small girl. The people loved Wulfhere. Whilst he was a big man, and fearsome in battle, he had a kinder, softer side which folk warmed to. Beornoth found himself alone amongst the crowd and walked to his hall to leave them to their greetings. He was their Thegn, and their protector, not their friend.

Beornoth entered the hall and the heat of the huge fire was warm on his face where it crackled and spat at the centre of the long room. Smoke twisted lazily up through the smoke hole in the thatched roof. Shafts of bright light shone in through open window shutters to show dust dancing in the sun. He marched up

the narrow corridor until he reached his rooms. A serving boy
came scuttling after him with a wash bowl, and a girl brought him
a jug of water, a crust of bread and some cheese on a wooden plate.
Beornoth nodded his thanks, and they shuffled out of his chamber
without meeting his eye. He unfastened the silver clasp and laid
his thick leather belt on the bed, along with his sword and seax.
Beornoth unfastened the silver cloak pin at his shoulder, fash-
ioned into the shape of a horse's head, and hung his dark wool
cloak on the back of the door. He bent over and grunted as he
pulled the heavy chain mail byrnie over his head and shook and
wriggled until the armour came off. Beornoth lay it carefully on
his bed; he would have Cwicca rub it down with sand, and then
cover it with fleece oil. He felt light without his armour, as though
he could float up to the timber joists in the ceiling. Beornoth took
off the leather padded jerkin he wore under his byrnie, and then
the wool jerkin beneath. He washed his face and body with the
cool water from the bowl and ran his wet hands through his hair
and beard. He groaned and felt gingerly at the bruises on his back,
face and shoulder from the fight at Watchet. They were purple-
green welts, but he was thankful not to have taken any cuts in the
battle. He turned to pull a clean woollen jerkin from a drawer and
caught sight of himself in the rippling water. Beornoth turned back
to the bowl and saw a broad-faced man with dark hair and a dark
beard shot through with grey and white. He saw a scarred warrior
with a fierce face. Beornoth pushed his tongue through the gap in
his teeth and there was a white, jagged scar running through his
beard on that cheek, and he traced his hands across the raised and
twisted scar tissue on his chest and shoulders, remembering each
cut in flashes of snarling men's faces and the white-hot pain of
blades in his flesh. His back and shoulder ached still from battle,
and Beornoth felt old. If he lay on his bed, he feared he would
sleep for days.

Beornoth pulled on a simple brown wool tunic and went to the small window of his room. A breeze blew in to cool his face and chest and he sighed. There was a fresh, late-spring floral smell on the wind, and he breathed it in deeply. He took in the beauty of the green pastures rising on the hills surrounding the burh, and then at the garden next to his hall where vegetables and plants grew amidst the buzz of beehives. His breath caught in his chest, Eawynn was there, sat on a chair, watching the plants sway in the breeze. The wind blew her dark hair away from her face, and she clutched a blanket around her shoulders. Beornoth swallowed against the hollowness in his stomach, and the catch in his throat.

He strode through the corridor, and through the wide hall, nodding a greeting at the men who tended the central fire, which always burned, and at the women who were covering the hard-packed earthen floor with fresh rushes. Beornoth opened a small door at the rear of the hall and emerged into the sunlight, squinting at the change from the darkness of his rooms and hall to the brightness outside. The sound of children playing and the people of Branoc's Tree talking and laughing filled the air, and it was a joyful sound. So different from the wailing and sorrow of Watchet. He walked around the hall until he came to the garden, and he approached Eawynn slowly. Bees hopped from yellow and blue flowers, and she turned her head as his boot snapped a twig on the soft grass. Beornoth stopped, the deep brown of her eyes so familiar, and yet so distant. She held his gaze, and Beornoth held his breath, unsure of what her reaction would be to seeing him. The corners of her mouth turned down and her lips turned up. It was a smile, of sorts, a sad but acknowledging smile. He took slow, careful steps until he stood next to her.

'It's a beautiful day,' he said, his voice stuttering. The words were clumsy, but it was hard to know what to say to a woman who had experienced so much pain, and with whom he had once shared such deep love and happiness. There was little trace of her younger self in the deep brown pools of Eawynn's eyes. But amongst the sounds and smells of the garden, he remembered her laughing and smiling on such a day long ago, beautiful, funny and happy. The sound of children laughing was also thick in that memory, and it soured it, too painful to contemplate. Their children, dead children. She nodded softly in answer to his statement, and he looked down at her pale face. The blanket slipped away from her neck and Beornoth saw the cruel and jagged scar which ran along her throat, white and savage where Vikings had unsuccessfully cut her throat after they had raided and burned their home in the north. He closed his eyes and raised his head, the sounds of the bees and breeze drowned out by the memory of that pain and, worse, the guilt. He had not been at home on that terrible day. Beornoth had been off fighting for his Lord, the Ealdorman of Cheshire, when the Vikings had struck and taken everything from Eawynn and from him. They had burned his hall and his children in it. Cruel and vicious men had brought ruthless violence to his wife and to his people, and left Eawynn for dead. But their cut had not been deep enough, and she had survived to live locked in a mind filled with dead children and the pain and suffering inflicted upon her on that day long ago. Eawynn had been driven mad by the pain, and Beornoth had fallen into drunken despair and had lost his lands and heriot. Eawynn had gone to live with nuns for her own safety and to be cared for, because he had been too drunk and had fallen too low to care for her.

'There will be honey soon,' she said quietly, almost as a whisper. His heart leapt to hear her speak, his one and only love, whom he had let down so badly, whom he had failed to protect when she needed him most.

'Yes,' he said, struggling for words to extend the discussion, unsure of what to say to her. He could count the times she had spoken to him since that terrible day on the fingers of one hand, and to hear her words made his heart leap and his mouth dry.

Silence passed between them. But Beornoth felt warm in it, like he was home. He wanted to tell her she would always be safe now, and that he would never let anyone hurt her again. But he had said such words before, and it was enough that she was alive, sat in the warm garden with the sun on her face. Beornoth jerked as he felt a soft warmth touch his hand. Eawynn had reached up and slid her small white hand into his own big, calloused paw and it sent a tingling rush up his arm. He swallowed down the lump in his throat and allowed himself to enjoy the moment, the feeling of her skin against his. It felt like happiness, like peace. He closed his hand softly around hers, and they stayed like that. Silent, but together, both remembering each other as they had been when they were young and happy, with two beautiful daughters filling their days with laughter and joy. He wished he could spend all his days like that, with his wife in the sun. But that was not his destiny, he was Beornoth Thegn and warrior, and two days later men came from Ealdorman Byrhtnoth, because his sword was needed again to protect the people of Saxon England.

## 7

A boy led Ealdorbana around the pasture on a long rope. The horse snorted and trotted, huge and powerful, and his coat had been brushed to a shine.

'Here,' Beornoth said, and gave the stable boy next to him three small silver coins. 'Share that with the other lads, the horse is well cared for.' The boy's eyes lit up, and he grinned broadly, holding the coins up to his face.

'Thank you, Lord,' he said, and scuttled off to show his mates their newfound fortune.

'That is a magnificent animal,' said a Norse voice behind him. Beornoth didn't need to turn to know the voice came from Brand, the Norse hostage. The boy had left Ealdorbana close to Beornoth to munch at a hemp nosebag hanging from a fence post. Beornoth leant in and stroked the warhorse's powerful neck. He reached into the pocket of his jerkin and fished out a red apple, which Ealdorbana ate hungrily, his lips tickling Beornoth's hands as he took the fruit.

'He was bred for war, trained not to fear the sounds and smells of battle,' said Beornoth, speaking Norse. The horse raised his head and Beornoth looked into the beast's large eyes and scratched under his chin and behind his ear.

'Like you and I then, Lord,' said Brand, and Beornoth nodded at that truth. 'We do not have many such horses in Norway. We have fine horses, but not for battle. Vikings ride the Whale Road, and fight on foot.'

'Where is your home?' asked Beornoth, not because he cared about the Viking, but because he was always keen to glean as much information on the Norsemen as he could, to better under-stand his enemy.

'Rogaland, close to Hafrsfjord. There was a great sea battle there, once.'

'I have heard the tale, King Harald Fairhair, wasn't it?'

'Yes, Lord, I congratulate you on your knowledge of our history. King Harald is Olaf's great-grandfather, and the first King of all Norway. That was the place of my birth, but my father served Olaf's father when he was King of Viken, which is further south.'

'So Olaf is a prince then?'

'Yes, he has led a life worthy of the greatest sagas.' Brand paused, and Beornoth turned to him. He was not as tall as Beornoth, but was broad in the chest and shoulder, a gift many Northmen took from rowing their warships across seas and up rivers. He had long blonde hair which rested on his shoulders in two thick braids, and a tattoo of a raven on his neck above a long beard. Beornoth raised his eyebrow and turned back to Ealdor-bana, stroking his coarse mane.

'Go on then,' Beornoth sighed. 'Tell me his story.'

'Harald Greycloak killed his father in pursuit of the throne. So his mother, Astrid, had to flee with Olaf whilst he was still growing in her belly. Harald was the son of Erik Bloodaxe, and he sent his killers on her trail, chasing Astrid first to where Olaf was born in secret on an island, then to Sweden, and finally Astrid fled to her kin in the land of the Rus. But pirates attacked her ship, and slavers took Olaf. They sold him on for the price of a cloak, and Olaf came eventually to his kin in Novgorod, who freed him from slavery. Whilst he was but a pup, Olaf killed his slave master with an axe, and fought his way up to become a leader of men and the master of his own ships. He will be King of Norway one day.'

'Unless he dies here in England.'

'He won't. The Gods favour Olaf. He will be King, maybe here in England as well. That is why I came here to fight alongside him with my father's men and ship.'

'I have heard your story many times, from other Vikings. You want to build your reputation and honour the Gods, so you sail with Olaf, a great war leader, to make your name.'

'Yes, that is my story,' said Brand, adjusting his belt and jutting his chin out. 'I left my father's lands in Rogaland to sail with Jarl Olaf, and I will make my name as a warrior.'

'You will make your reputation by making war on my people and write your reputation in their blood. You bring your ships and your axes here, to places like this,' Beornoth waved his arm around the fields of Branoc's Tree. 'And make corpses of the simple folk, the peaceful families, all for your adventure. I suppose you think Olaf honours you by making you a hostage?'

'He does. It means I am an important warrior in his army. We fight to honour the...'

Beornoth raised a finger to stop Brand. 'We will bury Padda later today, a good man injured fighting at Watchet. He took a wound to the gut and had spent the last three days writhing in agony from the infection in the wound. He has a son who you can comfort as we put his father's corpse into the ground. His father, who would be alive now if you and Olaf had not sailed to our shores in search of glory. You fight because you like to kill, and know this: if Olaf raids our shores again this year, I will kill you myself.'

'You will try,' said Brand with a shrug. Brand stared at Beornoth, and he stared back. The Northman was a fighter, Beornoth could see that from the scars on his hands and face, but so was he, and as Beornoth stared into his eyes, part of him wanted the Viking to try him, to lunge at him or hit him. Because if he did, Beornoth would tear him apart. And, Beornoth spoke the truth, he would kill the man in a heartbeat. They kept their eyes locked until a voice called to Beornoth from the stables.

'My Lord, riders approach. They look like Ealdorman Byrhtnoth's men.'

'Thank you for your hospitality, my Lord,' said Brand, and he smiled at Beornoth, breaking the stare and reaching out to stroke Ealdorbana.

'I will feed you and provide you with ale and warmth. But next summer you will leave our lands, and you will not return if you value your life.' Beornoth strode across the pasture towards the stables.

'Looks like Aelfwine of Foxfield, and Leofsunu of Sturmer,' said Alfgar, standing by the stables, staring at the approaching riders.

'Have Aethelberga prepare food and drink for them.'

'Surely Olaf cannot have attacked again already,' said Alfgar. He glanced across Beornoth's shoulder towards Brand.

'Who knows? Let's see what they have to say.'

The two Thegns rode through Branoc's Tree's gate and came with a party of six warriors, all mounted on splendid horses. Beornoth met them with a hand held up in greeting, and they returned the gesture.

'Beornoth, your burh is in fine order,' said Aelfwine with a smile splitting his handsome face.

'Welcome, friends,' Beornoth said. 'What brings you to Branoc's Tree?'

'The King summons us to Winchester,' said Leofsunu. He dismounted and Alfgar sent a boy to take the horse. Leofsunu clasped Beornoth's forearm, and they nodded in greeting. Beornoth knew both men as high-ranking Thegns of Essex, and part of Byrhtnoth's hearth troop of trusted warriors. They were brave warriors with well-earned reputations, and Beornoth had fought alongside them at Mersea Island and at Watchet. Leofsunu was a warm man, quick to make a joke and laugh, but he was the ugliest man Beornoth had ever seen. He had bulbous eyes and huge ears which stood out from his head like the handles of an ale jug. He was bald apart from wisps of brown hair which grew around the bottom of his skull, and his lips were small but thick.

'Trouble?' asked Beornoth.

'There will be if we don't get some ale soon,' said Leofsunu, and Aelfwine laughed. 'Aye, trouble. But not the bloody Vikings this time, thank the Lord. Come, let us drink and we will talk together.'

Aethelberga greeted the warriors and fussed around them, making sure they were sitting at benches close to the fire inside Beornoth's hall, and that they were brought bread, cheese and ale. Beornoth brought Wulfhere and Alfgar with him to sit at an eating bench with Aelfwine and Leofsunu.

'Wulfhere, you fought like a bear at Watchet. I hope Beornoth has rewarded you,' said Aelfwine.

'Well, he hasn't tried to hit me, or cursed at me since the battle. So, you could say that he has,' said Wulfhere, and the men inside the hall laughed. 'I am rewarded, my Lords.' Wulfhere slipped off a silver arm ring which Beornoth had presented to him after the battle at Watchet and held it up for the warriors to see.

'A good Lord keeps his men in rings,' said Aelfwine, and raised a tankard of ale to Beornoth.

'Which is why I am so poor,' said Leofsunu. 'Because my men fight like Beowulf himself.' The warriors in the hall laughed again and drank their ale. The chatter of warriors filled the room, along with the scraping of plates and cups on the wooden benches as they ate their meal.

The thirst in the back of his throat pricked Beornoth, and there was a nag in his head to drink with the visitors. The ale looked frothy and cool, and he imagined the joy of it as it filled their bellies, warmed their chests and dulled their minds. A serving girl appeared over his shoulder and poured Beornoth a cup of water. He nodded thanks and took a drink; it was dull and tasteless.

'No ale for you, Beo?' asked Leofsunu.

'Just water,' Beornoth replied, and he met Leofsunu's gaze firmly and with an upside-down smile that told Leofsunu to press the matter no further. Beornoth could not drink ale, because if he took a taste of it, he would never stop. Drink had cost him his ancestral heriot, his family's lands in the north, and he had almost fallen into a pit of drunken despair from which he could never return. 'So, what news from the Ealdorman?' he asked, leaning into the table and changing the subject.

'Trouble in the north,' said Leofsunu.

'A Northumbrian Thegn has attacked lands in Westmoreland. Good people killed, cattle taken, and halls ransacked,' said Aelfwine.

'Who was it?' asked Beornoth.

'I forget you are from the northern shires yourself,' said Aelfwine. 'Thered is the scoundrel's name, son of Oslac, who is Ealdorman of Northumbria.'

'I know of Oslac,' said Wulfhere. 'The man I served before

Beornoth was a Thegn in his lands, north of York. They once banished Oslac during the reign of the last King.'

'King Edgar, Æthelred's father?' asked Alfgar.

'No, his brother Edward.'

Leofsunu and Aelfwine exchanged a glance and cast their eyes at the table.

'Edward banished him for taking land belonging to the Church. Also, he is of Danish heritage, and is close to powerful men in Denmark, or was when I lived in those lands, at least.'

'Is Oslac still banished?' asked Alfgar.

'No, he returned when Æthelred became King, when he was a child and his mother, Lady Ælfthryth, ruled on his behalf. Thered is Oslac's son, as I remember it,' said Wulfhere.

'The King has summoned Byrhtnoth to Winchester, and his messenger said that the King needs the Ealdorman to quell troubles in the north. So, we will ride for Northumbria,' said Aelfwine. 'And we should talk no more of traitors. One man's traitor is another man's hero, depending on who is King.'

Wulfhere opened his mouth, but Leofsunu shook his head, and so Wulfhere kept his peace and took a swig of ale instead. Beornoth saw the exchange and saw the strange look in Aelfwine's green eyes as he spoke.

'Strange that the King would send Byrhtnoth to deal with a troublesome Thegn, and not one of his own men of Wessex?' Beornoth asked, trying to change the subject slightly.

'It's strange, all right,' said Leofsunu. 'Smells like the goings-on of the great and good to me, dangerous work, shadow work. Not for the likes of us who fight our battles in the shield wall.'

'Forgive my simple nature,' said Wulfhere, 'but I don't understand?'

'There is a tale to tell here, dear Wulfhere,' said Leofsunu, 'but I will spare you the long version. Byrhtnoth was a supporter of

King Edward, the heir of King Edgar. Æthelred's mother killed
Edward, so that Æthelred could become King, and she could rule.
He was only twelve years old at the time.'

'Lady Ælfthryth killed King Edward?' whispered Wulfhere,
leaning across the table on crossed arms, his eyes wide and flitting
from Aelfwine to Leofsunu.

'No, Wulfhere,' said Leofsunu. 'She weighs less than my byrnie.
Her men killed Edward at Corfe Castle.'

'Why?'

'She was not Edward's mother, she did it so that Æthelred
could be King.'

'Or so they say,' said Aelfwine. 'Byrhtnoth was a supporter of
Edward, and so not a friend of the King's mother. Also, there is the
subject of land and the Church.'

'Don't start with that, or we will be here all night,' grumbled
Leofsunu, and he called for more ale.

'What about the Church?' asked Alfgar, fingering absently at
the wooden cross hanging around his neck.

'It's a long story,' said Aelfwine, stroking his neatly trimmed
beard. 'As you know, Ealdormen often grant land to the Church in
return for prayer, or for God's good graces. Those lands keep the
priests or monks in silver and food, through rents and the bounties
of the various farms and mills within them. King Edgar gave a lot
of land to the monks, under instruction from the great Archbishop
Dunstan. When Edgar died and Edward came to power, they took
those lands back from the monks, and new Ealdormen were
created to support Edward. Obviously, that did not sit too well with
the monks, or with the Ealdormen who supported Edgar's land
gifts.'

'This is all making my head hurt,' said Wulfhere. 'Just show me
who we have to fight. Leave this nonsense to the men who wear
fine clothes, not the men who wear leather and iron.' He stood and

strolled to a different table where, moments later, the warriors there erupted into raucous laughter.

'He is right,' said Leofsunu. 'Let us not talk about such things. Tomorrow we must ride for Winchester and to the King. Byrhtnoth is our Lord, and we will do as he commands, no matter what goes on in the shadows.'

Beornoth ate his food and thought on all Aelfwine and Leofsunu had said. The summons from the King was dangerous. Beornoth remembered how warmly the warriors at the Witan outside Watchet had welcomed Byrhtnoth. They had greeted him with more support than the King himself, which would not have gone unnoticed. There were more dangers to fear than Viking raids and Viking blades. Beornoth knew that all too well. Only last year his enemy Osric of Cheshire had taken his wife Eawynn captive. Beornoth chewed on a crust of bread and the talk at the table drowned out into noise. He wondered how the great men of the Kingdom could play their games of power with Vikings back raiding Saxon soil. They must be united and fight as one if Olaf struck again. To ride to Northumbria would be a distraction, and he would be weeks away from Branoc's Tree should the Vikings strike. He stared at the fire, and in the flames he saw Olaf's harsh, angular face and his threat to find Beornoth in the west, and he worried for the fate of the people he was sworn to protect.

# 8

Beornoth stood in a bright courtyard filled with vivid flowers of blue and yellow. It was a garden haven set within the buildings of the royal palace at Winchester. The city had long been the seat of the Kings of Wessex, and there were reminders of Alfred and Athelstan, and the other great Wessex Lords in tapestries and carvings all over the palace. The courtyard was a small square between two halls, with a cobblestone walkway linking the buildings meandering its way around the plants and bushes, which smelled fresh in the morning sunlight. Ealdorman Byrhtnoth sat on a bench, leaning forward on his knees, his right leg jigging up and down like a ferocious twitch, and a thunderous look on his lined face. They had been waiting in the garden for over an hour. Byrhtnoth had brooded and glowered ever since they had arrived in Winchester, and waiting so long to be brought before the King soured his mood even further .

'Anyone bring any ale?' asked Aelfwine, from where he leant against a stone wall.

'You drank enough ale last night to drown a herd of cows, and that whore you ended up with had a face like a slapped arse,' said

Leofsunu of Sturmer, and the men in the courtyard laughed, until Byrhtnoth shot them a baleful look, and their laughter reduced to quiet sniggers.

'She looked like you then,' said Aelfwine, and winked at his friend.

'Are you saying you humped her because she looked like me?' said Leofsunu, and the men bent double in fits of stifled laughter. Leofsunu waggled his huge ears and stroked the tufts of brown hair around the base of his skull, making the men crumble into fits of painfully silent mirth. Byrhtnoth growled and shook his head. Beornoth had met the Ealdorman and his hearth troop the night before in the Dog and Duck, a tavern at the heart of Winchester's merchant quarter, and the ale had flowed freely. There had been no more talk of the King, or of the suspicion of the shadow manoeuvrings of the eminent men and women of Wessex. Beornoth had thought of little else during the ride to Winchester, where Leofsunu and Aelfwine had continued to talk of how suspicious they were of the King, his mother, Lady Ælfthryth, and the Ealdormen of northern England. Beornoth was surprisingly glad for the talk in the tavern to descend into the boasting of Byrhtnoth's men. Godwin and his brothers talked of their deeds at Watchet, and the feats of bravery and daring they would accomplish should the Vikings attack again. It had been empty talk. The last time Beornoth had seen Godwin at Watchet, he was vomiting and scuttling to the rear ranks with illness. Nevertheless, it had been a cheerful evening, and Byrhtnoth had asked Beornoth to attend this meeting with the King, along with Leofsunu, Aelfwine and a handful of his other Thegns.

Beornoth came to the palace wearing his byrnie chain mail, which the servants at Branoc's Tree had polished to a shine. He had been forced to leave his sword and seax at the palace gates, as had the others in Byrhtnoth's party, because blades were not permitted in the presence of the King. Aelfwine had whispered something about King Edward and a lesson learned, but Beornoth kept quiet. He had never been to Winchester before, and the palace was a thing to behold of neatly cut stone and high pillars.

Beornoth heard soft footsteps shuffling along a corridor leading to the garden, and a small man dressed in the King's livery appeared. He was a thin man with a long nose, and he bowed towards Ealdorman Byrhtnoth. The stomp of heavy boots followed him, growing louder and echoing around the corridor like the beating hooves of a horse. The small man stepped aside, and three men in byrnies snaked past him and into the garden. They paid no heed to Ealdorman Byrhtnoth, not to any of the Thegns in the garden. The man at their head had short red hair and a long, thin beard, which moved with the breeze. As he passed through the courtyard, Beornoth noticed that one of the red-haired man's eyes was milky white, like a strange boiled egg sat within his face. The three warriors disappeared as quickly as they had arrived, and the little man in the King's livery cleared his throat.

'The King will see you now, my Lord,' he said.

'Very well,' grumbled Byrhtnoth, and groaned as he pushed himself to his feet. They followed the small man along a dark corridor, and their heavy boots echoed around the cold stone walls as they marched. The man pushed open a tall oak door on black iron hinges, and led them into a wide and airy room flanked on each side by windows with wooden shutters pulled open to allow the breeze in. Another door opened at the rear of the room, and the King floated in on light feet and dressed in royal finery. A jerkin of dark green and a jewelled belt at his waist. He walked with his hands behind his back, stooped and pensive. Æthelred came to a stop by a table and four chairs and stared thoughtfully at the warriors. His pale eyes rested on Beornoth for a moment, and then he saw the Ealdorman.

'Ealdorman Byrhtnoth, thank you for coming. It is so soon after our victory at Watchet, but I fear we need you again.'

'I am at your service, Lord King,' said Byrhtnoth. He stood straight with his thumbs tucked into his belt, and his bulk and height dominated the room, making the King seem small and frail in comparison. The King gave a half-smile and inclined his head towards the door. There was a pause, which dragged on to become awkward. Leofsunu coughed, and another warrior shuffled his feet. There came a faint tapping sound beyond the door, which became louder and drew closer. The door swung open with a creak, and a grey-haired woman hobbled in using a dark wood cane as she walked. She turned and scowled at the open door and shook her cane until an unseen servant beyond pulled it closed. She came to stand next to the King, and fixed Byrhtnoth with a withering frown, blue eyes in a dark, wrinkled face glittering despite her age. The King kept his eyes on the stone floor.

'Ealdorman Byrhtnoth, the hero of Watchet and every other battle, it seems,' she said in a cracked and croaking voice. The King winced as she spoke.

'Lady Ælfthryth,' said Byrhtnoth, returning her frown.

'There is trouble in the north. A Northumbrian Thegn has taken it upon himself to raid and plunder a fellow Thegn's land in Westmoreland. There is lawless violence up there, and we would have it stamped out. Who better to uphold the King's law and his word, than his greatest warrior, the hero so acclaimed by the Witan at Watchet?'

'I am the King's Ealdorman, my Lady, and I will do whatever is asked of me.'

'I am sure you will,' she grumbled, and she hunched almost double as a wracking cough shook her frail body.

'I hope you are not very sick, Lady Ælfthryth.'

She laughed between coughs, a dry and mirthless laugh. 'I am sure you do, Lord Byrhtnoth.' She raised a crooked, shaking finger.

'Those Lords in Northumbria are of Danish stock. Watch them, they are Vikings at heart, and we fear treachery. There is something afoot up there, Byrhtnoth. Find out what it is. The Thegn you seek is Thered, son of Oslac.'

'Oslac, who is the Ealdorman of Northumbria?'

'The very same,' she croaked.

'Surely my Lady knows Oslac well, having lifted his banishment and allowed him to return to his lands and titles many years ago?'

She licked her lips and stared at Byrhtnoth. 'Will you do as your King commands, or shall we find another loyal Ealdorman to do it?'

Byrhtnoth bowed his head to the King. 'I will ride at once, Lord King.'

'You ride with the authority of the King, Ealdorman Byrhtnoth,' said Lady Ælfthryth. 'You have the power to convene a Witan. Gather the Thegns up there and punish this Thered so that they can witness the crown's power and justice.'

Byrhtnoth nodded solemnly and then held the King's mother's stare. Her head shook slightly from side to side, but her eyes were bright and keen. A slight smirk played at a corner of her thin mouth, before she turned and shuffled out of the room, her cane tapping on the stone floor as she went. Æthelred stayed and lifted his head for the first time to look at Byrhtnoth. He opened his mouth as though to speak, but then glanced at the open door as though waiting for it to close before he spoke. The tapping stopped, and there was a pause, and the door did not open. The King offered Byrhtnoth a wan smile, and then trudged after his mother and the door closed behind them.

Byrhtnoth said nothing following the strange meeting with the

King and his mother. He simply marched the men out of the palace. Byrhtnoth strode briskly through the town with long strides, and there was no talking amongst the Thegns as they trailed behind him. Beornoth walked beside Leofsunu and Offa, but they marched in silence. He wanted to ask Offa about the strange meeting, about the King and how he had deferred to his mother, but he kept quiet. There was a deep tapestry of history between Lady Ælfthryth, Æthelred, Byrhtnoth, the former King Edward and this Ealdorman Oslac of Northumbria, but now did not feel like the time to pick that scab. Byrhtnoth barked an order for the men to make ready to leave, and Beornoth left the Thegns to go to his own men. He had brought Wulfhere and Alfgar to Winchester, along with Wuffa and four of his household warriors. Beornoth had also brought Brand with him. The Norse hostage had caused a stir at Branoc's Tree, and his presence had soured Aethelberga. Fearing unrest whilst he was away, Beornoth thought it better to bring the Norse warrior with him, so he could keep an eye on him. He had not permitted the Norseman to carry his weapons, about which Brand had complained, but Beornoth kept them wrapped safely on his own saddle. The rest of his men had remained at Branoc's Tree to protect the people and the burh.

'Well?' said Wulfhere as Beornoth approached and took Ealdorbana's reins from a stableboy. 'What happened, Lord? Did you see the King?'

'We saw the King, and his mother,' said Beornoth. 'We ride for Northumbria.'

'We might see your old home, Wulfhere,' said Alfgar.

'Aye, we might. Hopefully, we aren't bringing our swords and axes to fight our own people, when there are Vikings circling our shores like wolves around a flock of sheep,' said Wulfhere.

'Do you think we will be gone for long, Lord?' asked Alfgar.

'Hard to say,' said Beornoth. 'A week maybe. We do as the King

and the Ealdorman commands us, but it doesn't sit well with me
either, that we should ride north when the threat is here, as you
say, Wulfhere.' He climbed up onto Ealdorbana's back and
scratched behind the horse's ears. The prospect of riding north
weighed heavily on him. Beornoth had thought he had left the
place behind when he had marched south a year earlier with
Alfgar's father, the Ealdorman of Cheshire, to fight the Vikings. He
had left his old home under a storm cloud, and his enemy Osric
loomed up there like a nest of bats in the high rafters. To ride
towards his past, and towards his enemy when he should protect
the people at Branoc's Tree from any potential Viking attack, felt
wrong.

'Don't tell me you are pining for Wynflaed already?' said
Wulfhere, mounting his piebald mare.

'No, it's the church I will miss,' said Alfgar, and his face flushed
red. 'There is a saints' feast coming up, and the priest will need
help with the preparation, that's all.'

'Aethelberga and the women will help with that, lad. Don't
worry. And our Viking friend is with us, so he isn't there to swive
your pretty Wynflaed,' Wulfhere said, and he laughed as Alfgar
cursed under his breath, and then crossed himself at the sin of it.

They rode out of Winchester in a long line of horsemen, with
Byrhtnoth at their head. There were thirty riders in all, and
Beornoth and his men rode at the centre of the column. The
people of the city moved out of their way, and bowed as they
passed, warlords in shining mail and powerful horses trotting
through the mud and stink of the busy streets and lanes. Their
journey would take them to Oxford and then Stamford, and then
on to York and Northumbria. The land around Winchester was
verdant and bright with summer sun and the sounds of birds and
farmers in the fields. They rode north until they picked up the
wide, flowing River Thames, which passed through the old Roman

city of Lundenburg on its journey to the sea in the south-east. Beornoth rode with Offa and Leofsunu, and they rode mostly in companionable silence until they came alongside the river, and the rushing flow of its waters filled the air.

'Tell us, Offa, for no one has fully explained it to me, what went on between the Ealdorman and Lady Ælfthryth, back when Æthelred came to the throne?' asked Leofsunu.

'It's a long story, my young friend. Probably one better told by Byrhtnoth himself,' said Offa, and he shifted uncomfortably in his saddle.

'We will ride for days, Offa. At least give us some of the tale now before we reach Oxford. You were there, after all, and you were probably ancient and wrinkled even then.'

Offa laughed silently and shook his head. 'I was there, but keep your voice down, Leofsunu. I don't want everybody to think I am gossiping like a maid at the milking stool.'

'I heard Lady Ælfthryth killed King Edward?' said Beornoth. Leofsunu and Aelfwine had told him as much, as though it was common knowledge, but the events of the royal family did not reach the northern shires, and when it had happened Beornoth had heard only that one King had died, and another now wore the crown.

'She was behind it, yes,' said Offa, and took a quick glance around to check who was in earshot. Satisfied that his audience was limited to Beornoth and Leofsunu, he continued. 'It's all to do with land, Church land. As you know, Ealdormen and Thegns such as our good selves often make donations of land to the Church, for the support of God, the support of the priests themselves, to have sins forgiven, or to sell the land to the Church when in need of silver.'

'I know that well enough,' said Leofsunu. 'My father granted a beautiful swathe of land on the edge of Sturmer to the abbey there, hoping the gift would wash away his sins, the miserable old bastard.'

'What you may not know, however,' continued Offa, 'is that Church land used to be exempt from the King's taxes and exempt from the duty to upkeep bridges and burhs and exempt from providing men for the fyrd. That practice was stopped in Wessex and Essex, but it still exists in other shires. As Thegns, we must fund the upkeep of our lands from the income of our own hundreds, and we must provide men from our lands to join the fyrd army when called upon. Æthelred's father, King Edgar, feared the growing power of the Church and was a supporter of the monasteries, rather than the traditional Church. He granted the monasteries land to increase their power and took that land from the nobles and Ealdormen of England, and from the Church.'

'So how does taking land from a priest and giving it to a monk cause the King's mother to have a problem with Byrhtnoth?' asked Leofsunu. He rubbed his fingers across his bulbous eyes, shaking his head.

'I was getting to that before you interrupted me,' said Offa. 'When Edgar died, there were arguments over who should be King: Edward or Æthelred. Byrhtnoth supported Edward, as did other powerful Ealdormen like Aethelwine of East Anglia. When Edward took the throne, the noblemen took back many of the land grants Edgar had made, and there was fighting throughout the Kingdom at the holy outrage of it. We fought against Aelfhere of Mercia, and the hatred was bitter. Many thought it was about who was the more legitimate heir, Edward or Æthelred. But really, it was about land and power. The land grants enabled the great families to put their second and third sons in charge of vast swathes of land as abbots or Bishops and become wealthy without paying taxes and paying for the upkeep of those lands. Some, like this Oslac in Northumbria, were banished during Edward's reign.'

'My father spoke of those days, now that you say it. I remember he said he fought alongside Byrhtnoth against the East Anglians,' said Leofsunu.

'They were dark days. Our own Aelfwine's father, Aelfric, was a convicted traitor. He is a descendant of Mercian nobility, and is a cousin of Aelfhere, Ealdorman of Mercia.'

'You southerners are always fighting about something,' said Beornoth, shaking his head. It was a hard tale to follow, but as far as he could tell, Offa was right. When the old King died, the Lords of England fought over Church land. They made their second sons Bishops or abbots and kept their land which had been granted to the Church, and became richer through the exemption from tax and upkeep duties.

'Many northmen were involved as well,' said Offa. 'Many Northumbrians, and East Anglians have Danish blood, as you know, Beo. Oslac, and Aelfwine's father were found to have been colluding with the Danes, inviting them back to our shores and guaranteeing support for their armies if they came. In the end, Lady Ælfthryth took it upon herself to have King Edward killed and put her son Æthelred on the throne. He was only a child, and she ruled the country in his stead. Men like Oslac were recalled from banishment, and she restored land to those in the nobility, and the Church, who had opposed Edward and supported her.'

'So, Lady Ælfthryth hates Byrhtnoth because he supported Edward, and fought against her supporters?' asked Beornoth.

'Yes,' said Offa with a long sigh.

'And she hates him more now that Byrhtnoth is the hero of River's Bend and Mersea Island, and she saw how the Witan acclaimed him at Watchet,' said Leofsunu.

'And now we ride towards Oslac...' began Offa.

'Who is the King's mother's ally, and Byrhtnoth's enemy. And we ride on her orders, given by her on the King's behalf,' said Beornoth.

'But aren't we supposed to be going to Northumbria to punish Thered? Who is Oslac's son?' asked Leofsunu.

'Yes, but there is a strange warp and weft to all this, don't you think?' said Offa. The question went unanswered, but Beornoth stared ahead at Byrhtnoth, huge and silent riding alone at the head of the column. Now he understood why the Ealdorman's mood was so sour. In the midst of their troubles with the Vikings, they were travelling north on the King's mother's orders. Riding into a wasp's nest of traitors and plots, right in the middle of the dealings of the most powerful people in the Kingdom, and a dispute which had led to the death of a King.

Byrhtnoth's warriors rode north, across a land fat with blooming crops and green forests. The company had followed the route from Oxford north, travelling across Watling Street, which once divided the old Danelaw from Saxon lands, and then into the lands around York. They asked the folk they met in the fields where to find Ealdorman Oslac or his son Thered the Thegn. Thered, they said, was Thegn at Loidis. Beornoth knew of the town, there was no burh or fortress there, it was a small place on the banks of the River Aire but there was a monastery there, and if the place had a Thegn, then there would be a gatehouse and some sort of wall to be defended.

Loidis sat almost directly between the place of Beornoth's birth, close to Mameceaster in the north-west, and the old Roman city of York in the north-east.

'Do any of you northerners know this place?' asked Aelfwine, leaning over the rump of his horse to look back at Beornoth, Wulfhere and Alfgar, who rode together with Brand the Norse hostage.

'I know it,' said Beornoth. 'Lots of Danes around here, descendants of Ivar the Boneless's army. Over a hundred years of Vikings in these towns and farms around York.'

'I was born only a day's ride from here. I lived and became a warrior there,' said Wulfhere.

'Should we visit your home once this business is over?' asked Aelfwine.

'There are no happy memories in that place for me any longer. I served my first Lord there, a Thegn like you, Lord Aelfwine. He was a good man, a good ring-giver. But there was a dispute with an Ealdorman and another Thegn, and we lost that fight. My Lord was killed, and I became a masterless man for a time. Until Beornoth brought me to justice with gentle persuasion. It's a shit-hole, anyway. Nothing to see but mud and sheep,' said Wulfhere, to much amusement.

'Danes?' said Brand, leaning towards Beornoth, his long blonde braids dangling from his head.

'Yes, there are many descendants of northmen in these lands, grandsons of the Ragnarsson army.' He raised an eyebrow at the Norseman, who had kept himself to a sullen silence throughout the journey north, his face fixed into a frown and his eyes firmly on the road in silent protest at being deprived of his weapons.

'Yorvik is close then, no?' Brand used the old Viking word for York, which had once been called Eoforwich by the Saxons, but the invading Danes had struggled with the word, and it had become first Yorvik, and then York.

'It's close, further north.' Beornoth saw the frown slip from Brand's face, and a thoughtful look fill his eyes. Beornoth knew what the Norseman was thinking, that there was a ready-made army up here in the north of Æthelred's Kingdom, men who might rally to a strong Norse or Danish banner should there be a war. Which was true, but it was not that simple. The settlers had been part of the fabric of Saxon society for so long that they were both

Saxon and Dane. Almost all were Christians and had lost the savagery of their Odin worship and the thirst for glory that religion brought. They were Thegns, and farmers, merchants and Ealdormen, and for many, it would feel like they were fighting their own people.

Byrhtnoth's men followed the directions of a shepherd up high pastures, until they reached a break in the hills and dales, where the land gave way into a flat shallow basin cut through by the River Aire. Bleak brown and black mountains rose in the distance where cloud sat low, thick and still like dragon smoke. At the centre of that basin and beyond a ford in the river was a small town. It was nothing more than a cluster of one-storey wattle houses with dark thatch, but there was a hall ringed by a timber fence, rather than by a ditch, bank and palisade. The wider town had no fortifications, and beyond the buildings was a fenced paddock filled with grazing horses.

'Loidis,' said Byrhtnoth as they approached the town. Wisps of smoke blew on a chill wind, and short, hardy grass covered the surrounding ground, punctured here and there by dark green bushes and plumes of bracken. Sheep grazed lazily, and the sound of the rushing river mixed with their bleating and the ring of a blacksmith's hammer to fill the fresh but chill summer air.

'They have spotted us,' said Offa, his brindled stallion moving slowly alongside Byrhtnoth's. A group of warriors strolled slowly from the hall and through its low wall.

'A lot of warriors and horses, for so small a place,' said Alfgar.

'They will still be drinking and celebrating their raid,' said Leofsunu.

Ealdorman Byrhtnoth grumbled and chewed his beard and stopped his horse just before the ford in the river, where its clear waters babbled noisily across rocks and shale. Beornoth reined in alongside him.

'There are thirty horses in that paddock, Lord,' said Beornoth, as he watched ten men stroll towards the river's edge. Two of them wore mail, and the rest were clad in leather breastplates. They were all armed, some with spears, and others with axes resting on their shoulders. The two warriors in byrnies both had swords strapped to their waists.

'One of the two in byrnies must be Thered,' said Byrhtnoth. 'And yes, likely there are more of them somewhere inside the village. Watch them, Beo.' He clicked his tongue and urged his horse forward. He reined in where the grass fell away into the river and leant over his saddle. 'I am Ealdorman Byrhtnoth of the East Saxons. I am come by order of the King, and with his authority to bring the Thegn known as Thered, son of Oslac, before a Witan to answer for his unlawful raiding and pillaging of Westmoreland.'

One of the mailed men coughed and hawked up a gobbet of phlegm which he spat into the river. Byrhtnoth's men bristled around him. Horse tracings jangled, and leather creaked as they shifted in their saddles, and hands fell to weapons. The men on the opposing bank saw it, and they shifted their feet, eyes flickering along the line of mounted warriors.

'Who is the King again?' said the man. He was young with short, dark hair cut close to his head. He had a long face and was clean-shaven.

'My Lord Æthelred of Wessex is your King,' said Byrhtnoth, sitting straighter and his voice hardening. 'Are you Thered?'

'Who did you say you were again?' said the young man. He yawned and scratched his arse.

'Are you Thered?'

'I am Thered, Thegn. This is my town, and you are in Northumbria. You are welcome to water your horses and then be on your way. You are far from home, grandfather.'

'You can come with us willingly, on a saddled horse and with one companion, to face the Witan. Or we can take you.'

'Take me?' Thered scoffed, and he looked back at his men. They laughed dutifully. 'You can try, if you like. You aren't Ealdorman here, no matter what your King says.'

'You are a Thegn and are oathbound to King Æthelred, will you come or not?'

'I am sworn to my father, who is the Ealdorman of Northumbria. You can take this up with him. Now, go.' Thered waved his hand at Byrhtnoth as though he were an annoying market trader or a pestering child.

'Wulfstan, Beornoth. Take him,' barked Byrhtnoth.

Beornoth climbed down from Ealdorbana and strode towards the river. Wulfstan joined him. Wulfstan was not a Thegn, but was a warrior of Byrhtnoth's household troops. He was an enormous man, taller even that Beornoth and with a neck as thick around as Beornoth's thighs. His nose had been broken in some distant fight, and his ears were cauliflowered from wrestling, at which he was widely held to be the best in all England.

'Wulfstan,' Byrhtnoth said as they passed his horse. 'Try not to kill anyone if you can.' Wulfstan grunted to confirm he understood the order. Beornoth rolled his shoulders to loosen his muscles as Thered's men fanned out into a line around their Lord. Thered himself took a spear from the man next to him and smirked at Beornoth.

'Look, these must be their best men. A crusty old bastard and a big simpleton,' Thered said, and his men laughed along with him.

Beornoth didn't break his stride and the chill of the river soaked his boot as he stepped into the ford. 'I can't believe he thinks I'm old,' said Wulfstan, grinning at Beornoth. Beornoth shook his head at the joke. Wulfstan was slightly cross-eyed, and with his vast frame and misshapen features, he did look like a lackwit. 'All right, big mouth, that's enough of your shit talking. Put the spear down, no one wants any blood spilled here today,' Wulfstan said.

'Who says no one wants blood? I'll piss on your dead face if you climb out of that river,' said the other man in byrnie chainmail. He was a slim man of an age with Thered, and so had seen around twenty summers.

Wulfstan strode through the ford and reached the far bank. He carried a long-handled war axe in two hands, and as he put one foot on the bank, Thered and his mailed friend lunged at him. The entire line of Thered's warriors leapt to back their leader, leaving only one man facing Beornoth on the riverbank. Beornoth heard the clash of weapons begin to his left, where Wulfstan exchanged blows with the young Thegn. The man facing Beornoth was a small, slight man with a balding head and a droopy eye. Beornoth didn't even draw his sword. He put one foot on the bank and the man levelled his spear. Beornoth ran up the river's bank so that he didn't lose his footing, and the spearman backed away from him. Beornoth strode towards him, and the man half thrust his spear forwards, not fully committing to the strike. Beornoth caught the spear just behind its blade and yanked it out of the little man's hands. As the warrior fell towards him, Beornoth punched him in the stomach so that he doubled over, and then cracked him over the skull with the spear's shaft.

He left the man unconscious on the grass, then strode to where the rest watched their leader exchange blows with Wulfstan, who was now out of the water and pressing the two mailed warriors backwards. The rest of Thered's men just watched the fight and shook their weapons at Wulfstan, threatening to strike at him, but clearly fearful of his monstrous size and fearsome weapon skill. A baying warrior turned just in time to see Beornoth's elbow connect with his eye socket, and another man cried out as Beornoth dragged him into a headbutt, his cheekbone shattering under the weight of the blow. He stamped on the groin of the man he had elbowed, and suddenly the rest of the warriors ran back towards the relative safety of Loidis's buildings.

Beornoth heard laughter from across the river as Leofsunu and Wulfhere mocked Thered's fleeing men and their feeble attack. Thered continued to circle Wulfstan warily, and the other man turned to face Beornoth, and he raised his sword, its point quivering five paces from Beornoth's face. Beornoth dragged his own sword free of its scabbard and batted away the man's blade. He tried to recover, but he was slow and there was no strength in the swing. Beornoth just stepped into it and the man's blow was fouled as his forearm struck Beornoth's chest. He twisted the warrior's wrist savagely so that he dropped his sword. Beornoth didn't let go and bent the man's arm backwards until it was fully extended, and he fell to his knees, yelping in pain. He slammed the pommel of his sword onto the warrior's forearm, and the bones there made an audible crack as they shattered under the blow. Beornoth kept hold of the man's hand and dragged him towards the river by his broken arm. The warrior scrambled across the grass on his knees, whimpering at the pain.

'You disrespected the Ealdorman of Essex,' Beornoth growled. 'Your bloody raid has forced me to ride halfway across bloody England, when I should be at home protecting my people against the sea wolves.'

'Please, stop,' the man gasped through sobs as Beornoth hurled him into the river. Beornoth slid his sword back into its scabbard, so that its precious blade didn't get wet in the river. The man cowered in the babbling ford, cradling his broken arm to his chest and shivering in the cold water. Beornoth kicked him in the chest, so that he went sprawling again in the river, and then grabbed a fistful of his hair to drag him up the bank before Byrhtnoth. The warrior left a brown smear in the field where his wet mail slid over the ground. Beornoth let go of his hair and kicked him in the face, smashing his nose so that blood spattered across the grass.

'Apologise to the Ealdorman and beg his forgiveness for your insolence,' shouted Beornoth. The man got to his knees, shaking, and apologised from a mouth filled with his own dark blood. Wulfstan brought Thered through the ford, pushing him forward with the haft of his axe, and the young Thegn had a split lip and a swollen eye. He stared at the ground as Wulfstan brought him to stand alongside his kneeling warrior.

'Get him on a horse and let's be away from this place before the others find their courage. We ride for York to call the Witan,' said Byrhtnoth, shaking his head at the two men before him. 'Only the Thegn comes with us, the other one can stay here.'

'I wondered why you only sent two men against their ten, Lord,' said Aelfwine.

Byrhtnoth twisted in the saddle to look at him with a surprised look on his face. 'Would you want to fight Beornoth or Wulfstan?' he said.

'No, I suppose not,' Aelfwine said laughing.

'Do you think you went a bit easy on that poor soul, Beo?' asked Leofsunu, and Byrhtnoth's men broke out into peals of laughter as they left Loidis behind and went to bring Thered before a gathering of the powerful men of Northumbria. That collective Witan would then discuss Thered's crimes, and moot what his punishment should be. Beornoth hoped it would not take long, each night his dreams were filled with Olaf Tryggvason's wolf face, and terrible images of dragon boats descending on Essex and killing their way to Branoc's Tree.

# 10
_____

Beornoth stood in the shadows of York's great hall. A trickle of sweat ran down his back beneath the padded jerkin he wore under his mail, and Beornoth wiped his brow with the palm of his hand. Thegns, warriors, Bishops and abbots were all crammed into the long hall. Benches and seats had been removed, so the high-raftered feasting room could squeeze in as many of the great and good of Northumbria as possible. The place was ripe with the earthy smell of leather and the acrid stink of men's sweat. Outside, the sun blazed down on York, and inside any man who owned one wore his byrnie. It wasn't just armour; the mail showed a man's status, wealth and fighting prowess. But Beornoth was baking like a morning loaf in a clay oven, and beside him Leofsunu shook his head and blew out his cheeks at the heat.

A ring of guardsmen kept the gathering away from the central floor with a square of spears ten paces long, in which the speakers could address the gathering without being jostled. A Bishop babbled a prayer in Latin, with one hand raised and another placed solemnly at his chest. The prayer went on for an age until eventually the Bishop finished his prayer, and every man in the hall made the sign of the cross. All except Beornoth, who was just glad the man had finished.

'We are gathered here today to form a Witan, a gathering of the Lords of Northumbria to make judgement on a Thegn of our great shire,' said the priest.

'There cannot be a Witan without the King,' shouted one man from somewhere in the mass of iron, leather and ecclesiastical robes.

'It's a Moot then,' shouted another voice. Which it was, Beornoth supposed. The only difference between a Moot and a Witan was that the latter supposed to advise the King.

'Who cares? Bloody get on with it,' Leofsunu hissed in Beornoth's ear.

'Oslac is the Ealdorman here,' Beornoth whispered back through the corner of his mouth. 'If it's just a Moot, then Oslac should preside, and he will not punish his own son, will he?'

'True,' Leofsunu said and pulled his byrnie away from his chest to let some air get behind it. 'I hope it doesn't take much longer.' Beornoth nodded. Guards made sure that only Thegns and any rank above that entered the hall, which meant Alfgar, Wulfhere, Brand and the other warriors were all waiting outside for the council's decision. Byrhtnoth had ordered them to be ready to depart quickly, just in case things turned ugly. When they had arrived in York, Oslac had sent a band of his Thegns to ask Byrhtnoth what his business was, and there had been uproar when Byrhtnoth said he was there to summon the Witan, or Moot, to be assembled to pass judgement on Thered. Oslac's Thegns had left Byrhtnoth to find lodging, which was rude. As a fellow Ealdorman, Byrhtnoth should have received welcome and food from Oslac, but the men had found taverns to accommodate them all, much to Wulfhere and the men's delight after many days of hard riding. Oslac's Thegns had come again to demand that Thered be handed over to them, but Byrhtnoth had refused, and within two days they had hastily arranged this gathering in York's main hall.

'Moot or Witan, it does not matter,' said the Bishop, and he banged his Bishop's crook on the stone floor to quiet the rumbling voices. 'Bring forth the accused.'

Offa emerged from the crowd carrying a three-legged stool, which he placed at the centre of the square. Wulfstan then pushed his way free of the throng and led Thered before him. The young Thegn stared around at the men in the hall and smirked at them. He winked at one man, and nodded a greeting at another. These were his people, and Beornoth wondered at the sense of bringing Thered here for judgement. Byrhtnoth should have dispensed justice on the banks of the River Aire at Loidis or brought Thered to Winchester for the King's justice. But then he remembered, Lady Ælfthryth had ordered Byrhtnoth to arrange a Witan in the north to dispense justice in the King's name.

'See that man, over there in the corner,' said Leofsunu, and Beornoth followed Leofsunu's gaze to the opposite corner of the hall, where a group of warriors stood together, looking much like the rest of the men in the hall, clad in mail, grim-faced and bristling with warrior's pride.

'Which one?'

'The one with the milky eye.'

Beornoth squinted, trying to focus his ageing eyes on the distant man. Then he saw him, a man with short red hair, and a red beard grown long but wispy, his left eye as white as cow's milk. 'I see him, I've seen him before somewhere. What about him?'

'I recognise him, but can't say from where yet though, and it's bloody annoying,' said Leofsunu. But then he went quiet, as did every other man in the hall, for the door at the hall's rear opened with a creak which echoed around the darkened timber rafters and through it came a stout man dressed in a blue tunic. He rolled purposefully on thin, bandy legs and his torso was like a keg topped by a bald head and a red face, which was twisted with a sour frown and pursed lips.

'Lord Oslac, Ealdorman of Northumbria,' shouted a bent-backed priest who scuttled along behind the red-faced Ealdorman. There was a hush in the room, broken only by a cough somewhere to Beornoth's right. Oslac marched through the throng, his boots slapping on the stone floor with his strange, short-stepped gait. He came to stand five paces before his son, tucked his hands into his belt and scowled at the men facing him.

'Well, we are all here. Where is the man who brings charges against my son?' said Oslac. His voice was low and loud, and it filled the room like pitch pouring into a bucket.

Byrhtnoth stepped forward to stand behind Thered. He looked huge compared to the seated Thegn, and Oslac, who had to look up to meet Byrhtnoth's broad face. 'I am Ealdorman Byrhtnoth of the East Saxons; I am here by order of King Æthelred and with his full authority. Thered is charged with raiding in Westmoreland, where he stole cattle, silver, and harmed good Saxon folk under the King's protection. He does not dispute that charge, and I gathered us all here today as a Witan to witness the decision of how Thered will be punished for his crimes.'

Oslac laughed silently and rubbed his eyes between two fingers. 'Punished? Witan? You are not the King, Byrhtnoth. We have all heard of your reputation for killing Vikings, and of your glorious victories. And, as far as I recall, you were a supporter of his illegitimate predecessor. This is a Moot, a gathering of the warriors and Lords of my shire, and I will decide what to do with my son, not you.' He shouted the last few words and jabbed a stubby finger towards Byrhtnoth. For a moment, Beornoth thought Byrhtnoth would reach out and snap that finger, but the

Ealdorman stayed calm and waited for the growls of ascent, and rumbling talk around the hall to subside.

'I am not here to argue with you, Oslac. The past is done, and I also remember the part you played in the succession of King Edgar's sons, and that there are many men in this hall who are descended from Danes and Norsemen, just as you are. But no man here is my enemy. I am here to follow orders.'

'You have brought armed men onto my lands and have laid hands on my son. You have attacked his village and injured his men, and I will not stand for it.'

'I am here in the name of the King,' Byrhtnoth shouted, and the hall went quiet as his fury erupted, the roar of it echoing around the stone walls. 'This Witan is arranged under the King's command, and I have invited you here, Oslac, to witness justice, not decide it. My ruling is that Thered will pay wergild to the people of Westmoreland for his unprovoked and unlawful attack. He will pay three hundred pounds of silver, six cows, three pigs and ten sheep before summer's end. That is the King's law, and this Witan is over,' said Byrhtnoth. The room erupted in anger. Men bellowed at Byrhtnoth's belligerence. The Witan was supposed to debate a case, and men would talk and discuss the evidence and make a mutual decision. They shook fists and wagged fingers at Byrhtnoth, and the throng pushed against the spears of the square as the guards struggled to hold them back. Oslac glared at Byrhtnoth, his face turning from red to purple.

Byrhtnoth turned to walk away, having laid down his justice, but Oslac raised his arms for quiet and a hush fell, putting out the collective anger like a blanket on a campfire.

'Whilst we have the people gathered here, for a Northumbrian Moot, or your Witan, Ealdorman Byrhtnoth. There is another matter requiring justice,' said Oslac, and he smiled, a cold, dead-eyed smile.

'Proceed as you wish. My work here is done. I leave York today,' said Byrhtnoth.

'This matter concerns one of your Thegns, I believe,' said Oslac, smiling thinly at Byrhtnoth, triumph glinting in his eyes. 'Now that we have met to pass judgement on my son in the King's name. This gathering will also serve as a Moot to provide justice for a real criminal. A man from the borderlands of Cheshire and Northumbria, a man who was a Thegn and, through drunkenness and low character, fell to the rank of reeve. A man who first assaulted a good man, an honest ceorl, and stole from him a pouch of silver and a good horse.' Beornoth froze, a sick feeling churned in his stomach and his cheeks grew hot. He swallowed. 'His thirst for the vile and ungodly not yet sated, this brute then freed a criminal, a murderer and a masterless man and fled south to join our fine Ealdorman Byrhtnoth here as a Thegn of the East Saxons.' There was a grumbling and hissing from the crowd. 'Then this cur, this scourge on our good society, returned to attack the Ealdorman of Cheshire in his own hall, assaulting him and killing his warriors.'

The warriors, Thegns and holy men crammed into the hall erupted into a roar of outrage. Beornoth saw Byrhtnoth jostled as men burst through the line of spears. Beornoth thought of trying to slip away, to run through the back door and find a horse to speed away, but there was no door and there could be no flight.

'What is it, Beo, you have turned as white as a dead man?' said Leofsunu.

'It's me he speaks of. Remember I rode to Mameceaster last summer? Ealdorman Osric of Cheshire took my wife captive, and I rode into his hall to rescue her. I killed his men,' said Beornoth, and Leofsunu's mouth dropped wide open.

'Oh,' he said, and passed a hand over his ill-shaped face. He put that hand on Beornoth's shoulder. 'We must leave this place. We can't let them take you.'

'I charge your Thegn Beornoth, who was once reeve of Knutsford, with murder, assaulting an Ealdorman, assaulting a ceorl, and theft,' bellowed Oslac, pointing at Byrhtnoth.

'This is an outrage!' bellowed the Ealdorman of Essex. He pushed the men away who had crowded him, and they cowered away from his fury and his monstrous size. 'How dare you bring false accusations against a man who is a hero? A man who fought valiantly against Vikings at River's Bend and Mersea Island?'

'I bring witnesses to support these accusations,' said Oslac with his arms held wide. There was movement at the rear of the room, and Beornoth swore under his breath as Ealdorman Osric of Cheshire strode into the hall. He wore a shining byrnie mail coat, and his hair was oiled and slicked back from his face. Osric swaggered through the throng as though he were the King of England. His eyes scanned the crowd until they locked upon Beornoth's own, and his tongue shot out to lick his lips like a serpent sensing its prey. He smiled and turned to beckon towards the doorway. A warrior emerged, pulling a tiny figure by the arm. It was a woman with brown hair shot through with silver and a dark-lined face. She resisted, and the warrior yanked her arm so hard that she stumbled.

'No,' Beornoth shouted, and anger blossomed in his chest like a kindling fire. He surged through the crowd, elbowing men out of his way. The woman was Blaedswith, she who had been his only friend during the darkest part of his life. He reached the circle of spearmen, and one raised his weapon to block Beornoth, but he grabbed it and hauled the man towards him and threw him over his hip. The crowd surged towards him, and Beornoth roared at them like a cornered bear. He cracked his elbow off a man's jaw and kicked out another man's knee.

'There he is, there is the criminal, seize him!' shouted Osric, and he took three steps back. Beornoth stood in the centre of the open space, his chest heaving, his frame huge and baleful.

'Beornoth is my man, and is a Thegn of the East Saxons,' said Byrhtnoth, addressing Oslac directly. 'He is not on trial here today.'

'He is now,' said Oslac.

Another figure shambled into the hall, and Beornoth recognised Swidhelm, the man from whom he had rented a room whilst he was reeve at Knutsford, and the man he had indeed beaten, robbed, and whose horse he had stolen. A short, stocky warrior followed Swidhelm. He wore a byrnie and had a balding pate of wispy brown hair above a heavy-jowled, ruddy face. It was Streonwold, a brave and reliable old warrior whom Beornoth had fought alongside countless times when he was a Thegn of Cheshire. Streonwold met Beornoth's stare, and his lips came together in a flat grimace. He led Swidhelm to stand alongside Osric and Blaedswith, but kept his eyes fixed on the ground. Streonwold was a fighter and a man of honour, and Oslac and Osric's deep cunning, such shadow work, was unworthy of a man renowned in the shield wall.

'Ealdorman Osric,' shouted Oslac, raising his hands to calm the din in the hall. The gathered men were a mass of red-faced outrage. Spittle trailed in beards and men shook their heads and spat curses towards Beornoth. Blaedswith smiled at him. Her eyes were sunken, and he saw bruising on her neck. She looked thin and old, and Beornoth wanted to lunge for her, to tear her away from the men who had dragged her to help punish him. She was a kind woman, a good woman. 'Who are these folk you have brought before us today?'

'This is ceorl Swidhelm, the honest merchant who was beaten and robbed by the beast Beornoth. He can swear an oath that these crimes are true, and that Beornoth also freed a masterless man and murderer condemned to death.' Which was also true, Beornoth had freed Wulfhere, and took him with him on his journey south.

'Good Swidhelm, do you so swear?' asked Oslac.

'I do, my Lord, this is the man Beornoth who did as you say,' said Swidhelm, and he pointed a bony, quaking finger at Beornoth, but kept his eyes on the ground and would not meet Beornoth's gaze.

'Is this crone the witch who helped him escape?'

'She is. She was one of us and part of our village. But she gave the criminal Beornoth succour.'

'Then she too is to be condemned,' said Oslac.

'Burn the witch!' shouted a voice from the crowd, and there was a cheer of approval.

'Ealdorman Osric, tell us of what happened, that grim day at Mameceaster,' said Oslac, and Osric told the story. He told how Beornoth rode his warhorse into the city and charged through his hall doors, how the horse was like a crazed hell-monster and had ripped open men's faces with its teeth, and how Beornoth had slain warriors to get to the Ealdorman. He told how Beornoth had cut his face with his sword. The crowd gasped and gawped at the tale, and Beornoth felt the hall closing in on him. The heat was close, and he couldn't breathe. He stared at Blaedswith and her eyes locked with his. He had spent years drinking himself into oblivion in her tavern, gorging on ale until it numbed his mind and washed away the pain of his dead children and tortured wife. Blaedswith had always looked after him, made sure he was fed and dressed his wounds whenever he returned from a fight in his capacity as reeve. He wanted to go to her. She was only five paces away from him, but it might as well have been across an ocean. Beornoth knew that if he moved forward, they would take him. Oslac had played the Moot well, and it had been a cleverly thought-out thing of cunning, needing time to prepare and execute. Thered's guilt was not disputed, but this fresh charge seemed worse. The men of Northumbria had not wanted to find their Ealdorman's son guilty and were apathetic to his punishment. But Beornoth was a foreigner. Byrhtnoth's belligerence pricked them, and they wanted blood. Furious faces surrounded Beornoth. Men who would string him up in York's main square in a heartbeat. Byrhtnoth was there at his shoulder, and so was Leofsunu. Aelfwine and the other Essex Thegns permitted in the chamber had forced their way to the front and stood in a line behind Byrhtnoth.

'So, we have a criminal in our midst, and as Ealdorman of Northumbria, I demand justice,' shouted Osric above the clamour, and he raised a finger towards the smoke-blackened ceiling. 'Should we seize this brigand, this murderer?' There was a surge from the crowd as they closed in, and a hand tugged at Beornoth's sleeve. He closed his eyes and breathed slowly, allowing the noise and pressure around him to melt away. Beornoth believed Byrhtnoth must give him up, to give himself and his men a chance to get out of this seething bear pit. He understood and was ready for it. He felt himself jostled but he didn't react, he hoped that Wulfhere and Alfgar would ride south and take care of Eawynn until another Thegn was appointed to his heriot at Branoc's Tree.

'There will be no seizing,' roared Byrhtnoth. 'I speak with the voice of the King. If you lay a hand on me or this man, then you lay hands on the King himself. Are you traitors? Are you not men of God?' Byrhtnoth paused and the rabble quietened. 'I have given my ruling, and Thered will make that payment to the men of Westmoreland. I will leave York now, and Beornoth comes with me. If you want to bring charges against my man, Oslac, you can bring your complaint to the King in Winchester. I will not have one of my Thegns lynched here by this rabble.' Byrhtnoth grasped Beornoth's arm and dragged him away, and he allowed himself to be pulled. Leofsunu, Offa and Aelfwine surrounded him, and they shuffled towards the hall doors. The throng fell quiet, eerily silent as the Essex men edged their way out.

'I will come for you,' Beornoth whispered to Blaedswith as he passed her, and she closed her eyes tight, a single tear rolling down her kind, weathered face.

# 11

_____

Oslac did not stop Byrhtnoth and his men from leaving York. The Ealdorman had marched from the great hall before his Thegns, just as they would in the boar's head battle formation to punch through an enemy shield wall. Byrhtnoth at the tip of the wedge, and Beornoth at its centre, with Offa, Leofsunu, Aelfwine, Wulfstan, Godric and his brothers on the wings. They had marched in grim silence from the hall, across the cobbled courtyard, and around the looming, magnificent walls of the city's great cathedral. Marching at double time, beneath the shadow of the old minster, where once Ivar the Boneless and his warriors had pillaged and stacked their looted treasure. They watched over their shoulders as they marched, fearful, just as Beornoth had been, that Oslac's Northumbrian warriors would pour after them like water from a dam to lay their vengeful hands upon Beornoth. They reached the rest of Byrhtnoth's force, including Wulfhere and Alfgar, and rode from the city without even securing provisions for the journey south.

They rode hard until the sun sat low in a crimson sky flecked with grey-tinged cloud, and stopped at a dense wood a half-day's ride south of York. Beornoth sat on a fallen silver birch trunk, warming his hands on a small fire. He had left his sword belt hanging over a branch five paces away, so he could sit comfortably after the long ride, and his escape from the trap Osric and Oslac had laid for him in York. Wulfhere crouched in the rotting leaf mulch, blowing into kindling and adding twigs to the nascent flame. It had rained earlier in the day, and the woods smelt like wet dog, with a close dampness beneath the canopy of branch and leaf. Ealdorman Byrhtnoth groaned as he sat down next to Beornoth, the wood creaking under his bulk.

'Thank you, Lord,' Beornoth said quietly, keeping his eyes on the flames.

'For what?'

'For not letting them take me.'

'I would never hand over one of my Thegns to another Ealdorman, unless commanded to do so by the King. Especially not to a bastard like Oslac, a traitor, a man once banished from these shores.' Byrhtnoth stroked his shovel-like beard. 'Did you do those things they accused you of, Beo?'

Beornoth looked around at the Ealdorman, meeting his bright, intelligent eyes. 'Yes, Lord. I am guilty of the charges Oslac spoke of. I am a murderer.'

'We are all murderers,' said Byrhtnoth, and he blew out his cheeks. 'What matters is that we kill in war, or within the law at least. We are warriors. Death is our trade. I pray we lived in a time where men like us were not needed.'

'Like I said, thank you, Lord.'

'No need to thank me, man. You are a Viking killer and a Thegn of Essex. We will need your sword, if and when Olaf and his crews attack again.'

'There was a man in that hall, Lord. A man I saw at Winchester,' said Leofsunu. He was crouched at the fire with

Wulfhere, and the flames threw shadows on his big ears and misshapen face, making him look like a troll of the forest. His usual humour gone, and his mouth set firm.

'Are you saying there was a Wessex man in Oslac's hall?' said Byrhtnoth, and the surrounding men who had been busy making shelters from branches and cloaks, or gathering wood for the fire, all now stopped and listened.

'Yes, Lord,' continued Leofsunu. He broke a moss-covered twig and fed it to the fire. 'There were three of them, and one was unmistakable. He had an eye as white and colourless as a goose egg. He walked past us in the courtyard as we waited on the King. Oslac and Osric, the bastards, would have needed time to bring their witnesses to York to bait their trap. There is low cunning there, and it runs against us like shit down a cow's leg.'

'What does that mean, what's going on?' asked Wulfhere. He took out his whittling knife and a piece of wood from a pouch at his belt and shaved thin slices from the timber.

'I don't know,' said Byrhtnoth. 'But whatever it is tastes foul. I knew it was strange for the King, or his mother, to send us north when the Vikings still threaten our coastline. But couldn't see what sort of plan had escaped her cunning thought cage. Whatever is afoot, Lady Ælfthryth's talons are all over it. This Osric of Cheshire is Aethelhelm's son, yes?'

'Yes, Lord,' said Beornoth. 'And he is Alfgar's brother.'

'Young Alfgar is the son of an Ealdorman?' said Byrhtnoth and clapped his hands on his knees.

'I am, Lord Byrhtnoth,' said Alfgar. He stood with a bundle of sticks in his arms and his eyes flicked from Beornoth to Byrhtnoth. 'A bastard son. My father put me into Beornoth's care when we rode south to fight at River's Bend, and when he died, my brother succeeded him.'

'I remember it now, and I remember your brother. Your father was a brave man, and he died with honour.'

'Yes, Lord,' said Alfgar, smiling wanly. There had been no closeness between Alfgar and his father. Aethelhelm had sent Alfgar to the clergy when he was a boy, as was the fate of many second sons of powerful men. But the Church had not suited Alfgar, despite his piety, and so the old Ealdorman had asked Beornoth to teach the lad to fight.

'Osric sent men to kill Alfgar, Lord. They came to Branoc's Tree last year,' said Beornoth.

'He sent men into Essex to kill Alfgar? said Byrhtnoth, his brow furrowing to create a deep knot at the top of his nose. 'What happened to them?'

'They died.'

'Of course they did. So, this Osric is our enemy. As is Oslac, and the mother of the King. She has never forgiven me or the other Ealdormen who sided with King Edward over her son, Æthelred.' Byrhtnoth sighed and looked into the fire, and there was silence, the flames crackling, and the men stared at the Ealdorman. All had whispered the question of why they had been sent north at such a treacherous time, and the rumour had spread of the Wessex men in Oslac's court. 'The Kingdom has not been the same since old King Edgar died. He was a good man, a fine King. Too much land and power has passed to the Church, and too many powerful men have family ties to the Danes, who are ever hungry for our fertile land.'

'My father is not alone in that, Lord, you are right,' said Aelfwine, and all eyes turned to the handsome young Thegn. 'He wanted the return of the Vikings and actively invited their return. To him, pagan Viking rule was better than a Christian Saxon ruler who took swathes of his land and wealth to hand to the Church or the monas-

teries. I, like many, have as much Viking blood in my veins as I do of
the old Mercian nobility. My father paid the price for his treachery
with his life. There are many Lords in East Anglia, Mercia and
Northumbria who feel the same way.' There was an awkward silence,
and then men continued at the business of making camp. They were
solemn words, and Beornoth worried for the future of England, the
country birthed of the old warring Kingdoms of Wessex, Mercia, East
Anglia and Northumbria. The Danes had done much to bring the
country into existence, their invasion forging the old Kingdoms into
one unified and powerful force under the steely determination of
King Alfred and his son Edward and grandson Athelstan.

There was a sudden commotion from across the clearing,
where the younger men of Byrhtnoth's force were brushing and
feeding the horses. Shouting erupted from the dank edges of the
camp, and birds flapped and sang in the treetops, disturbed from
their evening calm. Beornoth stood, as did Byrhtnoth, to see what
was happening.

'Blades, blades,' came a shrill, panicked voice. No sooner did
the shout go up, than an arrow whistled through the twilight to
thump into a tree only five paces from where Beornoth sat with the
Ealdorman.

'Shields,' shouted Beornoth, and he ran towards where he
thought the arrow had come from. His instinct told him to charge
towards the enemy. If the enemy had them surrounded, or even
caught in a crossfire of bowshot, there was no point staying still. He
dashed towards his weapons belt and pulled it from the branch.
He drew his sword and seax, threw the belt away and kept moving.
Around him, warriors moved, grasping blades, shouting and
crouching to avoid the iron-tipped missiles. He heard a man cry
out and saw one of Byrhtnoth's young warriors clutching at
feathers sprouting from his chest, blood gurgling at his mouth.

'We just want Beornoth. Hand him over, and you can all live,' came a shout from the trees. The voice rang around the treetops, and Beornoth moved towards it. He ran in a low crouch, moving from tree to tree, blood pounding in his ears. They had come for him.

'Show yourselves,' Byrhtnoth called from behind him. 'Who is it who attacks us on the road, we who travel with the authority of the King?'

'Just hand him over, or you can all die here in this forest, and no man will ever learn your fate. You will be lost, slain by masterless men, perhaps. You will be forgotten and left to rot here without prayer or priest.' The voice was closer, and Beornoth had his back against a tree trunk. He was breathing hard. He went to move towards the voice again, but an arrow sang past his face, and he fell to the damp leaf mulch of the forest floor. Beornoth scrambled back to the safety of the tree and another arrow thumped into the trunk. It hit the other side of the tree, and Beornoth felt its power through the wood. He made to dart around the tree but ducked back around the opposite side. The feint worked, and an arrow whipped past the space he would have occupied. It would have torn out his throat, and he would have died in the forest, leaving the people who needed him at Branoc's Tree unprotected and vulnerable. He saw the bowman standing behind a bush with shining leaves, and he roared as he charged towards the enemy. The man's face drained of colour as he saw Beornoth charging. He reached for his quiver and pulled free a long shaft and nocked it to his bow, its white feather fletching bright in the evening half-light. Beornoth raised his weapons wide and bellowed again, and the bowman raised his bow, but the weapon shook, because Beornoth was upon him. He loosed the arrow, but it shot high and wild, and Beornoth swung his sword. The blade snapped through the bow stave, and its edge chopped into the man's face with a crunch. He fell shaking, his head a mess of blood and mangled skull bones.

And Beornoth had to saw his sword back and forth to wrench the blade free from the gore.

He knelt and checked over his shoulder and nodded to himself as he saw Wulfhere and Alfgar edging forward behind shields, with Brand the Norseman on Alfgar's left side, shield raised and ready to fight. There was a rustle in the undergrowth to his right, and Beornoth saw the barbed tip of an arrowhead poking from behind a thick tree trunk. He darted towards it and came around the tree to drive the point of his sword through the archer's back, the blade travelling through his leather jerkin and his torso to punch through the other side in a spray of blood. The archer screamed in pain and Beornoth dragged his blade free and kicked the dying man to the ground. There was a roar from the forest's darkness, the voices of many joined together into one war cry. They came from the trees then, a score of warriors armed with spears and shields crashing through the undergrowth, snarling and hungry for blood. More of Byrhtnoth's warriors joined their shields to Wulfhere's small shield wall to meet the attackers, but Brand had peeled away and charged at the enemy, a spear in his hand and bellowing to Odin. He must have snatched the spear up from where weapons had been piled for the night, but he came at the enemy now and he tore one man's throat out and danced around another attacker to swing his spear low, tangling the legs of a running warrior, and then bringing the edge of his shield down to crush the falling man's face.

More of Osric's men surged forward, and three of them surrounded Brand. He crouched behind his shield, and they jabbed at him with spears. Beornoth ran towards them, he dodged a spear coming for his head and backswung his sword at the attacker, but the blade sang through the air and missed its target. He kept moving and saw Brand had taken a spear to his thigh and the Viking had fallen to the ground, where he squirmed and fended off spear blows with his shield. Beornoth brought his sword around and as he reached the warriors around Brand, one turned to him with bright blue eyes. He was too late to stop Beornoth, and those eyes went wide with terror as Beornoth stabbed the point of his sword into his stomach. There was some resistance from his boiled-leather breastplate, and Beornoth withdrew the weapon before it went too deep and became tangled in the man's guts. In one fluid movement, he crashed his shoulder into the injured warrior and rolled around him to plunge his seax into the next spearman's side, feeling the hot, wet blood pulse over his hand. He pulled the seax free, and the third spearman stopped his attack on Brand, and turned his weapon on Beornoth, showing his teeth in a filthy, bearded face. He jabbed the spear at Beornoth, but he batted it aside with his sword. The spearman came on again but cried out in agony and fell to one knee as Brand had scrambled around in the fallen leaves and twigs of the forest floor and stabbed his spear point through the spearman's calf. The man closed his eyes and whispered a prayer to God, but as his mouth opened, Beornoth rammed his seax blade into his maw and drove the point through the back of his skull. Brand clapped Beornoth on the shoulder as the man died.

'You saved my life. I swear to Odin and Thor that I will repay that debt.' He nodded solemnly. The surrounding forest was alive with battle, the clang of iron on iron, and the thud of weapons against shields. War cries melded with shrieks of pain, and Wulfhere and Alfgar were hard-pressed by the enemy, who had formed a shield wall of their own.

Beornoth was about to dash to their aid when he saw Brand's mouth fall open, and something fixed his eyes over Beornoth's shoulder.

'Look out!' Brand shouted in Norse, and Beornoth tensed his muscles, expecting a blade in his back, but felt only the weight of something heavy on his chest and arms. He looked down to see a thick rope looped around him and twisted to peer over his shoulder where a long face grinned, with one white eye staring straight at him.

'Go,' the man with the milky eye shouted, and Beornoth felt himself yanked from his feet by a terrible force. He flew backwards and clattered onto the forest floor; his blades fell from his hands with the impact. Pain shot through his head and chest, and it knocked the air out of him. Beornoth was being dragged through the forest, and he could hear the hoof beats of a horse above the crunching of leaves and branches as he was pulled along at terrible speed. He tried to wriggle against the rope around him, but his head slammed into a dull force, and all turned to darkness.

## 12

---

Beornoth woke to skull-splitting pain in his head, like someone was driving a long iron nail through the top of his forehead and into his brain. He groaned and spat dust and grit from his mouth. He was lying on his side, and tried to roll over, but his bonds clenched him in position. They had tied a thick rope around his arms and chest, and his skin and muscles pulsed and burned where the rope had dug and torn into his flesh as they had dragged him through the forest. He tried to move his feet, but they had also tied his ankles. Beornoth groaned as he rolled onto his back. He opened his right eye a crack and saw only darkness. His left eye would not open. There was swelling on that side of his face which throbbed and made it hard to breathe out of his nose. Crusted blood had dried all down that side of his head, from his scalp, over his eye and down to his chin. He could feel the hard flakes of it against his beard, and he opened his mouth wide and winced at the pain in his jaw. It wasn't broken, but there was a sharp pain behind his right ear.

He bucked against the rope and growled, remembering the ambush in the forest and how he had been caught in the rope like a pig for slaughter. For some incongruous reason, he remembered hearing a tale from a Danish merchant as a boy about how the Norse Gods had tricked Fenris-wolf, the mighty beast who guarded the underworld and was the son of Loki, the trickster God. The other Gods had bound him with a magical fetter to keep him prisoner and at bay until the day of Ragnarök, that end of the days the Norse folk believed would come when their Gods would do battle with the monsters and beasts of the Loki brood. Through the slit of his right eye, he glimpsed stars flashing between the shadows of fast-moving cloud. He bucked again at the ropes binding him, violently rolling and trying to wriggle the rope higher on his biceps so that he could move his arms and free the pressure on his chest.

A boot rested lightly on his shoulder and pushed him onto his back, and the rope bit further into his chest, crushing it and making his breathing quick and shallow.

'He's awake,' said a man in a drawling voice. A face appeared above Beornoth, boyish with a thin, blonde beard. He heard voices talking, and then another face appeared above him, a long, lantern-jawed face with a white eye, strange and ethereal in the night's gloom.

'Take off the ropes and get his byrnie off, and his arm rings. I'll have them before the Ealdorman gets here,' said White-Eye. 'Strip him down to his underclothes, Kari, but watch him. He's as strong as a bull this one, a man of reputation he is. A Viking killer. Leof, you help him.'

The young man rolled Beornoth onto his side and he could feel him working at a knot at his back.

'Here,' said an unfamiliar voice, low and gruff. 'I'll do it, lad. It's a bugger of a rope. It's thicker than your arms.' More pressure and movement at his back, and then the bindings came away and Beornoth breathed out in a gust of air and flopped onto his chest, soft grass wet with dew pressing against his face. 'Lift your arms,' said the gruff voice, the man named Leof. A meaty hand grabbed Beornoth's shoulder and rolled him over, and he saw a large head with bulging eyes and bristling black beard. As he allowed himself to be rolled over, Beornoth snarled and cracked his elbow into Leof's nose and whipped his other arm around to punch him in the guts. The big man cried out and blood spurted from his nose to splatter on Beornoth's face. He heard the younger man cry out and Beornoth dove towards the sound. He couldn't stand because of the ropes around his ankles, but he grabbed a boot and twisted savagely. The young man cried out in terror, and Beornoth flopped onto him, clawing his way up the scrawny body, batting away thin arms as they beat at him, desperately trying to fend him off. Beornoth found the soft flesh of the young man's face and clawed at it, driving his other fist into the man's ribs. Hands grabbed him and yanked him backwards, and Beornoth turned to see the big man clambering on top of him.

'Pin him down, get him,' shouted White-Eye. Leof tried to clamp his arms around Beornoth's torso, but Beornoth got one arm free and clamped his hand around the back of Leof's head and forced his face close so he could drive his forehead into Leof's face. The big man grunted and twisted away. Beornoth roared and flailed his arms around, grasping for another of his captors, rage bursting from him. Something thudded into the back of his head, and it was like being kicked by a horse. Beornoth slumped, lights crackling behind his eyes. As the deep darkness enveloped him, he wondered what had become of Wulfhere and Alfgar, he thought of Eawynn and Branoc's Tree, and the last thing he saw was a vision of Olaf Tryggvason's axe-like face whipped by a sea wind as he drove his dragon ships along the Saxon coastline.

The next time he woke, the sun's warmth was on Beornoth's face and chest. His head rang like a bell, and they had propped him up against a rock. He could feel its cool, rough surface against his bare back. They had stripped him of his mail, and he was naked except for his light trews. Even his boots were gone. His left eye was still closed shut by the swelling in his face. With his good eye, he saw a pale blue sky, warm and free of cloud. The sun shone bright and warm, and he guessed it was still early in the morning from the sun's height above the horizon. Leof and Kari bustled around in front of him. Leof stamped out the remnants of a small fire, his face bruised where Beornoth had attacked him, and Kari tightened saddle straps on a chestnut gelding.

A figure crouched next to Beornoth, and he twisted his head so he could look upon the man with his right eye. White-Eye smiled at him, brown teeth showing in his heavy-jawed mouth.

'Ealdorman Osric is here for you,' he said, and sniffed. 'He wants you bad. Can you hear his horses?' White-Eye cocked a hand to his ear, and Beornoth could indeed hear the rumble of horses in the distance.

'You are a Wessex man,' said Beornoth, the words thick in his swollen face.

'I am indeed.'

'You came north to warn Oslac of Ealdorman Byrhtnoth's coming?'

'I did, just as I was ordered. I follows orders, I do.'

'The King's mother wants Byrhtnoth out of the way.'

'His reputation is grown large, too popular amongst the Thegns and other Ealdormen. Men cheer him more than they do the King himself. Imagine that?' White-Eye tutted and shook his head. 'He should have died in the forest, your Ealdorman. We got you, but we was supposed to kill him. But your Ealdorman will be busy up here in the north for a while yet, I think. He's not amongst friends, the Lords up here are loyal to the old Queen. We'll keep your

Byrhtnoth nice and quiet, out of the way. Maybe we'll get him next time.'

'What if the Vikings attack whilst we are stuck up here? Did you think of that?' Beornoth spat.

White-Eye laughed. 'You think you are the only fighters in England? You think you fight better than Wessex men? Arrogant bastard. We can fend for ourselves. Osric approaches. You are going to make me wealthy, big man.' White-Eye grabbed Beornoth's cheek between his forefinger and thumb and gave it a shake like he was a chubby-cheeked child, and then he laughed again before striding towards where Kari prepared the horses. They were on a low hill between two steeper slopes thick with forest, rising high on either side to create a valley within the woodland. Beornoth could hear water babbling, and the sound of hoof beats drew louder and closer.

'I'll give you a drink if you promise to be good,' said Kari, walking gingerly towards him, holding out a water skin before him.

'I won't hurt you,' said Beornoth, his voice croaking. His throat felt shrunken, and his lips dry and cracked, his tongue like a dried piece of leather. Kari knelt and held the skin out at arm's length, trying to keep himself at a safe distance. He bore red, lurid scratches down one side of his face where Beornoth had clawed him. Beornoth leaned forward awkwardly. Rough hemp rope secured his hands behind his back and his ankles together, so he had to jut his chin forward so that Kari could pour the liquid into his mouth. The water was cool, and it washed away the foulness in Beornoth's mouth and slid down his throat like ice from a frozen lake.

'Good, eh?' smiled Kari. 'Fresh from the brook below the hill there.' He nodded to the west.

'Thank you,' said Beornoth. 'What happened in the forest?
Were many killed?'

'There was a hard fight. The Ealdorman of Northumbria's men
came in hard and fast, but your boys made the shield wall and beat
them back. Fierce fighters, them East Saxons. I think the fight
ended after we nabbed you. Osric's men fell back then. He had to
go back to York to meet some other noblemen. I saw some Danes
in York. Big men like you, with gold and silver on their arms and
tattoos on their faces.' Kari spoke excitedly, his eyes wide in
wonder at what he had seen in the old city.

'Shut your cheese-pipe, Kari,' shouted Leof. 'Leave the bastard
alone. Look what he did to my face.' The big man's face looked like
Beornoth's felt. Swollen, purple and sore.

Beornoth winked at Kari, and the boy smiled and then ran to
join White-Eye by their three horses. Beornoth sighed with relief.
Byrhtnoth and the others had survived the ambush, whose sole
purpose seemed to have been to capture him and kill Byrhtnoth.
There was an ill warp and weft to the midden pit he and Byrhtnoth
had walked into at York. Beornoth knew Osric hated him, and his
belly soured at the thought of what the Ealdorman of Cheshire
would do with him once he was his prisoner. But it was a thing
crafted like one of Wulfhere's carvings that Oslac and Osric had
become aligned against him. Their shires were on either side of
the Pennine mountains, and the borderlands between those shires
were badlands of border disputes and cattle raids. Someone, or
something, must have brought them together, and the King's
mother's low cunning dripped from the thing like warmed honey.
Kari had said there were Danes in York, which made Beornoth
shiver. He had only ever thought about the world in terms of his
own lands and people; he was aware of course of the wider country
and the lands beyond the seas, but to him, his heriot and the
people within it were everything. That was his world. Beornoth

had never understood, or considered, how riven the country was. Powerful men fought and plotted over land and taxes, Ealdormen, churchmen and monks all working in the shadows to make themselves richer and more powerful. He had always known of the close blood ties between the men of the north and their Viking forefathers, but those ties also spread down into Mercia and East Anglia. It made sense, he supposed. They were descendants of Guthrum and his army, the Dane who had made peace with King Alfred back when the Danelaw was formed. Beornoth had also been unaware of the murder of King Edward, and how much power Æthelred's mother wielded over the country. Powerful Saxons fought amongst themselves, and others would welcome the return of Danish rule in the old Danelaw, and all for more land and more power. Beornoth despaired for the Saxon people, should Olaf or any other Norseman land on Saxon shores with an army. Byrhtnoth and the Ealdormen and Thegns of Essex, Wessex and the southern shires could mobilise their warriors and the men of the fyrd, but should the Vikings land elsewhere in the country, they could row their shallow-draughted warships up long rivers and find a country unable to resist them. They would find Thegns and Lords who would welcome them with open arms, like a long-lost lover, coming to free them from the burden of taxes and Church land grants. The presence of Danes at York told Beornoth that there was already open talk between the northern Ealdormen and the Vikings, perhaps an offer of a safe port or supplies should the Danes bring their warriors to England's shores.

The sound of hoof beats rose like thunder until a line of riders crested the hill. Beornoth sighed, and the pain from the wound in his head throbbed and stabbed at his brain, and the countless bruises and scrapes on his body where they had dragged him through the forest stung and ached. Beornoth bowed his head. Osric had arrived, and he would find Beornoth beaten bloody and stripped half-naked. He searched the forests rising on either side of him and hoped to see Byrhtnoth leading his warriors in a charge through the pine trees to strike at Osric and free him from his bonds. But there was no heroic charge, and he doubted his Ealdorman knew if he was alive or dead.

'The mighty Beornoth,' Osric shouted, his voice high-pitched in his moment of triumph. The Ealdorman of Cheshire strode towards him, peeling off riding gloves and smirking through his shining, oiled beard. He was tall and slim, golden hair tied back from his face at the nape of his neck. 'Look at you now.' Osric turned to White-Eye and clapped him on the shoulder, untied a heavy purse from his belt and tossed it to him. 'Your plan worked; I'll give you that, you clever bastard. You should travel west with us and see how we dispense justice in my shire.' White-Eye hefted the purse and nodded his thanks.

Ealdorman Oslac of Northumbria's son, Thered, strode from the group of horsemen. He swaggered across the hillside to stand next to Osric. Streonwold was there also, but he busied himself barking orders at Osric's hearth troop to prepare the horses for camp, refusing to look upon Beornoth.

'I remember this one from Loidis. He broke the arm of one of my men. The bloody cheek of these Essex men. Still, I suppose my father's little ruse wouldn't have worked if they weren't so prideful,' said Thered, looking Beornoth up and down. 'You can go back to the King's mother and tell her we held up our end of the bargain,' he said, turning to White-Eye. 'And we expect confirmation of the land that was promised to be returned to us.'

'My Lady will be most pleased, Lord. Although, I do not think your father could kill the Essex Ealdorman, as was asked,' said White-Eye, still fumbling at his pouch of silver.

'We attacked them, and we tried. That is enough. If Lady Ælfthryth wanted a massacre, she should have sent more than you and your dull-witted friends north to aid us,' Thered snapped, and White-Eye, appearing to think better of continuing the discussion, bowed and walked away.

Osric came close to Beornoth and stood over him. 'You attacked me in my hall. Did you think that would go unpunished?' Beornoth kept his eyes on the grass beneath his feet. 'I am going to take you back to Mameceaster, and we shall have a Moot of our own. Just like your little gathering at York. I want my people to see what happens to men who challenge my authority. I'll hang you, stretch you, and cut you in pieces. I shall send a piece of you to all corners of my shire as a warning to masterless men and traitors.'

Beornoth could feel Osric's eyes on him, waiting for him to respond, to show fear or anger. He didn't want to give him the satisfaction, so kept his head low and his eyes fixed on the grass.

Osric snorted and turned away but thought better of it and turned back. 'I almost forgot. It won't just be you meeting a traitor's fate, I have your hag in a wagon back there. The crone from the tavern. She'll dangle from the rope as well. She has already suffered hard for your crimes, my men have been rough with her, I fear, even though she is old and ugly.'

Beornoth snarled and lashed out with his tied feet, and Osric threw his head back, laughing with delight. They had Blaedswith with them, and the thought of her being hurt and mistreated made him want to vomit. He heard the creak and jangle of a cart as it rolled onto the hilltop led by two horses.

'Tie him to my saddle, I want to drag the bastard to Mameceaster barefoot,' Osric crowed, and Beornoth's heart sank, because his ordeal had only just begun.

## 13

---

Beornoth pulled on the hemp rope which bound his wrists. It was thick and coarse and felt like a piece of flaming iron fresh from a smith's forge twisting around his forearms, biting and cutting. He curled his hands around the fetter and hauled, the horse's weight helping him to rise to his feet. He grunted as the muscles in his arms and shoulders screamed at the strain. Beornoth had lost count of how many times he had fallen to be dragged along by Osric's horse. Beornoth stumbled, half falling and half running on the leash, his bare feet a mess of cuts, scrapes and dirt from the road.

'Come along, great warrior. Viking killer, not far now,' Osric called cheerfully over his shoulder, and his men dutifully laughed along. Leof rode beside Beornoth on a small, dappled mare, and he tapped at Beornoth's naked shoulders with an alder branch switch. He had goaded Beornoth all day long, stinging him with the branch, clicking his tongue and urging him on like a cow led to market. Beornoth spat mud from his mouth, and it came out with a gobbet of blood. His lips had been mashed to ruin as they had dragged him along on his chest, the small stones and rocks of the well-used pathway driving into his face as he had tried to regain his feet. It was not one of the fine Roman roads of southern England, paved and crafted into a camber to allow rainwater to run off. The ancient Rome-folk, giants and men of ken far beyond that of the Saxons, had built those roads. Where the Romans built in stone, the Saxons built in wood and thatch, and mud. The road across the Pennine mountains was little more than a well-used goat track, a bare patch in the heather and rough grass of the high hills, hard mud baked solid in the summer sun. That road had ravaged and clawed at Beornoth's torso, his chest, stomach and back a mix of cuts, gashes and blood mixed with dirt and dust, and the horseshit which dropped from Osric's mount and which Beornoth could not avoid whilst the beast dragged him along behind it.

Beornoth made a strange murmur with each step, a rhythmic humming to keep him moving, his head lolling and spittle dripping from his ruined mouth. All day the journey had gone thus, pain and humiliation, exhaustion and despair. The wagon behind him creaked and groaned as it rumbled along, its wheels rolling through the ruts in the road where countless carriages had gone before it. Blaedswith was in that wagon. She had once been Eawynn's friend and one of the few people to show Beornoth any kindness during his dark days, when he had been a drunk and at his lowest ebb. She was back there alone and afraid, and ill-treated by Osric's warriors. Hate and hunger were all that had kept Beornoth from slipping into darkness during that long day: hate for Osric and the hunger for revenge. His wooden locket bounced against his chest as he shambled along and closed his eyes. White-Eye had not stripped that from him, being of little value to the man. It was just a simple, flat piece of smooth wood, similar in size

to a man's thumb, and fastened around his neck by a piece of dull
chain. It had no value to anyone but Beornoth. The rhythm of its
banging reminded him he needed to live. He had to stay alive and
free himself. Olaf Tryggvason and his fleet would be somewhere,
moving like a pack of wolves, looking for a place to strike on the
Saxon coast. Beornoth had to live and get back to Branoc's Tree to
protect his people, and to protect Eawynn, for he had let her down
once before with life-shattering consequences. More than once
during that day of pain and suffering, Beornoth had turned to scan
the hills, hoping to catch a glint of sun on a helmet or spear point,
or any signal that Byrhtnoth came for him, or that Wulfhere and
Alfgar were on his trail. But there had been nothing, and he was
alone with Osric, a man who hated him and wanted to make him
suffer.

The call went up to make camp as they came upon a half-circle
of large, marbled rocks beneath a clutch of sprawling rowan trees,
misshapen by the wind and harshness of the high hills. Beornoth
thought he would weep as they untied his bonds from Osric's
horse and he could slump to his knees. But he did not weep. He
took deep breaths and tried to conserve whatever sliver of strength
remained in his body from the arduous journey, just in case a
chance presented itself, a moment of opportunity. Osric slid from
his horse and strode towards Beornoth, a smirk creasing his handsome face.

'I hope you enjoyed that jaunt as much as I did,' he said, and
cuffed Beornoth around the skull with a gloved hand. 'Bring the
wench out and secure them both for the night,' Osric ordered. He
made to walk away but then spun on his heel and kicked Beornoth
in the back so that he sprawled into the heather, and Osric's
warriors laughed. White-Eye led Beornoth to the base of a crooked
rowan tree and tied him to its trunk by his neck with a loop of
coarse rope. White-Eye then also secured the tethers around his

wrists and ankles together with another length of rope, so that they were only a foot apart. Beornoth had to lie on the damp earth, the join between ankles and hands making it impossible for him to sit up. As the sun went down, casting long, dark shadows which danced as the trees swayed, Osric's men made camp. They tied the horses on a line between two trees and three young lads set to brushing and feeding the animals. Other men lit a fire within the shelter of a huge white rock which jutted from the earth, bright and looming in the sunset. Kari approached Beornoth with a water skin and knelt to pour some water into his mouth. Beornoth gulped it down, twisting his head awkwardly to reach the liquid from where he lay on his side.

'What are you doing, boy?' Osric barked, and Kari shuffled away, mumbling an apology. 'This dog only drinks when I say so. He is mine, my prisoner. My slave, if I wish it. I have a drink for you if you are thirsty.' Osric lifted his byrnie and dropped his breeches and pissed into the heather, so close to Beornoth's head that the hot, foul spray splashed onto his face and hair. Again, the warriors dutifully laughed at their master's cruelty. Beornoth glowered at them all, vengeance burning in his heart like a molten, broiling pit of hate.

'Ah, your crone is here to keep you company,' Osric said as a stocky man threw Blaedswith onto the ground next to Beornoth and secured her neck to the same tree. Osric marched away and his men prepared a meal and sat around their fire talking and laughing as evening turned to night.

'Blaedswith,' said Beornoth, his voice hoarse and croaking. He shuffled around in his bonds so that he could see her.

'What have they done to you?' she said, and she reached out to touch his face softly, her hand shaking and flinching at the touch of crusted blood.

'I'm sorry, I...' he began, but struggled for the words. She shook her head and placed her hand on his hair. 'They have hurt you to get to me.'

'These men are evil, they are not men of God,' she said, and then cried in pain as a long branch whipped against her arm, and then across the top of her head. It was Leof, swinging the switch he had used to beat Beornoth all day long.

'Don't touch the prisoner,' Leof barked, and took a long drink from an ale skin. 'I might come back and keep you warm later, hag. You aren't much to look at, old and ugly, but you can still keep me warm.' He licked his lips and strode away.

'How did it come to this?' Blaedswith said softly. 'I remember when we were young, Beo. In the summer, playing with the children by the river.'

Beornoth remembered it too. Blaedswith had been Eawynn's closest friend, like an older sister. She had been married to a wealthy merchant who owned a tavern and two trading ships. Her husband was often away at sea, and so Blaedswith would stay with Eawynn and Beornoth and play with their girls. They were happy times.

The ropes bit into his wrists, ankles and neck as he tried to move and relieve the burning pain wracking his body. After the Vikings burned his hall and killed his children, Blaedswith had tried to help Beornoth care for Eawynn, but her mind had been as ravaged and torn as his lands. As Beornoth had fallen into a spiral of drink and despair, Blaedswith had been his only friend. He had always known there would be a meal for him at her tavern, even in the darkest times. He wanted to tell Blaedswith what she meant to him, how kind she was. But the words died in his throat as he looked upon her bruised face. She was grey-haired and wrinkled; she was old and defenceless, her husband having died of the chest sickness years earlier. Beornoth couldn't say anything to make her feel better. Osric had brutally snatched and hurt her to punish

Beornoth. Osric had presented her at York to gild his charges and furnish that cunning trap with evidence.

'God help us,' she said, and winced as she sat back against the tree. Beornoth ground his teeth. He had given up on God long ago. What God could allow such cruelty to exist in the world? How could a good, honest woman like Blaedswith end up like this? There was no God. There was only the power and cruelty of men.

Evening turned to darkness and Osric's men unfurled their bed rolls and snored beneath a clear sky, huddled around the camp-fire's warmth. Beornoth could not sleep. He was in too much pain and his bonds made it too uncomfortable.

'Beo, look,' Blaedswith whispered, and Beornoth craned his neck. Blaedswith had a small stone in her hand. It was long and pointed like the tooth of a hunting dog, and its edge glinted in the darkness, sharp and napped with tiny chips along its edge. 'I found it on the road to York, and have tried to sharpen it whenever I could, waiting for the right moment.'

Hope flared in Beornoth's chest. A chance, a small opportunity. Blaedswith: strong, clever and dependable. 'This is the right moment; I can always rely on you, Blaedswith.' He spoke as softly as possible; the night was still young and Osric's men still slept. They had one chance to use the stone to cut their bindings. If they woke any of the warriors, that chance would be gone.

He could hear Blaedswith fidgeting in the darkness next to him, but he couldn't stretch his neck far enough to see.

'I can't cut my own bonds,' she hissed. 'I'll try to do yours first.' She shuffled towards him, slowly and quietly. Blaedswith leaned into his hip and scraped the rock on his hemp rope bindings. She rubbed at his fetters, and in the darkness, when any sound increases tenfold, the noise of it sounded like the crashing of the sea. Beornoth grimaced and turned his head to look at the sleeping warriors, shadowy mounds rising softly around the embers of their fire. If they woke, this chance at freedom would be lost, and Beornoth's hate seethed at his captors.

'Did they post a sentry?' he whispered. She paused and leant towards him.

'What?'

'Did they order a man to stay awake and keep watch? If so, we need to know where he is in case he catches us.'

'I can't see anyone. They all look asleep,' she said, and carried on cutting. Beornoth rocked gently as she worked at his rope.

'Is it working?'

'It's working, but it's slow. Mary and the saints in Heaven...' she cursed, and Beornoth heard her scrambling in the undergrowth for the dropped stone. For what seemed like an age she searched, hand scrambling in the grass, probing under his body. 'Thank you, Lord,' she said to her God, and worked again at the rope which tied his wrists together. That made the most sense. Once his hands were free, he could untie the rest of the bindings, and then hers. As she worked, Beornoth formed a plan. Once the bindings were loose, they still had to get away from Osric's men. He had noted only one bow amongst them, and over ten of the enemy were mounted. If he and Blaedswith were to escape and then evade their pursuers, they needed horses. Otherwise, even if they sneaked sway in the darkness, it would be a small matter for Osric, Thered and White-Eye to ride them down like prey. So, they needed horses. White-Eye had also taken Beornoth's byrnie, his sword and seax. The trappings of the heriot he had fought so hard to earn and restore his family's honour. He couldn't leave without that. Ealdorbana would still be with Wulfhere and Alfgar, or so he hoped, and Branoc's Tree was still his, unless he died at Osric's hand, or unless Olaf Tryggvason was there, burning and killing. Beornoth scrunched his eyes tight and told himself to focus on the matter at hand, one thing at a time. First, he had to get free of his bonds, then he had to get off this hilltop and away from his enemies. If he could get his weapons and mail back, all the better. But the most important thing was to live, to get Blaedswith to safety, and to get back to Branoc's Tree alive and be able to protect his people.

Blaedswith worked, and the night grew long. She had to pause more than once because the effort of cutting burned at her shoulders, but she kept going, rubbing and cutting at the thick, coarse fibres.

'Are you nearly there?' he asked countless times during the dark hours, which felt as though they lasted an eternity. Each time he asked, she tutted and hushed him. The soft spring of a rope fibre, or a grunt of triumph in Blaedswith's voice, and he knew she was making progress, painfully slow progress.

Beornoth's eyes stung from exhaustion, and his body shook with pain, and just as he was about to ask her to stop cutting so he could roll and change his position, he saw a pale light emerge over the distant hills. It was a sickly thing, little more than the orange-green colour of a faded bruise, but it meant the sun was coming up, and panic welled in his chest. The prospect of another day dragged behind Osric's horse, his bare feet already torn and bloody, and his body littered with scrapes and gashes, was horrifying.

'The sun,' he hissed.

'I am almost there. Pull, Beo, try to snap the rope.'

He bunched his shoulders, balled his fists and pulled his wrists apart. Nothing. He tried it again and his arms flung wide, the rope snapping and springing away. Beornoth sat up with a groan, his wrists finally free and no longer attached to his ankle bindings. Blaedswith had a wolfish grin on her face. The hurt and sadness replaced with hope and hunger for freedom.

Beornoth untied the knot at his ankles and then untied his

neck from the tree before untying Blaedswith. They embraced, and he held her tight into him. Her body was small and frail against the muscled breadth of his chest. 'Thank you,' he said, whispering into her hair.

'Let's get moving,' she said, and pointed at the sunrise as it creeped from its slumber, pushing back the darkness. Beornoth grabbed her hand, and they moved off slowly, treading softly and carefully around the crooked tree and taking a wide arc around the white boulders, towards the line of hobbled horses behind the camp. He halted as he saw a pair of boots move in the half-light. Beornoth grabbed Blaedswith's arm. She stopped dead and covered her mouth with her free hand. The boots shifted again, and a horse whinnied. They took slow steps forward, Beornoth holding his breath and placing his back against a boulder, its stone cool on his scabbed, bloody back. Beornoth stopped and leaned around the boulder, peeking through his open eye, the other still shut by the swelling of his face. He saw a warrior huddled under a wool cloak. The sentry. He was leaning against the rock, his head on his shoulder and feet outstretched, mouth open and fast asleep.

Beornoth turned to Blaedswith and signalled for her to wait. He could not risk edging past the sleeping man. He might only be half-asleep and if he woke and raised the alarm, they would be done for. Beornoth loomed over him and lowered himself onto his haunches. He reached out and steadied himself, then snapped his arms out as fast and lethal as a serpent, one hand grabbing the man's mouth and gripping it, and the other wrapping around his throat. Beornoth was a large man, and he had always had big hands, calloused and rough from a lifetime at weapons practice and battle. His hand covered the bottom of the man's face and his fingers dug into the flesh like a claw, his other hand squeezing and crushing the soft tendons in his neck. The sentry's eyes popped open, brown and panicked. Beornoth snarled, squeezed tighter, feeling a muffled, wet cry of terror beneath one hand, and the crunch and collapse of gristle and meat beneath the other. The warrior's boots scraped and kicked at the earth in his death panic and Blaedswith threw herself across the dying man's knees to stop the movement and stop the noise. The man went still. Beornoth's heart pounded, one enemy dead. He dragged off the man's boots and shoved them on to his own feet. Beornoth unbuckled the dead man's belt and fastened it around his own waist. There was a seax fastened to its front by two thongs, and now Beornoth was armed. He wanted to strip the man's jerkin from him but feared it would make too much noise and so he moved on towards the horses. The beast at the end of the line was a dappled mare, and Beornoth stroked her muzzle and forehead as Blaedswith untied her from the line.

Beornoth glanced back towards the camp and his hand dropped to the simple wooden grip of the dead man's seax. He thought about striding into the camp. He could kill Osric, Thered and White-Eye before they even knew he was amongst them. Death on a Saxon hillside. But the other warriors would overpower him, and he owed it to Blaedswith to get her to safety, so his thoughts of revenge and death slept, for now. Blaedswith led the horse away from the line, its hooves sounding like hammers striking an anvil they were so loud. Beornoth winced at the noise, and he thought he heard a movement in the camp beyond the stones.

'I'll climb on first, and then pull you up behind me,' he said, and Blaedswith nodded. Osric's men had brushed the horse before nightfall, and so she bore no saddle and just a simple wool blanket. Beornoth grabbed a fistful of the horse's mane and tried to leap onto her back, but she skipped away from him, and he slipped back to the ground. More sounds of movement beyond the stones.

He tried to mount again, but the horse moved away, and he could not climb onto her back.

'Wake up, wake up!' the cry came, peeling out across the early morning. Beornoth came closer to the horse.

'Please, girl. Help us,' he whispered in the mare's ear. He wrapped an arm around her neck and threw his leg over her back, and this time, she held still. Beornoth sat on her back and reached down for Blaedswith and hauled her up behind him. The first time Blaedswith fell away, and the mare whinnied, prancing around in a circle.

'There they are, stop them!' came another shout.

Panic, hot and searing in Beornoth's throat and chest. He grabbed Blaedswith's forearm and hauled her up, grabbing her waist as she rose, and helped her clamber behind him.

'Bastards!' men called, other curses ringing out, and Beornoth clicked his tongue and dug his heels into the horse's flanks, and the mare bunched her muscles and surged down the hillside.

Beornoth heard a whistling sound, and his head shrank into his shoulders involuntarily. The archer. An arrow whipped past the horse to sail into the distance. Another one sank into the ground and disappeared as the horse picked up pace, the wind blowing against Beornoth's face, its coolness drawing a reactionary tear from his left eye. He heard a slap, and the horse skittered and almost fell. Beornoth turned to see an arrow had struck the meat of her back leg, blood showing around the shaft. The horse carried on running, but she limped now, her gait impaired by the pain. More whooshes of arrows around him, and a grunt from Blaedswith over his shoulder

'We'll make for the cover of the trees,' Beornoth said, and pulled the horse's mane, directing her towards the towering hillside beyond, dense with ancient woodland. The horse would not be able to outrun Osric's mounted warriors, she was injured and carrying two riders. The deep forest and its tangle of branches and undergrowth was their best hope.

Blaedswith whimpered behind him, and he felt her arms loosen where they gripped his waist. As they rose and fell with the mare's gallop, Beornoth felt a warm wetness on his back, and his heart sank.

## 14

The green of heather gave way into the dark gloom of twisting branches as the forest came closer. Beornoth clasped Blaedswith's hands together tight at his waist. The mare slowed in her race to the treeline with every hoof beat, and Beornoth gritted his teeth, desperate to escape his enemies. The horse limped and laboured, her eyes wide, and she bravely tried to run as fast as she could with the arrow in her rump.

'Nearly there, old girl, you can make it,' said Beornoth, the words as much for Blaedswith as the injured horse. Both courageous, and both hurt. Blaedswith lay against his back, flopping with the horse's movement. Beornoth could hear the pounding of hoof beats behind him, and he leaned forward and bent to glance over his left shoulder. Horsemen streamed down the sloping vale, chasing him, dark iron showing in their fists.

The white foam of her sweat flecked the mare's neck and flanks, and the forest was still thirty paces away. Suddenly, the horse's rear legs buckled, and the mare jerked sideways. Beornoth leapt from her back to avoid being trapped under her bodyweight and hit the ground hard. He rolled, and the seax scabbard at his waist drove into his stomach like a punch. Beornoth came up, gasping at the pain, but ran to where the horse floundered on the earth in a snarl of kicking forelegs and terrible high-pitched horse screams. He dashed around her head and sighed with relief to see Blaedswith on the ground, but free from the horse's body. She lay on her side, and her face was ashen, bubbles of blood bright and speckling her white skin.

'Can you walk?' said Beornoth.

'No, I'm done, Beo,' she rasped, shaking her head. 'Leave me, go. They are upon us.'

Beornoth searched her back for the wound and felt the broken shaft of an arrow in the centre of her back. He shook his head and cursed. Beornoth slipped one hand under the back of her knees and another under her arms and lifted her, grunting at the weight. He turned and ran for the forest, taking short, quick steps and ignoring the burning pain from the wounds across his chest, back and arms. She rested her head on his chest, and as he ran, Blaedswith's breathing came in ragged and wheezing bubbles. He pounded for the forest, making for the darkest point he could see amongst the high trunks and branches.

'Ride the bastard down.' He heard a voice behind him, and felt the ground under his feet rumble under the weight of the chasing horsemen.

Beornoth ducked under a branch and swerved around a gnarled trunk thick with lichen. Five more steps and he was treading on deep leaf mulch, and the damp, heavy smell of the forest was all around him. The horses milled and churned the ground at the forest's edge, a seething mass of snorting animals, and the shouts and arguments of men. They would need to leave their mounts to enter the tangled wood. Horses would be no good in the tangle of fallen branches and treacherous footing. They would have to hunt him on foot, bringing their spears, knives and bows after Beornoth as though he were a killer bear or wolf who had been terrorising the countryside. His thighs screamed at him as he charged deeper and further into the mass of bush, branch and leaf. Beornoth could feel his arms shaking, and he shifted Blaedswith's weight higher upon his chest. His neck muscles were taut, and his head held high and back against the burden. He blew out his cheeks and kept on marching, twisting and turning, leaning into his strides as the forest floor turned into a steep hill.

He did not know how long he had kept up that ordeal, before his legs had buckled into the shallow bank of a babbling brook. The suffering, and his determination to master it, had sent Beornoth into a focused trance. Eyes fixed ahead, he had tried to take a breath for every two steps, the screeching pain of his body fading away into a determined madness. He dropped to his knees in the foul, thick black of the brook's edges. It reeked of decay, but the water flowed downhill, and it was cool on his legs. He lay Blaedswith down and dropped onto his elbows, spittle trailing from his lips into his beard as tried to get his breath back.

'I can't hear them,' he said, glancing over his shoulder. 'They will come, but they are not close. We can rest for a time.' Her face has grown paler, looking like a fetch, with sunken eyes in the forest's shadows. Beornoth placed a hand on her chest and snatched it away. She was cold and still.

'Blaedswith,' he said, his heart stopping. He knelt over her and listened for her breath, hoping to feel the lightness of it on his cheek, but there was nothing. Beornoth sank onto her, clutching her to him, his fingers digging into her back. She was dead. They had killed her. Beornoth should have protected her, he should have known they would come for her after he had rescued Eawynn from Osric's hall. He should have taken Blaedswith south with him. Anger bloomed inside Beornoth, mixing with the deepest sorrow and pain to create something new, something visceral and powerful that charged his limbs with strength. He let out a cry, more a scream than a battle cry. It was feral and wild, and birds flew from the treetops, away from his crazed fury.

Beornoth pounded his fists into the black soil, its damp foulness flecking his face and chest to cover him in black, wet mud. He looked at his hands, and then around him. He would not run any more. Kneeling next to Blaedswith's corpse, Beornoth was going to do the only thing he had ever been good at. He was going to kill. He was going to find Osric, and Thered, and White-Eye, and rip their lives from them. Beornoth slathered himself in black mud. He would become one with the forest and the darkness, like an ancient woodland demon, and strike at his pursuers with vengeance and fury.

The first voices came brash and flat, drifting through the snarl of wood and weed. Their numbers giving them the confidence to stomp through the forest without a hunter's care and stealth. Boots crashed through the undergrowth, heavy and clumsy, as unconcerned with the noise they made as a drunk leaving a tavern. They came fast, the sound of their footsteps quick and getting closer. Beornoth huddled between a plume of ferns, green and brown and wider than him, and a tall pine. He crouched in the darkness, at one with the shadows.

'This way,' he heard a voice call, a gap-toothed lisp in the sound of it.

'We've got him now; the Ealdorman will reward us if we catch him. Hates the bastard, he does.'

They referred to him, and he reciprocated that hatred. The boots came closer, crunching and sliding through the undergrowth, and Beornoth was still, his captured seax held low at his side. Waiting. He held himself still until he could hear their breathing, laboured and heavy, and when he saw a boot crash into the mulch a foot away, he attacked. Beornoth rose from his bunched crouch, slicing his seax up wool breeches and grasping a fistful of tunic with his free hand. The man cried out in pain, and Beornoth kept the seax moving, twisting and cutting until it reached the hunter's belly, and Beornoth grunted as he drove the broken-backed blade deep, rending and tearing, feeling the hot wash of blood on his hand and wrist. Beornoth stood to his full height and stared down into the dying man's eyes. They were blue and frenzied, panicked at death's arrival. Beornoth ripped the blade free, and he pushed the dying man towards the warrior who appeared behind him, levelling a spear. The falling man fouled the spear, and the warrior tried to thrust his dying friend aside, but he was slow. Beornoth grabbed the spear just below the blade and pulled it wide and turned his seax so that he held it overhand, and drove its point into the warrior's face, punching it through eye and skull, ripping it free in a gout of blood and eye jelly, and stabbing it into the warrior's throat. Beornoth threw his head back and roared. He bellowed at the treetops like a blood-mad bear, feral and savage. Two men were dead, but it did not sate his anger. He knelt and took the spear and set off on the hunt again.

Beornoth heard boots crashing towards him through the forest, and he stopped and crouched beneath sprawling foliage. The bushes were heavy and spiky and scraped against his bare skin. He had only travelled twenty paces from the two dead warriors before he heard their comrades rushing towards their screams. Beornoth waited in the shadows. The mud covering his naked torso helped him to blend into the forest's gloom. He had become one with the wood, and he felt like a creature from a folk tale, like a forest wight or demon lurking in the darkness. He heard voices drawing closer, and his heart leapt because one of those voices was White-Eye, confident with his drawl from the southern shires.

'Careful now, spread out and we'll surround the bastard,' White-Eye said. Leather-clad bodies moved about Beornoth, appearing and disappearing between shafts of light and gaps in the heavy forest.

'He's killed Mani, oh Lord, help us, there's blood everywhere,' came a voice, quivering and unseen.

Beornoth charged from the undergrowth, growling. Spear in his left fist and seax in his right. He ran towards the voice, and a short man turned and howled in fear just in time to see Beornoth racing straight at him. The spear took him in the belly and Beornoth forced him backwards until the spear point drove right through his baked-leather breastplate and on through his body. The man came off the ground, hurtling backwards under Beornoth's wrath until the spear pinned him against a tree trunk, the point having passed right through his body. He clutched at the spear and coughed up a gout of blood.

'Help!' he cried. 'Help me, please, help!' Beornoth crouched again and kept himself low amongst a clutch of dark brown ferns. The man groaned and wept. Soon, more of the enemy came to help their injured friend.

'Get the spear out of him,' said a balding man with a lisp. He tugged at the spear pinning his friend to the tree, but the injured man wailed from the pain. Beornoth sprang from the ferns, the lisping man spun and swung his seax, but his eyes were closed, and fear dripped from him like honey. Beornoth batted the seax aside and plunged his own weapon into his enemy's chest and put his left hand on the hilt along with his right and ripped the man's body open. The blade carved a terrible wound, opening him up from breast to navel

'It's not a man, help me!' the second man wailed, and he fell to his knees, hands clasped together in front of his face in whispering prayer as the lisping man's butchered corpse toppled beside him, slopping his purple and red insides into the brown-black leaves.

Beornoth stood over the praying man. His chest heaved from the exertion. He knelt and picked up the dead man's seax in his left hand and smelt the pungent smell of urine as a dark patch spread across the praying enemy's breeches. He was not a threat, and not a vessel with which Beornoth could slake his thirst for vengeance for Blaedswith's death, so he turned and stalked through the wood, gore dripping from his weapons and his body dark with mud and the blood of his enemies.

'Careful, boys. Watch him,' came a familiar voice from Beornoth's left. His stomach lifted, and he clenched his hands on the hilts of his weapons. It was White-Eye's voice. Beornoth turned, bracing his feet in the undergrowth and raising his blades, a short seax held in each hand. White-Eye came from the shadows slowly, his lantern jaw set firm. He had Beornoth's sword raised before him, and his byrnie slung across his back in a net sack. *My heriot.*

Beornoth sensed movement to his right and a sudden crashing erupted through the branches. He turned and luckily the attack came from the uninjured side of his face, because from Beornoth's good eye, Leof raced towards him with a rope stretched between his hands. White-Eye and his men were trying to repeat the same trick they had used when capturing Beornoth the first time, and for a split second the pain and suffering of his capture scissored through his mind like the lash of a whip, each of the wounds he had taken pulsed, burning and aching. It would not happen a second time. Beornoth stepped into Leof and lowered his seax, allowing Leof to throw a rope over his head, and enjoying the momentary look of elation on his oafish face change to pain-wracked horror as Leof realised he had run into one of Beornoth's seaxes. Beornoth stopped the weapon's stab when only a hand's breadth of its vicious broken-backed blade had entered Leof's belly, and then he snapped it back and stabbed again, four times in short rapid bursts. Then, Beornoth leapt back and roared into Leof's face, recalling each blow of his stinging branch whip across his back. Beornoth shrugged the rope from his neck and turned to face White-Eye, leaving Leof to fall into the decaying leaf mulch, mewing and dying from the punctures in his guts.

White-Eye licked his thin lips, and his eyes flicked around him, searching for support. 'I have him. On me, lads,' he shouted, and edged backwards, the tip of Beornoth's sword wavering in his hand. 'Lord Osric, I have him. Come to me, come now!' White-Eye shrieked, and he turned, as though he would run away. But it was too late. Beornoth leapt upon him. The sword had lowered as White-Eye turned, and Beornoth surged at him, lunging with his leg to trip his captor. White-Eye yelped as he tripped and turned to strike at Beornoth as he fell to his back, his long face drawn back in a rictus of terror. Beornoth just stood on White-Eye's sword arm, pinning it to the earth, and fell upon his chest, driving the air out of him as he sat upon him. White-Eye closed his eyes and clenched his teeth, waiting for the death blow.

'Look at me,' Beornoth growled, but White-Eye shook his head and kept his eyes scrunched closed. A tear rolling down his face. 'Look at me!' Beornoth shouted. The eyes snapped open, one brown and large, mottled with flecks of green, the other milk-white and dead.

'I'm just following orders,' said White-Eye.

'Whose orders?'

'Lady Ælfthryth, the King's mother, she is my mistress, my ring-giver.'

'She wants Byrhtnoth gone?'

'She does, and you. Taking the shine away from her son, she said. Kill them both in the north, says she. Let the King be the hero of the Saxons. She has poets making songs of his victory at Watchet.'

'I do not die so easy,' Beornoth whispered, and he cut White-Eye's throat, dragging the blade of his seax across his neck, leaning into the blow so that it severed his windpipe and cut down to the bone with a spurt of blood which washed over Beornoth's face. Beornoth rose to his feet, but heavy breathing came from behind him, so Beornoth turned with a snarl and raised his blood-soaked weapons. White-Eye's youngster, Kari, was there, staring at him with wide, frightened eyes. Blood dripped from Beornoth's face, hands and blades, slapping into the forest floor as he stared at the boy.

'I won't hurt you, lad,' Beornoth whispered, lowering his weapons. 'You showed me kindness. Run, if you like. Or you can come with me, join my men.' Kari had offered Beornoth drink and food on the road, and he seemed like a good lad. Also, he was a living testament to the betrayal of the King's mother and her orders to White-Eye the cut-throat. Kari just nodded, staring at his former friends lying dead on the ground. Beornoth pulled his own sword from White-Eye's dead hand and tugged the sack containing his byrnie from White-Eye's back, slinging it across his own shoulder. 'Take this and follow me,' he said, handing the boy one of his seaxes.

Beornoth set off again through the wood, turning back on his tracks and making for the edge of the forest. The boy followed, and Beornoth heard no sound of Osric or his men as he stepped over branches and through thick ferns. The shafts of light punching through the heavy canopy increased, and the density of alder and birch decreased until he emerged from the treeline and felt the soft give of grass under his feet. Beornoth saw three men staring at him. They stood with a line of Osric's horses, guarding them whilst the Ealdorman and his men had charged into the wood after

Beornoth. Those warriors were still in the woods. The three men were open-mouthed and stunned as their eyes washed over the terrifying beast of blood and death stood before them. The filthy mud from the forest brook still caked Beornoth's face and chest, mixed with the blood and gore of the dead, and he looked like a feral demon. He walked towards them and barked like a dog, clashing his sword against his seax, and the men ran. One of those men was Swidhelm, the man whom Beornoth had beaten at Knutsford, and whom Osric had brought to York to give evidence to support the charges against Beornoth. Swidhelm and the two men took one look at Beornoth, left the horses and ran across the pasture, fleeing from the filthy, blood-spattered and ungodly creature emerging from the forest's depths. Beornoth did not hate Swidhelm. It had been Beornoth who had wronged him, not the other way around. He did not deserve to die.

Beornoth strode to the horses, and some of them stomped the earth and whinnied at the smell of blood on him. He chose a fine black mare with a burst of white on her nose and white socks on her hind legs. Beornoth stroked her nose and whispered in her ear that she should not be afraid. She was already saddled and Beornoth climbed onto her back. Kari stared from the horses to Beornoth.

'Take one and come with me, if that is your choice,' Beornoth said. The boy grinned and mounted a chestnut gelding, and they rode up the hillside and away from Osric and his warriors. Blaedswith's body was still in the wood, and he could not leave her there to rot. She was a godly woman and needed a Christian burial. Osric would suffer for her death, and that vengeance burned in Beornoth's chest like fire as he and the boy rode towards the pine-covered hills to the east. And as they reached the crest of the valley ahead, Beornoth laughed. The boy looked at him incredulously, but Beornoth threw his head back and laughed at the sky because riders approached. Their mail shone and glinted in the sun, and their spear points bristled above their heads so that the line of them looked like a great shining dragon snaking across the high hills between Northumbria and Cheshire. Beornoth laughed with joy because he saw Wulfhere and Alfgar, and Byrhtnoth. The Ealdorman and his war band had come for him.

## 15

Beornoth sagged in the saddle and allowed his horse to halt. The sight of his Lord and war band flooded Beornoth with relief, but that also quelled his fury and blood madness like a red-hot blade taken from the forge and plunged into a bucket of cool water. Beornoth closed his eyes and grimaced, pain suddenly searing at him from the bruises, scrapes and cuts which covered his body. Weariness washed over him and he shivered. The wind in the high hills whipped at his bare torso and the mud on his face, arms, chest and belly had dried and turned into hard flakes, constricting and itching his skin. Beornoth's horse cropped at the short brown grass, and then it whinnied at the sound of so many horses approaching, the sound of their approach a rumble as though a God shook the earth from deep within the hill itself.

'They will know I was with the others,' said Kari, coming alongside Beornoth. 'They will hurt me. I should go.'

'They won't hurt you. Just stay quiet.'

'But they will know we rode north to harm you and the Ealdorman.'

'They won't care about you,' Beornoth snapped. 'There are greater things at stake here than your miserable life, boy. Stay, or go, the choice is yours.'

The riders came close, Wulfhere and Alfgar racing ahead of them to reach Beornoth first, their mounts galloping and reining in before Beornoth in a flurry of hooves and flying clods of earth. Brand was close behind them, the Viking's golden hair bouncing in thick braids as he rode.

'My God, Lord,' said Alfgar, making the sign of the cross above his breast and staring with horror at Beornoth's face and filth-covered body.

'What did the bastards do to you?' asked Wulfhere, the change from wide-eyed shock to grim anger playing out across his wide, flat face like a saga tale.

'Osric is down there. If we ride now, we can take him,' said Beornoth, his voice low and thin from exhaustion. Wulfhere and Alfgar looked at each other, and back to Beornoth.

'I have a spare jerkin in my pack. Let's get you looking like a Thegn again,' said Wulfhere, and he leant over the rump of his horse to delve into a hemp sack tied to the back of his saddle.

'Praise the Lord you are alive, Lord. We feared the worst,' said Alfgar.

'How did you know they had taken me?'

'Godwin saw them take you during the ambush. And we tracked you here.'

The rest of the horsemen reached Beornoth at a canter, and he slid from his horse, grimacing at the throbbing pain of his injuries. He let the sack containing his byrnie fall to the ground, the iron inside clanking. The bruising on his face ached, and he opened his mouth wide to stretch it, the pain flashing for a moment but then fading. Beornoth fished around his mouth with his tongue and was relieved that he had lost no other teeth from Osric's beating.

'Here, Lord,' said Wulfhere, tossing a brown wool jerkin to Beornoth. 'Put this on before you talk to the Ealdorman.' Beornoth caught it and slipped it over his head, just as the riders swirled around him.

'We knew you were alive, Beo. I told the men that it would take more than a ragged band of cut-throats to kill a Thegn of the East Saxons,' said Byrhtnoth, his voice loud and gruff above the ind's whip. Beornoth nodded at his Ealdorman, thanks and relief in the gesture. 'It looks like you freed yourself without our help,' the Ealdorman continued. 'Though not without feeling the wrath of their cowardly tortures, it seems. My God, man, but you look like a demon from the devil's pit itself.'

'Ealdorbana?' asked Beornoth, his voice croaking and broken from the ordeal.

'With us, safe and well. Some water, Lord,' said Alfgar, and he handed Beornoth a skin. Beornoth took it and took a long drink to slake his thirst, and then lifted it to pour the contents over his hair and face before washing away what he could of the mud and blood caked into his skin, hair and beard.

'They are running,' a warrior shouted from along the line of horsemen, and Beornoth recognised the voice as Cwicca's. Beornoth turned to see Osric and his men had returned from the wood, and were hastily retrieving their horses and galloping away at the sight of Byrhtnoth's war band.

'Let's ride them down, Lord,' said Leofsunu of Sturmer, rising high in his saddle to point at the enemy at the bottom of the hill.

Byrhtnoth leant across his pommel and scratched his iron-grey beard. 'We have Beornoth back now. That is what we came for. And we have fulfilled our task here in the north.'

'But the men who attacked us, and who took Beornoth, are within our grasp?' Leofsunu said, looking around at the other warriors for support.

'Aye, they are,' said Byrhtnoth. 'Men here in Northumbria and Cheshire have wronged us. I know that. But there is a foulness here in the north, and it would keep us here for months fighting our own Saxon people when we should protect our homes and families in Essex. If we ride down Ealdorman Osric now, then we could start a war in the north.'

'We should be at home, watching for Vikings,' said Offa, a frown splitting his wrinkled brow.

'This boy here came north with the Queen's man,' said Beornoth, nodding at Kari. 'Lady Ælfthryth sent him and his master to set a trap of deep cunning for you and I, Lord. The Ealdorman, who was a traitor, Oslac of Northumbria, was to keep us busy here in the country's north. I was to be put into the hands of Osric, to pay for the crimes of my past. You were to be killed. You could see for yourself how that played out in York, and in the ambush where they took me.' Beornoth wanted to get back to Eawynn and the people under his charge at Branoc's Tree. But Osric had caused Blaedswith's death, and he could not let that go.

'Lady Ælfthryth hates me still, after all these years. She is a ruthless woman and would do anything to further the position of her son, the King,' said Byrhtnoth.

'The King's mother plots against us?' asked Godric, sat astride a pale white stallion at Byrhtnoth's shoulder, his lopsided eyes wide with disbelief.

'She fears Byrhtnoth grows too popular with the people, that our Lord's reputation outshines that of her son, the King,' said Beornoth. 'So, she sent us north, into this snake pit, with knives at our backs and black hearts weaving withy nets for us at every turn. She wants Æthelred to take the glory of fighting Olaf and his Vikings, not Byrhtnoth.'

'There is no glory to be had from a ravaged Kingdom,' said

Aelfwine. 'Without us, I do not think there is a force in Wessex, Essex or East Anglia to stand against Olaf.'

'The Vikings will take a foothold in our country again. We would have a Danelaw once more, or a Kingdom ruled by Danes,' agreed Leofsunu.

'Some would welcome that,' Byrhtnoth growled. 'We have learned as much. Men with Viking blood in their veins, who call themselves Saxons. Men who stand to prosper if Vikings rule in England again. No more swathes of verdant land owned by the Church, a chance for men with Viking forefathers to welcome their kin from across the sea, and become richer and more powerful.'

'We are on a knife edge, the Kingdom waivers,' said Leofsunu, and the surrounding warriors rumbled their agreement. 'Viking dragon ships on our shores, traitors within who would welcome them. Saxon fighting against Saxon.'

'We must act, if we are to protect the people from the butchery and rivers of blood that would flow if the Kingdom fell to these men of greed and dark ambition,' said Byrhtnoth. He shook his head and gnawed at his shovel-like beard, his brows furrowed deep, like clashing clouds in a thunderstorm. 'Times are desperate, and sometimes better judgement must die on the blade of necessity. We must return to our homes, but we cannot leave this nest of vipers at our back. Beornoth, take your men and put an end to Osric of Cheshire. I will return to York and deal with Oslac. Be at your heriot before the waxing moon is full.'

'You mean to kill two Ealdormen?' said Godric, the blood running from his face.

'We are here with the King's authority to resolve the issues in the north. So, resolve them we shall. I don't like it, and I order it with a heavy heart. But these men must die to protect the Kingdom, the black souls of two Ealdormen for the lives of many hundreds of the simple folk of our shires and dales who would suffer under the Viking invasion we must prevent.'

'But the King's mother, and the King himself, will surely be enraged if we kill Ealdormen? Was it not Lady Ælfthryth who allowed Oslac to return from exile?'

'These Ealdormen have attacked me and my Thegns,' Byrhtnoth snarled. 'I will not leave enemies at my rear when there are Vikings prowling our coastline like wolves. These are my orders, and may God have mercy on me for it.'

'I will hunt Osric down, and end this feud,' said Beornoth. He would have followed Byrhtnoth south and left the scab of Osric festering in Cheshire, if the Ealdorman commanded it. His priority was to protect the people of his hundred at Branoc's Tree, but the warrior in him rejoiced in the order to kill Osric. The young Ealdorman had planned to kill Beornoth, after a show trial to demonstrate his power to his people, and he had killed Blaedswith. Now he would meet justice and vengeance.

'Good. See to it, and I will see to my business with Oslac of Northumbria. We will meet again before the full moon.'

Byrhtnoth wheeled his horse around, and his hearth troop followed him. Aelfwine and Leofsunu clasped forearms with Beornoth and wished him luck before they left. Beornoth opened the sack he had taken from White-Eye and pulled out his byrnie, its weight requiring both his hands to lift it. His helmet was also in the sack, wrapped within the links of his iron coat of mail. Beornoth lifted the coat and slid his arms into it, shrugging over him, slithering into it as though it were a second skin. He tied his helmet to his saddle, and with his heriot of sword, mail, helmet and seax, he was a Thegn once more.

'Let's get after them then,' said Wulfhere, watching Osric's riders disappear around the edge of the forest to the south-west. 'We must kill an Ealdorman. Who is also your brother, Alfgar.'

Alfgar sighed and stared at the empty field from which Osric and his men had fled. The young man said nothing, but Beornoth could see his mind working in the thought cage behind his clever eyes. If Osric died, then Alfgar would be the next in line to be the Ealdorman of Cheshire. He and Osric were both sons of the previous Ealdorman, Aethelhelm, and Osric had not yet sired any sons to succeed him. Byrhtnoth was aware of that fact, but he was a clever and cunning man and a fearsome war leader. Beornoth assumed that Byrhtnoth's mind wrestled with the sensitivities of that which must be done to protect the people, and the realities of the wolf pit that was King Æthelred's court. For Byrhtnoth to slay two Ealdormen and appoint others in their stead would be a step too far. It was one thing to kill another Ealdorman who had attacked the Ealdorman of Essex on the road whilst he was acting in the King's name. That was self-defence and Beornoth was sure that the Witan in Winchester would not condemn Byrhtnoth for that. But it was another entirely to appoint the new Ealdormen. That task would fall to King Æthelred. Clearly, however, it would serve Byrhtnoth, and the people of England, to have an Ealdorman in Cheshire who was an ally of the Ealdorman of Essex, the Viking killer. Beornoth watched his friend, and knew that same story unfolded in Alfgar's mind, and the taste of it would be sour in his belly. Alfgar would not welcome that responsibility. He was a warrior and happy to be betrothed and a man of Beornoth's war band. To become an Ealdorman was a fearsome prospect.

Osric and his hearth troop of warriors had taken the horses and made a hasty gallop through the dales and paths of the Snake-Pass, a well-worn passage which wove its way around the high hills and bleak mountains which separate the north of England like the curved spine of a long-dead monster, huge and jagged, buried deep beneath the land with only the high curve of its back above ground. It was a place of rough grasses and heather, of browns and yellows. The trail was an easy one to follow, and Beornoth led ten of his men in pursuit of the fleeing Ealdorman. He had sent Cwicca and Kari to recover Blaedswith's body and ordered them to treat her with the respect she deserved. In their haste, Osric's men had left the cart which had borne Blaedswith and Swidhelm to and from York, and Beornoth ordered the two young men to place her body in that cart and to bring it to Knutsford, where the people there would bury her properly. She was a godly woman, and she deserved a good burial. Beornoth made sure Kari and Cwicca had enough silver to give to the priest at Knutsford, to ensure that he performed the correct service, and that prayers were said for her immortal soul. She would have wanted that.

They tracked Osric and his men through the rest of that day until their trail of earth churned by horses gave way to lower land and greener pastures. Afternoon turned to evening, and the land became patched with rain-heavy clouds, black and brooding against the white and blue of the sky beyond. They had left the mountainous pass behind, and rode through fields of yellow and green, passing into Cheshire. Osric's shire. Beornoth had pushed his men hard. The enemy's trail was easy to follow, and it made no sense to blow the horses in pursuit. Throughout the long day's ride, Beornoth would often stroke Ealdorbana's ears or pat his neck, he was relieved to see his friend safe and well. When they ate or drank, Beornoth would whisper to his horse, and the beast would bob his head and nuzzle Beornoth's chest. Cwicca had looked after the horse, and his coat gleamed. Ealdorbana was as much of a friend to Beornoth as Wulfhere and Alfgar, and a trusted war companion, and being alongside the warhorse again calmed Beornoth. The silent companionship soothed the rage which bubbled inside Beornoth like a pot on a hearth. The anger at Blaedswith's death, frustration at being kept from his duty at Branoc's Tree, and hate for Osric and his attempt to kill him, had become white-hot inside Beornoth, and almost too much to bear.

'We ride too slow,' said Alfgar, who rode at Beornoth's flank. 'They have half a day on us and will be deep within Osric's own lands by now.'

'They will,' agreed Beornoth. 'But they must stop soon, and so must we. Osric will grow confident within his own estates, and we will catch him.'

'Then what?'

'Then he will die,' said Beornoth, grinding his teeth, brows furrowing into a snarl.

'Of course,' sighed Alfgar, shaking his head.

'And then you will be an Ealdorman,' said Wulfhere, cheerfully. He had nudged his horse into a canter and slowed to come alongside Alfgar. 'Only a year ago, you were a snot-nosed lad who had walked away from becoming a priest. You could barely hold a spear steady and look at you now. Lord Alfgar.' Wulfhere bowed his head, and almost toppled from the saddle, bringing peals of laughter from the men.

'Don't call me that,' Alfgar mumbled.

'When Osric is gone, you will be next in line to be Ealdorman,' said Beornoth, and the laughter subsided at the sound of his voice. 'You are Aethelhelm's son, and it is your right.'

'What if I don't want it?'

'When has want ever made a difference in this world?' said Beornoth.

'I don't want to be Ealdorman. I want to stay and fight for you, to live at Branoc's Tree with Wynflaed.'

'I'll look after her for you, lad. All that beautiful red hair...' said Wulfhere, and he leant away quickly as Alfgar swung at him. Wulfhere laughed, and the rest of the men chuckled along with him.

'It is your duty,' said Beornoth. 'Before the Vikings strike again, which they will, we need the north secure. We can't go into that fight with enemies at our back. The men of Cheshire will accept you as their Lord. Your father was well liked, and I dare say that Osric, the piece of goat shit, is not. You have grown into a fine man and a solid fighter. You will make a good Ealdorman.' Beornoth shifted in the saddle as he spoke, jutting his chin forward and avoiding eye contact with Alfgar. Kind words came not easily from his lips, but Alfgar had earned it, and the words he had spoken were true.

'*Drengr*,' said Brand, which meant warrior in Norse. He spoke in a laconically even tone, matter-of-fact and without alarm. Beornoth looked at him, and the Norseman nodded his head to the south-west, where a line of horsemen had appeared on a distant rise. They were still, a line of twenty horsemen, spears bristled above them, and they were cast in black against the setting sun.

'It's Osric, with more warriors,' said Wulfhere. 'We should charge them now, Lord. Get it over with here and now.'

There were grunts of ascent from the rest of Beornoth's men, but Beornoth wasn't so sure.

'They haven't come to fight,' he said.

'Of course, they have, Lord. Look at the bastards. They are armed to the teeth, and all mounted. They haven't come for a Yuletide barn dance,' said Wulfhere.

Beornoth raised an eyebrow at him. 'If you were going to attack a group of warriors who you know have a reputation as Viking killers, would you wait in full view on high ground? Or would you use your thought cage and attack where you would have a chance of killing your enemy without losing half of your own men, or risking your own life?'

'I would attack,' Wulfhere said, and he grinned at Beornoth. 'But that's why I am me, and you are a Thegn and our Lord. It's not my job to think. You tell me where to hit, and I hit hard.' Which was true enough.

'They don't want to fight, not yet at least,' said Beornoth. He clicked his tongue and urged Ealdorbana forwards to meet his enemy.

# 16

---

The sun crawled its way to a night of slumber, casting a soft red hue across the sky. Beornoth led his men to within one hundred paces of where the enemy horsemen sat still on a shadowed hill-top, spear points glinting and faces grim.

'Wulfhere, and Brand, come with me. The rest of you wait here. If they attack us, or you see my signal, attack,' said Beornoth.

'What signal?' asked Alfgar.

'Me killing them.'

Alfgar shook his head. 'How can you be sure that once you get beyond our lines, that they won't ride you down and butcher you?'

'I can't be sure, but like I said, if they wanted to kill us, they would use more cunning than waiting on top of that hill.'

'Why are you bringing him with you?' grumbled Wuffa, his pockmarked face twitching as he glared at Brand.

'Because he looks like a man who could kill three of theirs,' said Beornoth. He rode forward. Wulfhere and Brand followed, one on either flank. Three men ambled their horses forward from the enemy line, and Beornoth recognised the stocky shape of Streonwold at their centre. If his old friend had come to talk, it meant Osric was not with them, and had escaped deeper into his shire.

Streonwold came on slowly, his horse picking its way through the gentle hillside dotted with ferns and bushes with thick green leaves and bright blue flowers. Two warriors flanked him, and just like Beornoth, Streonwold had brought two big, scarred men. One rode with a spear held upright in a fist like a hammer. He had a wide face with a tiny, flattened nose, and small eyes below a wide forehead. The second man had a long-handled war axe resting on one shoulder. He was an enormous man, dwarfing his horse with his broad shoulders and thick legs as though he were riding a pony. The axeman wore a helmet with rings around both eyes, which cast his face in shadow save for his mouth, which had a white, jagged scar running across it and down to his chin, cutting through the red of his lips so that his lower face was a permanent snarl.

'Streonwold,' Beornoth said, and nodded his head in greeting. Ealdorbana dipped his head to crop at the long grass.

'Beo,' said Streonwold, his jowls wobbling as he spoke. The weight of his years had made his face strangely fat and loose, but Beornoth knew that belied the strength and war skill of the man. He and Streonwold had survived shield walls together, killed together, and there were few men he would trust more to protect his left side when the linden wood wall comes together, and blades come for neck, face and groin. 'You got away, and I can't say I wasn't sorry about that. But I was sorry to see the woman killed. I don't make war on women and children.'

'I know that. She was a good friend to me, in the old days. Now, she is dead. Osric should not have dragged her into this.'

'No,' agreed Streonwold.

'Where is Osric?' Beornoth growled, shifting in the saddle. A sour look stretched Streonwold's face. From his opening remarks,

Beornoth could tell that the old warrior was less than proud of his Ealdorman's reputation and actions.

'There is a town, half a day's ride from here. Like as not, he is in the tavern there, drinking off the dust from the road, and his anger at your escape.'

'He would have dragged me to Mameceaster, tortured me, and killed me.'

'Yes, he would. You should not have charged into his hall last year. He is an Ealdorman. Aethelhelm's son.'

'He had my wife.'

'I know.' Streonwold sighed and rubbed two thick fingers into the corners of his eyes and shook his head. 'Osric is not the man his father was.' Streonwold stared at Beornoth, and they held one another's gaze for a long moment, and in that look Beornoth saw Streonwold as he was, when they were young, and saw the same in him. Sharing horns of mead following a hard fight, riding to battle with Ealdorman Aethelhelm in their war glory. There was honour then. Brotherhood in arms. It felt like a different time, a different life.

'I am going to kill Osric,' Beornoth said, slowly.

'Go home, Beo. Back to the East Saxons. Leave Cheshire and never come back.'

'I cannot. You were at River's Bend; you know the Vikings have returned. There are men in the north who must be put down before the Kingdom can stand together against the northmen. Men who plot against the throne, men who would welcome Viking rule.'

'Those men are everywhere, not just here. There are more grandsons of Viking Jarls in East Anglia than there are in Cheshire. Æthelred is weak, a usurper King whose mother had his own brother killed so he could take the throne. The days of the great King Edgar are long gone. Powerful Ealdormen, Thegns, and worst of all churchmen, scheme and plot for land and wealth. Killing Osric will not stop that.'

'True,' Beornoth allowed, because Streonwold summed up the state of the Kingdom perfectly. 'But he killed Blaedswith and took my Eawynn last year. He is a piece of weasel shite, and I am going to kill him.'

'I am oathsworn to protect him, Beo. I can't let you pass. Just turn around, lead your men home to a warm fire. There are other enemies to fight.'

Beornoth sighed and stretched his back in the saddle, his shoulders ached from the ride and his wounds were many and sore. 'Alfgar is with us, see?' He turned and nodded back to his men.

'I would not have recognised him,' Streonwold said, and a half-smile split his solemn face. 'He has doubled in size, so you made a warrior of him.'

'Just as Aethelhelm wanted.'

'Aye. I am glad to see him well.'

'He is also a son of Aethelhelm, and brother of Osric. Who has no sons?'

'Don't say it, Beo.'

'No more men need to die here. Just one. Clear the road, and I will ride to this town and kill Osric. Then, his brother can become Ealdorman in his stead.'

Streonwold's tongue flicked out across his lips. He glanced at Alfgar and then back at Beornoth. 'Alfgar is a good lad, an honest, God-fearing lad. But I can't just let you ride on past and kill the Ealdorman.'

'Yes, you can. There is no oath-breaking in it. If Osric were dead, Alfgar would be next in line to be Ealdorman. Would you not rather serve a man you can love and respect?'

'I said no, Beornoth.' Streonwold raised his voice, and the big man with the split lip shifted his war axe on his shoulder. There was steel in Streonwold's voice, but his eyes told a different story. Beornoth saw them flick again to Alfgar, saw the future play out quickly in his old friend's mind, of an end to serving a man he couldn't respect, a glimpse of the chance to return to the sense of honour and respect he had enjoyed when they had both served Ealdorman Aethelhelm.

'Very well,' said Beornoth, and he dipped his head to Streonwold. He leant to his left as though he would wheel Ealdorbana around and return to his men. As he turned, Beornoth lowered his right hand and grabbed the hilt of his sword. The leather wound about its grip was warm and soft in his hand, and as he curled his fingers around it, Beornoth felt its strength course up his arm. He dug his heels into Ealdorbana's flanks, and the warhorse leapt forward, powerfully strong leg muscles bunching as the animal responded to his training. Beornoth dragged his sword free and as Ealdorbana lunged, he brought the sword to rest low at his right-hand side, waiting for the horse to draw closer to Streonwold and his men. Behind him, Beornoth heard Wulfhere call, and a look of surprise sagged Streonwold's face. The huge axeman grimaced and shifted his war axe from his shoulder, but it was too late, and he was too slow.

Ealdorbana picked up pace and reached the axeman in the blink of an eye, and Beornoth snarled as he drove the point of his sword underhand and upwards, piercing the axeman's mail and shattering its links with a loud clinking sound. The blade went on into the soft flesh beyond and Beornoth swayed aside to avoid the falling axe. The axeman's eyes showed white beneath the eyeholes of his helmet, and Beornoth whipped his sword free before it became entangled in the dying man's corpse.

'Do not kill Streonwold,' he shouted over his shoulder, and charged up the hill alone, sure that his warriors would follow close behind now that he had provided the sign to attack. Beornoth rode Ealdorbana hard towards the line of warriors atop the hill. He had his shield, which had remained on Ealdorbana's saddle after the ambush in the forest, slung across his back, its weight banging against his shoulders as he rode, and his bright, blood-tipped sword in his right hand, reins held firm in his left. If he was to kill Osric, then these men had to yield or die. Beornoth growled encouragement at Ealdorbana, and he raced up the hill, towards the line of horsemen who kicked their own mounts forward to meet Beornoth's surprise charge. He heard weapons clash and the shout of warriors behind him, and he hoped Streonwold had lived. He would need him if Alfgar were to become Ealdorman. Ealdorbana was in full flight, his power pulsing beneath Beornoth as he rose and fell, keeping time with the horse's charge. Ahead, he saw bearded faces coming towards him, some helmeted, others with hair streaming behind them as they charged. A golden-haired warrior howled as he came on, spear outstretched before him, and a shield held in his left arm and braced across his body. Beornoth applied pressure to Ealdorbana's flank with his left knee, and the horse followed his command, veering slightly to the left, towards the oncoming warrior's shielded side. The charging line bunched together, coming for Beornoth, but their line was a single rank deep, the length of them spreading wide, instead of bunching into ranks, and so Beornoth knew that once he was through their line, then he would be behind them with his men in front. Unless he died on the point of the sharp, shining spear blade racing towards him, couched in the fist of the golden-haired warrior, charging on the back of a rowan mare.

The sound of galloping horses was as loud as winter thunder, and the hillside shook under the weight of it. Beornoth held his breath as the enemy horsemen drew close, snarls, roars and sharp steel coming for him, coming to kill him and drive his bones into the earth. The golden-haired rider lifted himself slightly in the saddle and the tip of his spear flicked upwards, and in heartbeats it would tear into Beornoth's throat, ripping into his flesh and splashing his blood across Cheshire's green grass. But Beornoth shifted his weight and leant away from the blow, ducking as it passed a hand's breadth from his face. Beornoth bunched his muscles and drove the point of his sword into the golden-haired man's shield. Beornoth slammed his sword in further, feeling the elation, the impossible relief that comes when a man tries to snatch away your life, but you instead prevail and live on to fight and kill. The golden-haired warrior grunted, and because he had dropped his reins to hold the spear in one hand and shield in another, he toppled from his horse to crash on the hard earth, racing beneath the hooves of his charging horse.

Beornoth heard a shout of challenge to his left just as he struck the golden-haired man and felt the scrape of a spear point across the left shoulder of his byrnie, but the blow had no strength because Ealdorbana crashed his muscled chest into the attacker's horse, throwing the rider off balance. Beornoth gripped the reins tight in his left hand, and slid in his saddle under the impact, but clung on to Ealdorbana. Then they were through them, blades behind and rolling hills beyond. Beornoth wheeled his warhorse around in a wild churning of the earth beneath them, clods of mud flying and Ealdorbana neighing and chomping at his bit. Beornoth bent low to keep his balance, and then the enemy was in front of him, riding towards Beornoth's own riders.

'Ride now, my friend, and help me kill my enemies,' he said, and Ealdorbana bunched his legs and sprang once more into the charge. Ahead, Brand the Norseman had also broken through the enemy line, his axe swinging above his head in a shining arc.

'Odin, Odin,' roared Brand, and he backswung his axe blade into the shoulder of an enemy rider as he sawed on his horse's reins to bring her about. Beornoth steered Ealdorbana towards the right flank, where the fighting was hardest. Streonwold's men outnumbered Beornoth's force, but the left flank had spread out, disjointed, scattered by Beornoth and Brand's charge. On the right, however, the horses and warriors were thick, locked in a frothing, heaving mass of warriors, steel and horseflesh. Wulfhere was there, and Beornoth saw the big man smash his axe into the face of an enemy horseman, but he was taking blows on his shield, and Alfgar was there next to him, fending off two warriors with his shield. Ealdorbana slammed his chest into a dappled mare as Beornoth charged into that terrible maelstrom of death and pain. Beornoth drove the point of his sword into the throat of the mare's rider, his eyes bulging wide with surprise as the cold iron cut through his gullet and burst through the back of his neck, blood slopping across his mail. Beornoth ripped the sword free and leant over his saddle to smash the sword's edge into a black-bearded rider's face, and he sawed the blade back, feeling it grate on skull and teeth as the man's face sliced apart like an overripe apple. A thud hammered into the shield on Beornoth's back, and he had to cling on to Ealdorbana's reins and neck to stop himself from falling. He heard a man roar his defiance, and another hammer blow thudded into his back, the shield crunching under the powerful blow. For a horrifying moment, Beornoth thought he would slip from the saddle and tumble to the earth, to be clattered, kicked and crushed. His stomach heaved with the panic of it, the fear of his skull being crushed by a black hoof, but he righted himself and relief washed over him as Alfgar slew his unseen attacker with a thrust of his spear, and the man let out a deep-voiced roar of pain. Suddenly the press of horse, the stench of their urine, of leather and the iron tang of blood dissipated and Beornoth found himself in the open. Streonwold was swinging his sword above his head and bellowing at his riders to form a new line, and his men wheeled about him, preparing for a fresh charge.

'There are still too many,' Alfgar shouted above the fray. 'If they charge again, they might break us.'

Beornoth gnawed at the beard on his top lip, his heart pounding from the fight. It could not end here. Osric had to die, and he had to get back to protect the people of Branoc's Tree.

'Hold,' Beornoth shouted. 'Hold. Let them retreat.' His men put up their blades and the Saxons drove their mounts away from the maelstrom of killing and back towards Streonwold's line.

'Brand, stop,' he called in Norse. The Viking was hammering his axe, over and over, into the back of a Saxon warrior slumped over the back of his horse. Blood sprayed brightly on the field and flew in great gobbets. Blood soaked Brand's face and beard, his teeth showing bright white against the dark crimson liquid as he grinned at Beornoth. 'Come with me,' he said to Alfgar. 'Just you.'

He cantered towards Streonwold's line and held his sword upside down, so that the point dangled towards the earth to show that he came to talk in peace again. The line of enemy horsemen bristled and churned as their warhorses scraped the ground with their hooves and their heads rose and fell from the thrill and danger of battle. The warriors pulled in their reins, spears swayed above them, and helmets glinted.

'Enough men have died, Streonwold,' Beornoth shouted over the battlefield. He could hear the groans of the fallen, and the shriek of injured horses where they rolled and howled amongst the dead. Streonwold had lost six men, Beornoth thought, and that might be enough to persuade the old warrior to give up the fight. 'Give us the road. The heir, and your new Ealdorman, is amongst us. Ride with us, rid the land of Osric. He is unworthy of his father's shire.'

Beornoth brought Ealdorbana to a stop ten paces before Streonwold. His old friend was in furious but hushed conversation with his men. Arms waved and fingers pointed, before Streonwold dug his heels into his horse and came forward to meet Beornoth.

'Men have died because you brought your warriors here,' Streonwold said, his eyes blazing and his mouth twisting to show his teeth.

'I come for Osric. He is not worthy of being your Ealdorman. Stand aside and let me kill him. Alfgar will replace him, and you can swear a new oath to him. You know Alfgar, he is a good man.'

'We will give you the road, Beo. But this feels like a fell deed. I don't want to fight you or Alfgar.'

'Thank you, old friend. What we do is no more fell than when Osric had me captured with cunning, and dragged with ropes from a fight. He has no honour; he is not a Lord to stand against in the shield wall. Not like his father. I will go to this town and find Osric, and I will kill him. Will you declare for Alfgar and support his claim when Osric is dead?'

'Just go, Beo, before I change my mind,' said Streonwold, and his eyes flickered from Beornoth to Alfgar, and the old warrior smiled wanly. He wheeled his horse around and led his warriors from the field. Streonwold might not have confirmed that he would support Alfgar's claim to succeed Osric, but the fact the grizzled, stoic fighter had conceded the road with superior numbers made his thoughts as clear to Beornoth as a freshwater pool.

'What did you say to him, Lord?' asked Wulfhere, riding up behind Beornoth.

'I told him if he didn't give us the road, that you would kill him and his men with your foul cow breath.'

Wulfhere laughed, and Beornoth allowed himself a chuckle. He had lost a good man in the fight, but the road to Osric was now open. The Ealdorman of Cheshire was a half-day's ride away, and Beornoth could almost taste the vengeance it was so close.

# 17

---

Beornoth and his men rode late into the night, pushing to get as close to Osric's location as possible before the darkness made the ground too treacherous for their horses. A broken leg or lamed horse would slow them up, and so they made camp amongst a tangle of hawthorns out of the night's bleak wind. They had finished the rest of whatever supplies each man had in his pack following the hasty ride from York, which meant their evening meal comprised stale, hard bread, and some salted pork.

Beornoth woke the following morning with a growl in his belly, and stiff aches from his wounds. His back was raw from where Leof had lashed him with the switch, and his arms and chest were a mess of thick, itchy scabs from where they had dragged him across Northumbria and into the high hills. The swelling in his face throbbed, but had subsided a little during the night. .

Beornoth ordered Wulfhere and Alfgar to ride out early, just as the sun crept into a red glow above the horizon to push back the night's dark shadows. Their task was to scout ahead and find the village where Osric and his men drank ale, waiting for Streonwold and his riders to return. Wulfhere and Alfgar returned at midday, horses flecked with lather from a hard ride, and Wulfhere grinning as he slid from his horse, bursting with news.

'Crowsford is the name of the place, a rat's nest of hovels, a merchant's barn, a church and a tavern. A thin river runs alongside it, and rich farmland surrounds the place.'

'You saw Osric?'

'No, Lord. But they've stabled their horses behind the tavern, and his men are inside drinking the place dry.'

'How many men does he have?' asked Beornoth, and he touched gingerly at the swelling on his face, opening his mouth wide to stretch it, the dull pain strangely satisfying.

'There are eight horses there, Lord. The rest of his men must have gone with Streonwold to attack us,' said Alfgar.

'Is Streonwold there?'

'No, Lord.'

'Just your brother and his household troops, then.'

'Yes, Lord.' Alfgar was pale, and there were dark shadows beneath his youthful eyes.

'I won't make you become Ealdorman, Alfgar. Not if you don't want it,' Beornoth said softly, placing a hand on Alfgar's shoulder. He had taken Alfgar in a year earlier at his father's request, and had turned him into a fighter, a warrior who was now a veteran of the shield wall and had bloodied his spear with the souls of vicious Viking warriors. Alfgar was still young, and far too pious for Beornoth's liking. But he loved him like a brother.

'I don't think want comes into it, Lord,' Alfgar said, and gave a sad smile, the corners of his mouth turning down rather than up. 'My brother's a turd, and unworthy of my father's hall. I fear I must become Ealdorman and take up my father's mantle to support Byrhtnoth in the fight against the Vikings. The north must be stable, and its warriors and men of the fyrd made ready to fight.'

Beornoth nodded, and his heart swelled because Alfgar was

right. Whether he wanted it or not, if they killed Osric, then Alfgar would become the Ealdorman of Cheshire and one of the most powerful men in Æthelred's Kingdom, a peer to the other Ealdormen of the state, and outranked only by the King himself.

'Well, I hope we can get home soon,' grumbled Wuffa. 'I miss my wife, her hips and her cooking. And that old bastard Streonwold cut off my finger and cracked my skull yesterday. The fat-faced bastard.' He raised a hand where dark patches of blood showed through cloth bandages.

The other men laughed at Wuffa's misfortune, and Beornoth took Wulfhere to one side, away from where the others made ready to ride with the jangling of tracings, and the grumbles of tired men filling the air.

'Only eight?' he asked.

'Only eight,' Wulfhere confirmed, and ran a hand over his bald head, grinning at Beornoth. 'If we go in when the sun goes down, most of them will be blind drunk. We can kill them in their cups.'

'Only Osric needs to die.'

'They would have killed you, Lord. And they killed your friend, the woman who Cwicca and Kari are off burying as we speak.'

'They would, but I am thinking Osric's men are more useful to us alive than dead. We will let them live, if we can.'

'There is some deep cunning in that skull of yours, Lord.'

'We'll see,' Beornoth said, and he stroked his beard. 'Now, tell me about this tavern.'

They rode towards Crowsford as the day pressed on, white clouds churning in a sky the colour of gruel. The land rolled into valleys and farms, and as the sun made its descent toward the hills, they saw the small village of Crowsford appear beyond golden fields of wheat and barley. Crowsford was a tangle of buildings, a barn and a church with a high-gabled cross rising above the village. Beornoth and his men waited on a ridge beyond the village until the sun went down, and until the sounds of laughter and shouting pealed out of the tavern to drift on the evening breeze.

'So, Lord. Do we surround the place? Or do we burn them out? What's the plan?' asked Wulfhere. They fixed their eyes on the tavern, torches inside it making the building glow and shimmer like the heart of a wood fire. Tendrils of smoke drifted from the chimney to leave a grey stain above the village.

'I don't want Osric's men to fight, if we can help it,' said Beornoth. 'I want to kill Osric, and for most of his men to live. So, we won't attack in force.'

'You said that before, Lord. But if we have the numbers, which it seems we do for once, why not just ride in there now and get the job done?'

'I want to frighten his men so that they yield, and when Osric is dead, I will make them swear an oath to serve Alfgar when he becomes Ealdorman.'

'Do you think they will?'

'They will if we scare them enough. Which is why you and Brand will come into that tavern with me. We might need to kill or hurt a few of them to frighten the others. They are men of war, warriors of Osric's hearth troop. This is how they earn their living. Death and injury is their trade.'

'Just seeing the three of us walk into the tavern won't be enough to frighten them, Lord, if they are warriors.'

'Fear can be a weapon,' Beornoth said, his voice becoming low. 'They will see three big men clad in byrnies, armed with swords and axes, and wearing iron helmets. Most of them will only have leather armour, because a man in mail must have enough reputation and war skill to afford to have one made, take one from a dead enemy, or inherit one and have enough skill to stop others from taking it from him. Each sword we carry is worth more silver than it would cost to buy that entire village. They will see proper warriors of the shield wall, killers. Not men who guard an Ealdorman who surrounds himself with flatterers. We are the men who fight, maim and kill so that our people can live peaceful lives, so that families can sleep at night without fear of raiders, without fear of violence. We are the ones who fight for those who cannot fight for themselves. The men in that tavern would have killed me slowly, they would have dragged me to Mameceaster and tortured me, before killing me slowly and painfully and denying my people at Branoc's Tree the protection of my sword.' Beornoth's voice had become louder as he spoke, his anger welling. The rest of the men had fallen silent to listen. 'Osric must die, and we must strike with terrible force and violence. His men must know that they face viciously ruthless killers whom they cannot possibly stand against. That is us. We are those men. When this is done, and Alfgar is Ealdorman, then we ride back to the land of the East Saxons to protect our people. So Wulfhere and Brand will enter the tavern with me. The rest of you will wait outside with Alfgar. Any man who runs from that tavern wearing armour or carrying weapons, take him, but do not kill him.'

Beornoth translated the plan into Norse for Brand, and they rode towards the village in grim silence. As they reached the drab houses, thatch dark and the place stinking of pig shit, Beornoth climbed down from Ealdorbana and handed her reins to Alfgar. He took off his black cloak and draped it over the saddle and checked that his sword was loose in its scabbard, and that his seax was secure where it hung from the back of his belt on two leather thongs. Beornoth shrugged his mail, its iron links heavy and secure, gleaming in the dark like the scaled skin of a dragon. He took a helmet he had retrieved from the fight with Streonwold's men; it was bright and well made, a conical join at its peak came down across the forehead in the shape of a boar, and it had two eye rings, carved with whorls. Beornoth pulled it on, its leather liner resting comfortably on his scalp, the eye rings darkening his face. He was huge and powerful, broad and strong. The pain of the wounds he had taken fell away, his heart beating faster. It was a risk, marching into the tavern with only Wulfhere and Brand. There would be at least eight warriors inside, and they could overwhelm Beornoth and stab their sharp steel into his flesh, rending and tearing him until he died. But three would be enough.

Wulfhere and Brand also dismounted, and they strode toward the tavern together. It was a long building, the wattle gaps between its building posts and lintels daubed in lime washed white. Someone had painted a crude picture of a horse on to a wooden sign which swung gently above the doorway, creaking each time it swayed back and forth. Beornoth's boots crunched on the small stones of the pathway leading to the place, and the sounds of iron clanking, and leather creaking, emanated from the three warriors as they marched to kill an Ealdorman, the son of the man who had once been Beornoth's Lord, and his friend. A man he and his father had both fought for. But he did not pity Osric. He had come for vengeance.

'Wulfhere, go around the back and come in that way,' he said. The big man nodded and set off, hulking in his mail, a sword buckled at his belt and his monstrous war axe gripped in two hands, the beard of its blade hooked, sharp and terrible.

'Brand, you follow me in through the front,' he spoke in Norse. 'If it comes to fighting, hurt them badly. Look for painful and bloody wounds, lots of blood. Shock them. If we must kill one or two, make it as grim as you can.'

'May Odin bring us battle luck, and his Valkyrie take us to Valhalla if we fall,' said Brand, and Beornoth could see his white teeth flashing in a grin beneath his blonde beard, which he wore in a long braid stretching down from his chin to rest on his mail. The

Viking loved to fight, and he had a fearsome look, hard and cruel.
The look of a killer.

As Beornoth drew closer to the tavern, candlelight danced
from the windows and the place overflowed with the voices of
men, low and rumbling, interspersed with laughter. There was a
flute playing, the sound of the wood instrument chirping into the
night, light and jolly. Beornoth clenched his teeth and his powerful
hands curled into fists, two shovels at the end of his scarred,
muscled arms.

'Shall we look first, to see where the warriors are sitting?' Brand
asked. Beornoth heard the slither of leather as the Norseman
slipped his axe from its loop at his belt.

'No,' said Beornoth. He didn't care where they were sitting, or
whether they were armed. It didn't matter. He reached the door,
two twin panels of oak fastened to the door frame on iron hinges.
Beornoth kicked the join between them with his boot without
breaking stride. The loop which kept them closed crunched and
sprang apart under the weight of the blow. He ducked under the
door frame and stepped into the tavern, filling the space with his
broad shoulders and thick chest. A wave of hot air hit him, like the
breath of a horse, but foul with the stench of ale and greasy meat.
He rose to his full height and grimaced, eyes passing over the
room. He counted eight men with weapons about them. None
wore mail, so confident must they have been that Streonwold
would kill Beornoth. The warriors wore their weapons belts, at
their waists or slung over their shoulders, most armed with
wicked broken-backed seaxes, and he saw at least two spears
amongst them. The rest of the people at the dark timber benches
were women, ruddy faced and draped around the warriors, or
village folk in simple woollen clothing and mugs of ale in their
dirty-nailed fists. They all stopped to look at the warrior who had
burst through the doors. The flute player was a young man, with

sandy hair and a beardless face sat by a crackling fire. On the bench next to the fire Osric lounged with two of his hearth warriors, a woman draped around his neck, her dress loose around her breasts and her hair falling in curls around her shoulders.

'Anyone who does not want to die should leave now,' Beornoth shouted. 'Except you, Osric son of Aethelhelm. I am Beornoth, and I have come to kill you.'

The people in the tavern just stared at him, open-mouthed. They looked at one another and back to Beornoth, still and unmoving. Osric shrugged the woman away from him and sat up straight, his pink tongue flicking across his lips as he looked around the room at his men, eyes wide with surprise to see that Beornoth had got through Streonwold's force.

'Get out now, or I will kill you all!' Beornoth roared, the sound of his voice thundering around the roof timbers like the roar of a mighty bear. He drew his sword, the rasp of it scraping against the wood lip where the fleece lining ended. That grating noise was ominous. Danger and threat pouring from weapon and wielder like poison from the fangs of a serpent. The women and village folk sprang away from the benches, scuttling for the doorways, crouched and avoiding eye contact with Beornoth. A woman shrieked from the rear of the room as she opened the back door, but found Wulfhere on the other side of it. His axe gleaming, the fire glow dancing on its edge and his hulking frame filling the space where she expected to see only the dark of night, where she could flee from the nightmarish warrior in the tavern's entrance. Wulfhere stepped aside, and the woman and three others slipped past him, and then he stepped inside the room, hefting his long-handled war axe in two hands.

Brand entered the tavern and the door behind Beornoth slammed closed once the people had left, and Osric and his men rose slowly to their feet, hands reaching for weapons, their eyes wide with fear.

'I just want him,' said Beornoth, and he raised his sword so that the tip pointed at Osric.

'Who do you think you are?' spluttered Osric, and he flicked a trembling hand towards Beornoth. 'Kill him, a pouch of silver for the man who takes his head.'

A warrior came forward, a big man with muscled shoulders straining at his jerkin. He drew a seax from his belt and strode towards Beornoth, his lips pulled back so that his broad face looked like a skull, snarling and furious. He sprang forward, driving at Beornoth with speed which belied his frame. The seax came for Beornoth's neck, the warrior aiming to cut his throat in a savage upwards swing. Beornoth snapped his left hand out and caught the warrior's wrist in an iron grip. The man's twisted snarl changed into a grimace of terror as Beornoth raised his sword high, and with a lifetime of weapons practice and training, and all the strength and hate in his body he brought the edge of the sword down into the side of the warrior's neck. The blade cleaved through neck and then chest, carving deep into the man's torso, ripping and tearing through flesh, muscle and bone. Blood sprayed bright in the tavern's darkness, and the warrior fell to his knees. He made a high-pitched mewing sound as air wheezed from the huge gash which had cut open his chest, his upper body carved in two in a horrifying mess of bone and deep red flesh. Then he flopped to the floor rushes and his thick, dark blood pumped out onto the tavern floor. Beornoth dragged his blade free with a grunt, and Osric's warriors took a step back.

'Bastard!' shouted a short man, the awful death of his friend and fellow warrior driving his voice into a shrill scream. He ran at Beornoth, drawing a seax from his belt as he ran. He screamed as he came, and Brand took a step forward and threw his axe overhand. It spun in a glittering circle, its blade making a low hum as it cut through the air before slamming into the charging warrior's face with a wet thud. It threw the warrior backwards off his feet, his screaming cut off instantly as the axe head smashed into his teeth and jaw with a loud crack. The man fell to the floor and twitched, a sucking sound emanating from the wound before he died, and Osric's men groaned.

'I just want Osric. No one else needs to die,' Beornoth said, slowly and clearly. Two men dashed for the back door, but then stopped and fell back against the rear wall when Wulfhere threatened them with his axe.

'Kill them, kill them!' Osric pleaded with his men, shuffling backwards.

Beornoth stalked towards him, the sound of his boots on the hard-packed earth floor loud and stomping. The room was quiet other than the fire crackling and the shallow breathing of terrified men. Beornoth held his sword low with the tip raised, blood dripping from it in fat gobbets. Osric's men gazed at him as he passed them, and they saw a huge warrior clad in iron, his face hidden by his helmet. They saw their deaths in a grotty tavern and the warriors shuffled away towards the edges of the room.

'You killed Blaedswith, and you wanted to kill me. Last year, you took my wife by force. You are not your father's son, and not fit to be Ealdorman,' Beornoth said as he closed in on Osric.

'I did not kill your hag; it was my archer. Him over there, see?' Osric said. He thought Beornoth would look at the killer of his friend, because as he spoke, Osric whipped a knife free of his belt and lunged at Beornoth. He darted inside the range of Beornoth's sword and slashed the blade at his face. Beornoth swayed away from the blow and pulled back his sword arm and cracked the iron pommel of his sword into the back of Osric's skull, and he cried out and dropped to one knee. With his left hand, Beornoth slapped the knife from Osric's hand, and the blade skittered across the floor, out of his reach. Osric threw himself on Beornoth's leg, and he sunk his teeth into the meat of Beornoth's thigh. Beornoth hit him again with the ridged pommel of his sword, this time on the side of his face, and Osric's cheekbone cracked under the blow, and he fell away, shouting with pain and clutching the side of his face.

Beornoth levelled his sword, the point a finger's breadth away from Osric's face, and the young Ealdorman stopped writhing, and stared at the dull iron point.

'I am Beornoth, Thegn of Branoc's Tree in the lands of the East Saxons. I am here with the authority of King Æthelred to quell the trouble in the north of his Kingdom,' he said. Killing an Ealdorman was stretching the King's mandate to the point of it being a crime in itself, but he needed to add credibility to Osric's death, if the next part of his plan was to work, and for Osric's warriors to accept what must happen next. 'Osric, son of Aethel-helm. You connived with traitors and cut-throats, with Oslac of Northumbria, a traitor to our people, to invite Viking rulers back to our lands. You attacked Ealdorman Byrhtnoth, who acts with the authority of the King, and an assault on the King's men is the same as an assault on the King himself.'

'What?' Osric spluttered. He had no evidence that Osric was part of any plot to invite the Jarls and Kings of the Danes and Norsemen to invade England, but again, the charges must be enough to justify the punishment.

Before Osric could object to the charges, Beornoth simply jabbed his sword forward. He gripped the leather-bound hilt tightly, and from the shoulder he pushed the heavy iron weapon, keeping his wrist locked, and the point of the sword passed into Osric's eye, silently and without resistance. Beornoth applied more pressure and twisted the blade until a hand's span of iron was deep in Osric's skull. The Ealdorman quivered on the end of the sword like a caught fish, and Beornoth pulled the blade free so that Osric collapsed dead on the tavern floor. Relief and sadness in equal measure flooded Beornoth, and he felt tired. Too many Saxons had died because of Osric's hate, and his death was like an extra byrnie lifted from Beornoth's shoulders. One less enemy.

'Osric is dead, and there must be a new Ealdorman appointed to the shire of Cheshire,' Beornoth said, looking around at Osric's warriors. They were all staring at their dead Lord, and at each other, fear and uncertainty on their open-mouthed and wide-eyed faces.

Suddenly, the tavern doors burst open, and Wuffa bowled into the room. 'Riders, Lord,' he said.

# 18

Beornoth's warriors stood ready in two blade-bristling ranks, spears poised and resting on shield rims so that the throng before them faced a wall of painted shields and war iron. They formed up before where a group of villagers broiled, shouting and brandishing wood axes and hoes. Two of the villagers held torches, the light from them catching on the spears and helmets of Beornoth's warriors. Beornoth strode from the tavern clutching Osric's sword which had hung on the edge of an ale table. It had been Osric's father's sword, a fine blade in a red fleece-lined scabbard, the hilt wrapped in silver wire. Beyond the villagers, mounted warriors milled in the tangle of Crowsford's lanes, shouting and growling, iron in their fists. The riders emboldened the villagers, who would not have stood so bravely alone in the face of a well-armed war band.

Osric's surviving warriors came through the tavern door behind Beornoth and came to a stop before him in a line, cowed and shuffling their feet. Their Lord was dead, their ring-giver, and they had done little to prevent that. Wulfhere and Brand came out behind them, with Wulfhere ushering a straggler on with the long haft of his axe.

'They don't look like much. These lads are broken men,' said Wulfhere, shaking his head in pity at the warriors. 'It's no simple thing to see your Lord killed, making you a masterless man. I know and remember it well. It's like an icy blade plunging into your heart.' Beornoth had captured Wulfhere when he was a masterless man, roving the land as a thief and a brigand. It was the fate a warrior feared most, to have his status and reason for being stripped away by the death of the Lord he had sworn to protect. Such a man had to find a new Lord quickly, or he was deemed a man outside of the law and could legally be hunted and killed.

'Who in all hell are they?' asked Wulfhere. He squinted into the darkness, but it was hard to make out the riders beyond the glare of the villager's torches. 'If they are Osric's men, they could ride us down and kill us here. These pitiful bastards wouldn't be slow in joining them.' He jutted his chin at Osric's sullen warriors.

'Let's find out. I want no more Saxon blood spilt if we can help it.' Beornoth marched towards his men, holding the Ealdorman's scabbarded sword high above his head, his hand gripping its centre to show that he did not mean to use the weapon. Wulfhere was right, and if the horsemen were fresh warriors sent for by Osric to help protect him from Beornoth, then it would be a grim fight in the streets of Crowsford, and the men on horseback would have the advantage, striking from the backs of their mounts, and the power of their warhorses would scatter Beornoth's men like chaff. His men had left their own horses at the edge of the village, Beornoth not wanting to alert the tavern's inhabitants of their approach with the sound of hoof beats.

'Let me through,' he said to his men, and Alfgar barked an order and the two lines of Beornoth's warriors lowered their shields and, in a well-drilled manoeuvre, they split into two rows flanking the edges of the path. Each man lowered his shield. Half of the company took a step to the left, and half to the right, and then took two steps back. All in perfect time, just as Wulfhere had drilled them on the practice ground. Beornoth strode through them, and Alfgar's eyes became fixed on his father's sword, and he swallowed hard, throat rising and falling like a bucket in a well.

Beornoth marched towards the villagers. Blood splashed his mail where he had cleaved Osric's man open, and he towered over the farmers and millers. They stopped shouting and the entire group shuffled back before his approach. He glared at them through the eyeholes in his helmet, and then at the riders beyond.

'I am Beornoth, a Thegn. I was born and raised near to here. Ealdorman Aethelhelm was my Lord, just as he was yours. Osric is dead, and this is his sword. He was not worthy to lead you and shamed the people of this shire with his back-stabbing and treachery.'

'Murderers! Assassins! Our Lord is murdered!' screamed a heavyset man in a blacksmith's leather apron.

'Who are you to tell our Ealdorman what to do?' shouted a man with missing teeth, so the words came out fumbled.

'Get out of the way,' growled one of the horsemen, and he forced his mount through the crowd, the size of the beast scattering the villagers to the side of the road. As the mounted warrior moved into the torchlight, Beornoth breathed a sigh of relief as he recognised Streonwold's grey beard and shaking jowls.

'Ealdorman Osric is dead. He committed crimes and has met the King's justice,' Beornoth shouted, so that the villagers and Streonwold's riders could hear. There was shouting and murmuring amongst the people, and Beornoth heard weapons hissing from scabbards and belt loops. 'But his father, Ealdorman Aethelhelm, had two sons. The other son is amongst us. He is Alfgar, a godly man, and a warrior.' Beornoth turned and held his open hand out, and Alfgar stepped forward. He removed his helmet and came towards Beornoth. Alfgar took a deep breath and squared his shoulders. His steps had started as a shuffle, but the young man forced himself to stride with the straight-backed confidence of a warrior.

'I am Aethelhelm's son,' Alfgar said softly.

'Osric had no children, so left no heir. Alfgar is next in line, and is now the Ealdorman of Cheshire,' Beornoth said, and he handed the red-scabbarded sword to Alfgar, who took it and bowed his head.

'You killed our Lord. Why should we do what you say? Southern bastards! Murderer!' came a shout from Streonwold's ranks, and a young warrior spurred forward. His white gelding came alongside Streonwold's horse. The warrior carried a spear, and his face was round and beardless.

'Paega, hold your tongue,' said Streonwold.

'Would you have us become masterless men, Streonwold?' said Paega. 'Wandering the land in shame, fighting for coin? We swore oaths to protect the Ealdorman.'

Streonwold frowned and shot Beornoth a hard look, and Beornoth looked to Alfgar. Alfgar's jaw worked beneath his beard, and he stared at his boots, and his shoulders slumped. The moment was slipping, and Beornoth could sense the reticence in Alfgar. He was about to take on the mantle of Ealdorman, a rank he had never been prepared for nor wanted, and without the blessing of the King. All Alfgar wanted was to ride in Beornoth's war band, and to be with Wynflaed at Branoc's Tree, but fate does not care for the dreams of men.

'Command them,' Beornoth said, stepping close to Alfgar and putting his hand on Alfgar's shoulder. 'You are a warrior of the shield wall, and the son of an Ealdorman. You are a good man, a better man than your brother. Take their oaths and lead them.

Prepare the north to defend itself against the Vikings. You are your father's son, and I am proud to have stood beside you in battle, and of what you have become.'

Alfgar stared into Beornoth's eyes. They shared a moment of mutual recognition and friendship, a bond that can only exist between men who have fought together, lost friends together, and shed blood together.

'Beornoth, I have news,' Streonwold said, clearing his throat, his voice sounding tired. Beornoth ignored him and nodded at Alfgar to reassure him once more. There were murmurs from the villagers who huddled at the edges of the pathway, and horses snorted and tack jangled.

'I am Alfgar, son of Aethelhelm, and brother of Osric,' Alfgar said. He spoke clearly and confidently, his voice sailing on the night breeze, sonorous and sure. 'This is my father's sword, and I am Ealdorman of Cheshire. We who have fought against one another should put that enmity behind us now. Start anew, with open hearts and in God's grace.' He held the red-scabbarded sword high and turned in a half-circle so that all could see. 'Streonwold. You were my father's oathman, leader of his hearth troop and his finest warrior. Will you swear an oath to serve me, as you did my father and brother?'

Beornoth held his breath. This was the moment of highest danger, if Streonwold refused the request to swear his oath to Alfgar, then there would be a bloody fight in the streets of Crows-ford, and the north would remain a hornet's nest at the tip of England when the country faced the great Viking threat in the south. Beornoth nodded at Streonwold, and his old friend frowned, and glanced at the young warrior next to him. Paega shook his head slowly. His lips turned in on themselves in disapproval.

'Serving your father was my life's greatest honour,' Streonwold said. 'Your brother was not a good man, nor was he an honourable man. Paega is right, and I swore an oath to protect Osric, and now my Lord is dead. But I say that he broke his duty to us, his faithful warriors. He led us in an attack on fellow Saxons, on Beornoth who was once my sword brother, and on Ealdorman Byrhtnoth, who is the killer of Vikings. We are now masterless men, but now we can swear oaths to a new Lord, a new ring-giver.' Streonwold slid from his saddle, leather creaking and his mail and weapons clinking against one another. He grunted with the effort and strode to face Alfgar, scars visible on his lined face and across the backs of his hands, his jowls shaking as he walked.

Streonwold offered a small nod to Beornoth, before dropping to one knee in front of Alfgar.

'I swear before God,' he said, pulling a silver cross from beneath his byrnie and clutching it in one hand, whilst at the same time reaching up to grasp the red scabbard in Alfgar's hand. 'On this holy cross, and on the sword of Cheshire. I will be loyal to Alfgar, son of Aethelhelm. I will love all that he loves, and hate all that he hates, in accordance with God's rights and obligations. Never will I willingly or intentionally, in word or deed, do anything which is harmful to him on condition that he keeps me as I shall deserve, and carry out all that is our agreement now that I subject myself to him, and choose his favour.'

These were the old words, the oath words that bound men to their Lord. Beornoth's men had said those same words to him, and now the warriors of Cheshire would swear to serve Alfgar as Ealdorman. Alfgar offered Streonwold his open hand, and he took it in the warrior's grip. Alfgar pulled Streonwold into a warm embrace, and Beornoth smiled. Streonwold clapped Alfgar on the back and then turned to his men, and to the villagers.

'I pledge my sword and my life to Alfgar, who is now the Ealdorman of these lands. You owe him your allegiance.' He glared

at the villagers, and one by one, they bowed to Alfgar, heads
lowered in respect. Streonwold's men followed his lead and
climbed from their horses to make a line and swear their oaths to
the new Ealdorman. Osric's hearth troop stood to one side of the
pathway, their heads still bowed, but where some shot spiteful
looks at Beornoth and Alfgar, others had hands clasped together in
prayer, and hopeful looks on their faces. Alfgar waved them
forward, and the warriors from the tavern joined the line to repeat
the solemn words and swear a new oath to a new Ealdorman. Pride
bloomed in Beornoth's heart. Alfgar seemed to have grown taller
and wider when he had accepted his father's sword. Gone was the
callow youth he had first met in Knutsford, and before him was a
powerful Lord.

'You have turned him into a fine man, Beo,' said Streonwold,
standing next to Beornoth as his men swore their oaths. Even
Paega had now joined the line to swear to his new Ealdorman.

'He made himself into the man you see before you,' Beornoth
said.

'When we left him with you, he weighed less than a kitten. His
arms were spindly and his hands soft from reading the word of
God. He was a disappointment to his father, and Aethelhelm was
sure Alfgar would die in the shield wall.'

'A good way to get rid of an inconvenient bastard,' said
Beornoth.

'Alfgar's mother might not have been Aethelhelm's wife, but
she was no whore. She was a gentlewoman, kind and beautiful, a
widow who fell into his arms. Aethelhelm loved Alfgar when he
was a boy, but he was gentle and kept away from the usual rough
and tumble between the lads in the burh. The Church was the best
place for him, but he did not take to it. So Aethelhelm gave him to
you.'

'And now he has killed Vikings and is Ealdorman of Cheshire.'

'Yes, he is.' Streonwold removed his helmet and its leather liner and passed a hand through his thinning hair. 'I have news, Beo.'

'What news?'

'We met riders on the road. They said that Oslac of Northumbria has been punished, and Byrhtnoth has taken his son Thered as hostage to ensure his loyalty to King Æthelred.'

'Good,' said Beornoth. 'Is Oslac dead?'

'He is. Oslac locked himself into the tower at York, and fortified it with warriors. But his own men handed him over when Byrhtnoth moved to attack them.'

'Spineless bastards.'

'Byrhtnoth killed him there on the steps of his tower. The riders who carried that tale also had more news, and we came quickly to tell you.

'Why did you have to come so quickly?'

'Because there have been Viking attacks in the south.'

# 19

Beornoth led his company south, and they met Cwicca and Kari past Knutsford where the straight stone road built by the Rome-folk forked west towards Chester and its great burh built upon the ruins of a huge Roman fortress. Beornoth gave Cwicca and Kari a pouch of hacksilver to share as a reward for taking Blaedswith's corpse to Knutsford. They had made sure that she received a proper burial close to the church, and that the priest was paid to say enough prayers to send her immortal soul safely into Heaven. Cwicca had assured Beornoth that Swidhelm had caused no trouble, not once Cwicca's seax had threatened him. So Beornoth left the north quelled of discontent, or so he hoped.

They pushed hard to the south fearing where the Vikings had attacked, not at the gallop, but with long days of riding punctuated by regular breaks for the horses. Ealdorbana was all power and size and built for war. He was not a horse for fast cross-country riding. In sight of Tamworth, a town at the heart of the English Kingdom, Beornoth sent Wuffa with Cwicca and Kari south-east on their smaller, faster ponies to pick up Byrhtnoth's trail and look for any sign of a Viking attack. Byrhtnoth had told Beornoth he would meet him at Branoc's Tree before the full moon, which was still four or five days away. As much as he wanted to see that Eawynn, Aethelberga and the people of Branoc's Tree were safe, he did not want to blunder past the Vikings who could have attacked anywhere along the south-east or south coast.

'Will you kill him?' Wulfhere asked, nodding in Brand's direction, as they cantered through a meadow of grass cropped short by a herd of fat-bellied cows who lowed lazily as they passed.

'If Olaf has attacked Branoc's Tree, yes,' said Beornoth.

'The lads won't be sorry. It irks them that one of the enemy rides with us, fights with us, and eats our food. They resent him. What if Olaf has attacked, but not at Branoc's Tree?'

Beornoth grumbled into his beard, because it was a good question. Brand was one of nine hostages against any further attacks from Olaf, and should the Norse warlord bring his sleek, high-prowed dragon ships back to the Saxon coast or its rivers, then Brand would have to die. Beornoth had grown fond of the Viking warrior. He was quiet and stern, but a fighter and had fought as well for Beornoth as any of his own warriors. 'We'll see,' was all Beornoth would say on the matter.

They stopped at Tamworth to take on supplies, and the city was busy with its market day, and merchants poured news of Viking attacks into the streets and taverns. The snarl of lanes and streets was thick with the talk of it, and Beornoth purchased a new whetstone for himself to hear the tale.

'They ain't like normal Vikings, this lot,' said the merchant, a bulbous-nosed man with a red face and a goitre on his neck, protruding like an apple under his skin. 'They are a scourge from God.' The merchant made the sign of the cross twice over his chest. 'Here to punish us for our sins.'

'Where are they?' Beornoth asked.

'In the east, Lord,' he said, pointing a stubby finger in that direction, from where he rustled in his cart for the whetstone. 'Wicked men, slavers, and murderers. Defilers. The sword of Satan, they are.'

'Have you seen them?'

'Well, not as such, no.'

'Have you seen them or not?'

'No, Lord. But I heard tell of it from a man in a tavern a day's ride from here. Said they sailed up the river at Gippeswic and struck inland, raining terror on the simple folk, Lord.'

'There is a burh at Gippeswic?'

'Sort of, Lord. But it's more of a port these days, since they threw the Vikings out of there in my father's time. God bless his soul.'

Beornoth pressed a small silver coin into the merchant's hand, and he flashed a brown-toothed grin at him before shuffling away, his cart jangling and rocking as he went.

'Do we go home then, or to Gippeswic?' asked Wulfhere. He was turning an ivory comb over in his hand and marvelling at the carving of a horse's head at one end.

'Byrhtnoth said he would meet us at Branoc's Tree. But if he came south after dealing with Oslac, then he would also have heard of this attack.'

'And he wouldn't ride on past a Viking attack.'

'No, he would not.'

'So, we ride for Gippeswic?'

'Yes. And hope that Olaf hasn't attacked at Branoc's Tree.'

Wulfhere turned his lips in on themselves and shook his head at the hard choice. Beornoth could ride to Branoc's Tree, and if Olaf was there, he would fight for his people. But if it was Olaf who sailed into Gippeswic and Beornoth carried on to find Branoc's

Tree at peace, then he would be two days' ride away from where Byrhtnoth and the peaceful folk of Gippeswic needed him.

'What did you buy that for?' Beornoth said, frowning at the ivory comb and glancing at Wulfhere's shining bald head.

'For my beard,' he said, and ran it through the tangles below his chin.

'You want to look your best? For when we go to Branoc's Tree?'

'Why would I want to look my best?' Wulfhere said, squinting so that crow's feet showed at the corners of his eyes.

'For Aethelberga, of course?' said Beornoth, and Wulfhere opened his mouth to protest, his face turning as red as a summer apple. The big warrior spun on his heel and stormed off, mumbling under his breath and keeping the comb close to his chest. Beornoth chuckled to himself, the moment of levity a welcome distraction from the hard decision he had to make. He was closer to Gippeswic than Branoc's Tree, and the northmen had already attacked the people there, where Beornoth only feared that Vikings were at Branoc's Tree. He owed it to Byrhtnoth to ride to him if the Ealdorman had engaged with the enemy, and so the decision of where to ride made itself.

'Wulfhere,' he called after his captain. 'We ride for Gippeswic.'

Beornoth led his riders south-east from Tamworth, spending the last night of their journey at a monastery at Beodricsworth, which was a day's ride from Gippeswic. The abbot and his monks made them welcome with a frugal meal of bread and fish and regaled the younger warriors with stories of King Edmund, a martyr who was buried beneath the monastery and for whom the monks said endless prayers. The King had become a saint after being tortured and killed by Ivar the Boneless over one hundred years earlier. Ivar and his Vikings had tied the defeated King to a tree and threw spears and shot arrows at him. Throughout his ordeal, the King of East Anglia had proclaimed the glory of God and Christ until Ivar cut off his head. Beornoth's men said prayers over Edmund's relics: a collection of yellow stained bones, a few brown teeth and three arrowheads. The abbot told them of the groups of ceorls and merchants who had fled the lands around Gippeswic, travelling north and west to flee the Viking raiders. He told of harrowing reports of slaughter, burning and rape.

The company rode out on a still morning where cloud sat low against the hilltops, close and oppressive. By midday, Beornoth saw the first smear of smoke in the distance. It angled away from the low hills, whipped by the wind to spread and bloom like a deathly flower, too thick for a hearth fire and a sure sign of suffering, pain and death. Beornoth led his men towards it, and they rode in grim silence, bracing themselves for what lay before them. Brand rode at the rear of the column, and Beornoth knew the Norseman avoided him, fearful that the attackers were his people, that it was Olaf Tryggvason attacking Saxon lands, and what that meant for his fate as a hostage against that very event. They reached the source of the smoke where a fishing village stood on the shores of a shimmering lake bordered on three sides by dense forest. The smell of the place hit Beornoth before he saw the devastation. The stench of burning meat turned his stomach, mixed with charcoaled timber and old thatch. It was a smell Beornoth knew well, a stench he dreaded, and one he had fought his whole life to protect his people from. Horses in the column behind him whinnied and snorted, but Ealdorbana trudged on, and Beornoth placed a hand on his muscled neck to keep the beast steady.

Beornoth saw the first body hanging by its feet from a burned-out church. The west-facing end of the blackened building was still crackling with heat and smoke, but the gable end with its high cross had survived the flame. From that gable, a man's naked body turned slowly, a hemp rope creaking under the weight. His skin was part pink, and part blackened by smoke. Beornoth wanted to turn away and vomit into the grass, but he forced himself to look upon the body, steeled himself to remember the man and understand the pain and suffering he had endured at the hands of his killers. They had sliced the hanged man's skin and peeled it back in long strips, and cut off his hands. As the corpse turned slowly at the end of the rope, Beornoth saw with horror that the man's genitals had been cut away, and they had shorn the rear of his scalp, leaving a bright red patch of skin on his skull.

'God save us,' said Wulfhere through a sharp intake of breath, reining in alongside Beornoth and making the sign of the cross between his face and the mutilated corpse.

'There is no God here,' Beornoth growled. 'Just death.' He clicked his tongue, and Ealdorbana picked his way around the detritus of the ruined village, around the pool of thick, dark blood beneath the hanged man, and came to a stop before a pile of bodies, white and stark against the burned-black timbers of the village buildings. Crows leapt from the grisly heap and hopped away to a safe distance, scraps of human flesh in their beaks and blood staining their black shining feathers.

'Does this honour Odin?' Beornoth shouted over his shoulder in Norse, searching for Brand amongst the column of riders. 'Does thing bring war fame? Is it how Norsemen build their reputation?'

'No, Lord,' said Brand. He cantered his horse out of the line and the beast shied away from the hill of corpses. He spat on the ground and sawed on the reins to bring the horse around to face Beornoth. 'This is not Olaf's work. He is a *drengr*, not a murderer of children.' Beornoth saw small feet and hands protruding from the stiff, bloody limbs and the locket at his chest felt heavy, as though it had suddenly become made of stone.

'Piss on *drengskapr*, and on Odin,' Beornoth snarled. A *drengr* was the Norse word for a warrior, and *drengskapr* was the Viking

Way of the Warrior. It was that code which drove northmen to fight and build their reputations in service of Odin, to forge a name for themselves and secure a place in Odin's great mead hall. Brand's blue eyes blazed, but the Norseman knew better than to challenge Beornoth at that moment. 'Whoever did this are not men.' He urged Ealdorbana into a canter and brought him around in a circle to ride amongst his men. 'This is why we fight. To protect our people from this. We have wasted too much time in the north fighting with our own people. This could be Branoc's Tree, or any Essex village or town raided by Vikings whilst we were away. We will hunt the dogs who did this, and we will kill them.' Beornoth was shouting, stoking the anger and revulsion on his men's faces, and the evil looks they cast in Brand's direction.

'The bastards must be close,' said Wulfhere. 'The place is still smoking. They can't be more than a day away, and look, some of them are mounted.' He pointed his spear to hoof prints in the grass and the hard-packed earthen path which skirted the church.

Beornoth led them on, through the skeletons of houses which had once been happy places where families ate and reared children. They rode past a headless corpse, stripped naked and mutilated, its head ten feet away, where a fat crow pecked at the eyes. To his right was the corpse of an old woman, her skirts hitched up around her neck and her legs a bloody mess.

'Killers of old women and children, slavers and rapers. We do not rest until we find them.'

The Vikings were easy to find, their horses having left a trail through the countryside as easy to follow as a Roman Road. The smell of their campfires drifted on the breeze, and their shouts and laughter rang loudly as the raiders drank and ate to toast their incursion into East Anglia. Beornoth rode through a field half cut for hay, tools left in the stalks where the ceorls had fled for their lives. The sound of the enemy was welcome, and Beornoth's heart quickened and his breath came short and sharp. He took his shield from the loop on Ealdorbana's saddle and slung it over his back, and his knuckles whitened on the shaft of his æsc spear, its leaf-shaped blade honed so that he could have used it to trim his beard. Ealdorbana sensed the change in Beornoth, and he quickened his pace, his huge head nodding as he cantered.

'Should we scout them, Lord? So we know what we're riding into?' called Wulfhere behind him.

'Yes,' replied Beornoth, 'we should.' But he would not scout them. He was going to kill them now. Beornoth had seen no warriors on the journey from Tamworth to East Anglia, no Thegns and no signs that the fyrd had been raised. He should wait, check how secure the Viking camp was, send men to ride around for a mile and look for the local Thegn and his hearth troop. He should examine the lay of the land, attack at night, or from high ground. Beornoth knew war and had been taught how to fight it from the time he could walk. That lifetime of knowledge and skill all paled against the white-hot anger and fury raging inside of him. He wanted to rend and tear at these men, he wanted to stab and cut them, to hear their screams and soak the land with their blood. He was vengeance and wrath and would use his strength and savagery to bring justice down upon the raiders.

Beornoth dug his heels into Ealdorbana's sides, and the beast responded, launching into a gallop. The wind rushed past Beornoth's face, and his lips peeled back from his teeth in a wolfish snarl. He did not look back to make sure Wulfhere and his men followed the charge, allowing his rage to drive him on. He saw an enemy rise from where he sat on a fallen silver birch trunk. The man shouted a warning to the camp and turned to run. But Ealdorbana was racing, and he was upon the fleeing northman in three heartbeats. Beornoth leaned forward as Ealdorbana made the jump over the tree trunk and, as the beast was airborne,

Beornoth took the man between the shoulder blades with his
spear. The Viking cried out as blood sprayed across Ealdorbana's
flanks. Beornoth brought the spear around in a circle and levelled
the blade again. He burst from a high hedge of gorse and thistle
into a clearing filled with men. Bearded faces turned to him,
mouths open and eyes wide with surprise. Beornoth roared and
charged into a group of them squatting by a small fire. He yanked
back on his reins with his left hand and plunged his spear into a
man's belly with his right. Ealdorbana twisted his great head and
snapped his teeth at a crouching warrior, catching hold of his nose
and lips and ripping the skin from his skull with a terrible sucking
sound. All around Beornoth was shouting and chaos. A man in a
leather breastplate reared up ten paces away. He had a bushy black
beard and brandished a war axe. Ealdorbana reared up and
crushed another warrior with his forelegs, cracking skull and chest
bones, and Beornoth launched his spear as he leaned forward into
Ealdorbana's neck. The æsc flew and took the bushy bearded man
in the chest, throwing him back into another campfire and scattering glowing embers into the air.

The camp was like a kicked wasp's nest, men running and
horses charging. Brand and Wulfhere thundered into a group of
four warriors, the force of their horses scattering them like rolling
barrels. Beornoth dragged his sword free of its scabbard and
wheeled Ealdorbana around, noticing a clutch of women and children tied and huddled on the far side of the camp. A voice peeled
across the carnage, loud and commanding, barking orders at the
Norsemen. Beornoth heard the word 'arrows' just as a missile
whistled over his shoulder. Beornoth saw a stocky warrior clad in
dark, rusting mail with a stringy beard and small, pale eyes. He
was big-bellied and bow-legged, and he held a sword in one hand
and a shield covered with pale, faded leather splashed with blood
in the other.

'Ride them down!' Beornoth roared, pointing his sword at the three archers stood alongside their bow-legged leader.

'Shield wall,' Bow-legs commanded, and men flocked to him, dashing around Beornoth's riders to grab shields all bearing the same strangely pale leather. Beornoth's men hacked at them, and a few fell, but more made it to the widening shield wall, and Beornoth counted over two dozen fighters. He cursed to himself because the Vikings outnumbered him, and urged Ealdorbana on towards the prisoners, to the Saxon women and children the Vikings planned to take to the slave markets in Hedeby, or Dublin. As he turned the horse, an arrow tonked off the shield slung across his back as it hit the iron boss, and Ealdorbana shuddered. Beornoth saw a shaft had struck his horse in his rear thigh, the fletching standing out white against his coat. Wulfhere buried his axe into the chest of one archer, and Brand tore out the throat of another from the back of his horse.

'We have the numbers. Ride away now and you can live,' shouted Bow-legs from the front of his shield wall. He was missing his two front teeth, and he smiled a dread death's-head smile. His dark hair fell greasy and lank around his shoulders.

'Give us the prisoners,' Beornoth replied in Norse.

'These dogs are ours now'. The man spoke with the clipped accent of a Dane, not with the burr of a man from far Norway. 'They are nithings like you, you Saxon turd. Maybe you can join them? Or maybe I shall flay you alive and make a new cover for my shield.'

Beornoth shuddered, realising the coverings on the Vikings' shields were not leather, but human flesh. 'On me,' he said, and held his sword high to rally his riders.

'There are too many,' said Wulfhere. 'Leave now, and we can strike when we are better prepared.'

'Kill the prisoners,' Bow-legs barked. Four warriors peeled

away from the back of the Viking shield wall and ran to the prisoners, who screamed and wailed. Beornoth dug his heels into Ealdorbana's flanks and launched the warhorse forwards, just as the first
Viking slammed his axe into the back of a prisoner who had curled
herself into a ball of fear on the ground.

'No!' Beornoth roared, and he charged towards the prisoners,
but Ealdorbana rocked to one side with such jarring force that it
almost threw Beornoth from the saddle. A short spear had
slammed into Ealdorbana's muscled chest, and another flew from
the Viking shield wall to land beneath the horse's legs. Beornoth's
heart sank. His beloved warhorse was injured by arrow and spear
and bleeding heavily from both wounds. The horse reared, his
eyes rolling white, and his teeth bared in panic. Beornoth sawed on
the reins to bring him under control and as the horse planted his
forelegs on the earth, Bow-legs was upon him with his double-
bladed war axe raised high, and a crazed look on his scarred face.
Beornoth raised his sword, but the axe was already on its way
down, arcing through the air with a speed and force which belied
the enemy leader's appearance. The blow brushed Beornoth's
sword aside, but the sword stopped some of the monstrous
strength in the blow. Instead of crashing into Ealdorbana's chest, it
sliced down his neck and into the meat of his foreleg, spraying
blood across the Viking leader's face.

Ealdorbana sagged and jerked away from the attack, and
Beornoth clung to his horse as he turned. The huge horse sank
down onto his forelegs but rose again and tottered away from the
fray as Beornoth's men forced themselves between Beornoth and
the advancing enemy shield wall. Beornoth allowed Ealdorbana to
flee the fight, and as he went, he saw the dreaded Vikings plunging
their blades into the last of the prisoners, howling and drenched in
the blood of both children and women. Beornoth roared as he fled,

an animal's cry, deep and undulating as pain and anger washed over him.

'I am Ragnar the Flayer,' Bow-legs' voice rang out behind Beornoth as Ealdorbana limped along, trying bravely to gallop but managing a limping half-canter, blood flowing from his wounds and lather thick on his flanks.

## 20

Beornoth and his men rode south, away from the defeat and the horrors of Ragnar the Flayer. They stopped where Ealdorbana fell, on the banks of the River Gipping, and beneath an outcrop of black rock mottled with white veins. The great warhorse stumbled onto his injured foreleg and Beornoth heard a bone snap as he leapt from his back. Beornoth scrambled in the dirt to kneel next to him, placing his hand on Ealdorbana's neck. The horse's lips peeled back from his lips, and he let out a long, loud scream. The whites of his eyes were huge and afraid. Beornoth touched his forehead to Ealdorbana's neck, and he felt the horse's pain as keenly as if it were a brother or kinsman.

'He won't rise from those injuries, Beo,' said Wulfhere. The big warrior crouched next to Beornoth and patted Ealdorbana's flank. 'Let me end his pain.' Wulfhere stood and took an axe from a loop at his belt.

'It must be me,' Beornoth whispered. 'I am the one whom he has carried so bravely. He has saved my life many times. I should not have ridden him with these injuries. He is as fierce a warrior as any of us, fiercer perhaps, for he carries no blade and wears no mail.' Beornoth held a shaking hand out towards Wulfhere, and he placed the axe in Beornoth's grip. Beornoth closed his fingers around the leather-bound haft and shifted himself around Ealdorbana's flailing legs to stand before his proud head.

'I am sorry, my brother. My friend.' Beornoth heaved the axe two-handed and brought it down hard and true between the horse's eyes, and mighty Ealdorbana fell silent. Beornoth fell to his knees again and stroked his trusty horse's mane.

'They were beasts, not men,' said Brand in Norse, leaping from his horse and striding back and forth along the riverbank. His horse plodded to the flowing water to take a drink. 'They were Danes, but not *drengr*. Just as I feared.'

'They were Danes,' said Beornoth in Norse, and he rose to his full height to hand Wulfhere back his axe.

'What are you saying?' asked Wulfhere, the other men dismounting and gathering around.

'That they were not Olaf's men. They were Danes,' Beornoth replied.

'There were so many of them,' said Wuffa, wiping a hand down his sweat-soaked face. 'Did you see how they killed the women and children?'

'We lost Ead back there. They dragged him off his horse and I saw him fall as we ran,' said a quiet voice. The last word spilled from his lips to shame them all, for they had run from Ragnar. Even if the Danes had possessed greater numbers, it was still a defeat. A defeat that had cost the lives of Ragnar's Saxon prisoners. Ead's dun mare had followed Beornoth's men as they rode away, despite the Vikings having dragged and slaughtered the rider from his back.

'They were devils. We should find the local Thegn and go back with greater numbers. They must be stopped. God help those poor people,' said another, and the warriors all made the sign of the cross upon their breasts.

'We will bring these fell Vikings to justice and find vengeance for those people,' said Beornoth, but there was little force in his voice and he could not meet the eyes of his men. He left them to make camp beneath the rocks and went to stand by the riverbank. He watched the water flow by, tugging at reeds and making its inexorable way to the sea. Ragnar had beaten him, and innocent people had died because of it.

Beornoth did not sleep that night. He lay beneath his woollen cloak, staring at the stars and lamenting the loss of brave Ealdorbana, regretting allowing his anger to master his judgement. Beornoth should have scouted the Viking camp, and if he had, then their greater numbers would have been clear. He told himself that at least he had struck a blow against the Danes. Some of their warriors had died. The screams of the dying prisoners filled his ears whenever Beornoth tried to close his eyes, so he kept them open. He looked at the heavens and hoped that whatever God was up there, whomever it had been who had created the world and people within it, would grant him vengeance over Ragnar the Flayer.

The sound of approaching riders woke the camp the next morning, and Beornoth surged to his feet, sword in hand, expecting to see Ragnar and his grisly shields galloping down the riverbank. There were two riders, and the men cheered to see Cwicca and Kari coming towards them, hands held up in greeting, Cwicca's curly hair bouncing around his ears. The men gathered around them, the good news of their arrival lifting the desperate pain of defeat. The two young warriors smiled and clasped hands with their friends, but Cwicca caught Beornoth's eye, and the smile fell from his face. Beornoth walked away from the group and Cwicca dismounted to follow him.

'You found us,' Beornoth said.

'It was not difficult,' Cwicca shrugged. 'We knew you would come home and would hear news of the Vikings' attacks, and you would head straight towards the trouble. There are not many armed bands of riders in these lands.'

'You found Byrhtnoth?'

'We did, Lord. He is in the south, patrolling the lands around the Thames, between Lundenburg and the coast. Olaf Tryggvason and his ships are raiding around Folkestone, and he fears they will strike further north. The King has left Winchester and marches towards Lundenburg.'

'So, Olaf raids the south-east coast, and drives north towards Essex, towards our home. Here in East Anglia, there are Danes raiding and killing. Then, we have bastards within our own lands who welcome the Vikings to return and will feed them, supply them, and help them kill our King and butcher out people.'

'So, it would seem... Yes, Lord.' Cwicca looked at his boots, frightened by Beornoth's raised voice, and feeling the tension from his Lord, understanding the overwhelming danger the Kingdom found itself in.

'Do Byrhtnoth and the King know that Danes have attacked?'

'There is word of a fleet of dragon ships, Lord. They sailed across from Frankia and news came of them in the north. Messengers came to the King just days past.'

'Two Viking armies then,' said Beornoth. He sighed. His mail felt heavy, and his eyes were stinging from lack of sleep. He felt suddenly old. Old and tired. 'Was Byrhtnoth not summoned by the King, or his mother, to explain Osric and Oslac's fate?'

'Not that I know of, Lord. Is that Ealdorbana?' Cwicca asked, looking over Beornoth's shoulder at the dead horse on the riverbank.

'Yes. We fought against a large crew of Danes yesterday. They have ravaged this entire area, savage and brutal men. Maybe a vanguard of this new force of Danes you speak of. Who knows? They are here, and they are murdering our people. We attacked them and they killed Ealdorbana, along with Ead.'

Cwicca made the sign of the cross and whispered a prayer. 'Byrhtnoth bids you ride to him, Lord. He will meet the King at Lundenburg, and the Witan will decide what to do.'

'Did Byrhtnoth say why the Ealdorman Aethelwine and his Thegns of East Anglia have not risen to fight off the Danes?'

'Not to me, Lord,' Cwicca shrugged. 'I am just your messenger. I heard the King has summoned the East Anglian Ealdorman and his Thegns to Lundenburg. But there are rumours...'

'Go on.'

'Well, Lord. The talk around Lundenburg was that there are Thegns in East Anglia, and elsewhere, who have called for the Danes. Who would welcome them. Some names were mentioned, some of Byrhtnoth's own shire-men.'

'Who?'

'Æthelric of Bocking, amongst others.'

Beornoth nodded and rubbed his thumb and forefinger into the corners of his eyes. He had heard of Bocking; it was north of his own hundred and close to the East Anglian border. East Anglia was akin to Northumbria in that the Vikings had ruled it within the Danelaw for one hundred years, and many of the people there to this day were descendants of Danish Viking invaders. Perhaps this Æthelric was one such man, a Thegn sick of King Æthelred's rule and his mother's scheming, sick of taxes, and sick of losing land to the Church. Beornoth allowed Cwicca to join the others to share his news. The weight of events fell heavy on Beornoth's shoulders. It appeared the entire Kingdom was on fire, and the King was hiding in Lundenburg, or so it seemed to Beornoth. He must answer the call of his Ealdorman and ride to Byrhtnoth, leaving the people of East Anglia to the horrors of Ragnar the Flayer and his beast-men.

They struck camp and Beornoth led the company south-west towards Lundenburg, away from East Anglia and from Ragnar the Flayer. He rode Ead's mare, who was much smaller than Ealdorbana but a fine horse with a dun coat, and a black mane and two black forelegs. There had been grumbling and long faces amongst Beornoth's men at the order to ride away from Gippeswic. The defeat stung, and they burned to avenge Ead's death. They spent most of that day heading steadily south-west. They travelled through a low, flat land of yellow grass and boggy fields. The riders crossed fast-flowing streams which tumbled down from high hills beyond sight. As the day wore on and they passed through Essex, the open grassland turned to farmland and in time they passed the River Chelmer so that by late afternoon they were in the lands between the rivers Crouch and Thames and within a half day's ride of where Cwicca had last seen Ealdorman Byrhtnoth.

Beornoth rode through empty fields of crops, and villages where the people locked themselves inside their houses, or had fled completely, seeking the safety of the burhs and their fortifications, designed by King Alfred to be used in just such circumstances when Vikings attacked. What villagers they did see opened shutters when they saw the riders were Saxons, and all pointed east towards Assandun and more news of Viking ships in the River Crouch. The day waned, but Beornoth did not want to camp for the night when he knew that both his Ealdorman and more Vikings were within reach. Keeping the glistening snake of the river on his left, they passed through verdant lowlands, until Cwicca and his keen chestnut eyes spotted the glint of iron in the dying sunlight. Beornoth quickened their pace, and he saw that ahead of them a company of warriors hurried towards them through a yellow patch of bogland. They marched with shields

and spears ready, and beyond them came a larger force, perhaps
double the size of the foremost war band.

'There must be thirty men down there in that first group,' said
Wulfhere. His horse was skittish and the big warrior allowed her to
turn in a circle.

'Must be Byrhtnoth,' said Beornoth, squinting across the plane,
but his eyes could not pick out a banner or sigil amongst the spear
shafts.

'So, the ones chasing him must be Vikings.'

'Let's find out,' said Beornoth. He drew his sword, having lost
his æsc spear when fighting Ragnar's men. He held the blade aloft
and wheeled his horse around in front of his men. 'The last time
we fought, we had to retreat. Ead, a good man, died and was left
unavenged. We are warriors, we are the Viking killers, men of
Essex and the victors at Mersea Island.' The men pulled axes from
their belts or from loops at the saddles, and others raised their
spears in salute. They released a cheer to shake the very river,
hearts thundering at the chance to fight again and kill the cursed
Viking invaders. 'So kill these Viking bastards instead!' Beornoth
allowed himself to release a war cry along with his men, and he let
the mare have her head, racing down towards the chase ahead of
them.

Beornoth made for the Saxon line and recognised Byrhtnoth
by the horsehair plume streaming from his bright helmet. Beyond
Byrhtnoth's men, the Viking line paused at the sight of Beornoth's
riders.

'Beornoth, well met!' called Byrhtnoth, teeth showing in a wide
smile beneath his silver beard. 'Shield wall.' The Ealdorman
turned and brought his shield up to overlap with the two men
flanking him, and Beornoth was pleased to see the ugly face of
Leofsunu of Sturmer next to the Ealdorman. Beornoth ordered his
riders to split into two, one company on each flank of Byrhtnoth's

men. He slid from the mare's back and pushed himself into the line next to the Ealdorman. Byrhtnoth's warriors greeted him as he moved through them, clapping him on the back. Offa flashed him a grim smile, and the old warrior looked weary and drawn.

'Olaf?' said Beornoth, overlapping his shield with Byrhtnoth's after Leofsunu shuffled aside.

'Olaf's men, not Olaf himself,' said Byrhtnoth, the marks of battle fresh upon both the Ealdorman's and his warriors' weapons and gear. There was dark blood crusting on Byrhtnoth's bright spear, and Leofsunu had a long cut on his cheek. Their mail was dusty and splashed with the blood of their enemies, and their faces were glistening with sweat. 'The bastard himself is at Folkestone. His ships, however, are raiding up and down the coast. We came across two crews of them landed in an estuary.'

'Too many of the sea wolves for us to fight, Beo,' called Aelfwine of Foxfield, whose shield overlapped Byrhtnoth's on the opposite side. The delicate features of his handsome face were strained and taut.

'But we fought them anyway,' said Leofsunu, and he grinned, and then regretted it, his ugly face twisting into a wince as blood oozed from the wound on his cheek.

The Viking shield wall edged closer, each third step forward accompanied by a deep shout from the lines of warriors until the leader, at the centre of their line, held up a leaf-bladed spear to call the halt thirty paces away from the Saxon shield wall.

'We fought a band of Vikings in East Anglia, and were also outnumbered,' said Beornoth as the two opposing lines caught their breath from the pursuit, staring at each other across the pasture.

'Norsemen?' asked Byrhtnoth.

'Danes,' said Beornoth. 'Murderous slavers who use the flayed skins of men to cover their shields.'

'Danes in East Anglia?' said Offa, his jaw dropping. 'So, it is true.'

'Let us win the fight in front of us before we worry about that,' growled Byrhtnoth, shifting the weight of his shield. 'We charged into them, Beo, but there were too many. This is a retreat you have rescued us from. They won't march too far from their ships, so our best hope was to outrun them.' He sighed and looked at the grass. 'We cannot waste good warriors and good steel on these skirmishes. Me coming here was a mistake. We need to put an army together, Beo.'

Beornoth knew that all too well, he had lost his warhorse, an animal he loved like a friend, and a young warrior in Ead. They had fallen because of Beornoth's hunger for blood and vengeance, and because he had not stopped to use his thought cage to make war. He had blundered straight into the fight like an untrained boy or a wild animal. Wulfhere and his riders were on the shield wall flanks, eager to test their mettle against Vikings and wash away the shame of their retreat from Ragnar with the blood of this fresh force of Vikings.

'We should not fight these men, Lord,' Beornoth said, the men around him looking upon him incredulously. Just like him, every man in Byrhtnoth's shield wall was a warrior or a Thegn. Each man raised to the blade from the time he could hold one steady. They were born to the warriors' code, arrogant and prideful of their skill and reputation. Before battle, the shield wall was a place of brave talk and boasts of deeds to come, of shouting and battle cries to work up the courage to trade blows with an enemy. To stand across from a man who has come to cut and rend your flesh with blades. He has weapon skill, just as you do, and he is bent on using all that skill to cause you pain, to kill you, or wield the blow that will grievously wound you and condemn you to a life as a cripple, begging for scraps in the dirt.

Three Vikings strode from the enemy shield wall, big men in byrnie chain mail and with bright helmets over their long hair.

'They don't want to die here either,' said Byrhtnoth. 'And Beornoth is right, we waste our swords and our lives here, when there is a bigger fight to consider. The real fight is with Olaf, the oath-breaking whoreson. We must bend our will and concentrate our minds to throw him back on to his cursed ships, having lost so many warriors that he will never return. These Vikings before us want to return to their ships and to their Lord just as much as we need to march to our King. So, let's end this.'

Byrhtnoth and Beornoth marched forward to meet the three Norsemen. They slung their shields across their backs and stopped ten paces away. The lead Norseman took the helmet from his head to reveal a tumble of hair as black as a crow's wing, and Beornoth recognised Einar Ravenhair, huge and muscled in his mail and his spear shaft as thick around as most men's wrists.

'Beornoth,' said Einar in Norse, his voice like the crashing of the sea. 'The Norns have woven the threads of our lives together once again. It seems we are destined to fight, you and I.'

'Einar,' said Beornoth, greeting him in Norse. 'Leave the field, and we will do the same. Take your men and your ships and sail back to Jarl Olaf. We will fight another day.'

'Is Brand still with you?'

'He is.'

'Brand, is that you over there?' Einar shouted to the Saxon lines.

'I am here, Einar Ravenhair.'

'You look like a Saxon; I hope you haven't become a Christ-worshipping nithing like these shit-stinking cowards.' A ripple of laughter shook the Viking lines.

'What is he saying?' asked Byrhtnoth, shifting his feet and a frown like thunder creasing his forehead.

'Calling to the Norse hostage with my men. Insulting us.'

'Will they attack us?'

'No. I don't think so, Lord.'

'So, let's get this over with, then. They withdraw, and we withdraw.'

Beornoth nodded, but he knew it would not be that simple. The Vikings were raised to axe and sword just like the Saxons, but they worshipped Gods of War, and for them to retreat in the face of an enemy was not possible, not without some honourable tale or deed to carry with them.

'Will you leave the field, Einar?' Beornoth said in Norse.

'We might. If you return Brand to us, and you leave all your weapons here, and your mail, and your horses.'

'I should have killed Brand the day you and Olaf broke your oaths and set foot on our soil again, and our weapons and mail come with us. We both leave the field now, with honour. Or we fight and both lose good men for nothing more than pride.'

'Pride?' Einar scoffed. 'You should have killed Brand, but you did not. If you were a Viking, his head would sit atop your hall's gable.'

'I am not a Viking; I do not take my warriors to other men's homes to kill and enslave their wives and children.'

'We make war to honour the Gods and make reputations that will live on in the sagas long after we are dead. Who will remember you when you are dead?'

'Who remembers Skarde Wartooth now that he is dead?' Beornoth levelled a flat stare at Einar. Beornoth had killed Skarde at the battle of Mersea Island, and Einar's belligerence was grating on him. 'My men and I only recall him when we need laughter in the mead hall, and we talk of how you thought you were safe on the island, but when the tide went out, we simply walked across the land bridge and put you to the slaughter. Skarde was a fool, and so are you. You and your men here are all walking corpses, dead men walking the land, until you fall to our Saxon blades.'

The muscles behind Einar's beard worked in his cheeks as he ground his teeth, and his dark eyes narrowed. 'I remember Skarde with honour, as do his warriors. I should kill you now, Beornoth of the Saxons, for killing Skarde. He was a fine warrior and a great war leader. He waits for me in Odin's hall where we will drink, feast and fight together for all time.'

'He was slow. And you can try to kill me, Einar Ravenhair. Why not make the fight worthwhile? Let's fight then, you and me. If I am victorious, your men will march away and sail back to Olaf and leave their silver and weapons on the field. If you win, our warriors will leave their weapons and silver here and leave the field, and Brand will return to you.' Beornoth knew how Vikings thought from a lifetime spent amongst them in the north of England. They were ever susceptible to a challenge of single combat. A true follower of Odin, Thor and Týr could not turn down a challenge to fight without harming his reputation and damaging his chances of taking his place in the Einherjar, the forces of Odin and Thor in the afterlife.

Einar rolled his shoulders and smiled at Beornoth, the crag of his face creasing. 'I will fight you, and it will be as you say. It will be a great honour for me to kill the Saxon bastard who killed Skarde.'

'It will bring me no honour to kill you, Einar. I have already killed your master and better, so killing his servant will bring me no greater honour than slaughtering a fattened pig.'

Einar's lip quivered at the insult, and his knuckles turned white as his huge hand tightened its grip on his spear shaft. Beornoth had enraged the Viking, just as he had hoped. It was time to use anger as a weapon in his own favour this time.

'Spears, axes and shields,' rumbled Einar, and Beornoth nodded and told Byrhtnoth what would happen. The Ealdorman objected and offered to fight Einar himself. But this was Beornoth's fight, and he wanted it. He needed to replace the shame of fleeing from Ragnar's murderers with a victory to lift the heart of his men. He had to fight and kill Einar Ravenhair to prevent more warriors' lives wasted that day, and because he wanted to. He wanted to kill Einar and all the cursed Vikings who came to kill his people. Byrhtnoth handed Beornoth his spear, and Beornoth prepared himself to fight to the death.

# 21

---

'Kill him, Beo,' said Byrhtnoth, handing over his æsc spear, its leaf-shaped point crusted with dried blood from the fight with the Vikings. 'I should be the one fighting him, though.' Byrhtnoth frowned and clapped Beornoth on the shoulder. Beornoth had seen Byrhtnoth fight in single combat before, and whenever there was a man to be fought, the Ealdorman preferred to do it himself rather than watch one of his men put himself before the scything blade of an enemy.

Beornoth hefted the spear, sliding his hand up to heft it over-hand, and then underhand. The weapon was well balanced. Beornoth nodded his thanks.

'I see you still have the Norse hostage with you,' said Byrht-noth. 'We should kill him; Olaf broke his oath. We should kill his man and toss his corpse in a midden pit.'

'Brand has fought well for me, and we can use his sword. I'll fight Einar Ravenhair. One more death to spare the lives of our men. We are being attacked on all sides. Killing Einar robs them of a leader. He commands the ships he has brought raiding up the coast. He is a warrior of reputation, so his death harms them, makes them fear our blades. If I fall, then we have lost a Thegn, but they believe themselves better fighters than us, anyway.'

'May God protect you,' said Byrhtnoth and made the sign of the cross. Beornoth raised his spear to the Saxon lines, and they let out a clipped roar in salute.

'Kill the bastard!' Wulfstan shouted, huge and baleful with his broken nose and cauliflower ears.

'Gut him, Beornoth,' called another.

They banged spear or axe blades against the iron rims of their shields in unison and kept a rhythmic beat going as Wulfhere shouted 'Beornoth' to the time of the weapon clash, and the warriors took up the chant until it rose to the sky and lifted Beornoth's heart in his chest. Wulfhere marched forward and handed Beornoth his war axe, and the big warrior held his gaze for a moment. He spoke no words, but in that look Beornoth saw a friend who wished him luck, a man whom he had once dragged down a mountainside to bring to justice, and whom he now loved like a brother. Beornoth glanced over at Brand, and the Viking showed no emotion on his face, but raised his spear to Beornoth. Beornoth turned and stalked across the grassy field, the shouts of the Saxon warriors ringing in his ears and his heart pounding.

Einar Ravenhair strode towards him, spear in one hand and shield in the other. He had removed his helmet, and his black hair flew behind him as he marched. The Viking warriors roared and cheered their leader and their champion, just as the Saxons lauded Beornoth, and the low-lying grassland was filled with the shouts of warriors. As Beornoth and Einar came together, the sound of the warriors died out, and Beornoth's heart slowed. He heard the wind in the grass, and the caw of gulls as they pecked at the estuary mud at low tide. Beornoth could taste salt water in the air, and his head filled with pictures of Einar Ravenhair tearing open his belly with his spear and the horrendous pain that would come with such a blow. He imagined Einar cutting off his arm, or laying open his face, searing pain and life-ruining injury. They were things to fear, things that might make a man run for his life. Beornoth remembered a rare moment with his father when he was a boy. They were sitting on the walls of Mameceaster, watching a horse race in the wide fields outside the Roman fortress. His father had an enormous fist, busted knuckles and scarred skin, resting on Beornoth's knee.

'Remember, Beo,' his father had said in his deep voice, always so stern and brutal. 'Fear is a thing to be welcomed. It sharpens us, makes us faster. But you must learn to overcome it, for bravery is the mastery of fear. Courage is doing a thing despite our fear. There is no greater horror than the shield wall, Beo. But there will always be war, and always men to fight. You will be a Thegn one day, and you must learn to fight and kill. You will be afraid, but to be a warrior who fights in front rank and a man who is respected by other warriors, you will have to learn to master that fear. Your enemy is as afraid as you are, all men fear. You must master it, Beo, and become a killer.'

Beornoth had been just a lad then, only seven summers old. His father had been a simple and savage man. He had been exactly the man he had to be in order to protect his people, and he had been right. So Beornoth swallowed and killed his fear, and thought of the things that would allow fury to master it. He thought of his dead daughters, and he thought of Ragnar the Flayer and the dead Saxons in his camp. Beornoth ground his teeth and marched faster, fear devoured and furious anger abounding.

'Are you ready to die, Saxon?' said Einar, coming to a halt and grinning at Beornoth through his raven-black beard. He was a tall man, of a size with Beornoth, but broader in the shoulder. 'When you die, I will strip your mail and your weapons and piss on your corpse.'

'I would have honoured your corpse, Einar Ravenhair, and returned you fully armed to your men for a funeral worthy of Odin. But now I think I will return the favour. I will strip your bright mail and your weapons and give them to my men to chop into hacksilver. Your mail alone will keep them in whores and ale for months, and we will laugh at you as we drink, just as we laugh at Skarde Wartooth, the fool who forgot about the tide.'

Einar's face turned a bright red at the cheeks, and the maw behind his crow-black beard opened to show bright white teeth, and he let out a battle-roar to shake the very land. The seabirds in the estuary screeched and took to the air at the din of it, flapping overhead and fleeing from the bear-man's war cry. Beornoth smiled to himself. His anger had got the better of him facing Ragnar and he had lost a good horse and a brave man. Now, he would use anger as a weapon of his own. Einar sprang at him, lunging with his spear with a speed belying his size. The spear point hissed at Beornoth's face, and he swayed to one side, lifting his own spear to bat the blow aside and block a reverse cut. Einar stepped in, raising his shield before Beornoth could raise his own and the iron-rimmed edge smashed into Beornoth's chest, shoving him backwards. As he took a backwards step, Beornoth lifted his shield high just in time to catch Einar's spear point in an arm-juddering thrust against the boss. Beornoth swung his own spear underhand, beneath his shield in a blow he hoped would tear open Einar's groin, but the Viking skipped away as light on his feet as a dancing maiden.

Beornoth was already breathing hard, the weight of his byrnie, shield and spear burning the muscles in his shoulders. The scabbed wounds from his time as Osric's captive chaffed at his mail and his hair was already wet with sweat. Einar, on the other hand, looked as though he was taking his rest at a mead bench, calm and ready to attack again. No sign of fatigue on his thick, oar-strengthened barrel chest. Beornoth snarled and whipped his spear around, sliding his hand down the shaft so that it extended to its full length. The blade sliced through the air in an arc aimed at Einar's face, but he ducked under the blow and lunged so that the point of his spear scraped across Beornoth's mail-clad belly and the force of it was like a punch from a troll. Beornoth grunted from the pain and stepped back again.

'I can do this all day. You are old and tired, Beornoth. Should I cut you to pieces and put on a show for my men, or kill you quickly, like a wounded animal?' Einar scoffed.

Einar was younger, stronger and faster, and if Beornoth continued to trade blows with the Viking, he would indeed become cut to pieces. But Beornoth had one thing he hoped Einar did not. He had hate, fury and savagery. Beornoth let his shoulders sag and his shield drop slightly and came on again, lunging low this time. Einar brought his spear across to use his shaft to parry the tired strike, just as Beornoth hoped he would. The Viking wanted to use the block to set up a lunge with his blade that would carve open Beornoth's throat and spill his lifeblood down his byrnie. Beornoth swung his shield across his body and put all strength into the blow, so that the heavy willow and iron of it smashed through Einar's spear, breaking the weapon in two. He then stabbed his own spear at Einar, trying to disembowel his enemy, but Einar dropped the snapped shaft of his weapon and caught Beornoth's spear, and dragged Beornoth towards him. Beornoth snarled and allowed himself to be pulled inside Einar's reach, so close that he could smell stale ale on the man's breath, and then he punched Einar in the throat and raked his boot down the instep of Einar's leg, and as the Viking grunted from the pain, he smashed his knee into Einar's groin.

Einar stumbled backwards, choking from the blow to his throat, and doubled over by the sharp pain between his legs. He

grabbed for the axe at his belt, but Beornoth charged him, leaping
on the Viking and wrapping his leg around the injured warrior to
throw him over his hip like a youth wrestling at a summer fair.
Einar smashed into the grass and his mail, axe and knife clanked
and his eyes were wide with surprise. Beornoth dropped on top of
Einar, clenching his knees on either side of the Viking's waist.
Beornoth had dropped his shield, and punched Einar in the face,
leaning into each blow so that the weight of his body thundered
through each fist to smash into Einar's cheekbones, nose and lips,
crushing and pulping them into a bloody mess. Einar roared and
tried to lift his hips and throw Beornoth off, but Beornoth locked
himself in place, and pummelled Einar's face with his fists, the
knuckles of his left hand shredding against Einar's teeth through
his mangled lips. Einar Ravenhair might have youth, and strength
and skill on his side, but now he was fighting a Saxon Thegn, a
savage warrior fighting to protect his people.

Einar kneed Beornoth in the back. He was bucking, roaring
and clawing at his attacker, but Beornoth held on and allowed the
momentum from the blow in his back to drive him forwards and
crunch his elbow into Einar's throat. The Viking's tongue poked
out, pink against the black of his beard, and his eyes bulged.

'Die, you Viking bastard,' Beornoth hissed in his ear. But Einar
wanted to live, and he grabbed a fistful of Beornoth's hair and
twisted it in his massive fist, dragging him sideways. As Beornoth
leant with the pain, Einar raised a hip and threw Beornoth off him
with a victorious shout of triumph. The Viking scrambled to his
feet and grabbed for the axe looped at his belt, but as Einar
coughed and choked, blood and spittle dripping from his face,
Beornoth snatched his seax from where it hung at the rear of his
belt and dove at Einar. The Viking drew his axe but before he
could bring it to bear, Beornoth was upon him, stabbing, slashing
and rending with his seax. He bullied the big Viking back and off

balance, and slashed low at his knees, and then up underneath his byrnie to jab the point into Einar's flesh in four short, stabbing bursts, each one no deeper than a thumb's length, and hot blood poured from the wounds, running down Einar's legs. Einar roared in pain, but Beornoth was too close to him for Einar to swing his axe, so he pressed the blade of the axe into Beornoth's neck and began to saw it back and forth. Pain seared through Beornoth, and his own blood seeped inside his byrnie as Einar's axe blade sawed into the soft, unprotected skin of his neck and the lobe of his ear. Beornoth could feel the axe cutting deeper, so he drove his seax into the meat of Einar's thigh and twisted the blade until he felt it grind against bone, and suddenly the pain in Beornoth's neck subsided and Einar crumpled to the earth clutching his thigh.

Beornoth groaned and stepped away from the fallen Viking, and the Saxon warriors in the distance let out a victory roar. Einar Ravenhair, the proud warrior, was curled into a ball, just like a baby, nursing himself and the countless wounds across his face, legs and groin. His eyes were swollen and closed and his nose and mouth a ruin; blood pooled thick on the grass from his groin and thigh wounds. Beornoth turned and raised his torn fists to Byrhtnoth and the Saxon Thegns, and he let out a brutal animal cry, undulating and savage. It was a release, both from the fear of fighting Einar, and the sheer exhilaration of surviving the struggle of life and death with his adversary.

'Let me die well,' Einar mumbled through his mangled mouth. Beornoth turned to him and remembered how the warrior had promised to strip his mail and weapons should Beornoth have been the man who fell. Einar would have left him dead, naked and pale in the grass for Wulfhere and the others to drag his shamed corpse back to Branoc's Tree.

'I will treat you as you vowed to treat me,' said Beornoth. He crouched and curled his hand around the antler hilt of his seax, where it was still buried in the meat of Einar's thigh. He ripped the blade free, and blood pooled in the ruined flesh and wool of Einar's trews. Einar gritted his teeth and shuddered at the pain. 'But I am a Saxon, not a Viking. Cruelty doesn't flow through my veins as it does yours, Einar Ravenhair. So, I will send you to Valhalla first.' He turned the seax around and pushed the hilt into Einar's shaking, blood-slick fingers and they curled around it, clutching it to his chest.

'Thank you, Beornoth. I will save a place for you there, and we will drink all night and fight again together until Ragnarök,' Einar said, the words mangled by his broken teeth and swollen lips.

'Give my regards to Skarde Wartooth,' Beornoth said as he pulled Wulfhere's axe from his belt. He leant forward and Einar moved his hands away from where they cradled his chest, to expose the soft skin of his throat. The big warrior closed his eyes tight so that the corners of them creased like crow's feet, and his face twitched in anticipation of the death blow. Beornoth sliced the sharp edge of the axe blade across Einar's throat and his lifeblood slid from the wound, thick and dark against his pale white skin. Then, Beornoth tossed the axe aside and made a pile of Einar's weapons, his broken spear, his axe and knife. He unbuckled his fine belt with its iron buckle in the shape of a boar's head and slid the intricately carved silver arm rings from his brawny arms. He could hear shouts of protest from the Viking lines and saw weapons waving above their heads in protest at Beornoth stripping the wealth from their fallen champion, but they would not attack him. Their twisted sense of honour that allowed them to rape and murder would also stop them from streaming across the plane to cut Beornoth to ribbons. He rolled Einar over and untied the fastenings at the rear of his byrnie, and then yanked and pulled at the heavy coat of mail until it slid over his arms and shoulders. Beornoth held up the mail to his own warriors, and their victory shouts erupted once more to shake the estuary. He picked up the haul of silver and war gear and marched towards Byrhtnoth, leaving Einar's corpse to dung the Saxon field with his blood. The pain from the cut on his neck throbbed, but he had saved the lives of his and Byrhtnoth's men and deprived the Vikings of a valuable war leader.

'One less Viking to kill,' shouted Byrhtnoth as he strode from the Saxon lines to clap Beornoth on the shoulder. 'Let's be done with this place. Our lands are under attack, and we need to talk.'

# 22

Beornoth warmed his hands on the hearth fire, glad of its heat after so many nights spent under the stars. Every day since he had left Essex with Byrhtnoth, Beornoth had been in the saddle, or marching all day and enduring nights of broken sleep, unable to find comfort in the long, cold nights. The churn of pain from his injuries, anger at his enemies, worry at the converging forces at the edges of the Kingdom, and being missing from Branoc's Tree, all swirled and folded in on themselves to make his head hurt. Beornoth watched the flames dance on the logs, trying to find a place inside his head that was empty, a place that could just be still. All he found was more worry, more pain, more problems to chew on.

It was a summer night, following a day heavy with rain, and as cold as autumn. The shutters of the mead hall rattled as the wind howled outside, and rain came through the smoke hole in the thatch to hiss as its droplets struck the fire. Byrhtnoth had led them north-west away from the coast and towards Lundenburg, and they had stopped to spend the night at the hall of an ageing Thegn who had grumbled and claimed poverty at the approach of so many armed warriors seeking shelter, food and ale. Beornoth had tossed the man one of Einar Ravenhair's beautifully carved arm rings, and now the men sat huddled at the few eating benches crammed into the small hall, which was more like a barn with a fire than a Thegn's feasting hall.

The old Thegn gave his name as Irmin, and his people had brought bread, pork, honey and cheese and rolled in a barrel of ale. And so the warriors were happy. Beornoth had eaten little. If he moved his jaw to chew, the cut in his neck and his ear stretched against where Irmin's ancient wife had sewed it closed with shaking hands. He ached from the fight with Einar. It had been brutal, and not for the first time that summer, he felt old.

'The men say you killed a Viking warlord?' said a croaking voice. Beornoth turned, wincing at the pain in his neck to where Irmin stared up at him. He had grey eyes in a face as creased and cracked as a parched riverbed. He had a thin beard which was as white as snow, and a pink mouth with three brown teeth beneath his trembling smile. Beornoth nodded and held his hands out again to the fire, the scabs on his knuckles pulling at his skin, spots of blood showing at the edges. 'I have never fought a Viking,' Irmin said, and kicked at a log with his boot to stir up the flames. 'They did not come in King Edgar's time, but they are back now that his son Æthelred is King. My father fought them in the old days, and his grandfather fought them alongside Alfred. They say the Viking's God has sent them here, smelling our weakness. That he wants to crush us, and our God, and fill our land with pagans.'

Beornoth sighed. 'Gods have nothing to do with it. Merchants from Dublin and the Vik bring tales north with their fleeces and ingots. They tell of a Kingdom split by greedy Lords and church-men, by tithes and taxes. They bring messages from men in East Anglia and Northumbria who are the grandsons of the men your sires fought, messages to say they would welcome the return of the Danes, for a rule without the Church and its hunger for their land.'

'Are there armies coming to our shores?'

'They are not coming, old one. They are already here.'

Irmin held Beornoth's gaze, and there was fear in the grey and yellow of his eyes. A fear that plucked at Beornoth's chest, because he knew it was the fear of all men, women and children. Fear that men with blades would come for them, to kill them and take all they have, and that there would be nobody to help them, no warriors to protect them from the wolves.

Beornoth walked to where Byrhtnoth stood with Leofsunu, Aelfwine and the other Thegns in his hearth troop. They went quiet as Beornoth approached, and Leofsunu nodded a greeting.

'So, we ride for Lundenburg in the morning,' said Beornoth. 'Away from the swords and axes, but towards the shadow blades and enemies we cannot see.'

'But they are just as dangerous. These are dark days we find ourselves in,' said Byrhtnoth and he lifted his leg to rest on the seat of an eating bench and leant upon his knee. 'We know Olaf is at Folkestone, and raiding north, we crossed swords with them ourselves. We also know that Lady Ælfthryth sent me north to die. She sent us to dispense justice to an unruly, raiding Thegn, but we found traitors and murderers and a trap for Beornoth and I set by our own people.'

'Beornoth would be dead now, if she had her way,' said Leofsunu, and there were hooms of agreement amongst the warriors.

'Beornoth says there are Danes in East Anglia, murderous slavers. They are the vanguard of a new army. Sweyn Forkbeard, son of Harald Bluetooth and King of the Danes, has brought his ships and his warriors here and is welcomed by our own people.'

'I heard Æthelric of Bocking is one traitor. One of our Thegns, a man of the East Saxons,' said Aethelwine.

'Either way, it means there are two Viking armies converging on our shores. We have not faced such a threat for over one hundred years. Our King doesn't seem to have the belly for the fight, and his mother's schemes and plots increase her son's popularity and keep his place as King secure.'

'Æthelred is an honourable King, Lord?' said Godric, looking at the others with arched brows.

'Is he?' barked Byrhtnoth. 'He holds the title because his mother had his brother Edward killed. A man I loved and fought to protect, just as his father King Edgar commanded me to. Æthelred holds the title, but he doesn't have the respect of the people, of the Thegns and Ealdormen of his Kingdom because of the way he came to power. That is why the word of a weakened Kingdom has sailed north, and why the sea wolves are here on our shores.'

'So, what do we do, Lord?' said Offa. He spoke for them all, for a band of warriors who understood that they faced enemies on all sides and fought for a Kingdom eating itself from within.

'We talk to the King. Try to give him the belly for the fight to come. He will need to fight with the strength and cunning of his grandsires, of Alfred himself, if our Kingdom is going to survive this threat,' said Byrhtnoth. He spoke slowly and deliberately, his eyes moving across each of his men, boring into them as though he searched them for their commitment, for their own will to get through the danger.

'What if he won't fight?' asked Godric.

'The King has no choice,' said Byrhtnoth, and he stood to his full height. His sheer size dominated the hall, filling it with power and strength. 'He has to fight, and we have to fight. Otherwise, our people will be slaughtered, all that we know and love, everything we have fought for our whole lives will be torn asunder under the boots and blades of the northmen. We need the King's army to fight them. Between Olaf and Sweyn, they could have three thousand men.'

There were gasps amongst the warriors, exchanged glances with wide eyes, and more than one man made the sign of the cross before himself.

'God save us,' said Irmin.

'God won't save you,' said Beornoth. He pulled his seax from its sheath at his back and held up the bright blade for all to see. 'This will save you, and it will save our people. If the King won't fight, then we will fight. If the King's mother drips poison in his ear, then let her. We can bring the fight to the Danes and Norsemen; and we can raise the county behind us. We are Saxon Thegns; it is our duty to fight for and protect the people in these lands.'

The men drew their own blades and held them high, and Byrhtnoth nodded.

'We go to the King first. I will ask him to raise the army, and if he refuses, then we will do it ourselves,' Byrhtnoth roared, shaking the roof timbers of Irmin's hall, and the hearth troop raised their blades to echo their Lord's war boast.

'We are lucky men,' said Aelfwine of Foxfield, and he walked amongst the warriors, each man now falling silent and watching the Thegn stalking across the floor rushes, the firelight glinting from the blade he held before him, and in the blue of his eyes. 'We are lucky because we are warriors, and we live in a time when our lands are beset by enemies. Men, it is our duty to cast down our foes, to defend our people and our God, to make reputations for ourselves that will live on through the ages.'

The warriors all grunted approval at Aelfwine's words, his voice every bit as rafter-shaking as Byrhtnoth's.

'Are we Thegns of the East Saxons?' Aelfwine roared, and slammed his boot into the hard-packed earth.

'Aye!' the warriors acclaimed, each man stomping his own boot into the ground.

'Are we the Viking killers of Watchet, River's Bend and Mersea Island?' Aelfwine called again as the men fell silent, each staring at him, hanging on his words like children hearing a faerie tale from a grandmother.

'Aye!' came the chorus again, and a crash of boots.

'Are we sworn blades to Ealdorman Byrhtnoth of Essex?'

'Aye!'

'Is Byrhtnoth not the greatest warrior on God's earth, the pagan-slayer, the justice-giver, our ring-giver?'

'Aye!'

Each warrior was alert, their faces open, eyes bright and fervent, jaws slack. Each man was a fine and brave warrior in his own right. Wulfstan: as hard a man as any Beornoth had met in his long life at the shield wall. Wulfmaer and Maccus: muscular arms looped across one another's shoulders, scarred faces staring in rapture at Aelfwine. Godric and his brothers Godwin and Godwig, young and fervent for the battle to come.

'We are brothers of the sword, oathsworn to a hero. Let us pledge ourselves to our Lord and to this war once more, but with an oath of blood this time. Who would become a bloodsworn brother of war, oath-bound to drive the Vikings from our land, to fight until our last breath and last drop of blood for our Lord and for our country?'

'Aye! Aye! Aye!' each man roared. Beornoth's own men, Wulfhere, Cwicca, Kari, Wuffa and the others, had all joined in the cries of acclamation, although sworn to him and not to Byrhtnoth. The Ealdorman himself stood with his brawny arms folded, his face a hard crag of stone, his eyes dark pits lost beneath the bluff of his brows and forehead framed by iron-grey hair, and his spade of a silver beard hanging over his byrnie. He watched his warriors, allowing Aelfwine to whip them into a war frenzy, preparing them with fervour for the horror of the shield wall that now surely lay in each man's future.

Aelfwine lifted the sleeve of his jerkin and held his bare arm up for the men to see. 'I swear with my blood that I will fight to the death for Byrhtnoth and for the Saxon people. I will not rest until the Vikings are corpses and their ships burn.' He ran the blade of his seax across his forearm in a red streak and held the bloody wound up for the warriors to see. They roared their approval, and each man followed suit and they clasped forearms together, milling and swirling, clapping one another on the back and mixing the blood on their forearms together in a war oath sealed in blood. Beornoth felt a shiver run down his spine. The men were oathsworn to Byrhtnoth already, but this was something different, something that went beyond King and country and the rules that bound a Thegn to his Lord. This was a death oath, a blade oath.

Offa and Byrhtwold stood by the fire watching their fellow Thegns, and Beornoth went to join them. Byrhtwold was a Thegn of an age with Offa, wrinkles criss-crossed the skin of his flat face and his close-cropped hair was as white as bone.

'Not swearing the blood oath?' Beornoth asked them, suddenly jealous as he watched Offa swig back a drink of ale, where he sipped tepid water.

'Byrhtnoth already has my oath. Young fools have let this sour sheep's-piss ale go to their heads,' said Byrhtwold, shaking his head.

'I have spilled enough blood for the Ealdorman. I need to spill no more to prove my loyalty,' said Offa, and drained his cup. 'Let's hope Byrhtnoth can rouse the King to summon the army.'

'Lady Ælfthryth tried to kill Byrhtnoth, and she did that so her son could take the glory of the fight with the Norsemen, so why hasn't the King already mustered the army from each shire, Thegns and fyrd?' asked Beornoth.

'Who knows what goes on in the twisted minds of the King and his mother, and the archbishops are no better. They would sooner see the Kingdom fall than see any other man than the King vanquish our foes. I'll never understand it,' said Offa, and the three men stared silently into the dancing flames as the surrounding warriors continued to shout and boast of how far they would go to honour their Lord and protect the Kingdom.

'If we go to Lundenburg,' said Byrhtwold, and he looked first at Beornoth and then at Offa, his face grave. 'Seems to me the King or his mother might find an easier way to kill Byrhtnoth than sending him north into a trap. A knife in the dark, an ambush at a false meeting. We must be on our guard.'

'They would not lower themselves to such an act, surely?' said Offa, his tone more hopeful than questioning.

'Lady Ælfthryth has done it before. She has killed a King to put her son on the throne, don't forget that. She wouldn't think twice about putting a blade in an Ealdorman's back. Offa, you and I fought in the last war for the dead King Edward, Saxon against Saxon. They were dark days, but not as dark as the sea of shit we are in now,' said Byrhtwold.

'Enemies at sea, and enemies within. They beset us on all sides, and we are only the men in this hall and whatever fyrd we can raise. Not enough to fight three thousand Vikings and the King's assassins,' said Offa. The three men fell silent again. All of what the two old warriors had said was true. Beornoth felt the deep fear twist in his belly like the blade of a knife. Never had he faced such overwhelming forces set against him, but standing and talking about it wouldn't sink any Viking ships or soothe the low cunning of an old Queen.

Beornoth stalked to the rear of the hall, licking dry lips, and

raised his hand to scratch at a parched throat. He had drunk his fill
of water, but this was a different thirst. His mind told him that ale
would make things better, that a horn of ale would make his
worries for Eawynn, for his people and for the Kingdom fade away.
He had to fight against his own yearning, because Beornoth knew
it would never be just one horn of ale. One would lead to ten, and
oblivion. But the price for that oblivion was the hole he would
crawl back into, the craving for more ale or mead or whatever he
could get his hands on, and that was not a cave of despair he
wished to experience again. Instead, he pulled a sack from underneath his cloak, which he had stowed behind a wall timber. He
carried the sack to where Wulfhere, Brand, Kari, Cwicca and the
other Branoc's Tree men sat at their cups. He sighed when he saw
the fresh nicks on their forearms, and what that meant for their
futures.

Beornoth dropped his heavy sack onto the bench, and it
landed with a chink and a thud. His men jumped at the surprise of
it, and their faces all turned to him. He fished his fist deep into it
and pulled forth one of Einar Ravenhair's silver arm rings.

'Cwicca, you have ridden the length of the country, and done
more than should be asked of a lad your age. You are part of my
hearth troop now, and this arm ring is for you.' Beornoth tossed
him the ring, and Cwicca's round face lit up like a sunrise to have
finally become a warrior. The lad had stood out amongst
Beornoth's men throughout the summer, and Beornoth had
rewarded him handsomely. Beornoth delved inside the rough
hemp sack again and pulled out a brass arm ring.

'Kari, you rode north with a killer and helped set the trap that
would lay our Ealdorman low and see me butchered by an enemy.
But you showed me kindness when your master and Osric treated
me like a dog. And, you have since shown yourself loyal. So, this
night you will swear your oath to serve me as a warrior and will

become a man of Branoc's Tree.' Beornoth handed the ring to Kari, who took it, gawping at the whorls in its craftmanship, and the warriors ruffled his hair and punched his shoulders in congratulation.

'Wulfhere, you are a loyal captain and a trusted fighter. This byrnie of mail I give to you, either to replace your own coat, for it is crafted by Frankish smiths unless I am mistaken, or give it to another man here who has earned it. That is your choice.'

'Thank you, Lord,' said Wulfhere, and he brought his fist to his chest and bowed his head solemnly.

Beornoth left them to congratulate each other, and drink to their rewards. He hoped it would distract them from the blood and death to come, that they would have at least one night of peace and joy before the world around them collapsed into spears and axes, blood and ruin. He was their Lord, their ring-giver, and it was his duty to provide them with silver and spoils of war, and their duty to stand and die for them. Beornoth sat alone and sipped his water and looked at the young faces around the hall. Their cheeks ruddy from the heat in the room and from the ale they had drunk, their faces smiling and laughing. Many of them would be cut and slashed, injured or dead in the months ahead, and there was little he could do to stop that. But, Beornoth would stand in the front line, just as he always had. Under the table he slid his knife from its sheath at his belt, and sliced the cold blade across his forearm, making the blood oath silently, promising to kill Byrhtnoth's enemies or die trying.

## 23

Byrhtnoth's company reached Lundenburg on a humid, drizzle-washed day. Rain swirled on a westerly breeze and shafts of sunlight punched through dark clouds to cover the old city in shifting shadows. Beornoth felt the age of the place as they rode through a stone archway in the Rome-folk wall built of huge, dressed stone. Some men said a race of giants enslaved by the Romans in the time beyond the ken of Saxon people had hauled those monstrous blocks into place. Beornoth ducked under the arch and reached out from the back of his horse to run his calloused hand along the pitted stones, which were cool under his touch. He could sense the spirits in the place, warriors who had fought for it over the centuries whispering to him from the after-life, asking to be remembered by those who followed.

King Alfred had rebuilt the city within the old Roman walls once he had cast out the Viking invaders. Once free of the Danelaw, it became an important Saxon trading city. Lundenburg sat on the banks of the wide Thames, which slashed into the south-east coast of England and therefore provided a thoroughfare for traders from Frankia, Frisia and the far north. It was a trading city rich in silver and its merchants stored their goods safely behind the high stone walls.

Beornoth's horse's hooves clattered on the cobblestone pathway, echoing around the walls as they ambled along to a stable where Byrhtnoth paid a man to keep their horses safe whilst he went to talk to the King. Beornoth could sense Alfred in the place, the great King who learned so much in his wars with the Vikings. He had turned England into a network of fortifications, burhs built to his specifications, and London was no different. Before Alfred's time, the Saxons had been naïve and wide open to attacks from the cunning Viking raiders who would sail upriver in their shallow-draughted warships to lay waste to a countryside undefended and unready for their depredations. Alfred had come within a hair's breadth of losing his Kingdom, beaten back to living in the fens like a fugitive. But he had fought back, beaten the Vikings, and then steeled his Kingdom against the marauders. Beornoth craned his neck up at the high walls, and the warriors atop them, and wondered how a man would even go about attacking the place. Winchester, the Kingdom's capital, and most other Saxon cities were things of wood, ditch and palisade, but the old Roman cities like Lundenburg, York and Chester were different. The stone would never rot or burn, and with enough men Beornoth believed a King could hold these walls against armies beyond reckoning.

'Beornoth, Offa and Wulfstan,' Byrhtnoth barked, frowning through the melee of horses snorting as boys led them to the stables, and warriors dismounting to marvel at the city. 'Come with me. Byrhtwold, you and Leofsunu find us somewhere to sleep tonight, and some ale and food for the men.'

Beornoth handed his reins to a stable boy and left his spear and shield with Wulfhere, who nodded grimly as he took the weapons and offered Beornoth a downward smile. 'Be careful, Lord. This old place makes me shiver,' he said, looking at the walls.

'There is ancient cunning flowing through it like blood through a man's veins.'

'I will,' Beornoth said. 'Make sure the lads get fed and keep them out of trouble.'

He followed Byrhtnoth through the snarl of narrow streets and lanes, each one crammed with merchants in fine robes, warriors in byrnies or baked leather, growling and supping ale from skins, and urchins gathered in every corner and cranny: the small, filthy children who scuttled around the edges of the place, searching for food or unsuspecting men to rob. The four men marched through the city in stony-faced silence, Beornoth's nose filled with the shit-stinking reek of the place. They knew the risks they faced here, but like an enemy shield wall, the King and his mother were an enemy to be confronted, not to run away from. They marched uphill until the city's enormous church came into sight, its high cross reaching above the buildings like a ship's mast on a swelling sea. This part of the city was ringed with warriors: men with spears and shields whose leather covers bore the King's sigil of the Wessex dragon. A scarred-faced warrior led them to a grand hall where timber patchings covered collapsed Roman stone. Its wooden entranceway was painted green, and swirling beasts were etched into its door lintels. Scarface ordered them to leave their weapons at the door, which they did with frowns and grumbling, although Beornoth understood the sense in disarming men before they came before the King.

Scarface led them to an antechamber within the hall, where they sat and waited. Servants fetched ale, fresh water and warm bread. The four men ate and waited, but before Beornoth had finished his small loaf, two hulking warriors clad in gleaming byrnies and armed with long æsc spears strode into the room, their boots heavy and their faces broad and hard.

'Just you, Lord,' said one warrior, nodding to Byrhtnoth. He had a long nose and wore his blonde hair close-cropped to his skull.

'Has the King arrived already?' asked the Ealdorman.

'You can go in, Lord,' said the man, avoiding the question. Byrhtnoth looked at Beornoth and frowned. The blonde-haired warrior opened an oak door with an iron circular latch and pushed it open. It creaked on its hinges and Byrhtnoth stepped into the darkness beyond. The blonde warrior closed the door and looked impassively ahead. Beornoth wanted to follow Byrhtnoth. He feared for his Lord. Behind that door could be a band of Lady Ælfthryth's assassins, all waiting to plunge daggers into the Ealdorman's flesh. Offa and Wulfstan both shrugged. Wulfstan looked huge inside the small room, like a bear stuffed into a small cage. Beornoth paced the room, listening but unable to hear anything that occurred beyond the small oak door. Time passed slowly, and Beornoth was sweating beneath his byrnie. The walls of the room felt as though they were getting closer, as though he would soon have to bend to stay standing upright. He stalked across and behind the dining table and pushed open a window shutter. The breeze was cool on his face, and he could see across the tangle of thatch and timber buildings down to where the broad river glistened and snaked around the high stone walls. He rested his hands and breathed in the cool air, fresh above the stink of the city below.

'Beornoth!' Byrhtnoth bellowed from beyond the door, sudden and clipped. Offa and Wulfstan both stared at Beornoth as he snapped his head around. The two royal warriors lowered their spears. 'Beornoth, to me,' came the Ealdorman's voice again. Beornoth stepped forward and grabbed the back of the dining chair in front of him and threw it across the room at the two warriors, who raised their spears to block its flight. He leapt over the table and in two strides, he was at the door. The chair clattered to the floor, and the blonde warrior looked at Beornoth with wide

eyes, and Beornoth grabbed a fistful of the man's byrnie and threw
him backwards towards Wulfstan, trusting that the huge warrior
would handle the man. Offa lunged at the second warrior and the
two men grappled, surging across the room. Beornoth turned the
door latch, but it was locked from the inside. He let out a roar, his
heart pounding at what might happen to Byrhtnoth beyond those
timbers. He slammed his shoulder into it, and it shook, dust
shaking from it to fill the air with drifting motes. Beornoth kicked
the door twice, and then took four steps back, ignoring Offa and
Wulfstan fighting the two warriors in the small room, and charged
at the door. His shoulder smashed into it and the iron lock burst
open under his weight. Beornoth fell through the door and into a
wide room lit by candles and filled with six warriors, all armed
with spears. He stumbled to the floor and scrambled to his feet.
The Ealdorman was in one corner, penned in by spears levelled at
his chest and blood showing on his thigh and a cut bright red on
his cheek. In the centre of the room was a small, old woman
swathed in a green cloak, her lined face twisted in a furious snarl.

'Kill that one, too,' she said in a tiny, croaking voice. But
Beornoth rose from where he had fallen to his full height, and he
glowered at the warriors in the room. They were all big men, just
like he and Byrhtnoth, but these men were royal guards, picked for
their size and strength to stand at doors and look threatening.
Beornoth, however, was a killer. He was a Viking fighter, gnarled,
scarred and as vicious as any Dane or Norseman. No sooner had
the words escaped Lady Ælfthryth's lips than Beornoth sprang at
the closest warrior. He was unarmed, and the man levelled his
spear at Beornoth, but he hesitated and Beornoth let its point bang
into the shoulder of his byrnie, confident that his mail would
deflect the blow. It did, and Beornoth reached out, his shovel-like
hand still scabbed from where he had mashed Einar Ravenhair's
face to pulp with his fists. He grabbed the spearman's face with his

hand and drove him backwards five paces, running with the man's face in his grip. The warrior's helmet toppled from his head and Beornoth smashed his skull into the far wall twice with a dull cracking sound, and let his limp body fall to the floor rushes.

Another guard charged at Beornoth, and he swerved so that the tip of that man's weapon sank into the timbers of the wall behind him. Beornoth reached up with both hands and sank his thumbs into his attacker's eye sockets, feeling the wetness of the man's eye jelly and wrapping his hands around the base of his skull. The man howled in pain, and Beornoth drove his thumbs deeper, digging them into the warrior's skull. The man fell to his knees and Beornoth threw him to the floor, his thumbs coming away bloody. Beornoth snarled and lifted his leg to crash the heel of his boot into the fallen warrior's throat and twisted his foot to crush the man's windpipe. Lady Ælfthryth gaped at him, horror replacing the anger on her face, and she shuffled towards the corner of the room.

'Kill them, now!' she shouted, waving a crooked hand towards Beornoth and Byrhtnoth. Wulfstan emerged, growling from the doorway. He dominated the space and two of the spearmen turned towards him, and as the huge warrior stepped forward, Offa followed him into the room, and the royal spearmen sidestepped slowly, the sharp points of their weapons flitting between the unarmed East Saxons.

'Stop!' roared Byrhtnoth, his voice shaking the walls in the timber-walled room. 'I am the Ealdorman of Essex, and I did not come for this. Hold your weapons. We came to talk, not fight.'

'Byrhtnoth,' hissed Lady Ælfthryth, drawling the Ealdorman's name as though it were a thing of putrid decay. 'Of old you are an enemy of my son. You fought for his brother, Edward, you fought against me. You are an enemy of the King.' She shook with rage, her lips parting in a snarl to reveal yellowed teeth.

'How dare you say that to me? I am loyal to the King and this country. Who fights harder for our realm than I?'

'There! You condemn yourself. You are not the hardest fighter or greatest hero of this Kingdom, as much as you want to be. My son, King Æthelred, is our hero and the greatest of Saxon Kings, and he will protect us from the invaders! You subvert my son at every turn.' The old woman was shouting, spittle flying from her mouth in a red-faced fury. 'I ordered you to kill them, attack!' she screeched at her spearmen.

Suddenly, another small door at the rear of the room burst open, and a figure charged in. It was the King, dressed in a fitted blue tunic and with a silver circlet on his brow which pressed down on his auburn hair. His lantern jaw dropped open at the sight of the spearmen facing Beornoth, Byrhtnoth, Wulfstan and Offa. 'What in God's name is going on?' he said, his fists bunching at his sides and his eyes moving from Byrhtnoth to his mother.

'This Ealdorman is a traitor; he comes here to attack you. Byrhtnoth has always been your enemy; he was a supporter of your cursed brother Edward. Seize him!' Lady Ælfthryth said, and she raised her hands in supplication to her son.

'If he comes to attack me, why is he unarmed?' the King said, and held up a finger to his mother and closed his eyes. 'Don't answer that. Byrhtnoth, what is happening here and why is my mother forced to defend herself with spears?'

'I came here to tell you, Lord King, of the threats to your Kingdom. Of how Olaf Tryggvason and his fleet of warships are embedded in Folkestone and are now, at this very moment, raiding up the south-east coast. I fought them there, as is my duty, to protect your Kingdom. Sweyn Forkbeard of Denmark is in East Anglia with his own force of Danes poised to attack, and what's more, traitors from within our own Kingdom have welcomed him. Beornoth fought those Danes and here we stand before you, with two enemy fleets off our shores, and enemies within our own Kingdom who are just as dangerous.' Byrhtnoth glanced from Lady Ælfthryth to the King.

'I have heard this news, Ealdorman. That is why I have gathered the Witan to meet this very evening. But what has that to do with my mother, and why are my guards injured or dead on the floor in my royal quarters?' Æthelred pinched the bridge of his nose and shook his head as his mother made to speak, and he again held up a long, pale finger to silence her.

'I asked for an audience with you, Lord King, to bring you this dire news and to discuss the defence of the realm,' said Byrhtnoth. 'But I was instead met by your mother and attacked by these men.'

'Mother, leave us,' the King said, his voice quiet in a room that had but a moment earlier been filled with violence and argument.

'I will not leave. This man is...'

'I know who Ealdorman Byrhtnoth is, Mother, and I would speak with him alone,' said Æthelred, fixing her with an icy stare.

'You need me here to advise you, my son. He is a snake, an enemy...'

'I am the King!' Æthelred shouted, and the force of it surprised Beornoth. Æthelred tugged at the hem of his tunic beneath his belt and his chin jerked to the side as he fought to compose himself. Lady Ælfthryth inclined her head to her son and flashed a murderous glance at Byrhtnoth and sauntered from the room, her stick tapping on the floor as she went. Her guards followed and dragged the fallen spearmen with them. The man whose eyes Beornoth had gouged out left a smear of blood on the floor timbers as they dragged him by his feet.

'Thank you, Lord King,' said Byrhtnoth, and he bowed to the King, and Beornoth followed suit.

'So, tell me, Ealdorman. What is happening here?'

'Your mother sent me north to bring justice to a Thegn who

had raided Westmoreland. This I did. I am sorry to say, my King, that it was a well-laid trap. Ealdorman Oslac of Northumbria was waiting for me there with assassins. I saw those men leave your palace at Winchester as we waited to meet you that day in spring. They ambushed us in a forest, and in league with Ealdorman Osric of Cheshire, they killed some of my men, and laid hands on Beornoth here in a savage attack. You know, Lord King, of this Oslac. He was a traitor once banished but permitted to return.'

'I remember him,' said the King, and frowned, clearly not wanting to dredge up the story of his brother, King Edward's, murder.

'Osric is dead, Lord King, and I took the liberty of appointing Aethelhelm's second son, Alfgar, as Ealdorman of the shire, pending your approval. Oslac is also dead, and the shire awaits your ruling on who should succeed him.'

'Are you saying that my mother tried to kill you?'

'Yes, Lord King. Is it so hard to believe?' Byrhtnoth said, and he folded his arms across his chest and stared at Æthelred. It was a challenging look; the Ealdorman held the King's stare and arched an eyebrow. Lady Ælfthryth was a notorious schemer, and the King was more than aware of that fact. Æthelred rolled his eyes and held up his hand to accept that it was indeed plausible that what Byrht-noth said was true. 'Also, there are other men like Oslac, men who sent word to the Danes, invitations to this King Sweyn Forkbeard, that they would welcome him to our shores, that he would receive succour in the form of food and horses for his warriors.'

'What?' said Æthelred, his face suddenly drawn and pale. 'Can this be true?'

'Yes, it's true. Forkbeard is already here. Between him and Olaf, they have over ninety ships. That's three thousand men. You are the King, and it is my duty to tell you, you are ill-advised, my Lord. I do not say this to hurt you, but to protect you and the Kingdom.

Every man on those Viking ships is a warrior, each one of them trained to fight with axe and spear from the time they can stand. We can field a similar force, if we call out the fyrds of Wessex, Essex, East Anglia, Defnascir and so on. But the men of the fyrd are not warriors, they are farmers, millers and woodsmen. To gather a force with enough warriors to meet the Vikings in battle, you will need to rouse the Kingdom and call out the Thegns in such force not seen since the days of King Athelstan. We need to fight our enemies, my Lord, not each other. I beseech you to seek good counsel. There has not been such a threat to the realm since before your father's time. We are on the edge of a knife blade here, my Lord. Every day we delay in marching against the Vikings, more of our people are killed or enslaved and the invaders gain more of a foothold in your Kingdom.'

Æthelred looked at the bloodstains on the floor and up at Beornoth, and across the faces of Offa, Wulfstan and Byrhtnoth. He licked at dry lips and his face was as pale as mare's milk. 'Be at the Witan this evening, Ealdorman, and we will decide how to meet our foes.' The King turned on his heel and left the room.

'Will he fight?' said Offa, blowing on bruised knuckles.

'The fight has come to him; I don't think he has a choice. He needs good advice, or all of our people will suffer,' said Byrhtnoth.

# 24

---

Beornoth waited for news of the Witan at the White Hart, a tavern on the Thames filled with merchants, sailors and whores. It was an enormous place, as long and wide as a barn with two floors, the bottom for drinking ale, and the top floor filled with women who could make a man forget his problems for the right price. The East Saxon warriors wasted their silver on ale and women. Beornoth sat at a bench with Wulfhere, Leofsunu and Aelfwine and picked at a loaf of bread whilst the others drank ale. The tavern keeper was a stout man with drooping moustaches, and along with a pimple-faced lad and two girls in aprons, did his best to keep the ale flowing.

The tavern door swung open, hinges creaking as a hooded figure strode into the room. He closed the door and fastened the latch, and the room went silent. Where before there was chatter, laughing and the rumble of men enjoying their ale, now there was stillness for the man who had entered was hulking and tall, and he threw back his hood to reveal iron-grey hair and a face creased by a frown like thunder. Byrhtnoth had returned from the Witan, and he searched the room with his steely eyes until he found Beornoth and Aelfwine and made for their bench, beckoning to Offa as he went. Wulfhere shuffled sideways to make a space at the bench for the Ealdorman and Byrhtnoth sat into it heavily, resting his arms on the table, running his hands through his beard. He brushed away the shavings Wulfhere had left on the tabletop whilst whittling at a piece of golden timber. Once Byrhtnoth had seated himself, the noise in the tavern sparked up again, the many voices melding together to create an undulating rumble. The tavern keeper's lad plonked a tankard of frothing ale on the table and slunk away, and Byrhtnoth lifted the cup and drank its contents in four long gulps, wiping the froth from his beard with the back of his hand.

'Well?' asked Offa. Watching Byrhtnoth drink his ale had seemed to take an age. The Ealdorman's throat contracted and expanded with each suck at the drink, and the silence felt so long that Beornoth could almost hear his own heartbeat in his chest. All he wanted to know was if the Witan had agreed to summon the King's army, and if there would be war.

'The King has sent his mother away, and she will no longer cast her decaying shadow over the throne,' said Byrhtnoth. There were hooms of ascent at that from Offa, Aelfwine and Leofsunu. She was a malevolent and controlling force in the King's life, and her removal from the King's closest circle would mean that men of action like Byrhtnoth, and not slimy courtiers, could now find a voice and influence the course of action against the Vikings. 'There was recognition of the threat posed by Forkbeard and Olaf Tryggvason, and from some of our own people,' Byrhtnoth continued. 'But the Bishops' voices proved more convincing than my own.' Byrhtnoth shook his head and stared at the tabletop, his face suddenly looking old. Wrinkles ran deep in his forehead and at the corners of his eyes and pale red veins traversed his nose.

'But we will fight?' asked Offa, placing his two hands palms up on the table.

'The Archbishop of Canterbury, Sigeric, and his cronies want to pay the Vikings to go away,' said Byrhtnoth, and shrugged his shoulders.

'They want to pay them?' asked Leofsunu.

'Aye. They say we cannot successfully fight such a force, or even muster the army in time to stop them from getting a foothold in our lands. They worry that Olaf and Sweyn will join forces and create an army to rival that of Ivar the Boneless back in Alfred's day.'

'It won't work,' said Beornoth. 'I have fought Vikings my whole life. If we pay them now, they will keep coming back for more until they bleed the Kingdom dry. Then they will invade anyway. Payment now just gives them a sniff of the greater prize. We must fight them.'

'My forefathers were men of East Anglia, eminent men, once,' said Aelfwine, staring into his ale as though he could see images of the past swirling amidst the froth. 'King Edmund, the last King of East Anglia, gave Ivar and his great army silver, food and land to winter upon. He gave them horses to ride, hoping that they would ride to another Kingdom and leave his alone. They did and ravaged Northumbria and killed its King before returning to Edmund's Kingdom and burning it and making him into a martyr. What Beo says is true. If you give the wolf the taste of blood, he can't get the stink out of his nostrils until his belly is full and the sheep are dead.'

'So, they will try to talk with Olaf and Sweyn?' asked Wulfhere.

'They will, the King's men and Bishops will gather a horde of silver before the month is out, and then the Bishops will seek talks with the Vikings,' said Byrhtnoth.

'They will bleed the Ealdormen and Thegns is what they

mean,' said Leofsunu, and spat into the floor rushes. 'The Bishops and their churches are as rich as Lords in Frankia, and they won't put up a pouch of hacksilver towards this goat's arse of a plan.' He crossed himself and threw his bulbous eyes up to the rafters.

'You have the right of it,' said Byrhtnoth.

'So, what do we do, Lord?' asked Offa.

'We do what we always do, old friend,' said Byrhtnoth, and he sat up straighter and pushed his shoulders back. 'We fight.'

'How can we when we don't have the support of the King and his warriors?' said Aelfwine. He stroked a hand across his neatly trimmed beard.

'Archbishop Sigeric will gather silver and go to talk to the Vikings. That will take longer than the month he says it will, probably until the end of the summer,' said Byrhtnoth. 'By that time, the northmen will look for a place to spend the winter once summer campaigning is over. They might stay at Folkestone or look further north. Then, in the spring their attacks will resume. That is always their way, just as Aelfwine says.'

'We can't fight them in the shield wall without more warriors. And the longer we wait to fight, the more of our people will suffer and die,' said Beornoth, and he placed an open hand on the table-top. 'But we can harry them, raid their camps, and kill their scouts. We can hurt them as they forage for food or strike out on raids. We can do to them what they do to our people.' Beornoth closed his hand and made a fist which he held up before the others, the skin on his knuckles turning white and the scabs there splitting to ooze blood down his scarred hand. 'We can squeeze and crush them. We can be the wolves and they the sheep. With a small force, we can perhaps hurt them enough to drive them back to the sea.'

'I like that plan better than the old, fat-bellied Bishops' plan,' grinned Wulfhere.

'And that is what we shall do. We shall attack them from the

forests and rivers, in the night and darkest places. We shall become
as a nightmare to these men who bring death to our people. We
will fight until our swords shatter, or our lives are lost, and soak the
land with the blood of our enemies,' said Byrhtnoth, his eyes blazing. He stared around at the men in the tavern, and Beornoth
followed his gaze. 'But we must also protect our homes, and we
cannot command our warriors to follow this path of slaughter, on
which many of us will meet our doom. So, most of our men should
return to our farms and hundreds. A small force of us will ride,
Thegns and a few warriors only. Men who have a son to succeed
them, or men with no family who rely upon them for food and
shelter. Let us gather fifty of our best fighters, men who are ready
to die, and the rest will return to keep our people of Essex safe.'

'We who swore the blood oath will ride,' said Aelfwine, and
Leofsunu banged the table with his fist in agreement.

'Return to your lands, and seven sunrises from now we will
meet at Sturmer and our war band will ride against our enemies,'
said Byrhtnoth.

'But which threat do we fight, Olaf or Sweyn?' asked Offa.

'We know Olaf and how dangerous he is, but I don't know
much about this Sweyn Forkbeard,' said Byrhtnoth. 'Beo, you
fought what you believed to be Forkbeard's vanguard. Who would
you fight first, Olaf or Sweyn?'

Beornoth closed his eyes for a moment and saw Ragnar the
Flayer and his hell-warriors. The memory of the slaughtered
Saxons etched like a brand into his memory. He shuddered at the
depredations Ragnar would have subjected the folk of East Anglia
to whilst England's swords hesitated and listened to the words of
Bishops and priests, men who had never fought in the shield wall
and with no idea what it takes to kill. Men of peace were making
decisions which would shape the future of the realm, and the
safety of Beornoth's own people at Branoc's Tree. These holy men

knew nothing of Vikings, men devoted to gods of war and for whom slaughter and death was the pathway to their Heaven.

'We should go first to East Anglia,' said Beornoth. 'Sweyn's man Ragnar is there, and he is a killer, a slaver and torturer.'

'But what of Olaf and his Jomsvikings?' said Offa. 'They were a different kind of Viking warrior when we fought them at Watchet. If we want our small force to strike the greatest blow against our enemies, then we should try and kill as many of the Jomsvikings as possible.'

'I remember the Jomsvikings, and I remember how Olaf looked at me when we slew Palnatoki, the man who had been as a father to him,' said Beornoth, and he leaned over the table to look deep into Offa's eyes. 'But this Ragnar is different. He covers his men's shields with the skins of our dead people. He is a killer and slaver of women and children. He is evil, Offa. The Jomsvikings are warriors, like us. They might be pagans, but they at least follow a warrior's code of honour. This Ragnar is a beast.' Beornoth turned to Byrhtnoth. 'If our duty is to protect the people, then we must stop Ragnar. Then, we can leave East Anglia and protect our own coastline from Olaf and his Jomsvikings.'

'Very well, Beo,' said Byrhtnoth. 'We go for Ragnar first, then we harry Olaf and pray that Archbishop Sigeric is right and that we are wrong, and that silver will remove the Viking threat from our homes.'

## 25

Branoc's Tree smelled like honey, wheat and barley. Simply being in the place made Beornoth lighter, as though it buoyed the weight of his byrnie, helmet and sword. Ceorls were tending the fields and the high crops moved like a golden sea under the wind, flowing like the tide. He had arrived the day before, he and his men weary from a summer spent in the saddle and at the blade. The people had flocked to them, their smiling faces and ruddy cheeks a joy to behold.

Beornoth stood in the shade at the corner of his hall on a warm day, the sun shining bright in a pale blue sky. He watched the garden at the rear of his sleeping quarters, where beehives nestled between beds of blue, yellow and red flowers. A single chair occupied the garden, and he waited for its owner to take her daily place to enjoy her flourishing garden, and to watch the bees at their work. Branoc's Tree's courtyard was busy with the bustle of daily life, laughter and chatter where the womenfolk welcomed back their husbands with delight; the hammer of the forge rang where the smith had already started work on repairing damaged horse tack and putting fresh edges on spears and axes.

Soft steps sounded on the timber boardwalk which ran from the hall doorway down to the grass, and Beornoth stood closer to the wall and peered around, hoping to remain unseen. A woman emerged from the shadows and seemed to glide across the green grass, so gentle were the footsteps of her supple leather shoes. She wore a plain green dress made of wool, and a blanket hooked over her two elbows, falling low across the small of her back. She stopped and looked up at the sky, and Beornoth's heart stopped as she turned to face the sun and a smile spread across her face as the summer warmth bathed her skin. He would have given his life to see that smile again, a thing he had not seen for so long, and a warmth bloomed deep inside him like the wings of a great dove enveloping his chest. Her hair shone like copper in the day's brightness, and Eawynn was as beautiful as she had been the first time Beornoth had ever seen her, years ago, when they were young together.

Eawynn walked to her garden and dipped to smell a yellow rose. She crouched and pulled a weed from the flower bed and ran her fingers across the leaves surrounding a blue flower and her slender shoulders rose and fell as she took a deep breath of the fragrant air. Beornoth had done his best to remove the worst of the grime from his skin and hair that morning and had run a bone comb through his beard and hair and tied his hair at the nape of his neck with a thin strip of leather. When he had stripped his jerkin and trews off, he examined how battered and bruised his body had been from the season spent fighting up and down the length of England. His ribs and stomach still had bruising from where he had been beaten in the north, and his thighs and fore-arms bore fresh scarring from combat. He had peeled the bandaging from his neck and ear, and washed the stitched wound, but it was still lurid and raw and was painful to touch.

Beornoth emerged from the hall's shadow, and the grass

beneath his feet felt like he was walking on a cloud. He wore a simple tunic and trews and moving without his weapons and byrnie was like floating. He was ten paces from Eawynn, and even though he had known her his whole life, his throat was dry and his palms sweating. Beornoth had brought her south from the nunnery a year earlier, and he still found it hard to be around her. The pain of their dead children and of what the Vikings had done to her mixed with his shame at not better protecting Eawynn and his family, which sat like a stone of guilt in his belly. She heard his steps and her head turned. Eawynn dipped her head slightly and brushed loose strands of her hair behind her ear.

'Hello, Eawynn,' he said, and cursed himself for being a clumsy fool. He stopped before her and couldn't prevent his cheeks from blushing. She flashed a half-smile at him and lowered her eyes to the grass. 'You look well,' he said haltingly. Which she did. Even the half-smile was more than the wildly furious rages Eawynn had flown into on the few occasions when Beornoth had visited her in the nunnery. Her cheeks seemed fuller, and there was colour in her face.

'Beornoth... I...' she said, and then shook her head and turned away. 'I am glad you are back. Glad you are... safe,' she whispered and Beornoth's heart leapt into his throat. He swallowed the lump down.

Beornoth took a step forward so that he stood next to Eawynn, and she looked up at him and smiled again. 'I am glad to be back. But not for long. I must leave again soon.'

'The Vikings have returned, haven't they?'

'Yes.'

He looked down and met her eyes, and they shared a moment of silence, eyes searching one another's face for signs of the young lovers they had been. Of the laughter and days walking by rivers or through fields, of the joy of having children together. She reached up a trembling, thin hand and held it close to his injured neck, and then traced a path across his scarred, broad face. He closed his eyes, the softness of her fingers making him shiver. He opened them as she took his hand in hers. His hand was a shovel-like paw of scarred and calloused skin with mashed knuckles, still scabbed from where he had fought the King's spearmen in Lundenburg, and her hand was small and pale, as fragile as a bird.

'Will the fight ever be over?' she asked.

'One day, maybe.'

'What will you do then, Beornoth?'

'Sit with you, my love, and watch the garden,' he said, the words catching in his throat. She nodded, and a tear rolled down each cheek. He placed his other hand on top of hers and leant in to kiss her on the cheek. The cheek above the scar across her neck where the Vikings had cut her throat. He released Eawynn's hands and left her in peace with the flowers and bees.

'Beornoth,' she called after him.

He turned to her.

'Kill them all,' she said, shuddering, her teeth clenched, and soft eyes suddenly turned hard as stone. He nodded and went to find Wulfhere.

He found his captain sitting alone in the stable. Wulfhere had his back to the wall and his horse's head bobbed in a stall above him, as though the two were deep in conversation. Wulfhere had his small whittling knife and worked at an intricate carving on a small piece of gold-bright wood. He heard Beornoth's footsteps on the dry hay of the stable floor and he looked up before scrambling to his feet.

'You have been working on that for weeks,' said Beornoth, pointing to the wood in Wulfhere's hand.

'Yes, Lord,' Wulfhere said. He looked at the piece and then

rested his head on his horse's neck, who returned the gesture by turning to nuzzle Wulfhere.

'Who is it for?'

'It's for… a friend.'

'A friend? Your horse there, or Cwicca maybe?'

'No, Lord. I made it for Aethelberga,' he said, and looked at Beornoth, and for the first time since they had met a year earlier, Beornoth saw fear in his captain's eyes.

'Give it to her then,' Beornoth said, smiling. 'Can I see it?'

Wulfhere sighed and nodded. He handed the piece to Beornoth.

'You missed your calling; you should have been a carpenter.' Wulfhere had carved a cross, like the piece he had made for Alfgar before, but smaller and with more shaping to the four corners. At its centre he had cut an intricate flower with petals which seemed to spring from the cross as though a real flower had been turned to wood by a sorcerer. Wulfhere had tied a length of leather cord to its top so that it would sit low on the chest of its owner.

'She is a Lady, and I am just a warrior. What use has a woman like that for a man like me?'

'Why don't you talk to her about it?' said Beornoth clumsily. He was the last person to be giving anyone any advice about how to use gentle words or soft gestures.

'In case she laughs at me, Lord.'

Beornoth clapped him on the shoulder. 'She won't laugh at you, but if you are going to give her your carving, then it must be today. You also have the comb you bought for her. Tomorrow, you, Brand and I will ride to meet Byrhtnoth and join his riders.'

'Just the three of us?'

'Just the three of us. The rest will stay here to protect Branoc's Tree in case Olaf brings his Jomsvikings into Essex.'

'Don't you ever get… well, lonely, Lord?'

'Yes. I miss Eawynn and my old life. But there is no way back to that now. I am what I am, and my people need me, just as they need you. We are alone, but we also have our brothers, our brothers of the blade. And we must fight so that others can live the peaceful lives we dream of. That is our lot.'

'I had a wife once, when I was a warrior of Northumbria, before they killed my old Lord. She died.' Wulfhere looked at Beornoth, and tucked his carving into his jerkin. 'All I want is a hand to hold in the winter, a good woman to reach out to in the dark of night. A hand to hold when the dreams come. Do you dream, Lord, of the men you have killed?'

'Yes,' said Beornoth, and that was all he would say on that matter. The faces of warriors he had slain came to him often at night, screaming and howling from the afterlife, and he would wake sheeted in sweat and unable to sleep again for fear of those fetches returning to haunt him. 'Go to her, Wulfhere. It can't be as daunting as facing a shield wall of spear-and-sword Danes?'

'It's much worse than that, Lord,' said Wulfhere, and he laughed. Beornoth laughed with him, and Wulfhere walked from the stable.

'Wulfhere,' Beornoth called after him, and the hulking warrior turned to him with the sun at his back. 'You are a good man, a fine warrior, and there is no man I would rather have with me in the shield wall.'

'Thank you, Lord.' Wulfhere inclined his bald head and strode into the sunlight. Beornoth stroked the horse along his muscled neck and gave him a scratch behind the ear. He would sit and eat with his people that night. He would enjoy their company and drink in their good cheer and the simple life of the people of Branoc's Tree. These were the people he fought for, the reason he would bring his sword and his strength and risk his life to fight the Viking invaders. He was a Saxon Thegn, and he would give his last drop of blood to keep the wolves away from the homes of his people.

Beornoth rose early the next morning and shrugged on his heavy byrnie mail coat, slithering it over his shoulders like a serpent's scaled skin. The weight of it was comforting, heavy, cold and sturdy, and hard enough to turn a blade. He strapped a thick leather belt around his waist, and it took some of the weight of the byrnie from his shoulders. Beornoth took his scabbard and fastened it to the belt. Kari had oiled the sword and had the smith put a new edge on the blade, and Beornoth slid it into the fleece-lined scabbard where the wool's oil would keep the blade clean and sharp. He took two leather wrist protectors and tied them in place with their leather thongs. Beornoth took the small wooden locket from his bedside table and slid it over his head. He kissed the smooth wood, inside which were strands of his lost daughters' soft blonde hair, and tucked it behind the chain mail. He bent and shifted his supple leather boots so that the thin metal plate greaves inside them were flush with his shins and tugged at the bindings there to make sure they were securely in place. Beornoth stood straight and cast his thick woollen cloak around his shoulders and clasped it together with an iron brooch pin. He marched from his chamber, clad in iron and ready for war.

The day was young, and there was still a crimson hue on the horizon. The courtyard outside his hall echoed with the clip-clop of three horses being prepared for their journey. Men who fussed at saddles and tack coughed and talked in hoarse voices, gifts from too much ale at last night's feast. Beornoth thanked the ceorl at his own horse. It was a beast from his own stable. A roan horse of good size, but they had not trained him for war as Ealdorbana had been. He patted his neck.

'Are you ready to ride, Hengist?' The horse was named for one of the first Saxon kings who had come to England's shores.

Beornoth checked the straps and tugged at the blanket beneath the saddle to make sure everything was secure.

'Sometimes I think you warriors love your horses more than people,' said a woman's voice. Beornoth rose and saw Aethelberga smiling at him. She had Wulfhere's crucifix hanging proudly on her chest, and she touched it as she saw Beornoth gaze upon the carving.

'Maybe we do. They are trustworthy, hardworking, and do not moan or ask for anything.'

'He is a good man,' she said, looking down at the crucifix.

'He is,' Beornoth agreed.

'We can never marry; I am a Thegn's daughter and was the wife of a Thegn.'

'You can do whatever you wish, Aethelberga. I will allow it, if you both desire it.'

She shrugged. 'I will pray and see what guidance the Lord provides.'

'I didn't get to talk to you last night,' Beornoth said. He had spent much of the feast either sat quietly with Eawynn eating and enjoying her silent company, or with his men enjoying their bawdy jokes and tales of bravery and daring. 'You have kept the place well.'

'It is my duty.'

'I leave most of the men here, they will guard the palisade in watches night and day. I have also ordered them to patrol the hundred. War is upon us.'

She nodded and crossed herself. 'We shall sleep safely knowing that you and Wulfhere fight for us.'

'If I do not return before the first frost, send a man to Byrht-noth's estate for news.'

'You will return,' she said, and reached to hold his wrist. She shook it warmly. 'When you first came here, I resented you. This was my husband's home, a place we had lived all our lives together. I thought you a cold-hearted brute, a vicious man who cared nothing for the place or the people. I was wrong about that, and for that I am sorry.'

'Wulfhere is a lucky man. Care for Eawynn.' Beornoth pulled himself into the saddle and Cwicca handed him his shield. Beornoth grunted as he hefted its weight, willow boards riveted to an iron boss and ringed with an iron rim. He slung it across his back and reached out for his spear.

'Be lucky, Lord,' said Cwicca, and he passed the long æsc spear with its leaf-shaped blade to Beornoth. He took Beornoth's two-handed war axe from Kari, thumbed the edge and slid it into the sheath on Hengist's saddle.

'My head feels like it's been kicked by a donkey,' grumbled Wulfhere as he strode across the courtyard. He bent to lay a soft kiss on Aethelberga's cheek, which made her blush and fuss at her dress. She glanced towards the church and shuffled away from Wulfhere. Brand was already sat astride his horse, and together the three warriors rode beneath the gatehouse in Branoc's Tree's palisade and their horses clattered across the timber bridge which ran across the ditch outside the walls. They rode to war, and Beornoth left the love and peace of his home behind and hardened his heart for the pain and slaughter to come.

## 26

Beornoth knelt forward, leaning into Hengist as the horse charged through a shallow river. Spume exploded from the water around the beast's flanks to spray horse and rider as they thundered along the riverbed. Beornoth held the reins with his left hand and in his right hand he gripped the leather-bound hilt of his sword, held away from his body and ready to strike. The horse pounded through the icy water at full gallop, the sound of its hooves splashing, and the whip of the wind roared in Beornoth's ears, and he bared his teeth as he closed on his prey. They were Vikings caught out of their camp, Ragnar the Flayer's men, and rage coursed through Beornoth's veins as he rode them down, hungry to lay vengeance upon them for the Saxon people they had murdered or enslaved.

The two Vikings ran for their lives, racing through the stream. One glanced over his shoulder and cried out in terror as he saw how close the mail-clad Saxon killer had come and he ran harder, his blonde braids flowing behind his head like a mane. Beornoth applied pressure with his left knee and tugged lightly to the left with the reins, and Hengist swerved his run, allowing Beornoth to lean slightly in the saddle. He waited until the horse's forelegs struck the riverbed and slashed the blade of his sword across the shoulders of the first Viking, who fell under the blow to splash into the river and turn its water crimson with his blood. The second Viking stopped his run and ducked underneath Hengist's neck as Beornoth sawed on the reins to wheel the horse around in the water. Beornoth twisted in the saddle to his right and brought his sword around in an arc to slice across the arm of the second Viking as he rose into a run. The man spun and toppled to his knees and Beornoth drove Hengist's powerful chest into the man, driving him into the water.

Beornoth snarled and brought Hengist around so that his heavy hooves trampled the riverbed, including the Vikings who lay upon it.

'Please, Lord!' called one in Norse, his voice gurgling on river water and his eyes wide and terrified.

'Feel Saxon vengeance!' Beornoth roared at him, also in Norse, teeth bared in a feral snarl. The two wounded men gasped for air as their faces showed in the water beneath Hengist's legs, and Beornoth pulled back on the reins to drive his horse across the Vikings once more, hearing the crack of their bones where Hengist trampled them. Their blood turned the stream crimson, both from the sword wounds on their bodies, but also from where the horse had crushed bone and flesh. The man who had pleaded for his life reached a hand through the water, his forehead cut wide open where Hengist's heavy steps had cracked his skull open. Beornoth leant from the saddle and swung his sword down overhand so that its tip smashed through the Viking's face, laying open eyes, nose and mouth and spraying his broken teeth into the churning water.

'That's the last of them,' said Wulfhere, short of breath as he cantered through the river to join Beornoth.

'Bastards,' growled Beornoth, and he clicked his tongue to urge

Hengist out of the river. From the bank he watched Leofsunu and Brand cut down another man in a knee-high pasture of dark green grass. Byrhtnoth's riders cantered across the pasture behind them and Beornoth rode to join them.

'More of the turds dead!' called Aelfwine from the line and raised his sword to salute Beornoth.

'Now we draw them out,' said Beornoth as he came alongside Byrhtnoth. 'I need their heads.'

'We have put ten of their men in the ground these last seven days,' said the Ealdorman, grimacing at Beornoth's request.

'They will feel that loss, Lord,' said Beornoth. 'These are Ragnar's men, warriors his men have shared rowing benches with, stood in the shield wall with, some may even be blood relatives. They will want to kill us, but they will worry that we have roused the shire fyrd, and we now outnumber them. If we can't get Ragnar and his dogs out of that palisade, this last insult might be enough.'

'So, we bring the heads, and give them a look at us.'

'Not all of us, Lord. If they see we have a score and half of warriors, all men in byrnies and therefore warriors of distinction and reputation, he won't come out.'

'So, let's bait the wolf then,' the Ealdorman said, and Beornoth reached for his axe, because he needed heads.

Beornoth, Brand and Wulfhere had met Byrhtnoth and his men at Leofsunu's home at Sturmer before riding north-east towards East Anglia in search of Ragnar and his beast-men. 'Time to let you loose on the Vikings, Beo,' Byrhtnoth had said, and so it proved to be. They were thirty riders, and all wore mail and carried swords, axes and spears. Most of the men had sworn the blood oath in Irmin's hall. They were Thegns and experienced warriors, for only the wealthiest of men could afford byrnie and sword. They were the marks of the warrior caste, men who held a heriot and who made their living fighting. As the war band heard the caw of gulls and smelled the sea in the air, they had met the depredations of Ragnar the Flayer and the scar he had carved into the land. There were no questions that pursuing Ragnar was the right thing to do when Byrhtnoth's men rode through the third village burned to ash. Swollen corpses rotted in the brittle remains of house timbers, where families had once laughed and lived. Crows tore at the skin of the dead men, women and children who had nobody to give them a Christian burial, with all their family and friends dead or fled.

Earlier that day, Beornoth and Byrhtnoth had watched Ragnar's camp from a high bluff around a sheer range of cliffs. The shore curled around like a scythe into a wide river mouth, and at its narrowest point a long finger-like sandbank topped with rock poked into the lapping water. Ragnar's camp centred around his two *drakkar* warships pulled up onto the shale beach within the river's shelter with their grey sails cast as awnings to make large tents, and a palisade of cut timbers surrounding that section of beach rising high into rolling dunes. The stakes of the palisade were only as high as a man, but to get across that obstacle and the dunes, with Viking axes swinging at heads and hands, would cost lives. So Byrhtnoth had decided that they would give the Vikings a taste of their own low cunning. Beornoth took the sack of heads towards Ragnar's enclosure, and on the night following the slaughter in the river, he and Brand stood on the edge of a strip of sycamore trees watching the Viking camp. It was late evening; the sun had retired for the day and a sliver of moon made the darkness as thick as day-old porridge. The fresh timber posts of Ragnar's camp seemed to glow gold in the night where they were lit by torches above the palisade at ten-pace intervals. Spears bristled beyond the posts of the palisade where warriors patrolled its perimeter, and beyond that timber wall, smoke rose in wisping tendrils from cook fires and Beornoth had the rich smell of roasting meat in his nose.

'Do you think this will work?' asked Brand, curling his lip at the bloodstained sack in Beornoth's fist.

'Yes,' said Beornoth. 'They won't want their pride pricked by fellow northmen. You should know that better than anyone. How many spears do you count?'

'Ten,' said Brand after a brief pause.

'Come on, then.' Beornoth marched into the darkness and stopped when he came into the glow carved into the night from the wall torches. The flickering light danced on the rings of his byrnie, and Beornoth stopped when he was sure the light bathed him in its orange glow. Brand stood next to him, his spear held forth and his long hair falling in two braids over his shoulders onto his chest. Beornoth emptied the sack of heads so that they fell with a dull thud onto the grass. He kicked three of them towards the gates.

'I am Halvdan Hrafnsson,' Beornoth lied, calling out in Norse. 'I killed some of your nithing warriors in the forest. They told me you have plundered silver and slaves from this land.'

'Do you know whose men you have killed there, little man?' came a shout from beyond the gate.

'Yes, I heard Ragnar the nithing is over those walls, and I also hear he and his men fight like old women. So, I thought I would bring my ships here and relieve you of your spoils. Come out and fight like men. Don't skulk in there like the cowards you are. Tell Ragnar that Halvdan is better than he. Come out and fight, unless you have pissed in your breeches at the mere sight of me.'

Beornoth watched as the spear points above the walls moved along behind the palisade, first in ones and twos, and then more until there was a bristle of them like a hedgehog's back. They came to see whose heads rolled, bloody and grim, before their camp, and because a Viking cannot resist a challenge to his honour.

'I think that's most of them drawn away from the edges to the front gate,' said Brand, counting the spear points.

'You murdering bastard!' came a shout from behind the gate. 'You are the nithing, coming here in the dark like a fetch. We'll find you and cut your balls off.'

'I am standing right here. Come and do it now, nithings,' Beornoth called back. There was a silence for a moment, and then two of the spear points jigged up and down and retreated from the gate.

'They have gone to get Ragnar,' said Brand.

'Good. Any moment now...'

A loud crunch suddenly shook the night air as though the earth itself had cracked open.

'Let's go,' said Brand, grinning at Beornoth. They turned and ran towards the trees and clambered up onto their horses. There was shouting and panic in the Viking camp, and the rumbling sound of horses galloping somewhere in the darkness. Beornoth leant to pick his spear up from where it rested against a trunk. He clicked his tongue and urged Hengist into a canter. Beornoth's heart pounded in his chest because he knew the plan had worked. While he had distracted the Vikings at the gate, Byrhtnoth and his men had looped hemp rope around the stakes on the western side of the walls and tied the other ends to their saddles. They had then raced their mounts away from the walls to tear that whole section of wall from the earth and create an opening for a company of Saxon warlords to ride into the Viking camp and bring swords, axes and shields to wreak revenge for the murdered Saxon souls in the burned and ravaged villages.

Beornoth heard the whoops of Byrhtnoth's men as they poured into the gaping hole ripped in Ragnar's palisade, and the shouts of alarm from inside the camp. He brought Hengist around towards them and the horse jumped over the snapped remnants of the stakes sticking up from the ground in jagged stubs like broken teeth. Before him horsemen whirled through a snarl of tents and running men, blades flashing in the torchlight. Beornoth reined Hengist in and slid from the saddle. He shrugged the heavy shield off his back and kept hold of his spear. A clutch of three spearmen were running from the gate shouting and making a charge towards Byrhtnoth's riders. Beornoth swept his own spear around into an overhand grip, took two steps forward and grunted as he launched the weapon through the darkness. It flew in a low, flat arc before slamming into the thigh of one of the three spearmen. He shrieked in pain and dropped to one knee. And before the other two men could identify their attacker, Beornoth drew his sword and charged at them. He held his blade two-handed and as a wide-jawed man hissed and stabbed his spear forwards, Beornoth batted it aside and with the strength in his shoulders, arms and wrists he slashed the edge of his sword down the chest of that man, slicing through his leather breastplate. Without pausing, Beornoth whirled and drove the point of his blade into the gullet of the man howling with Beornoth's spear in his leg. The man gurgled and choked on blood and steel, before Beornoth yanked his sword point free and slashed the edge across the face of the man whose breastplate he had cut open.

The iron tang of blood was in the air, and the Vikings were dying. They were dirty-faced men with greasy hair and brown, foul teeth. They were evil men, but Beornoth was meaner and more vicious than their evil, and he had come for them. He looked up to see a rider thundering towards him with a spear levelled. Beornoth's heart stopped because the rider was Brand, and for a horrifying moment he thought the man he had taken as a hostage but who had become his brother in arms was coming to kill him, but the spear flew over his shoulder and Beornoth heard a guttural cry behind him. He spun to see the third spearman falling to his arse with Brand's spear in his belly. The man had been about to drive his spear into Beornoth's back, and Brand had saved his life. The Viking had sworn he would repay that debt and Beornoth raised his sword in salute, and Brand nodded, before wheeling his horse around to find more men to kill.

Beornoth strode through the camp. Viking bodies writhed and moaned on the ground, clutching at wounds and, as he passed by them, he struck with his sword, sending their screaming souls to hell. In the dark shadows, amidst swirling smoke wafting from a flaming tent, Beornoth saw a gigantic figure swathed in mail and a black bear-fur cloak. That figure clutched a long, two-handed war axe, and he swung it with an ear-rattling war cry to pluck one of Byrhtnoth's riders from the saddle. The Saxon flew backwards in the air whilst his horse continued riding. The big Viking swung his monstrous war axe again and its oversize bearded blade arced through the shadows and slammed into the earth, taking the fallen Saxon's head as it did so. Beornoth strode towards the Viking giant, who stood a head taller even than he.

'Nithing!' Beornoth roared at the man, and he turned to face him, flashing a gap-toothed grin. The Viking had one eye missing, a black pit in place of his left eye, and a beard folded into a thick braid falling to his mailed chest. Beornoth had seen no mail-clad warriors in the Viking camp, and though this man was not Ragnar the Flayer himself, he must be one of their champions.

'Saxon turd!' the Viking spat back at him, and he wrenched his axe head from the dirt and came at Beornoth, swinging his axe around him in great twirling circles so that it moved in a blur, swishing through the smoke and darkness and coming towards Beornoth like a wheel of death. Beornoth gripped his sword and stood his ground, watching the blade flow around the giant faster than the eye could follow. The Viking grinned at him, a murderous, slanted grin. Beornoth imagined the pain this man had caused the people of East Anglia, the women and children, and swung his sword low. The blade swept towards the Viking's ankles, and he had to leap backwards to avoid the low blow. The jump fouled his intricate axe swings and as the axe faltered Beornoth kicked the axe haft back towards the Viking, and because his sword was low, he followed the kick in to slam the cross guard of his sword hard into the Viking's face, sending him stumbling back. Beornoth kept moving and brought his sword up above his head, ready to strike down and end the life of his enemy, but the Viking came up with a snarl and punched Beornoth in the gut and the wind whooshed out of him like a gale, and he almost fell over from the pain and surprise of it. The Viking was fast, and it was Beornoth's turn to spin away in pain.

'I am going to use your skull as a pisspot,' the Viking said, and he unclasped the heavy bear-fur cloak from his shoulders, letting it fall to the ground. He shrugged his boulder shoulders and came on again, two hands on his axe and ready to kill. Beornoth sucked in huge gasps of air, but it seemed to go nowhere, and his body felt as though a giant hand squeezed him as he desperately tried to get air into his chest. The axe head came at him, and he parried it with his sword, the blow jarring up his wrist and arm, the weight in the strike sending pain screaming through Beornoth's bones. Another blow came, and he twisted away from it, kicking his attacker in the knee. The Viking grunted as his leg extended, and he had to pause and regain his balance.

'No,' growled Beornoth through gritted teeth. He had come here to kill Ragnar and his slavers, not to die under the axe of this Norse monster. His breath came back and he held his blade before him in his right hand and slid his seax from his sheath at the back of his belt. The fight raged around him in the smoke and darkness, hoof beats, the clash of iron, and the shouts and screams of men. The Viking came for him again, and Beornoth parried the over-hand below with his sword and seax, and then slid his seax down the long axe haft and felt the blade catch on the Viking's finger bones. Beornoth sliced the blade harder and twisted away as the Viking roared in pain. Beornoth ducked and sidestepped around his attacker and dragged the edge of his sword across the Viking's left calf and the warrior fell to his knees, howling up at the night sky. The giant backswung his axe desperately, but it was a clumsy strike weakened by his wounds and Beornoth stepped away from it and brought his sword blade down onto the Viking's forearm, cracking the bones. The enormous axe fell to the earth and Beornoth stalked around to face his enemy. The warrior looked up at Beornoth, his face twisted into a rictus of hate. He was about to speak, but Beornoth stepped in to ram his seax blade underneath the man's beard and up through his mouth so that blood pumped dark across Beornoth's hand and down onto the man's byrnie.

'They are running,' a shout came from somewhere in the dark-ness, and Beornoth searched the dark, smoke-filled camp, fearful that Ragnar was escaping the vengeance Beornoth had come to lay upon him.

## 27

'The ships, to the ships,' screamed a Norse voice, high-pitched and desperate.

Beornoth cursed and dashed through the camp, horsemen thundered around him, and he swerved and leapt over corpses and the writhing figures of wounded men. Ahead, torches gathered through the gloom, and as he approached them a curved prow reared from the night, its snarling beast head glaring down at him. Where there had been two ships, there was now only one. Men were in the water, splashing and shouting.

'Where is the other ship?' Beornoth said, grabbing one of Byrhtnoth's men by the shoulder.

'Bastards fought their way to the shore and got one of their ships away. Their leader is amongst them,' said the man, his face spattered with the blood of his enemies. 'Look at those poor souls,' he said, and made the sign of the cross. He pointed his spear towards a fenced pen on the shore, from which pale hands reached out to them, with long faces as white as the moon, their mouths curled into terrified arcs. Saxon slaves taken by Ragnar and his men.

'No,' Beornoth whispered. He remembered the slaves murdered by Ragnar and his men during their last encounter, and the Saxon flesh stretched over the Viking shields. He could not allow Ragnar to sail away. Beornoth thought about pushing the remaining ship into the water to pursue them, but he was no sailor and nor were any of Byrhtnoth's men. The Vikings sailed the vastness of the Whale Road in their sleek warships and a pursuit on water would be no pursuit at all. Ragnar's camp lay beside a river, but on the cusp of where that waterway opened up into the wide sea. If he didn't act quickly then the Vikings would be surging across the white-tipped waves and gone. He saw a riderless horse stood idly, chewing on a patch of grass, and Beornoth ran to it and hauled himself into the saddle. He dug his heels in, and the horse set off at a canter, following the coastline. The men in the water had waded up to their waists, Saxon warriors who had tried to stop Ragnar from slipping away. Torches bobbed ahead of him, the flaming staves held by men who rode after Ragnar's ship. Beornoth urged the horse into a gallop and felt the power of the beast beneath him as it raced across the muddy riverbank. He caught up with the group of horsemen and slowed as he recognised Wulfhere and Leofsunu amongst the riders.

'How many are on the ship?' he shouted.

'A dozen,' yelled Wulfhere. The ship was level with them on the black but shimmering water with a flaming torch flickering in the darkness gripped by one of the crew, two banks of four oars dipping into the water and hauling the ship along. They were moving slowly with so few oarsmen, but they were moving. The Vikings could keep up that pace forever, and there was little he and his men could do about it. Then he remembered the view from the bluff where he and Byrhtnoth had observed Ragnar's camp. Along the shoreline, towards the sea, was a spit of sand and rock which stretched out into the water like a long finger. There were old and rotten posts across its length as though it had once been a jetty of sorts. Beornoth clicked his tongue and rose with the power of the horse as he drove it into a gallop again. Beornoth heard Wulfhere calling after him, but rage had overcome him like a madness. If he could reach that spit of land stretching into the river then there was a chance to stop Ragnar from getting away: a desperate, wild chance, but Beornoth rode towards it like a maddened bull.

He rode with his sword in one hand, and his seax in its sheath at his back. Beornoth glanced to his right, and he raced past Ragnar's ship. Ahead of him, the sandbank emerged from the darkness to cut into the smooth surface of the water like the neck of a sea beast. He drove the horse up onto the bank, and he had to drive it hard across the treacherous surface of rocks, sand and dirt, but the horse ran, and the ship approached. Beornoth's heart pounded in his chest because he suddenly realised the madness in what he was doing. He wore his heavy byrnie, and to fall into the deep water would mean death in its icy embrace, but he could not allow Ragnar to survive again. The ship drew closer, oars splashing and her crew shouting desperately at one another to pull harder. Beornoth dug his heels in savagely to the racing horse's flanks and sawed on the reins so that the beast leapt into the air. Beornoth jumped from the saddle, the fear of what he was doing hot like a fire in his belly. He closed his eyes and flew through the darkness, curling himself into a ball as he did so, and then suddenly he crashed into the hard timbers of the ship's deck. He landed heavily on his front, and the impact drove the sword from his hand and sent him rolling across the deck. The horse snorted and splashed behind him, where it had plunged into the river. The desperate leap had worked, and Beornoth raised himself up on his forearms just as a boot thudded into his ribs to send him sprawling. Beornoth grunted at the pain and rolled into the ship's sheer strake. He looked up and saw a boot coming for his face and

Beornoth grabbed it and twisted it, rising on his haunches to throw the man backwards. A spear came at him and Beornoth swerved to his right, but the blade punched into his chest, knocking him backwards. The links of his byrnie held, and the blow did not pierce his skin, but the force of it was like a hammer.

Blood rushed in Beornoth's ears, and his chest was hot with panic. His breath came in short bursts and his cheeks blew out with quick exhalation. Death was close. He could feel its dark hand on his shoulder. An axe blade whistled through the air and Beornoth twisted again just as the bearded blade thudded into the deck next to him. A boot came for his head again, and Beornoth raised his forearm to deflect the blow. He had dropped his sword and had jumped recklessly into a ship of Viking murderers. But they were men he had to kill.

'No, no, no!' Beornoth shouted, his sheer rage like a living thing, refusing death at the hands of his enemies. He roared like a caged bear and surged to his feet, punching the man trying to stomp him in the face and driving him backwards. The spearman was a short warrior with a grizzled beard and Beornoth wrenched the spear from his hands as though he were a child. He slammed its stave into the warrior's nose and kneed him in the groin. Beornoth shouted again and turned the spear in his hand and threw it down the deck at a fat man who stood on the steerboard, leaning to push the tiller away from the sandbank. The spear took the Viking in his gut, and he sprawled backwards against the stern, dragging the tiller with him so that the warship lurched towards the spit of land. The crew who had been coming for Beornoth with blades and snarls now toppled in the bilge from the ship's sudden lurch. Beornoth grabbed the sheer strake behind him to steady himself and whipped his seax free with his other hand. Five Viking warriors struggled to rise amongst the tangle of ropes, oars and each other, and Beornoth charged them, stabbing and slashing with his seax, its broken-backed blade opening terrible wounds in their faces, arms, legs and necks. Beornoth lost himself in the blood frenzy. He moved amongst them, cutting with his left hand and punching, clawing and raking with his right. Beornoth was bellowing incoherently, but he gave himself over to that wild fury, knowing that each strike was a blow of vengeance for his Saxon people who had suffered at the hands of these men. He took blows in return, but the blood-madness dulled them. Beornoth felt thuds against his back, face and shoulders, but these men would not kill him. He was the killer.

The ship lurched again, and it threw Beornoth from his feet and he landed heavily against a rowing bench. He grabbed the rough rope of an oar plug, which dangled from its hole, and hauled himself up. The ship had run aground on the sandbank, and Wulfhere leapt over the side to slam his axe into the chest of a Viking who came to meet him. There was blood sloshing in the bilge, and more Saxons climbed aboard the slavers' ship, their eyes hungry for the hated invaders' blood.

'Drop your weapons and you will receive mercy,' Beornoth called to the Vikings in Norse, and they looked at one another, and then across their shoulders at a figure waiting at the prow. A bow-legged stocky man was there, and he nodded slowly.

'They will surrender. Let them live,' Beornoth said to the Saxons, who advanced on the enemy.

'We have no use for prisoners,' said Byrhtnoth as he clambered over the side with a wolfish look on his lined face.

'We might have use for this ship and the one on the beach,' said Beornoth, the cloak of fury lifting from him, and the pain from the blows he had taken aching and burning across his body.

'We aren't sailors, Beo,' growled Byrhtnoth.

'These bastards are though,' said Beornoth. 'Maybe the ships will be of use to us when we go to attack Olaf.'

Byrhtnoth glared at Beornoth and then at the Vikings, who saw the grim look on the Ealdorman's face. They dropped their weapons and knelt on the canted deck. 'Sounds like you have a plan in mind,' said Byrhtnoth, nodding at Beornoth. 'They can live, but I want them chained to these oar benches. Chained with the fetters they used on our people.'

'You can live, but the price of your lives is that you will row these ships where we command,' Beornoth said in Norse to the kneeling Vikings, walking amongst them. 'You will swear oaths to our Ealdorman that you won't try to escape or do us harm. But not you.' Beornoth pointed his bloody seax at the bow-legged man at the prow. It was Ragnar the Flayer, and he smirked at Beornoth and stood to pick up his axe from the deck.

Ragnar hefted his axe in two hands and rolled his shoulders. It was the same axe with which he had struck Ealdorbana, and the weapon had drunk many innocent souls. Beornoth searched the deck for the sword he had dropped when making the leap from the sandbank and found the blade resting against a crutch which held the lowered mast post. He picked it up and advanced on the Viking leader. Ragnar came at Beornoth with alarming speed, his lips peeled back from his rotten teeth and his axe extended to chop Beornoth's arm in half. The edge of Beornoth's sword caught the axe haft as he parried the blow. He slid the sword down the haft to slice into the Viking leader's hand, but he whipped the axe away and brought the butt end up towards Beornoth's face. Beornoth ducked underneath it and came up inside Ragnar's arm's length and headbutted the Viking in the nose. Ragnar twisted away in pain, his nose mashed to a bloody pulp, but Beornoth followed him and chopped his sword down hard just above Ragnar's hand so that the axe fell from his grip. The Viking gasped and reared up, his eyes wide and waiting for the death stroke.

'No simple death for you, slaver,' said Beornoth, and he rested the tip of his seax at Ragnar's throat and smiled at his enemy because the fight was over.

The captured Vikings swore their oaths and Beornoth translated the words between Norse and Saxon for Byrhtnoth and Ragnar's captured men. Wulfhere freed the captured Saxons from the slave pen inside Ragnar's camp, and those pale figures spat and swore curses at the Vikings. Wulfhere took the Viking captured at the camp to the ship which had been driven into the sandbank and they rowed the warship back to the beach. They secured the heavy iron collars and chains which had been taken from the Saxons to the new prisoners. All the while, Ragnar glowered at the Saxons from the beach where Beornoth had tied him to a post. Beornoth allowed the Saxon prisoners to do as they would with the Viking leader. Most of them just trudged past him, some spat at the bow-legged leader and others struck him with fists or feet. One woman clawed his face and tears streamed down her cheeks as she screamed at Ragnar. Once that was over, Beornoth and Byrhtnoth came to Ragnar and the Viking sneered at their approach.

'Is Forkbeard here to raid, or to invade?' asked Byrhtnoth, and Beornoth translated the question into Norse.

'He has Jarls like me for raiding,' said Ragnar, laughing through his filthy beard. 'Do it like the Boneless. They were his orders. So that's what I did, just like Ivar the Boneless.'

'Where is his army?' asked Beornoth.

'Ask your kinsmen,' Ragnar said, and cackled again. 'They welcome him, like a hero. He is north of here, ready to settle in for winter, nice and warm with Saxon bed slaves and plenty of Saxon meat.'

'So, he will attack in the spring?'

'I'm not telling you anything, nithing. Kill me and have it done with,' said Ragnar, and he spat at Beornoth's feet.

'He won't say any more, so I'll make an example of him, Lord.

I'll hurt him so bad the Vikings will talk of it all the way to the Vik and across Jutland. He will tell us everything he knows, and his pain will deliver a message for us to Olaf and Sweyn,' said Beornoth, and he beckoned to Wulfstan and Leofsunu to carry across the brazier they had prepared for him. Beornoth slipped his seax from its sheath and waited for Wulfstan to spark the kindling into life, and as Leofsunu added sticks to the rising flames, Beornoth placed his seax into the brazier.

'God help us, Beo, but I think you hate these Vikings even more than I do,' said the Ealdorman, shaking his head. 'Making that jump today to their ship was madness. No one would believe it if a poet told the tale.'

Wulfstan added timber to the fire, and the flames licked the seax blade, heating it, casting orange and red sparks into the evening air.

'We should have killed the man in the fight, not brought him here to torture him,' said Godric from within a knot of Byrhtnoth's men, gathered to witness Ragnar's fate. 'This is not the honourable thing to do. Are we not Thegns and men of honour here?'

Beornoth stared at the young Thegn and his golden curls. 'What do you think Ragnar here would do if he caught you, Godric, and wanted to extract details of our army and plans?' Beornoth said, too tired from the fighting to be annoyed with the man.

'So, we are to become as beastly as they are then, to reduce ourselves to acting just as the pagans do? God sees all, Beornoth. But then, you are not a godly man. I have warned you before, Lord,' Godric said, making the sign of the cross in Beornoth's direction and looking to Byrhtnoth. 'Beornoth does not fight like a man of God. we should treat our enemies with respect and in a godly manner.' There were hooms of ascent from Godric's brothers and some of the younger Thegns.

Byrhtnoth waved his hand to quieten Godric. 'To defeat the Vikings, and make them fear us, we need to be more savage than their evil ways, Godric,' he said. 'What Beornoth does, and how he fights, does not fit with the warriors' dream the poets conjure for us when we listen to their tales of battle and heroes at our fathers' firesides. But it's because of men like Beornoth, and Wulfstan, Leofsunu, Aelfwine, Offa, Wulfhere and all of you here that we have now put a band of rabid Viking slavers to the sword. Beornoth fights like a Viking, and it's because of the things that he and I do, our people can sleep at night knowing that their children are safe. We stand in the shield wall and trade blows, risking our lives to throw back men who would come and kill, rape and enslave them. So, if you don't agree with what must happen here, go and say prayers for our companions who fell in battle today. What Beornoth does is the face of war against the northmen, and they must fear us, for they think of us as sheep and themselves as wolves.' Godric bowed his head and muttered to his brothers, and Byrhtnoth nodded to Beornoth to continue.

'Tell me everything you know of Sweyn and his army, how many warriors he had, how many ships. What his plans are and the names of the Saxons who brought him here,' said Beornoth.

'I won't tell you anything, you shit-stinking Saxon,' Ragnar said, and he shifted uncomfortably in his bonds, eyeing the seax in the flames which glowed red.

'You will, because I am going to make you into a *Heimnar*, Ragnar. Do you know what that is?'

Ragnar licked his lips and shook his head, looking at Byrhtnoth as though he was considering begging for his life.

'Don't look at him, Ragnar. You are mine now. You said Sweyn ordered you to scourge our country just as if you were Ivar the Boneless, and you did. Our people have suffered at your hand. I am the sword of revenge and justice for those people. So, I will do to you what Ivar did to his enemies. I will cut off your feet and hands, then your legs and arms to knee and elbow, then down to shoulder and groin. You won't die because my seax will burn the wounds closed. That, Ragnar, will turn you into a *Heimnar*. You will keep your eyes and ears so you can see the horror on people's faces when they see you and hear their screams of horror at what you have become. You will keep your balls so you can still desire women, even though they will despise you, and your tongue so you can cry out in despair.'

'No, not that. Please...' Beornoth pulled his seax from the flames and held the heat of it close to Ragnar's face until the Viking twisted away from it and the glow of the blade shone in his eyes. 'I'll tell you all about Sweyn...'

## 28

The two captured Viking warships hugged the coastline as they sailed south, moving from the flatlands of East Anglia into the rising hills and gaping estuaries of Essex. Summer waned, and it was a bright morning where a wolf moon still stood low and proud in a pale sky, not yet yielding the heavens to the sun even though its golden disk had risen hours earlier. Despite Brand's insistence that he could sail the ships, and that he had forgotten more about the Whale Road than any Saxon would ever know, Beornoth had found a fisherman and his two sons on an East Anglian river mouth to help them keep the ships in good order. He did not trust the Viking captives and knew nothing of the sea himself and nor did any of his men. Beornoth liked Brand, which was why he was still alive, but he was still Olaf's oathman. The fishermen had grumbled, scratched at the lice in their beards and refused to help until Beornoth paid them two arm rings taken from Ragnar's men, which was enough wealth to buy their fish-stinking village ten times over. The fisherman was short and lean and his age was impossible to guess from his weather-burned face and bald head. His name was Cena, and he knew the confusing business of rope, sail and knot enough to keep the ships underway. It was slow-going, and for much of the journey Beornoth stood at the prow watching the heave of the grey-green sea and peering out to the distant horizon.

'I hate the sea,' said Wulfhere, wiping vomit from his beard with the back of his hand. The hulking warrior had been heaving his guts over the side ever since they had left East Anglia.

'It is quiet out here,' said Beornoth. The sound of the white-tipped waves crashing on the hull and the gulls cawing towards the shore were strangely soothing.

'It's noisier than rutting pigs,' said Wulfhere, taking a swig from an ale skin and sloshing the liquid around his mouth to wash away the foul taste of his seasickness. 'Between the constant noise of the water, the groaning of these bastards as they row, or the barking of that lice-ridden, fish-stinking bastard you dug up to sail this bloody thing, this is what hell must be like. That's without mentioning your creation back there, howling to the heavens whenever he wakes up.'

Beornoth chuckled at his friend. They had only been at sea for a day, and at first the ships had moved clumsily under oars, the Vikings surly and staring at their captors with barely disguised hatred, despite their oaths. It had horrified them when the Saxons had carried the *Heimnar* aboard and placed him below the raised platform at the prow. Ragnar was terrible to look upon without his arms and legs. He lay upon a cot stuffed with straw and flitted in and out of consciousness, suffering from his terrible wounds seared shut by Beornoth's red-hot seax. 'Ragnar suffers for what he did to our people. The bastard stretched the flayed skins of dead Saxons across his warriors' shields.'

'He did, and the bastard deserved what you did to him. But let's just toss him over the side now. Looking at him makes the lads sick.'

'I don't think it's Ragnar's wounds that are making you sick.'

'No, it's this bloody ship. Sooner we get our feet on dry land, the better.'

'We are in Essex now, I think. Cena tells me we aren't far away from Mersea Island. So, we should be with the Ealdorman Byrhtnoth by tomorrow. If this wind keeps up.'

'Aye, well. Can't come soon enough for me. Will the King fight Olaf, Lord?'

'I don't know,' said Beornoth. He listened to the sigh of the sea and looked at its rolling mass stretching away into the distance. 'I don't think Olaf or Sweyn are going to leave without a fight. They haven't brought their ships and warriors here to raid a few coastal towns and settle for carts of silver.'

'What do they want then?'

Beornoth shrugged. 'Power, land, glory and the silver. Our land. Just as our forefathers came here long ago and took the land from the Welshmen, pushing them back into the corners of the island.'

'And you think these ships and your *Heimnar* can help us defeat Olaf?'

'Maybe. If the King fights, but it does not seem like he wants to.'

'What other bloody option does he have?'

'He could pay them to leave, just like the Franks do, like his Bishops want to. Or he could cede them land, just like Alfred did with the Danelaw.'

'God help us,' said Wulfhere, and then clasped a hand to his mouth and dashed to the side to spew whatever morsels remained in his stomach. The Vikings on the nearest rowing benches shouted at him, because Wulfhere had not grasped the significance of not vomiting into the wind.

Beornoth left him to it and picked his way along the deck,

passing his hand from rope to rope along the intricate web of rigging to keep himself steady. The Vikings kept their eyes down to avoid his gaze, their chains clanking and shackled to their rowing benches. He smiled as he saw Brand at the tiller, his fair hair loose and long, whipped by the wind behind him. His eyes looked ahead, and he leaned on the tiller, a look of pure joy on his face as the ship ploughed through the waves.

'You miss this?' Beornoth said, joining him on the raised platform at the ship's stern, upon which a man stood to handle the tiller and steer the ship.

'Yes, Lord,' said Brand, and he smiled broadly before the grin faded, to be replaced by a wistful look in his eyes. 'I miss my home and my people. We leave Forkbeard and his Danes behind us then?'

'We do,' said Beornoth, frowning. 'We are but a few men, and our first duty is to protect the people of Essex. Forkbeard is in East Anglia. Olaf is close to Essex and will raid near Branoc's Tree before long.'

'If Sweyn and Olaf meet and can share power, the Saxon Kingdom will fall, I think. They would have close to one hundred ships.'

'Not if we kill them, they won't.'

'You can't kill them all, Lord.' Brand smiled. 'There are few enough Saxons like you and the Ealdorman Byrhtnoth. Your Æthelred is not a War King. Seems to me his mother and the Christ priests tell him what to do.'

'Byrhtnoth says Lady Ælfthryth is out of favour, but there is nothing to be done about the priests. More's the pity.' Beornoth felt a heaviness, knowing that all northmen shared Brand's reasoning. That was the reason the Vikings were plaguing Saxon shores. They smelled weakness, like a starving wolf. They would pour into the festering wound of a fractured Kingdom with their warships, strip it of wealth and then crush its rulers with axe, spear and shield. The Vikings did not bring thousands of warriors across treacherous seas without some certainty of success. 'Your time as a hostage may soon be over,' said Beornoth, changing the subject. The doom of the Kingdom made his belly sour. Brand stared at him and raised an eyebrow.

'It should have been over when Olaf attacked again. By rights, you should have cut my throat then.'

'I should. But you fight well, and maybe I am getting soft in my old age.'

'I think Ragnar might have something to say about that.'

'Will you fight for us against Olaf when we meet him?'

Brand looked over his shoulder to the west and smiled into the wind. 'This ship, and the one behind us being steered by that toothless fisherman's sons, are splendid ships,' he said and stamped his boot against one of the clinker-built strakes. 'When I sailed to join Olaf, I brought my father's ship and she will still be with Olaf now, with the warriors from my village. The fighters who drink ale in my father's hall. Her name is *Fjord Eagle*. That ship is a little longer than this one, and faster, I think. It took the women of my village two years to make her sail from the fleeces of two hundred sheep. She is beautiful. I have fought for you this summer, Lord, just as I swore I would. You are a good Lord, and you have given me these two arm rings.' He held up his right arm and shook the silver rings Beornoth had given to Brand for his service and then tapped the pouch he wisely stored beneath his armpit. 'And my purse is full of silver. But I cannot fight against my people, my kinsmen and my friends. I swore an oath to fight for Olaf.'

'And you swore an oath to me.'

'Too many oaths.' Brand sighed and chewed at the triangle of yellow beard below his bottom lip. 'I should not have sworn my oath to you, Lord. I should have stayed in your lands, even tied like a pig in a sty, but I have fought for you and killed fellow northmen. Your men hated me at first, but they have become my friends. I do not want to fight against you either.'

'So, you must decide where your path will take you next.'

'The Norns laugh at me at the foot of the great tree Yggdrasil. Those three witches who determine the fates of men spin the threads of our lives, and they are plucking at mine for their amusement, or so it seems. If I leave you, Lord, would you try to kill me?'

Brand had first come to Beornoth as a hostage, but he now thought of him as one of his men, even as a friend. 'I won't stop you if you want to return to your people, Brand. But if you join Olaf's shield wall, and we face each other, I will kill you.'

'I know you would try, Lord, and Odin would not have it any other way,' Brand said, and he flashed a wide smile at Beornoth. It was a smile that said he thought of him too as a friend. They had become sword brothers, but such things were difficult to talk of between men. 'I think you should pray to Odin, you fight like a Viking, and you have no love for the Christ God.'

Beornoth shook his head at that. He had lost his faith when the northmen had killed his children and hurt Eawynn, leaving her for dead. There seemed little point in praying to a God who spoke of peace but allowed such terrible atrocities to happen to his flock. The Viking Gods urged them on to battle and violence, and they sought it out to please Odin, to burnish their reputations bright with the blood of their prey. Beornoth was a man of violence, but only because he had to be. He did not sail to other men's homes to kill and rape and make himself rich with stolen silver. 'I have no love for my God, but less love for yours.'

'That's a pity, Lord. For you would be a welcome warrior in Odin's Einherjar and we would feast and fight together in Valhalla for eternity whilst your Christ followers float in the clouds singing prayers.' They both laughed.

'That's Mersea Island,' said Beornoth, pointing to where the coast curved away to reveal a hump of land shimmering in the distance. 'Steer a course for it. Byrhtnoth will be there with the horses and news of Olaf.'

'So, we will learn if there will be a fight or not?'

'Aye,' said Beornoth, and let his hand fall to the hilt of his sword. He was tired and sore, the wounds from the hard fighting that summer still raw and aching on his neck, legs and body. But he wanted the fight. He wanted to kill Olaf and all of his Odin-worshipping axemen. He wanted them gone so he could get back to Eawynn, and he hoped Byrhtnoth waited with news of that fight, and if he could use the captured ships and Ragnar the *Heimnar* against Olaf Tryggvason.

'The King is still in Lundenburg,' said Byrhtnoth. The Ealdorman stood with his foot raised and resting on a log of bleached driftwood. Beornoth stood next to him, and they both looked out at Mersea Island. It was high tide, and the sea hid the causeway linking the island to the mainland.

'And the Vikings ravage our lands without opposition,' said Beornoth, shaking his head.

'Some Thegns fight where they can. Trying to protect their land. But the King and the Ealdorman in Kent have not raised the fyrd, so the people cower. They try to gather their crops now that the evenings draw in, but the Norsemen harry them looking for food and plunder.' Byrhtnoth folded his arms across his thick chest. 'It wasn't so long ago we fought on that island. Last year, we fought Skarde Wartooth there and put his men to the sword. Now we face a threat too large for me to fight alone.'

'Has the King moved his fleet east to pick off their raiders, like Einar Ravenhair, who take one or two ships looking for spoils?'

'Not that I have heard or seen. The fleet remains in the southwest. It is no match for Olaf or Sweyn, anyway. A handful of ill-crewed cogs compared to their dragon ships able to sail the deep seas.'

'So, the Bishops are still gathering enough silver to pay Olaf and Sweyn to go away?'

Byrhtnoth nodded. 'That remains the plan. They are travelling to every shire, hundred and tithing. Collecting a tax large enough to pay them off.'

'They won't leave, though. They will take the silver, winter in our lands eating stolen food and then in the spring they will attack again.'

'Aye. Just like Olaf and his empty promise at Watchet. You still have your hostage.' Byrhtnoth glanced behind them to the rolling sand dunes, where Brand and Wulfhere stood talking to Offa, Wulfstan, Leofsunu and Aelfwine.

'He is a fighter, so I let him live, despite Olaf breaking his oath. What became of the other Watchet hostages?'

'They are dead,' said Byrhtnoth. 'I ordered it, Olaf broke his word, so his men had to die.' He made the sign of the cross on his chest and looked up at the sky. 'So much death, Beo. So much cruelty,' he whispered. 'Is this God's plan? Is our God at war with the pagan God? If so, then maybe their Gods are winning. We become more like these Vikings, I think. More savage.'

They were not questions Beornoth could answer, so he left the thoughts of them hanging in the air. Beornoth knelt and picked up a stone and cast it into the gentle waves lapping at the dark sand. Making Ragnar into a *Heimnar* had been a cruel and terrible act, and Beornoth regretted it. It had been hard, grim work cutting away the Viking leader's limbs. His stomach churned, thinking of the horror of it, the stink of the burned flesh and blood. It was foul work. Byrhtnoth was right, they were becoming more like the Vikings. There had always been fighting, always been wars, before the northmen came to Britain. Beornoth's own ancestors had taken

Britain by force, and were in those days pagans, just like the hated Vikings. But the Saxons had found God and Jesus, the saints and a sense of trying to follow the teachings of Christ. Men still killed and fought for land and silver, but not with the brutal savagery of the Vikings. Beornoth supposed that across the span of his life, a life filled with death and war, he had become every bit as brutal as his enemies. He wondered what his mother would make of him, if she could see him now? It was a strange thought, and he found it hard to remember her kind face. She had been a godly woman, dedicated to the Church and to running a good house for his father. Beornoth's father had been a brutal boar of a man. Beornoth shut such thoughts from his head. His mother would be ashamed of how he fought, of the things he did to protect the people. But his father would understand, would see the need the Kingdom had for Beornoth as a hunter and killer of Vikings.

'So, do we wait for the King to make his offer to Olaf, or do we fight?' Beornoth asked.

'I know that deep down you hope the King will fight, that he will rouse the fyrd of each county and bring a host of Thegns to crush Olaf and Sweyn. But his Bishops have too much power, Beo. They will try to pay the Vikings off. But, we keep our war band together,' said Byrhtnoth, taking his foot off the log and turning to face Beornoth, his face a frowning crag. 'Olaf is still in Kent, at Folkestone. We will go there and harry him, fight him, make his life hard. Maybe that will make him more likely to accept King Æthelred's silver when he grows tired of our blades.'

'If Olaf has his fleet in a harbour, then we can use Ragnar's ships to hurt him. Instead of many weeks of ambush and killing his men in forests and valleys, we can strike an actual blow against him.'

'We only have a few men, Beo, just the men who rode against Ragnar. I won't raise the men of Essex to fight in Kent and leave their homes unprotected. We can't attack Olaf in Folkestone; he still has over a thousand men.'

'We don't need to attack Folkestone, Lord. Just hit Olaf where it will hurt him most. His ships. There is little a Viking loves more than his *drakkar* warships. If we can hurt his fleet and force him out of his camp in a rage, even with our small numbers, we can kill a lot of the bastards. Soften them up so that the offer of silver is more appealing than facing our blades all winter whilst they forage for food. I don't want the Vikings paid off. I want them dead. But if the silver at least buys us a winter to prepare for war, then let's help the King make that happen.'

Byrhtnoth chuckled: a silent, chest-shaking laugh. 'Maybe God sent you to us, Beo. I granted you a heriot here last year because you earned it. You came down from the north, and your appetite for war matches my own. I am thinking we should return to our homes. Let the King and the swords of Kent deal with Olaf. We can prepare ourselves over the winter for the war to come in spring, when Sweyn and Olaf will certainly renew their attacks.'

'What if they never attack, Lord? What if Olaf and Sweyn both have their footholds in Kent and East Anglia and just creep across the country, killing Thegns and Ealdormen and adding land to those footholds? The Great Heathen Army was here for thirteen years in the time of King Alfred. It could be a year or more before the King musters the courage, and enough men to fight them. More Norsemen will come, smelling our weakness like ravens flocking to a rotting corpse. If we go home now and prepare for a war that might not come, we just await the inevitable. They will come one day, but will it be next spring or summer, or in two years' time when Sweyn has made himself King in East Anglia and Olaf King in Kent?'

'I breed horses, Beo. On my estates, magnificent animals. I wish I was there now, watching them grow and caring for them. I must find you one to replace your warhorse,' Byrhtnoth said. He was smiling as though they were old friends talking on market day.

'Thank you, Lord. I would like to see that, one day.'

'One day,' said Byrhtnoth and he gnawed at his beard, the smile falling from him like night descending over a balmy evening. 'For now, we will take your ships and our blades and force Olaf to fight. We shall stab him and cut at him and make him uncomfortable. I imagine he sits like a Lord in his war camp at Folkestone, growing fat on Saxon meat and rich on Saxon silver. Let's hurt him before he hurts us. Tell me what you plan to do with the captured *drakkars*.'

## 30

Beornoth stood in the prow of the Viking warship, staring out across the surging, white-tipped waves. The churning sea rolled beneath him, and the timbers of the ship groaned, and its seal-hide ropes creaked as the ship rode the swell like a sea dragon. It was a bright, sun-filled day, and the surface of the water twinkled and shimmered as though the night's stars lay upon its surface. They had sailed south from Mersea Island under favourable winds, with the sail snapped full for most of the journey. The ship flew along faster than a galloping horse under sail and on the calm coastal waters. Beornoth stared into the wind, enjoying the fresh whip of it in his face and hair. The Viking prisoners sat hunched at the rowing benches, their shackles chinking every time the ship lurched or one of them moved. They were a silent mass of bodies rolling with the heave of the waves, hunched shoulders and dark eyes, glaring with undisguised hate through the folds of their unbound hair.

'One day, Lord, I hope you get to take a journey far across the sea,' Brand had said to him earlier. The Norseman had grinned the whole way, his hand on the tiller and delighting in the thrill of being at sea. 'The waves at the edges of Midgard are as high as your hall at Branoc's Tree, and monsters appear from the deep to look at you with dark, dead eyes.'

They raced across a wide bay, like a high-sided bowl cut in half. The bluff was white, run through with iron-grey rock and topped with green grass, and Beornoth could see villages dotting the shore leading down to a strip of golden beach. They made for where the lip of that bay jutted out into the sea, sloping tree-covered headland disappearing into rock where the waves crashed in white frothing spume. Beyond that headland was another smaller bay, and Beornoth could see the black shapes of warships at rest there, a forest of masts and prows huddled into the protective embrace of the small sandy bay, shielded from the sea's fury should a storm rise from her bowels.

'Wulfhere,' Beornoth shouted. The huge warrior sat glowering against the stern. His face was corpse-pale, and he clutched his axe in two hands. Wulfhere pushed himself to his feet with a groan and clutched a rigging rope to stop himself from falling as the ship rolled beneath him. He wore only his jerkin and trews, and went barefoot, as did Beornoth.

'Please tell me this nightmare is nearly over. I hate the bastard sea. I'll never set foot on a boat again when we get off this bloody thing,' said Wulfhere, taking deep breaths to stop himself from becoming sick again. 'Are you going to tell me now what in all hell we are doing sailing one ship towards an entire Viking fleet, and why I had to take my bloody boots off?'

'When we get past that headland.' Beornoth pointed to the sloping bluff, squinting from the bright sun. 'We are going to cut a hole in the hull of this ship. You and I will cut a hole big enough to allow Ragnar's men to row her into that port, but so that she will sink and foul the bay, cluttering the ships there with her wreckage.'

'What if the ship sinks before it gets into port?'

'The prisoners will need to row hard, or drown,' said Beornoth with a shrug. 'So, we must cut a hole to allow the sea to pour in, but not too big that she goes down quickly.'

Wulfhere grinned and kissed his axe blade. 'That, I can do. What about that?' He pointed his axe towards the cot resting beside the mast post, where Ragnar the Flayer, who was now Ragnar the *Heimnar*, lay beneath a blanket. He was asleep, which thankfully was his usual state as he suffered from his appalling injuries. When he was awake, he would scream and roar and spit and curse until falling unconscious again.

'He will probably die soon; all I need him to do is deliver a message to Olaf for me.'

'What about Brand?'

'Don't tell him what we plan to do. He is a good man, but we are sailing towards his people, and I don't want him to know our intentions.'

'You don't think he would betray us?'

Beornoth shrugged. 'Better safe than sorry.'

The ship raced towards the headland, and Beornoth made his way carefully along the deck, using the ropes to keep his balance, just as Wulfhere had done.

'Cena,' he said, calling to the fisherman, who fussed at a knot on the halyard.

'Yes, my Lord.'

'If we lower the sail now, how long will it take the men to row into the harbour?'

'Not long,' Cena said, peering over the side and looking into the wind. 'Tide will help them.'

'Very well. Get the sail down, don't waste time with it. Throw the bloody thing over the side, if you must. And get the *faering* ready.'

'Yes, Lord,' said the fisherman, and he grinned his gap-toothed smile and cackled, before hirpling off to bark orders at his sons. They let out the rigging and the mast came down in halting jerks on its yard. Cena didn't bother to tie the sail up. They just furled it and left it dripping from the yard, but tied that off so it wouldn't swing about loose.

'Oars,' Brand shouted once the sail was down, and the prisoners removed the oar-hole plugs and slipped their oars through the holes, and made themselves ready. Cena hauled at a rope over the side, and turned to nod at Beornoth, showing that the small four-man rowboat, or *faering*, was ready for them. Beornoth had ordered the *faering* to be dragged along behind the *drakkar*, and he stared at the headland, trying to judge how long it would take to row the small vessel to land.

'A ship, leaving the harbour,' Wulfhere called. Beornoth made his way back to the prow and wrapped his arm around the snarling beast head to peer ahead across the sun-glistening water. A warship was slithering from the harbour, its curving prow pointing right at them, and its oars rising up and down, like the wings of a dragon.

'Start chopping,' Beornoth said. Warmth kindled in his belly and blood rushed in his ears. Fear. His plan had seemed so simple, but now Beornoth feared that he had left it too late, and even if he could cut a hole quickly now in the ship's deck, the approaching warship would smash their little *faering* to pieces as he Wulfhere and the fishermen rowed for the safety of the headland before Folkestone's harbour. He grabbed his own axe where it rested against the prow and he and Wulfhere chopped their blades into the perfectly carved planks, overlapped at one edge and riveted together by dark iron nails. Shouts erupted from the prisoner crew, curses and howls of panic. They were fastened by iron collars and wrist shackles to their rowing benches, and they knew that if the ship went down, they would sink with her into the embrace of their Sea God: Njorth.

'Row hard, you bastards,' Beornoth shouted to them in Norse, 'and you will live. Row this ship into the harbour and your fellow northmen will save you. Waste time now bleating like old women, and you will surely die here today.'

The oars dipped and sliced into the surging waters, and the ship heaved ahead. Ragnar the *Heimnar* began to howl and roar from his cot at the mast, calling to Odin and spitting curses at Beornoth and all Saxons. Beornoth swung his axe and as he wrenched its head from a plank, the timber shivered and split, and cold sea water flowed through the hole and washed down the deck to collect in the bilge. Wulfhere smashed his axe down twice in the same spot, and the water ran freely now, flowing around the oar benches and splashing against the feet of the Viking prisoners who cried out in alarm.

Beornoth leaned out over the prow and saw that the Viking ship was much closer. He could make out figures on her deck and see the gleaming droplets of water on her oar blades. The ship moved so gracefully, like a bird in flight, but that ship meant death. It meant the cunning of his plan brought to ruin and so Beornoth ran along the deck, towards the *faering*. He reached the mast, and Ragnar's face snarled at him from his cot, his mouth spewing spittle.

'I curse you, Saxon. I ask the Gods to put a growth in your children's belly and to send warriors to rape your wife a thousand times like the whore she is, I will...' Ragnar didn't get to finish his threat because Beornoth kicked the *Heimnar* off his cot so that he flopped into the pooling sea water. Ragnar cried out, panic twisting his blood-drained face. He was just a torso and a head, with rotting joints at groin and shoulder, and would surely soon die of his wounds, but drowning is a terrible fate and Beornoth left the man who had cut the skins from Saxon men and women to flounder like a fish.

'Come on, quickly,' he called to Wulfhere, and the big man was at his shoulder. They reached the stern, and Cena's two sons were already in the *faering*, bobbing next to the *drakkar* and looking up at Beornoth with anxious faces.

'That ship is getting too close, Lord,' hissed Cena.

'Get in the boat then,' Beornoth replied. And the fisherman, with a nimbleness belying his crooked frame, lowered himself into the *faering*.

'Brand, you are next,' said Beornoth, as he held on to Wulfhere's wrist and helped the warrior clamber into the small boat.

'I won't be going with you this time, Lord,' said Brand, his voice even and stern.

Beornoth turned to him, and Brand smiled, the tendons in his neck stretching his raven tattoo.

'Thank you for not killing me, as was your right. I have enjoyed fighting alongside you, Beornoth. But it is time for me to return to my people. Ill steer the ship into the harbour. You go now and row quickly, for that ship will be upon you before you know it.'

Brand reached out his hand, and Beornoth took his forearm in the warrior's grip. They shared a look for two heartbeats and then Beornoth went over the side and dropped into the *faering*, scrambling to a seat so he could grab an oar.

'Row!' Cena barked. Beornoth heaved back on the oar, but his stroke fouled, and the oar blade crashed into Wulfhere's oar. 'Do it in time, and twist your bloody wrist,' Cena said, his voice becoming like a screech, the Viking ship so close now that Beornoth could hear its hull crashing through the waves. He had his back to shore. 'Pull,' Cena shouted. Beornoth brought his oar down and heaved back on it so that the muscles in his back stretched. The *faering* moved away from the *drakkar*, and Beornoth hoped the warriors aboard the warship which had come from the harbour would be more interested in that than the small fishing boat which now made for the finger of the headland. He couldn't yet see the beach, but he trusted Leofsunu would be there with his and Wulfhere's mail and arms, and their horses, just as they had arranged.

The oar blades on the *drakkar* continued to pound the water, and as he pulled on his own oar, Beornoth hoped the ship would make it far enough into the harbour to do as he intended, far enough so that it would sink and foul the inlet for the rest of Olaf's fleet, making it difficult for those ships to enter and leave the secure harbour around the sunken timbers of Ragnar's ship.

'How far away are we?' Beornoth shouted, not wanting to risk looking over his shoulder because, if he did, he might miss his oar stroke and lose valuable time in the race to shore. The Viking warship heading out of the harbour passed by the *drakkar*, and her oars paused as she glided by.

'Close, ten more strokes. Pull!' Cena shouted. The prow of the warship reared up on the crest of a wave, and Beornoth could see the barnacles on her hull at the break of the waves, and the snarl of her painted beast head, a red maw growling at him across the water. The ship came about, the bank of oars facing Beornoth poised above the glistening waves as she turned. Then, there were bearded faces glowering over the sheer strake, and a spear flew from the deck. It arced high in the air and fell two spear's lengths away from the *faering*.

'Ha!' Cena cackled. 'They fear the rocks. They won't come any closer, the pig-humping bastards.'

Beornoth hauled on his oar and watched the warship turn and make a course back towards the sinking *drakkar*. Beornoth thought, or hoped, that Ragnar's ship looked lower in the water and seemed to cant to one side. The *faering* banged against the slippery rocks at the foot of the sloping finger of the headland before Folkestone bay. Sure enough, Leofsunu was there to help them clamber off the rowboat and up the rocks to where their horses waited for them.

'You did it then,' said Leofsunu, shielding his eyes from the sun with his hand. 'I think it's sinking?'

'It's sinking,' said Beornoth.

'So, the first part of your low cunning scheme has worked. Now for the next part.'

Beornoth nodded and wiped the sweat from his brow. He had been sure the Viking ship would run them down, and it had been a close thing. Beornoth wanted Olaf's men to be rescued before the ship went down, and he hoped Brand would get off safely. Above all, however, he wanted Ragnar the *Heimnar* to be brought before Olaf. Beornoth had made him into a thing of nightmares; he wanted Ragnar's fate to sting Olaf, and spark fear in his Viking heart. Ragnar had killed Saxons, and Beornoth had struck back in terrible revenge. Beornoth wanted Olaf to know he was coming for him, so he could tempt him to come out and fight, so that he could feel Saxon steel and know that not all the Saxon people were sheep for Viking slaughter.

## 31

Darkness shimmered on the sea, making the churning mass appear like thick birch-bark tar. Beornoth shivered as the chill night wind cut through his jerkin and its cold air kissed the hairs on his chest. He stood at the stern of the second of Ragnar's captured Viking warships, unarmed and unarmoured, the wind billowing the sail and driving the ship around the same headland where he had fled from one of Olaf's *drakkars* earlier that day.

'Shall we light it now?' asked Aelfwine. He, too, wore only his jerkin and trews, for they were not expecting a clash of blades beneath the bright glow of the wolf moon above them.

'Light it up,' Beornoth said. He glanced over his shoulder to where Cena tied the tiller with a length of seal-hide rope to the sternpost to keep the ship on track.

'That'll hold her, my Lord,' the fisherman said, and rubbed his gnarled hands together, hopping from one foot to the other in excitement. 'We'll stick it to the buggers, won't we, Lord?'

Aelfwine took a flaming brand from a brazier they had lit beneath the thwarts and set it to the foremost rowing benches which they had soaked in fish oil. The fire crackled and spat along the timbers, a blue hue at its centre. Beornoth nodded and gritted his teeth. Ahead of them was Folkestone's harbour, packed with Olaf Tryggvason's precious warships. The town was only visible as dots of torchlight, and the occasional, distant sounds of a dog barking or muffled shout were almost lost on the rippling waters.

'Let's go,' Beornoth said, and they clambered over the side into the same *faering* they had used to escape from the sinking warship. Beornoth took his oar and leant into the strokes. This time no ship came to intercept them, no boats patrolled the sea. So confident was Olaf in the supremacy of his Viking sailors and their *drakkars* that they would never expect an attack from the Whale Road, where the Norsemen reigned supreme. Beornoth watched the flames spread slowly but inexorably across the deck and creep onto the sail, so that the ship burned brightly, casting dancing shadows and shuddering light across the bay and cliffs above it. Lights on the shore moved towards the harbour, Olaf's men noticing that a fireship sailed towards their fleet. They would feel panic, and Beornoth hoped they felt fear. He wanted them to feel that heat in their bellies, and the catch in the throat as the fire came for them. He wanted them to feel pain and suffering as the ships built from the sacred trees in their homeland, from logs cut by their fathers, brothers and cousins, were burned to ruin by Beornoth's fireship.

The *faering* reached the rocks, and they clambered ashore, helped up by Wulfstan and Wulfhere. Beornoth took his mail and slipped the byrnie over his head and shook it over his shoulders. Wulfhere handed him his sword and seax, and Beornoth saw three corpses bleeding on the rocks. Viking sentries sent by Olaf to watch the headland, in case of any more surprises. Those sentries were dead now, cut down by Wulfhere and Wulfstan.

'Thank you, Cena. You have served your people well today,' Beornoth said to the fisherman who stood with his sons, eyes fixed on the harbour, waiting to see if their fireship would glide into the Viking fleet.

'We did it, Lord, look,' he said, pointing as the ship's mast crumbled under the flames, but the ship continued on its path, passing by where the remains of the sunken *drakkar* poked through the tip of the water like a skeleton, visible now under the bright, flickering flames of the fireship. Beornoth slid another arm ring from his wrist and handed it to Cena, who cackled and showed the silver ring to his sons.

'It's beautiful,' said Wulfstan, his deep voice rumbling and full of gravel. He was staring at the bright glow of the fireship, which was now in the harbour itself. Beornoth strode to where his horse, Hengist, waited, hobbled behind the rocks. He untied her forelegs and clambered into the saddle, and the others followed him. He was silent and grim-faced, for there was work to be done. Sword work. Blade work.

Beornoth rode Hengist at a canter along the headland's shore; Wulfhere, Wulfstan and Aelfwine rode with him. Across the bay, the fireship nuzzled gently between the first two of Olaf's ships at the harbour's edge. She barged her way through before coming to rest between the tightly anchored fleet. The shore was busy with torchlight, and above the crack of burning timbers and the lap of the sea against the rocky shore, panicked shouts peeled out as the Vikings raced to stop their precious fleet from burning to ash. There was a glint of moonlight on steel ahead of Beornoth, and through the darkness, figures appeared. Men with helmets and spears, whose helms flashed and flickered with orange from the flames across the bay.

'You did it, Beo,' came a shout from the band of warriors.

'Let's hit them then,' Beornoth shouted to the men, and the war band climbed into the saddle. He passed his tongue through the familiar hole in his teeth where an arrow had once punched through his face. He had felt old and tired in the weeks leading him to Folkestone. His wounds had hurt and ached. Now he felt young and strong as he watched the fire spread to more ships, the light of it dancing on the water. The fireship cracked and groaned and slipped in the night-black sea water, and as she did so, more of her flaming timbers fell onto an adjacent deck. A warrior handed Beornoth his shield, which he slung onto his back, and a long æsc spear. He kissed its blade and turned to grin at Wulfhere.

'Are you ready?' he said.

'We are all ready Lord, let's attack them for a bloody change. Let them feel fear.' Wulfhere glowered under a furrowed brow, and his jaw set square below his flat, hard face.

'Let's kill them, kill them on the beach, men!' Beornoth shouted, and he dug his heels into Hengist's flanks. The war band rode, the sound of their hooves like the rumble of thunder in the night. They came around the headland, pushing uphill onto the summit of the white cliff, which was grey in the moonlight. Short grass and ferns covered the top of those cliffs, and the horses pounded along rhythmically, Beornoth rising and falling with Hengist's gait. Traces jangled and his shield banged against his back. He was hungry to bring the fight to the Vikings, to hurt them. He led the riders around the bay and then down a hillside strewn with briar towards Folkestone itself. There was a beach where dark timber jetties stretched out into the water and where the Vikings had moored their fleet.

'Carry me to the fight, friend. Do not be afraid,' Beornoth said, leaning into Hengist's neck. The horse laboured up a sandbank tipped by long, hard grass, and then they were on the beach, the sound of hooves muffled by the soft sand. Ahead, men gathered in huddles, and others ran towards the chaos of the burning fleet. Leaders bellowed orders, and men clustered onto slim jetties, filling them as they hurried to board their ships and save them from the flames. They would try to pole the burning ship away from the fleet with oars and timbers, but the sunken ship in the bay would make this task difficult, just as it would be if they tried to pull anchor and sail their vessels away from the flames. The Vikings would need to navigate their *drakkars* around the fireship, and the sunken ship in the darkness. The glow of the flames illuminated the carnage that Beornoth had wrought amongst his enemies, and his heart swelled at the joy of it. He pounded down the beach, flanked by a dozen riders. They were twelve against a thousand men, but Beornoth did not want to fight them. He wanted to hurt them. He wanted Olaf angry, so that the Sea Lord made rash decisions in his fury.

'Strike fast and hard,' Beornoth shouted over his shoulder. 'Don't get yourselves killed.'

He saw bearded Viking faces turn to him on the beach, faces which had looked anxiously at the flame-lit bay now showed panic in wide-white eyes. Three men turned to run, but Beornoth's horse was at the gallop, and he took the first man between the shoulder blades with the leaf blade of his æsc spear. He allowed Hengist to drive into the second Viking with his powerful chest hurling the warrior from his feet before Beornoth struck across his saddle to spear the third man in the shoulder. Screams erupted around him, mixed with shouts of alarm as his riders drove into the Vikings. They were in jerkins and unarmed, come in a hurry to save their ships, and he laughed as the battle joy came. The thrill of war came not only from the death of one's enemies but also from using your mind to hurt them, to kill men bent on killing you.

Beornoth led Hengist in an arc, he and his riders curving around the beach like a flock of swallows on the wing. They struck at the fleeing Vikings, and Beornoth's spear was red with the blood of the Norsemen. Wulfhere whooped and shook his axe above his head, and Beornoth saw Leofsunu's ugly face split by a wide grin.

They came around again to face the enemy, but now there was a glint of byrnies on the beach and a deep voice called, '*Skjaldborg*,' which meant shield wall in Norse. The man organising that defensive formation was thick-set with a rope of a beard which reached his belt, and it swayed as he bellowed at his men to form a line. It was the right thing to do, because horses will not charge into a shield wall. Beornoth cantered Hengist forward and raised his spear to point at the warrior with the rope-beard.

'Bring me Olaf Tryggvason,' Beornoth shouted in Norse.

'Our Jarl does not talk to nithings who attack in the dark,' snarled Rope-Beard. Hengist skittered, and Beornoth fought with the reins to bring her back to face the enemy. She reared up on her hind legs, and as he leant forward to stay in the saddle, Beornoth brought his spear back and, with a grunt, flung the weapon into the flame-lit night. The æsc spear slammed into Rope-Beard's chest and threw the warrior from his feet, and the shield wall shuffled back a few paces at the surprise of it. Rope-Beard had not expected the attack from Beornoth whilst his horse was off balance, which was why he had launched the spear. Beornoth wheeled Hengist around and drew his sword, pointing his blade at the shield wall.

'Is your leader afraid to face Saxon blades?' he called.

The Viking shield wall surged forwards, the front rankers knocked off balance by a line of men armed in mail byrnies, spears and shields. A lone warrior barged through both lines, his chest heaving and a war axe clutched in his hand.

'I remember you, Saxon, from Watchet,' the leading Viking shouted, pointing his axe at Beornoth. A line of men who all bore the same device on their shields, a rune painted in white on their dark leather shield coverings which glowed in the fire-drenched moonlight, flanked the Viking leader. The rune was two arrow-like lines facing away from each other, and though Beornoth knew the

Norse language, he did not know their letters. He recognised the runes and the shields, however. They were Olaf's Jomsvikings. The man who had burst through the line of grim-faced men was young, slim-waisted and broad-shouldered. He had a long, angled face with a wide slash of a mouth, and the soot of his burning ships marked his cheeks. It was Olaf Tryggvason. 'You are a nithing who strikes in the darkness. You have burned some of my ships and sent some captured Danes to me. One of them made into a *Heimnar*. Are you Loki come to prey on me disguised as a Saxon?'

Loki was the trickster God of the Norsemen, cunning and able to change his shape. 'I am Beornoth, and I killed your man Palna-toki at Watchet,' Beornoth called, and cantered Hengist towards the sea and back again, parading in front of the Viking lines with his sword raised. 'I have come here to see if you want to fight, Olaf Raven-Starver, or if you are content to sit here and raid farms for grain and pigs. Have you come to our lands for war, or to grow fat?' he shouted in Norse.

Shouting erupted from the Viking lines, enough to drown out the roaring of the men behind them who struggled to put out the fires amongst the fleet, because Olaf made to run forward and attack Beornoth, but his warriors held him back. He struggled in their grip, and his warriors were wise to hold him because Beornoth would ride him down and butcher the Jarl in front of his own men. Raven-Starver was a pride-stinging insult for the Viking leader. Beornoth had learned it in his youth fighting Vikings in the north. No Viking could ignore such an insult, to be accused of being one who starves the ravens of corpses.

'We are here now, Saxon, if you want to make a shield wall on the beach, and we will see who the Raven-Feeder is,' Olaf spat, shrugging off his men waving at them to show he would not run into the attack alone. There was an edge to Olaf's voice, and his knuckles showed white on the haft of his axe. He was angry, and

Beornoth continued to ride along Olaf's line, trying to annoy him even more with arrogance and belligerence.

'I only have twelve men, Raven-Starver. So, we won't fight here,' Beornoth shouted as he rode. 'Follow me beyond the dunes and we can have our fight. Maybe I will make you into a *Heimnar* also? Like that raping, murdering Dane I sent to you as a gift. I am the Viking killer; no man here can defeat me. Or maybe I am Loki, sent here by Odin to punish you for your cowardice. I will make you all into *Heimnars*. That is all you are fit for. You are all cowards and nithings. Look at how I have burned your ships. It is like fighting children.'

'I will kill you, Beornoth. I swear it—' Olaf bellowed, but Beornoth cut him short with a forced laugh.

'I challenge you to fight then, boaster. Bring your blades and your warriors. Follow me now, Olaf Raven-Starver, or your men will know you for the weakling you are.' Beornoth pointed his sword at Olaf, and then wheeled Hengist around and galloped down the beach, away from the furious Olaf.

'I think you've annoyed him, Lord,' said Wulfhere, riding alongside Beornoth, shouting above the din of the wind in their faces and the pounding of their horses' hooves.

'I hope so. Vikings can't refuse a challenge. With the fireship and the *Heimnar*, let's see if we can't get them to come out and fight.'

'What's the sense of it though, Lord?' Wulfhere called from the back of his mount. 'We are few, and they have a thousand warriors. We cannot win?'

'We don't have to win, just fight them. We have burned some of their ships, and I hope that's enough to keep them in Kent and not sail to Essex and our homes. If we can fight and kill enough of them, we can keep them in Kent for winter if the King makes peace with silver. Maybe even persuade them to sail away and winter somewhere else.'

'But what if they kill us all?'

Which was the fear also growing in Beornoth's belly. He had kicked the beehive. He had poked the honour of a Viking leader with a thousand warriors, who would bring his axes and spears howling down upon Beornoth and Byrhtnoth's small band of fighters. Beornoth rode up over the sandbanks and towards the headland, hoping that Byrhtnoth had found a defensible position where they could make a stand, where they could make the shield wall and kill Olaf's men. Where he could strike with his sword and put enough terror into Viking hearts to keep them away from Branoc's Tree. Or die trying.

## 32

'They are coming, Lord,' said Godric, red-faced and his horse lathered from a hard ride. He climbed from his mount and shook his head, pointing towards twin hills over which the sun had just risen, casting a bright hue on the underside of low clouds.

'How many?' said Byrhtnoth, eyes searching the hills for signs of the enemy.

'Hundreds of them,' said Godric, and he looked up at his brother, who nodded vigorously from the back of his horse. Byrhtnoth had sent them to watch the enemy march through the night. 'Too many, I fear, Lord.'

'Good,' said Byrhtnoth, and he glanced at Beornoth, who gave a small nod of his head.

'But there are too many, Lord. They will butcher us in short order,' said Godric, his tongue flicking across his thin lips. His gaze ran across the faces of the rest of Byrhtnoth's men but found no support amongst the warriors, who had already started to tighten belts and check weapons. 'They can simply march through the river and surround us.'

'The river is too deep, and we will fight them here,' said the Ealdorman, and turned away from Godric.

'Lord, I am sorry, but what is the sense of we few making a stand here to be slaughtered when the King comes soon to make peace?' Godric said, turning and looking to the other warriors for support, but finding only stony faces.

'I let Beornoth loose on the Vikings to show them we can fight, that we can hurt them just as they hurt us. They know we are men of Essex, and I want them to fear bringing their ships to our lands. If the King is to make peace, then maybe if we have taught them the strength of our steel, then they will accept that peace and buy us more time to organise the defence of our Kingdom.' The Ealdorman took a deep breath to calm his anger. He didn't need to explain himself to Godric, but it was good for the men to understand the reason they would stand now against such a large Viking force. 'We don't have to fight here until the last man. We just need to show them how we fight and kill some of the Norse bastards. I want us to hold this ford for as long as we can, and then we all have our mounts here. Once the Vikings are hurting, and the river runs red with their blood, we will ride away during a lull in the fighting.'

Byrhtnoth looked into each man's eyes, and each man nodded to show he was ready for the fight, ready to stand and die if necessary. They were warriors, and most were Thegns, their duty was to fight wherever their Lord commanded. Stout warriors like Byrhtwold, Maccus and Wulfmaer, grim-faced and war ready. Byrhtnoth let his gaze linger on Godric, but the young Thegn could not hold his Lord's eye. He looked at his boots, fingering the gold wire on his sword's hilt, and then turned away to prepare himself to fight.

Byrhtnoth touched Beornoth's elbow, and they marched towards the river. It was ten paces wide and fast-flowing, carving through a pasture of soft grass. Its meander was high-banked and filled with thick bush and briar, but Byrhtnoth had found a knee-deep ford slashed through by a well-worn pathway, no doubt used by the farmer of this land to move his cattle or sheep between pastures.

'Seems like you made Olaf angry, Beo?' said Byrhtnoth, grinning behind his iron-grey, shovel-shaped beard.

'Looks that way, here they come,' Beornoth said, gesturing to where a column of men wound around the hillside. Their spear points and helmets caught the morning sun, and their mail glistened so that the marching ranks looked like the coils of a great serpent slithering across land, stalking its prey.

'Let us hope that this has all been worth it.'

'At least we have brought the fight to them and not cowered behind our burhs. Olaf won't march far from Folkestone now that his fleet is damaged. He will want to repair and secure his ships before he makes any strikes that would threaten the King.'

'Summer grows long, and they will look for winter quarters soon. Let's hope they stay in Kent.'

'Or piss off back to Norway,' said Beornoth, and they both laughed softly.

'We'll hold the ford for as long as we can and kill as many as we can. But Godric is right, we won't give up our lives here today. If we can get them to fall back, we shall ride away, and leave them with a sting they won't forget. Every day we keep them here saves Saxon lives.'

'We have drawn them out of their camp. If we had an army here, we could have crushed them for good.'

'Aye, we could. Olaf is so angry he leads his men out without even scouting the hills. We could have fallen on them like waves crashing on the shore. But all we have is our men, and this is as good a place to stand as any. We shall fight alongside one another today, Beo, at the centre of our shield wall. Put some fear into the rotten bastards.' Byrhtnoth clapped Beornoth on the shoulder and strode to his men. They stood taller at his approach, chins rising and shoulders back, and the men busied themselves hefting shields and checking grips on their spears, swords and axes. It was a good place to stand. The river was deep enough to prevent the Vikings from outflanking the Saxon line with their vastly superior numbers. Beornoth stepped into the water, and its chill seeped into his boots and around the iron strips he wore there to protect his shins. He bent to cup a handful of it and splashed his face, the icy wetness washing the tiredness from his eyes. A good fight here would buy his people a winter of peace, so he slung the shield from his back and slid his arm through the leather strap for his forearm, then his fingers grabbed the wooden grip. He rolled his shoulder with its weight and brought the shield up before him to test the grip and loosen his muscles. The Vikings marched across the valley basin, and they sang rhythmic war songs, the rumble of their voices spreading across the field like a fog. Olaf's men broke out from their marching column into a line facing the Saxons.

'How many do you think?' Wulfhere said, joining Beornoth in the river. He had a helmet on his bald head, a riveted bowl with a nasal strip to protect his nose.

'A few hundred.'

'Ten times as many as we have?'

'More or less,' Beornoth shrugged, and Wulfhere laughed at the lack of concern.

'So, all we have to do is kill twenty of them each?'

'You can kill at least that many with that axe of yours,' Beornoth grinned, and Wulfhere laughed again.

'Brand might be out there. Come to kill us.'

'He might. If he is, he can die like the rest of them,' said Beornoth, but he didn't mean it. He hoped Brand wasn't with Olaf's force, that he was with the rest guarding the fleet at Folkestone and so their blades wouldn't cross.

'We are in a bit of a spot here, Lord. We can't kill all of them.'

'No, we can't. But when have you ever fought a battle where everyone was killed? We just have to fight them. Hurt them enough to put fear in their bellies and then withdraw.'

'Just like that.'

'Just like that.' Beornoth smiled at the big man. Of course, it would not be that simple. There was the terror of the shield wall to face, the press of bodies where you can feel the heat of your foe's breath on your face as he tries to kill you. Where blades come from above and below, trying to force their sharp edges into the soft flesh of your body and rip you to ruin.

'Shield wall!' Byrhtnoth shouted, and the Saxons gathered on the bank facing the Vikings, in front of the ford. They were thirty men armed with shields, spears, swords and axes. Many of them were Thegns and wore gleaming byrnies and helmets. The rest wore hard baked-leather breastplates. Beornoth took his place beside Byrhtnoth, with the Ealdorman's oldest companion Offa on Byrhtnoth's left. Wulfhere stood on Beornoth's right, and beside him was the enormous figure of Wulfstan. Leofsunu and Aelfwine were in the second rank with Godric and his brothers.

'Remember your oath. We are brothers, bloodsworn to fight for our Lord and kill our enemies. Death to the Vikings!' Aelfwine roared, and the lines responded with a clipped shout of ascent.

'Are we men of Essex?' Aelfwine called, and the Saxons shouted again in ascent, and banged their spears on their shields. Beornoth's heart pumped harder. The Vikings were close now. He could see their teeth and eyes white beyond the browns and greys of their armour, weapons, beards and helmets.

'Are we the Viking killers?' came Aelfwine again, and the men roared louder this time, and the bang of spear on shield was as loud as a thunderclap.

'Then let's kill the bastards!' The spears battered iron shield rims, and the sound of it was like a horde of horsemen racing through the valley. Beornoth was breathing hard, and the Norsemen came on, bellowing their own war cries and their front rank interlocked their shields to create their own shield wall. It was twenty warriors wide and outflanked the Saxon line, which they had limited to ten shields.

A figure came before the Viking shield wall dressed in shining mail, slim of hip and broad of shoulder. It was Olaf, and he levelled his spear at the Saxons.

'Is this all you can muster, Saxons? A gaggle of crusty whores beside a river. I thought you had invited us to battle, so I brought my warriors to feed the ravens with your corpses and entertain Odin with your deaths.' Olaf's voice was as clear as a church bell on a cold, silent, frosty morning. He waited for Byrhtnoth or Beornoth to meet him for the customary exchange of insults, but Byrhtnoth stayed silent. Olaf shrugged and turned to his warriors. 'For Odin, Valhalla and glory!' he roared, rising his spear to the heavens, and his men bellowed in response, beating weapons on shields in a rhythmic drumbeat as their shield wall advanced, each step accompanied by the beat of their weapons on the iron rim of their shields.

Beornoth's stomach clenched, and his throat was dry. He rested his spear on his shoulder and took the locket from beneath his byrnie and kissed the timber casing, warm from where it had rested against his chest. The locks of his murdered children's hair were ever close to his flesh. He thought of their golden curls bobbing as they ran in the sunlight, of their laughing faces as they bounced on his knee, and of their shrunken burned corpses in the remnants of his northern hall. Beornoth delved deep for the memory of Eawynn curled into a ball in the ashes and filth of his destroyed home, her throat cut, and body violated. Vikings had done that, ripped Beornoth's life away with axe and blood. They had sailed to England to do that again, to rend and tear at the happiness and dreams of other families. Beornoth would not allow that, not whilst he could hold a sword. He let the rage take him, felt it flood his body with strength and anger. His chest heaved and the muscles in his neck, shoulders, chest and arms bunched. Beornoth tucked his locket away and grabbed his spear.

'Make ready!' Byrhtnoth shouted, and brought his shield up. Beornoth overlapped the left side of his Ealdorman's shield, and Wulfhere did the same for Beornoth. He felt Leofsunu of Sturmer's spear point to the left of his face and brought his own spear up to rest on the tip of his shield. Beornoth's helmet made his head hot, and he clenched his teeth under the heady, exhilarating mix of fear and fury. The Vikings came on. Beornoth could see eyes shining behind shields and helmets. They were ten paces away when an order barked across their lines, and a wave of short spears flew from their rear ranks. The weapons flew low and deadly, whipping across the space between the lines as fast as a hare. Beornoth grunted as a spear slammed into his shield, driving his shield back into his chest. A man cried out along the line, and as he recovered from the blow, Beornoth gasped to see the Vikings running towards him. They had used the disruption caused by the spear throws to charge the Saxon line, and they came in a snarling, cursing wave of blades, iron and wood.

Beornoth braced his shoulder against his shield as a Viking shield crashed into him, the force of it pushing him backwards. Leofsunu shoved his shield into Beornoth's back, and Beornoth drove his legs into the enemy, shoving back with all his strength. He could smell the acrid sweat of the Viking's leather, and the stale ale breath of the man opposite him. Beornoth saw a glimpse of a grey, grizzled beard and pale blue eyes. The press was suffocating. Men grunted and shouted, spear arms pinned in the press of warriors. Beornoth wriggled and pushed so that his right elbow came up out of the press. The weight of the larger Viking numbers felt like a mountain falling on the Saxons. Beornoth slid backwards, boots slipping across the grass. He pushed his spear forward; he could only move a fraction and saw the delight in Greybeard's eyes as the spear point stepped a hand's breadth from his face. The enemy stamped on Beornoth's foot, and he cursed from the pain. He drove forwards again, and the point of his spear went close to the enemy but stopped two fingers away from doing any damage. The grey-bearded Viking was bellowing and twisting his head away from the spear, and the surrounding lines pushed and shifted like the waves of an angry sea. Beornoth shook his shoulders, trying to make space to fight, and Wulfhere sensed what he was trying to do and shuffled to his right. Suddenly there was space, and without hesitation Beornoth punched his spear point into Greybeard's eye, bursting open the jelly and washing the man's face with blood. He pulled the spear free and jabbed it into the throat of the man opposite Wulfhere and then turned his wrist to jam the spear blade through the cheek of the warrior pushing against Byrhtnoth's shield. The spear point burst through the other side of that man's face, spraying smashed teeth and blood against Byrhtnoth's shield. Where the shield wall clash had been a surge of shields pushed together, a test of strength, now it became a blood-soaked place of horror and savagery. The men wounded by Beornoth's spear fell away, recoiling at their injuries, and he forced himself into the gap. He let go of his spear and it stayed above the fray, resting on the shoulders and shields of the press of men around him. Beornoth reached behind him as he stepped forward and whipped his seax free. He stabbed it furiously below the rim of his shield. It hit upon the resistance of mail, and then the soft give of leather and flesh, and then warm liquid on his hand. He roared and jabbed the blade again, pushing forward as he did so.

Beornoth then stepped backwards to rejoin the shield wall, and the Vikings before tripped forwards, the mass of shields behind them pushing them into the space he had left, and Wulfhere and Byrhtnoth stabbed their spears at that new front rank. Shouts and cries of pain filled the air, mixed with the sour iron smell of blood. This was the shield wall.

'Four steps back. Now!' Byrhtnoth bellowed above the battle din, and the Saxon line took four long steps backwards. They moved into the ford and Beornoth felt the cold of the river through his boots. The Vikings stumbled forwards again, and their front rank died on Saxon spear points. Byrhtnoth had made his shield wall on the Viking side of the bank just to execute that manoeuvre, and it had worked. The Vikings now had to clamber over the corpses or writhing, injured bodies of their front rank into the river water.

'Hold here,' Byrhtnoth ordered, and Beornoth was breathing hard from the exertion. He looked to Wulfhere, who had a livid red cut bright on his cheek, and the big man nodded at him to show he was ready to continue the fight. At a barked order, the whole Viking force shuffled backwards out of the river, stepping up onto the bank. The front rank lowered shields, and each man turned to the side to let a new line take their place. This line, however, was different. Each man bore the shield marked with the white rune, and all wore byrnies and bright helmets.

'Jomsvikings, forward,' came an order in Norse, and the fresh line moved forwards. These were the warriors Beornoth had fought at Watchet, Palnatoki's men renowned for their organised savagery. It seemed Olaf had seen enough of the small Saxon force getting the better of his greater numbers, and he now sent his elite force to crush Byrhtnoth's men. The Jomsvikings came on with their spears resting on the top rims of their shields. They came to the corpses on the bank and flowed over them like running water. Beornoth and the rest of the Saxon line braced themselves for the onslaught and it came as a surprising, fast clash of shield on shield as the Jomsvikings crashed into them, but then they withdrew as quickly as they had come on, and now it was the Saxons' turn to stumble forwards, pushing against shields which were no longer there. The Jomsvikings had charged them, and then leapt back two paces as one unit.

Beornoth's shield lowered as he surged forward, trying to recover his balance, and a spear point hammered into his chest. His byrnie held, but the force of the blow threw him backwards, and another bright spear blade came at his face, and Beornoth twisted his face away, but not before the point carved open his forehead so that blood spilled into his eyes. The Saxon front rank was in disarray, and they moved backwards as the Jomsvikings came on again, spears jabbing forwards with brutal efficiency. The river ran red with the blood of Vikings and Saxons alike, and Beornoth turned to see Byrhtnoth's face straining and pale with the panic of it.

Beornoth continued to shuffle backwards, and his feet came out of the water and onto the far back of the river. The Jomsvikings paused, their shields perfectly held in a straight line, all at the same height, each man glaring above the iron rims. They did not shout or curse, they were a calm killing machine.

'Beornoth,' Olaf called, he was in that line somewhere, but they all looked the same, like a long line of twins. 'You challenged me, and here I am. We are the Jomsvikings, and no men can stand against us. I will rule this land, I will be King here one day. And it starts with you, now.'

'We can't hold them,' came Godric's voice in the rear rank, shrill and shaking.

'Hold them,' Byrhtnoth growled.

And the Jomsvikings came on again.

# 33

Beornoth's shoulders burned with the ache of keeping his shield high. He struck with his seax but each time the blade met the relentless force of a Jomsviking shield, there were no openings for him to slide his blade under, over or between. Wulfhere grunted alongside him, panting and trying to strike with his spear over his shield, but facing the same implacable wall as Beornoth. Byrhtnoth yelled at his men to keep the line, to hold their position. Beornoth pushed and shoved against the Jomsvikings' shields, but they were as strong as Roman-built walls. If the Saxons yielded any more ground, they would be beyond the ford and the riverbank would be open for the Vikings to flood around the Saxon flanks, and then it would be a massacre.

'Are they across the river?' Beornoth shouted.

'Some tried to wade through, but our lads speared them as they struggled across,' called Leofsunu from over Beornoth's shoulder. As the ford widened, the river fell to the depth of a man's chest, and beyond that it was not passable. Byrhtnoth had chosen well.

'We must break off, Lord,' came a voice. Beornoth thought it was Godwin, Godric's brother. Byrhtnoth did not reply.

'They are not even trying to kill us,' Wulfhere hissed, his face bright red from the exertion. The Jomsvikings were not bothering to strike at the Saxons. They were content to push them back, to heave and open the way for their larger force. They were disciplined warriors, controlled in the heat of battle. Beornoth admired and hated them at the same time.

'Kill them,' Byrhtnoth bellowed. 'Kill them or we will all die today.'

Beornoth ignored the pain in his shoulders and tried to wipe the crusting blood from his eyes with the back of his jerkin sleeve. 'I'll try and drive through them, open up their line,' he said.

'Do it, Beo. I will follow you,' snarled Byrhtnoth. 'We can't get away from this unless we can be rid of these Jomsviking bastards long enough to get to our horses.'

'Wulfhere, watch my back,' Beornoth said, and Wulfhere frowned at him, because he would do that without needing to be asked.

Beornoth closed his eyes and whispered the names of his daughters. He flexed the fingers of his right hand around the bone handle of his seax and took a deep breath. The force against his shield was unyielding, but he let out that breath and with it came a war cry to shake the roots of the earth. Beornoth knelt, and with all the strength in his body, he banged his shoulder into the bottom of his shield, forcing it into the bottom rim of the shield opposite him. That shield was overlapped on left and right, just as Beornoth's was, but Byrhtnoth and Wulfhere let Beornoth's shield pass theirs so that only the three shields facing them dipped forwards. Then, Beornoth leant back, and quickly surged to his feet so that a space opened for a fraction of time between his shield and the Viking shields, and he drove the upper rim of his shield into the Vikings' so that their shields which had pitched forwards now sprang backwards to bang into their bearded faces. Grunts of pain came from those granite, bearded faces, and Beornoth let go of his shield.

He grabbed the edge of a Jomsviking shield and yanked it down, and then drove his seax into the throat of a man who stared in disbelief as a Saxon blade ripped through his gullet. Blood sprayed from the wound as Beornoth sawed his weapon free, and he pushed himself into the ranks, propelled from behind by Wulfhere and Byrhtnoth. They tried to create a wedge, a swine-head formation to punch through the Jomsviking ranks, and Beornoth slashed and clawed, spat and snarled at the enemy. It was a blur of blood and pain. He felt blows striking his chest and back, and his vision went dark for a moment as they battered his helmet from his head. Beornoth saw shining lights and shook his head. He shoved his seax blade into the armpit of a red-bearded man who tried to headbutt him and felt the hot wash of that man's blood on his hand and wrist. Beornoth was moving forward, and then he wasn't. The Jomsvikings were not summer warriors arrived in England to raid and plunder before going back to their farms. They were professional and experienced warriors, masters in the trade of war. A powerful hand gripped his wrist, and another twisted the seax free. Shields pinned him on either side and Beornoth could not move. He wriggled and bellowed, but they pushed him backwards and cries of alarm erupted from the Saxons behind him.

'That one is mine, let him go,' came Olaf's voice. The pressure on Beornoth fled, and he dropped to his knees from exhaustion.

'The Ealdorman is hurt. Back, back,' came cries from behind him.

'Are you ready to die? Maybe I should make you into a

*Heimnar*?' said Olaf in Norse, grinning, the hard angles of his face demon-like in his fury. 'The riverbank is open. Kill them all.'

Beornoth glanced over his shoulder and the Saxons were retreating, dragging bodies with them. One of them was Byrht-noth's. Wulfstan lay dead. The huge warrior had been cut down, his face laid open by a savage cut, and his blood ran into the river. So brave in war, and a good man. Beornoth's heart sank to his brother of the sword lost to Viking blades. They had tried to split the Jomsviking line, but the attempt had failed. The plan to hurt the Vikings in the ford, and then escape to leave them bloodied, had also failed. Beornoth climbed to his feet and dragged his sword from its scabbard. Around him, Vikings splashed through the ford, water spuming around them as they whooped for joy at their victory. Beornoth did not feel fear for himself. He felt afraid for Eawynn and his people at Branoc's Tree. Who would protect them if he died? But if he were to die here, then Beornoth hoped he would meet his daughters in the afterlife, in Heaven perhaps. He was ready to die.

Olaf dropped his spear and drew his own sword. He removed his helmet, the horsehair tail at its top flowing in the wind. He raised his sword and came at Beornoth, lunging and cutting with perfect form. Beornoth parried the blows then edged backwards under the assault. Olaf was fresh, young and skilled. He got his blade inside Beornoth's own and it raked across his belly. The byrnie did not break under the blow. Beornoth went down on one knee with a curse, slipping on a rock. Olaf smiled and leaned in for the killing blow, to take everything from Beornoth with a sweep of his sword. But Beornoth had pretended to slip on the rock, and as Olaf swung to take out his throat, Beornoth twisted around the strike and punched Olaf in the face with the pommel of his sword and kicked him savagely in the groin. The Viking leader crumpled to his knees, and Beornoth stepped forward and brought his blade down overhand. Even if Byrhtnoth and his warriors were all killed, at least Olaf Tryggvason would die, and dung the Kentish field with his blood. Olaf looked up at Beornoth, and in the heartbeat it took for Beornoth's sword hand to strike, he saw the dreams and ambitions of a Viking Lord fade away in those bright blue eyes. Beornoth's arm jarred as someone suddenly parried his strike.

'No, Lord. Not today,' said a familiar voice. It startled Beornoth to see that the man who had blocked his death blow was thick-chested, fair-haired, and a tattoo of a raven stood proud on his neck. It was Brand. Clad in a bright byrnie and holding his sword in two hands. Other men dragged Olaf away, the Jarl staring at Beornoth, his face twisted into a snarl of hate. 'Go. Fight with your Ealdorman,' Brand said. He lowered his sword and smiled wanly at Beornoth. Beornoth turned to where the Vikings swarmed around a circle of Saxon shields. They were like flies on a corpse and Beornoth believed his time had come.

A deep, undulating sound rippled down from the closest hill, a pure, low musical note from a war horn. Beornoth looked to the hills, and a wedge of horsemen galloped down the hillside like birds in the sky. They were Saxon horsemen, leaning into the charge with spears levelled and screaming their battle cries. The Vikings shouted in alarm, and fled back across the river, retreating from the circle of Saxon shields. They dashed past Beornoth, not bothering to strike at him, and he let them run. He watched Brand loping off after the men who had dragged Olaf from under Beornoth's sword. Beornoth dropped that blade, his hand throbbing and swollen from the tight grip he had held on his sword and seax.

The horsemen tore into the Viking warriors with the crack and crunch of spear and thundering horses on flesh and bone. Olaf and his Jomsvikings ran with the rest of the Norsemen towards Folkestone, and Beornoth stumbled across to the circle of Saxons, his breath held in his chest, desperate to learn the fate of Byrht-noth, Wulfhere and the rest. Beornoth fell on the riverbank, his limbs exhausted, and the pain of the wounds he had taken forced their way through the cloak of war-frenzy. He stood and dragged himself towards the Saxon shields. Leofsunu greeted him and cast an arm around his chest to help Beornoth walk. Wulfhere was there, grimacing at a spear wound in his thigh. Byrhtnoth was there also, but he was unconscious, and blood was in his hair.

'Will the Ealdorman live?' Beornoth gasped.

'There is hope, the wound is not deep,' said Leofsunu.

'Look, a rider,' said Aelfwine. The Thegn leant on his spear, scowling at the pain from a wound in his shoulder which had ripped through the rings of his byrnie.

Beornoth turned to see a warrior astride a black warhorse. He had peeled away from his company to ride towards the river and reined his horse in to splash in the shallow ford. He wore a fine byrnie, and he removed his helmet to reveal a young and familiar face.

'Alfgar, you beautiful little bastard,' exclaimed Wulfhere, pushing himself up on his elbows.

Beornoth laughed and raised his hand in greeting to his friend, Alfgar, Ealdorman of Cheshire, whose riders now chased Olaf Tryggvason's warriors back across the bloody field of battle.

## 34

King Æthelred and his Bishops arrived the day after the fight, along with the King's hearth troop and wagons filled with silver. Alfgar had stopped his charge beyond Folkestone, his riders no match for the larger mass of Olaf's warriors inside the fishing town. Olaf licked his wounds within the harbour, his fleet, and his pride, singed by the Saxons.

'I won't have any arm rings left soon, lad, if you carry on like this,' Beornoth said. He took a drink of cool water from a skin, his face aching and swollen where his skull had been cracked in the fight against the Jomsvikings.

'I rode as soon as you left, Lord. And brought Kari with me,' grinned Cwicca, the smile splitting his round face. 'I thought you might be angry, but we got here in the nick of time.' He turned over the silver Viking arm ring Beornoth had presented him with on the battlefield.

'We'd be dead men if you hadn't gone north, Cwicca,' said Wulfhere. He was sitting on the grass with his wounds bound and his leg outstretched. They were gathered outside the walls of

Folkestone, watching a parlay between Olaf Tryggvason and the Lords of Saxon England.

'Alfgar, Streonwold and his men rode the very day after I arrived in Mameceaster,' said Cwicca. 'We rode hard across the whole country to find you, Lord. As soon as I told him you fought alone, and against two Viking armies, Ealdorman Alfgar didn't hesitate.'

The men around the fire hoomed and nodded their respect at that, even Godric. 'He will make a fine Ealdorman,' said Beornoth. Leofsunu handed him a piece of fresh bread, and a slice of the duck which roasted above the small fire around which they gathered. Most of Byrhtnoth's men had suffered wounds in the fight with Olaf, and they all took care to clean and wrap their injuries because all men knew that the prospect of infection was a worse killer than the blade wielded by an enemy.

'He stands alongside the King now,' said Wulfhere, shaking his head. 'Only a year ago, he was a snot-nosed stripling fresh from the Church. The only callouses he bore then were on his knees from praying.'

Alfgar, King Æthelred and Byrhtnoth met Olaf Tryggvason before the timber-staked walls of Folkestone harbour. Archbishop Sigeric presented Olaf with chests of silver in exchange for his oath not to attack Saxon lands again. He had, of course, sworn that oath before. The wound to Byrhtnoth's head had indeed been shallow. His helmet had taken the brunt of the spear blow, which had knocked him unconscious on the battlefield. Beornoth ate his food and watched the holiest man in all England bowing and scraping to the Viking Jarl, and Olaf placed his hand on his chest and said the words that would bring peace to Saxon lands, for the winter at least.

'I almost had him,' Beornoth said, mopping up the meat juices from his wooden plate with the last morsel of bread. 'Olaf was under my sword, but Brand saved his life.'

'Brand,' said Wulfhere, coughing scraps of food in his surprise. 'The ungrateful bastard. He has always been our enemy. A cuckoo in the nest.'

'He saved his Jarl's life. But he did not raise his blade against me.'

'Oh, well then. Let's invite him to spend winter with us,' said Leofsunu, throwing his arms wide. 'Why not let him sit in the high seat and I can clean his boots for him?'

Beornoth chuckled, and Leofsunu tapped him on the shoulder and nodded to Alfgar, who approached on horseback.

'Beornoth,' Alfgar said. He nodded to the others in recognition and smiled warmly at Wulfhere.

'So, there is peace?' asked Beornoth.

'So, it seems. For now, at least,' Alfgar said. He twisted in the saddle to watch the Vikings march back into their harbour. 'They are rich with silver, and Archbishop Sigeric has committed to providing them with supplies for the winter. To avoid further raiding.'

'Thank you, Lord,' said Beornoth.

Alfgar waved a hand at him, as if to waft away the words like a fly. 'You never need to call me that.'

'I do. You are an Ealdorman now. Lord. You didn't have to come, but you did. You saved our lives, and Byrhtnoth's.'

'Once Cwicca told me of the peril you were in, I had to ride. It is what my father would have done.'

Beornoth smiled and nodded. 'Yes, he would. I hear the King has approved your investment as Ealdorman of Cheshire?'

'He has; I will swear a royal oath in Lundenburg. We leave for there now, along with the King and his Bishops.'

'Good,' said Beornoth. He stepped towards Alfgar, and the

young Ealdorman grabbed his outstretched hand. 'Your father would be proud of you. You reminded me of him, charging into the Vikings.'

'After Lundenburg, I will call to you at Branoc's Tree. I must see Wynflaed, and I will bring her north, if you agree, Beornoth,' said Alfgar. Beornoth smiled and nodded his agreement. 'Thank you, Beornoth. For everything.'

'What about me?' barked Wulfhere. 'I taught you to fight. All he did was growl and bark at you.' The men laughed, as did Alfgar. He nodded again at Beornoth and rode to join the King and his men. 'Can we go back to Branoc's Tree now, Lord?'

'Yes, Wulfhere, we can,' said Beornoth.

'Don't get comfortable though,' said Leofsunu, a frown splitting his ugly face. 'Sweyn Forkbeard is still in East Anglia, and it looks like Olaf will still be here in the spring. Enemies still surround us.'

Tendrils of smoke rose from behind Folkestone's buildings and Beornoth wondered if it was from cooking fires, or the smoking ruin of Olaf's burned ships. The wind snatched at the smoke, making it dance against a sky rolling with dark clouds fat with rainwater. He would go back to Branoc's Tree and see Eawynn and the rest of his people. They would gather close for the winter, bring the livestock in from the cold and the days would grow short and dark. Then, in the springtime, when the mornings were no longer laced with sparkling frost, and the swallows returned from their travels, the Vikings would strike again despite the silver and their oaths, and Beornoth would be ready for them.

# ACKNOWLEDGMENTS

Thanks to Caroline, Nia, Claire, Jenna, and all the team at Boldwood Books for their belief in Beornoth's story, and in me as an author, with special thanks to Ross and Clare for all their effort and amazing eye for detail.

# HISTORICAL NOTE

The first book in this series, Warrior and Protector, provided an introduction to what is a fascinating period in the history of England. King Æthelred, known as the Unready, came to power after a rare period of peace in the Viking Age. His father, Kind Edgar, ruled from 959AD to 975AD and oversaw a prosperous period for the nascent Kingdom of England where the country was largely untouched by the Viking raids which had dominated the Anglo Saxons for over a hundred years.

When King Edgar died, there was a significant dispute over the succession. King Edward the Martyr succeeded Edgar in 975AD and ruled until his death in 978AD. Edward was murdered at Corfe Castle in circumstances shrouded in mystery. Edward was not his father's recognised heir but was supported by powerful churchmen like the famous Bishop Dunstan. There were some who supported the claim of Edward's half-brother, Æthelred, who was the recognised heir and son of the Queen Ælfthryth. It is suspected that it was the Queen who had Edward killed so that her son could take the throne.

In Storm of War, Beornoth finds himself caught up in the aftermath in that fight over the succession. There were indeed factions who had supported the martyred King Edward, and others who supported Æthelred. Byrhtnoth allied with Aethelwine, Ealdorman of East Anglia, in support of Edward and so it is logical that the Queen Dowager, Ælfthryth, would remain hostile towards him. To add to the complexity of the politics of the time, the succession was also wrapped up in a dispute between supporters of the monastic church, such as the famous Dunstan, and the church itself. During his reign, Kind Edgar had forced monastic reforms upon his Kingdom, and had taken land from lesser nobles to support the Benedictine monasteries which sowed discontent and paved the way for conflict.

All of this provided a fractured Kingdom for the Vikings to take advantage of. The Vikings of Denmark and Norway found an England weakened by its years of peace, and struck in increasing numbers throughout Æthelred's reign, coming to a head in the 990s. I set this story in the years leading up to that larger attack, and specifically the years before the Battle of Maldon in 991. That battle shocked the English court and led to new policies which would halt the Viking conquest, at least for a time.

The reference in the novel to Æthelric of Bocking is historical. He was accused posthumously of treason and treachery. The Essex Thegn allegedly plotted to receive the Danish King Sweyn Forkbeard in the early 990s, around the time of the Battle of Maldon, which shows just how close the ties were between the Vikings and the peoples living in Æthelred's kingdom.

Byrhtnoth and Olaf Tryggvason are historical characters, but Beornoth is fictional. He is a man of his time, a brutal warrior whose existence revolves around his skill at arms. His role as Thegn is to serve his Ealdorman, and the King, as a warrior and to fight for them when required and to protect the laypeople of his shire. Leofsunu, Aelfwine, and the other Thegns of Byrhtnoth's hearth troop are also historical characters and held lands in Essex. It was a time of Oaths and brotherhood in arms, and I have tried to weave that into the weft of the story. It must have been a powerful thing to fight in hand-to-hand combat, trusting your life to the man next to you, and those men would have shared an incredible bond.

The Viking raid on Watchet is a historical event, and the Thegn Goda was indeed killed by the raiders who had sailed down from their secure base in the River Severn to launch a series of attacks on Saxon lands. Olaf Tryggvason and Sweyn Forkbeard will have a larger part to play as this series continues. The story of England in the late tenth century is one of Viking invasion and warfare, leading up to the St Brice's Day massacre, and eventually to the attacks of Sweyn Forkbeard and his son King Cnut in the early eleventh century. Beornoth's fate is to be at the heart of that conflict, so his battles are far from over.

## MORE FROM PETER GIBBONS

We hope you enjoyed reading *Storm of War*. If you did, please leave a review.

If you'd like to gift a copy, this book is also available as an ebook, large print, hardback, digital audio download and audiobook CD.

Sign up to Peter Gibbons' mailing list for news, competitions and updates on future books.

https://bit.ly/PeterGibbonsNews

*Warrior and Protector*, the first instalment of Peter Gibbons' fast-paced Saxon Warrior series, is available now...

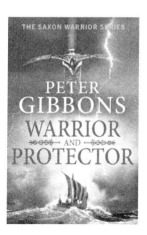

# ABOUT THE AUTHOR

**Peter Gibbons** is a financial advisor and author of the highly acclaimed Viking Blood and Blade trilogy. He comes to Boldwood with his new Saxon Warrior series, set around the 900 AD Viking invasion during the reign of King Athelred the Unready. He lives with his family in County Kildare.

Visit Peter's website: https://petermgibbons.com/

Follow Peter on social media:

twitter.com/AuthorGibbons
facebook.com/petergibbonsauthor
instagram.com/petermgibbons
bookbub.com/authors/peter-gibbons

# Boldw∞d

Boldwood Books is an award-winning fiction publishing company seeking out the best stories from around the world.

Find out more at www.boldwoodbooks.com

Join our reader community for brilliant books, competitions and offers!

Follow us
@BoldwoodBooks
@BookandTonic

Sign up to our weekly
deals newsletter

https://bit.ly/BoldwoodBNewsletter

Printed in Great Britain
by Amazon